Annie O'Neil spent most of her childhood with her leg draped over the family rocking chair and a book in her hand. Novels, baking and writing too much teenage angst poetry ate up most of her youth. Now Annie splits her time between corralling her husband into helping her with their cows, baking, reading, barrel racing (not really!) and spending some very happy hours at her computer, writing.

Three-times Golden Heart® finalist **Tina Beckett** learned to pack her suitcases almost before she learned to read. Born to a military family, she has lived in the United States, Puerto Rico, Portugal and Brazil. In addition to travelling, Tina loves to cuddle with her pug, Alex, spend time with her family and hit the trails on her horse. Learn more about Tina from her website, or 'friend' her on Facebook.

NEW YEAR KISS WITH HIS CINDERELLA

ANNIE O'NEIL

THEIR REUNION TO REMEMBER

TINA BECKETT

MILLS & BOON

First Published in Great Britain 2021
by Mills & Boon, an imprint of HarperCollins*Publishers* Ltd,
1 London Bridge Street, London, SE1 9GF

www.harpercollins.co.uk

HarperCollins*Publishers*
1st Floor, Watermarque Building,
Ringsend Road, Dublin 4, Ireland

New Year Kiss with His Cinderella © 2021 by Annie O'Neil

Their Reunion to Remember © 2021 by Tina Beckett

ISBN: 978-0-263-29785-0

12/21

MIX
Paper from
responsible sources
FSC™ C007454

NEW YEAR KISS
WITH HIS
CINDERELLA

ANNIE O'NEIL

MILLS & BOON

This one is with gratitude for the wonderful Tina Beckett,
who made this SUCH fun to write.
I am deeply jealous of her upcoming trip to Dollywood.

CHAPTER ONE

CARTER LET OUT a low satisfied whistle. He'd never seen a woman ride a mechanical bull like she was doing a ballet before. Some kind of dance anyway. She was undulating with the erratic whips and spins of the longhorn as if she could predict it. Not jerking around like her predecessors, most of whom, courtesy of too much tequila, had been flung onto the mats within seconds.

Not this woman. Her right arm was up in the air, hand cupped like she was royalty, her left wrapped around the leather-bound handhold as if she were idly steering a shopping cart with wheels that worked. That made her a leftie, then. Like him. A confident one.

She had a gorgeous billow of hair blowing in the light wintry breeze, snowflakes catching in it like they were diamonds. Skin the color of coffee with the perfect dollop of cream in it. Sexy as hell is what she was. Sexy enough to require a shift to his belt buckle at least.

Her dark eyes were lit up by the myriad of neon lights vying for competition out here in the heart of Nashville's party street. Honky Tonk Row. Everything blinked and glowed at maximum party levels. He guessed tonight was a party for most folk. New Year's Eve wasn't anything special to him. Just another day. A busy one if he were at work. But that didn't start until tomorrow. First day of another New Year in another new town. One he might actually learn the street grid for this time. Maybe.

If this woman were a sign of things to come, maybe Nashville wouldn't be so bad after all.

She wasn't smiling, but her lips weren't pressed into a thin line of grim determination, either. They were pushed forward in a thoughtful pout. Fancy people would probably call it a *moue*. But fancy was the last thing he was.

He reckoned this was her thinking face. He liked it. Could easily imagine cupping her jawline in his hands, stroking his thumb along her cheek and pulling her to him to turn her expression into something that looked a lot more like a smile. He let his gaze shift down past the sheepskin collar buttoned up close around her neck, beyond the flannel-lined jean jacket and slide down those long legs of hers, also clad in denim. They were holding onto the hide covered "bull" as if they genuinely wanted to. Not like most folk did—for dear life. He laughed. She knew she was good. That she was going to win the cash prize. Upward of two thousand dollars now and growing by the minute. The more takers, the bigger the pot.

And then she looked at him.

He felt it at once. The connection. A carnal one that lit him up like electricity, heating every primitive cell in his body quicker than fire.

Carter's lips curved into the first happy smile they'd made since he'd arrived here in Nashville. Next thing he knew, the mechanical longhorn was flinging her to the mat, landing her at his feet.

When he reached down to help pull her up, it was like trying to hold onto a wildcat. She was raging. Not in a screaming, angry way. In a low deliberate way that for some reason made him want to pull her into his arms and direct all that energy into something a bit more... not productive exactly.

"Thanks for nothing," she growled.

"Hey." He body-blocked a couple of drunken twenty-somethings trying to push their way into the cordoned off ring around the bull, his gaze never leaving hers. "I was just standing here, minding my own business."

"Ruining my chances of walking away with the cash is what you were doing,"

"Is that what the goal was?"

Something flickered through her defiant expression. A vulnerability. One she instantly hid with a jutted chin and a slight curl to her top lip. She'd betrayed too much to him and was regretting it.

They both looked at the leaderboard. She was ahead of the previous riders by ten seconds. He could tell by the look on her face she'd been hoping to secure that lead by something much more substantial.

"You need that money?" he asked.

It was bold. Putting it out there like that. No one liked their pride dented, but he wasn't one to step away from a bit of straight talking. Most of the time anyway. He crossed his arms and waited. He'd seen what she was made of physically and mentally atop that bull. Now it was time to see what sort of emotional grit held her together.

"I don't recall informing you that it was any of your business." There was a smile on her face, but it wasn't a warm one.

Okay. Good. He got it. No one said laying your cards on the table was a smart thing to do. Especially with a stranger. Even so, he could see they both knew her answer meant yes. She needed the money and blamed him for cracking that laser sharp concentration of hers that had all but guaranteed a bulging wallet come midnight.

"I'll win it for you," he said.

She laughed. "Yeah, right." Her dark brown eyes flicked up to his Stetson. "This isn't the state fair, cowboy. I don't need a stuffed toy."

Shame. It was pretty easy to picture the two of them walking through a fun fair. Him with a deep-fried pickle—yeah, it was a thing—and her with a huge old teddy bear balanced on that curvy hip of hers. He tipped his head toward the line of people waiting their turn to ride the bull before the clock struck midnight. He gave his chest a thump with a fist. "Nothing but blood and bones in this prize. Carter Booth, at your service." He took off his hat and bowed.

When he rose, her arms were crossed, and her expression had shifted from irritated to something trickier to read. He reckoned he had about a sixty-second window to win her over.

He had some height on her, but somehow she was smiling down her nose at him even though her chin was practically vertical. Nice trick. It could definitely put someone on edge. Not him. But somebody.

"If you actually could ride longer than me, it'd be your money you'd be winning." She didn't tell him her name. But the comment told him a lot about her character.

"No." That wasn't how he saw it. "I wasn't planning on riding tonight, and I'm guessing you would've been up there a while longer if my good looks hadn't thrown you off balance."

She made a noise of protest. And this time, she definitely blushed. He knew he wasn't a pretty boy. More rough than ready. But his gut was telling him she liked the look of whatever it was he had going for him and, for tonight at least, that was good enough for him.

Her eyes narrowed. "What do you want in return?"

"A kiss."

Well, what do you know? He hadn't known he was in possession of that much temerity. His brain threw him back to the moment he'd told his last boss to stuff it. Then again, maybe he did.

Her eyebrows were raised almost up to her forehead. "What? On the cheek?"

He shook his head and tapped a finger on his lips, enjoying himself that little bit more when he saw her fight a shiver of anticipation. "Stroke of midnight," he continued. "Then just like Cinderella, I'll disappear out of your life."

She laughed out loud at this. "I thought that was my role."

He shrugged. "You can be the princess. I've never been one to kowtow to the so-called patriarchy." He believed in a lot of things. Democracy. Freedom. Looking after the people you loved. Especially family. Respect. Honesty. When it was required. He also believed in moving in and out of town without setting down roots because, as sure as the seasons would change, his sister would be doing something that meant he'd have to throw his duffel bags and guitar in the back of his truck and hit the road again.

"You're that confident, are you?" she asked, her tongue dipping out for a quick swipe along her lips.

She was warming to him. Good.

The guy who'd climbed on the bull after her had been thrown off and someone else was climbing on. Carter would glue himself to the bull if that's what it took to stay on the longest. But it wouldn't take that. Back in Texas, he'd called his riding paying the bills. His sister had called it sheer stupidity. They'd both been right.

"Never met a bull who didn't take to my winning personality." He tipped the brim of his hat to her.

Her eyes didn't leave his. "If you win my money, I'm not taking it."

"And I'm not letting you walk away empty-handed."

She frowned. "I guess you'd better come up with something else, then. I don't steal prizes that aren't mine."

He held his hands out, then ran them alongside his body. "Apart from my guitar, this is the only other thing I've got on offer."

He wasn't actually broke. He wasn't a thief, either. That role in the family was already taken.

A loud roar from the crowd filled the air as another contender climbed aboard the longhorn.

She tilted her head to the side, and he took the few moments she was assessing him to do the same. Skin that looked so soft there probably wasn't a thread count high enough for it. A body that rocked the hell out of her double-denim getup. A pair of cowboy boots that definitely weren't just for show. God*damn* she was sexy.

"Well, then," she said. "I guess you'd better get on up there and show me what you got." When she met his gaze, he was pretty sure he wasn't only seeing neon lights flaring in her eyes.

She put out her mittened hand. They were going to shake on it, apparently.

Carter smiled. Progress. She liked him, too. Enough to want to see him show his stuff atop a mechanical bull anyway. Maybe she merely wanted a good laugh. Either way, he could work with that. Not that he'd be seeing her again, but...it was New Year's Eve. The bit of him that believed in destiny, that hoped that fate wasn't something only poets spoke of, wanted her appearance in his life to signify something more than a chance meeting. Yet another moment in time that would slip through his fingers when reality reared its head and cut things short. Again.

It surprised him how much he wanted her to be a sign of good things to come. Needed it, even. Perhaps if he won that kiss...

He put his thumb and index finger on the tip of her thumb. "May I?"

She didn't say anything, but she didn't refuse. Just watched, mesmerized, as he tugged off her mitten, slowly, so that when their hands finally met, it would be flesh on flesh.

The atmosphere changed. The sounds of the crowd dulled and somehow, the way the world can sometimes, everything stilled so that it seemed like it was just the two of them out here in the middle of Nashville with nothing but a few flakes of snow between them.

When he finally cupped her hand in his, her eyes widened. A sound escaped her throat. One that gave the impression she'd just been touched somewhere much more intimate than her palm. And that she liked it. He barely managed to stop a guttural exhalation from escaping his own throat. It pleased him that she felt the connection, too. It'd been a while since he'd pulled out his flirtation skills and chances were they were real rusty.

"Avery!"

She pulled her hand away, turning toward the sound of the woman's voice. He saw a tall slender dark-haired woman waving in their direction. She was beautiful, too, but didn't catch his eye in quite the same way the one in front of him did.

This woman—"his" woman—waved. "Over here, Lia."

Okay. First mystery solved. Her name was Avery. Nice. It tasted good. He liked the way his teeth had to scrape against his bottom lip to say it. Now all he had to do was figure out if this Lia was her friend, her wingman or both.

"Hey, Avery." Lia, bundled up to her chin in a thick winter parka, hip-bumped her friend. "Who's this?"

They both turned to look at Carter.

Avery shrugged. "He claims he's my knight in shining armor." They shared a complicit look. "Don't worry. Not worth remembering."

As if the words were some secret code, the two of them started giggling.

"I think you'll find otherwise," Carter said. "I'm going to win that money."

"What money?" she riposted. "You mean my money?"

They looked at the leaderboard and though only a few seconds stood between her and the last rider, she was still in pole position.

Lia's smile dropped away. She lowered her voice and

asked Avery something he couldn't quite catch with all the hullabaloo around them. Another joker climbed on board the longhorn. Lia and Avery were sharing a look that spoke to him loud and clear. She'd genuinely been banking on that cash.

The guy fell off in about three seconds flat. Another contender clambered up. A woman who fell off the second they set the bull in motion and was whisked away by a group of friends.

He glanced at the clock. Time was running short.

"If you'll excuse me, ladies." He tipped his hat to Lia first, then Avery with whom he held eye contact. "I'm off to win my kiss."

Avery, clearly emboldened by her friend's arrival threw him a wicked smile. "I don't recall giving you permission to have that kiss."

"Well, we'll see about that. Here, keep an eye on this for me, would you? I presume you're trustworthy enough not to make off with a man's guitar?"

Avery nodded, her eyes fleetingly taking on a look of longing as they set on his guitar case.

Five minutes later, the crowd was counting down to midnight and Avery's name was still ahead on the leaderboard. She hadn't cold-shouldered him after he'd fallen off two seconds short of her time, but her focus had definitely narrowed in on the bar owner who was poised to hand out the prize—now double what it had been twenty minutes ago when he'd first seen her.

Once she had the envelope safely tucked inside her jacket, he was surprised to find her standing in front of him as the counting hit the single digits. Fewer than five seconds to go and it would be a New Year. Three. Two. And then they were kissing.

He didn't need fireworks to feel lit up inside. The touch of her lips, warm and soft and interested in exploring his was all the heat he needed. If he hadn't been holding a guitar in one hand, he'd have hooked her legs up and around his hips faster than she could've blinked. Carried her back to his soulless serviced apartment and spent the rest of the night setting her on fire. He heard a hint of a moan as he drew his thumb down her throat to her collarbone. The sort that meant he'd give his right arm to elicit a proper one.

She pulled back first.

He shifted his stance. Had to. His jeans were officially uncomfortable. In the drollest voice he had, he said, "Well, that was unexpected." It was a massive understatement. "I feel like I collected on something I didn't earn."

She considered him for a moment, running her index finger along those lips of hers. Fuller now that they were bruised from kissing. "Well, I guess you owe me, then." She smiled, turned, then walked away. Before he could get his brain working straight, she'd disappeared into the crowd.

He smiled. Laughed to himself. It had been a risk to fall off the bull early, but something had told him she wouldn't have taken the money if he'd grandstanded in front of her. And he'd still got his kiss. All in all, it was a good start to the New Year. Though, with his luck, he wouldn't hold his breath that it would continue.

CHAPTER TWO

AVERY TOOK A long draught of coffee. She leaned against the counter, eyes closed, as the warm liquid slid down her throat and into her nervous system. My goodness, she'd needed that. Whoever made the hospital shift-change roster hadn't taken midnight kisses and sleepless nights thinking about sexy cowboys into consideration.

Valentina, the ER charge nurse, sidled up alongside her, slipping her own enormous reusable coffee mug onto the counter Avery was using as a support.

"Late night?" Valentina asked.

Avery laughed and *mmm-hmm'd*. It had been, but not for the reasons Valentina's saucy tone was implying.

Well...

For about thirty deliciously juicy seconds it had been. And after that—after walking away from a man who could get a full-time job as a city power grid—surprise, surprise, she hadn't been able to get to sleep. It was the kind of chance encounter the most heartbreaking love songs were written about. But she didn't sing them anymore, so instead she'd just lain there, brushing her fingers along her lips, wondering what it would've been like to have more. Then stridently reminding herself *over* and *over* that she didn't do relationships anymore. Especially not with guitar-wielding, mechanical bull–riding sex gods. Not that a relationship had been on offer. She couldn't see a guy like that hanging up his hat long enough to gather dust, so…

So long, Carter Booth. May your ride into the sunset be as beautiful as your behind.

She tipped her head toward Valentina's impressive mug. "How many cups can you fit in that thing?"

Valentina gave an indignant little huff and said something in Spanish that sounded a lot like, *Takes one to know one, chiquitita.* "I'm not as young as I used to be, *mija.* I need two cups just to get my eyelids open. Then I pour the rest of the pot straight on in. Any room that's left gets filled up with creamer."

Avery leaned in and sniffed. "Hazelnut?"

Valentina tapped the side of her nose, then turned her attention to the board where staff were gathering for the morning handover from the nightshift crew. The night nurse manager looked burned-out and, because it was still busy, was fastidiously moving from curtained bed to curtained bed. Saint Dolores Hospital—aka St. Dolly's—was full to the brim with people who'd been hoping for a spectacular start to the New Year. They'd got that, all right. Not necessarily the type of spectacular they were hoping for but…they'd have a story to tell and, with any luck, the vim and vigor to tell it.

"Looks like we've got a lot of leftovers from last night," Valentina said, nodding at the full patient board. "New Year's Eve seems to bring out the stupid in people."

Avery quickly scanned the list of injuries. There were, of course, a few of the "bread and butter" cases.

Chest pain. Abdominal pain. Foreign objects where they shouldn't be. A "concerning" growth.

She grimaced. She'd try to steer clear of that one.

Because there'd been a lot more alcohol flowing on the streets of Nashville last night and the snow had frozen as fast as it had fallen, a truckload of sprains and breaks and...ha!...a fractured coccyx from riding a mechanical bull. She wondered if... No. A man with a butt as firm as Carter's—yes, she'd watched as he'd walked away and climbed up atop that bull—a butt like that wouldn't bruise. Which meant the man behind that particular curtain wouldn't be Carter. No. That ship had definitely sailed. Shame. She'd never been one for one-night stands, but...there were always exceptions to rules. And if there weren't, there should be in his case. She closed her eyes and could practically feel his lips descend upon hers again.

"What're you thinking about?" Valentina gave her a nudge. "It looks naughty, whatever it is."

Avery smirked. "Nothing. Just thinking that New Year's Eve has a lot to answer for."

Valentina clucked her tongue. "Pray do tell. I've got to live vicariously these days."

Valentina had been married over twenty years and was allegedly enjoying being an empty nester, but as soon as her kids had up and left for college, she'd pretty much adopted Avery. Not that Avery was an orphan, but her own parents had... Well... She refused to judge them after what they'd been through. What they all had. They'd run away from the painful memories and she'd dug in. Around the edges anyway.

Valentina lowered her voice to a whisper as the gathering of staff around them thickened. "I forgot to ask. Did you get the money? From the bull-thingy?"

Avery grinned. "Sure did." Her brain circled right back to the kiss she'd stolen afterward. She forced her smile to appear more innocent. "I should be able to put the deposit down as soon as I can get to the realtors."

Valentina gave her a side hug. "I'm so proud of you, honey. It took a lot of work to get to this point."

About two hundred overtime shifts, upgrading her nursing degree from oncology nurse to acute care nurse practitioner and pinching her pennies on an apartment that had just about enough room to turn around in. With her lease soon up, she would've moved back home, but her parents had decided traveling around the country in a Winnebago was their new destiny. They'd offered her some money toward the deposit, but the sting of their departure had made her refuse it. She wanted to do this on her own. For April.

Her brain slammed on the brakes as it usually did when she thought of her sister. But then, remembering the milestone she'd reached last night, she forced herself to think the words, *Now that April was gone, things were different.*

And they were. For the four hundred and twenty-seven days and—she glanced up at the wall clock above the patient board—two hours and nineteen minutes since her sister had died.

Her jaw clenched. Thinking about those final moments, April's hand in hers, still felt as raw as it had on the day itself. Like losing an actual physical part of herself.

Being able to put a deposit down on the house the two of them had dreamed of owning was the first time in a long time she'd felt a genuine sense of achievement. Sure, getting her nurse practitioner certificate had been big, but the main reason she'd done it was so that she never had to go back to the cancer ward again. In fairness, the work here in the ER was amazing. So, no regrets on that front.

And since the cancer had proved to be a stronger force than they'd thought, the future she and her sister had dreamed of leading in the house wouldn't happen. April teaching, Avery nursing, the pair of them singing down at The Bluebird Café on Thursday nights, hoping to be discovered.

So, yeah. That was different, too. She'd need a housemate to make the mortgage payments. A loan to pay a builder to help her get the place weatherproofed. And a list about as long as her arm for everything else the place would need, but, even so, she still felt proud. As if she'd reached a proper crossroads moment when she could finally visit April's grave and say, *You know what, big sis? I've done it. Made one of our dreams come true.*

As for the others…

"All right, everyone!" Dr. Leah Chang, the head of the ER Department clapped her hand against her tablet to get their attention. Her ebony hair was broken up by her trademark neon streak. Hot pink today. As usual, the entire slick of hair was pulled into submission by a high-set ponytail. "First things first. Happy New Year. I hope you all had fun but that none of you need Breathalyzers today. Ha-ha." Her smile turned serious. "I'm not kidding. If I have any doubts, you're out on your ear."

Avery and Valentina exchanged a look. It was a risk not worth taking. Pity the fool who showed up in Leah's ER nine sheets to the wind.

Leah continued, "New Year. New staff. First up, we've got Rocky Martinez, joining us as an orderly. He is replacing KC Burns, who has moved to Georgia to be closer to his grandmother. Can we have a round of applause welcoming Rocky, please?"

Avery followed Dr. Chang's finger. Her eyes landed on a Latino man about her height who was swirling a set of car keys on his pinkie finger. He pocketed them when he felt the crowd's eyes on him. He was quite obviously a gym buff. He looked like he'd dragged his car here by his pinkie finger rather than driven it.

After a quick round of clapping, Dr. Chang carried on. "He's won an actual medal in the actual Olympics for boxing, so please do not try to arm wrestle him. You will not win. And now, to my... Where'd he go? There he is, behind Avery... Also joining us today, from the wilds of Texas, is Dr. Carter Booth! Another round of applause please."

Avery was midway through putting her hands together when the name registered.

Every hair on her body stood at attention as little sparks of excitement shot through her. She could've turned around and checked. Apparently, he was that close. But looking Carter Booth in the eye after she'd kissed him the way she had felt like throwing herself into a river she'd never be able to swim out of. His current was too strong. Too intoxicating. Not to mention the fact she'd told him he owed her. Would he try to pay his debt? Just thinking about it swept a fistful of glitter through her erogenous zones.

Well, then. Looks like she knew where her body stood on the issue of payback. The only question was could common sense overrule it? It better had, seeing as they were at work.

Rather than turning around and finding out if it was the same Carter Booth who'd all but imprinted himself on her DNA, she sniffed. Last night, she'd inhaled him like he was her last breath of oxygen. He had smelt that good. Pine needles and beeswax. Maybe something else, too. Pheromones that spoke to her with a loud-speaker. Her body shuddered as the scent poured into her nervous system.

"What?" She heard his voice low and sexy in her ear. "Not good enough for applause?"

His tone wasn't accusatory. More…amused. His bari-tone was so rich it practically vibrated down her spine, lighting up body parts that shouldn't be sparking right here in the middle of a staff meeting. Or ever.

She tilted her head to the side, popped on a smile, pitter-pattered her hands together and stage-whispered, "Happy?"

"Very."

Damn. She shouldn't've looked. For whatever reason, she hadn't noticed his eyes last night. Maybe it was all the neon lights. The chaos he'd wrought in her brain. Maybe it was the fact she hadn't been able to stop star-ing at his mouth that, annoyingly, looked just as edible now as it had last night. Especially when he dragged his top teeth across his bottom lip when he said words with Vs in them. Like *very*. And *Avery*.

She forced herself to look back up into those eyes of his. Framed by blacker than black lashes, they were just about the most beautiful shade of green she'd ever seen. And green was her favorite color. He still had that "rough and ready" look he'd worn last night: unshaven, tousle-haired, eyes bruised with a lack of sleep. An aura hung around him—a vital potency—that suggested he'd pile into a fight for honor if need be, his or someone else's, but he'd rather not. It wasn't reluctance. It was more…he was a thinking man. The type who didn't just leap into things willy-nilly, which did make her look at what happened last night in a brand new light. She'd taken him for a chancer, but she saw now that she was wrong. Sure, he still had a sting of danger about him, but standing tall, shoulders back, body filling out his dark blue scrubs the way only a few men could, there was something…capable…about him. Something that suggested he'd hang around. For the duration of his shift anyway. And that scared her. Because ten minutes of his time last night had made a deep enough impression on her. And now a ten-hour shift? She wasn't sure if she had the backbone for that.

Avery felt Valentina's eyes bouncing between the pair of them. Her stomach clenched. She couldn't ignore her. Neither did she want to answer the question she knew was coming.

"Do you two know each other or something?" Valentina asked. "I'm getting a *vibe*."

Avery said, "No," at exactly the same moment Carter said, "Sure do."

"Oh?" Valentina arced an eyebrow.

Shoot. Valentina really was living vicariously through her colleagues.

"He was one of many in a very large crowd down on Honky Tonk Row last night."

"From the looks of things, he stood out." Valentina didn't even try to wipe the smirk off her face.

Carter looked at Avery expectantly, as if he, too, was

curious to know whether or not he'd stood out from the crowd. Idiot. Of course, he had. But he was meant to be riding off into the sunrise right now, not showing up in her ER in her city on the first day of the rest of her life.

"She doesn't look best pleased to see you," said Valentina.

"No," Carter agreed. "She doesn't."

"I am perfectly happy to see him," Avery spat back.

Carter laughed. "In which case, thank you for the warm welcome." He tipped an invisible cowboy hat.

"Whittacker." Dr. Chang was making a beeline for her. "Can you take Dr. Booth here on the grand tour? Help him through the first couple of patients so he knows where to get things and who to call if he needs help." She didn't pause to find out if Avery was amenable to this request. Which, for the record, she was not. "After that, they need you up on the executive floor to discuss this year's benefit. They know it's a tough one for you. Especially after last year, but…" She held up her hands. "I'll leave it to you to discuss the particulars." She gave them a stern look. "Thirty minutes max for the whistle-stop and first two patients. After that, I want both of you moving on double time." She disappeared in a cloud of barked orders.

Talk about being squished between a rock and a hard place.

"C'mon, then," Avery said, turning her back on Carter and swinging her arm in the direction of the busy ER. "Tour first, then we'll get ourselves to work."

"Want to go up to the executive floor first?"

She glowered at him.

He shrugged as if it meant nothing to him, which,

of course, it shouldn't. "You just looked as if you might want a bit of backup."

"I can handle it," she said with a bit too much flair.

No, she couldn't. Singing in a benefit for the cancer ward in a concert she usually sang with her sister? Not. A. Chance.

He locked her into one of those impenetrable gazes of his. "I'm sure you can handle whatever you set your mind to, Avery Whittacker."

He took his time saying her name. Deliberately. And, as if he knew it was a lure, he dragged his teeth over his lower lip again. Her breasts gained about ten pounds in that nanosecond. Jerk. He wasn't playing fair.

"We'd better get a move on, Dr. Carter. Dr. Chang likes patients admitted within thirty minutes of arrival and discharged or reallocated to another department within the same amount of time."

He let out a low whistle that ribboned around her chest. "Guess we'd better maximize our time together, then."

She race-walked him through the area as if they were being timed. Ambulance entrances, walk-in registration, trauma, resus, staff lounge, medical storage, critical-care beds, triage and the double doors that led everywhere else: labs, radiology, inpatient wards and, for his purposes, the operating theaters. The moment they hit the supplies cupboard and paused for breath, she knew it was a mistake.

They were alone for the first time and her parting line to him last night kept rolling through her head—*I guess you owe me, then.*

She was the one who owed him. She'd seen what he'd done. Fallen off when he could've ridden that mechanical bull till the sun rose if he'd wanted to. That's why she'd kissed him. Okay, sure. She thought he was hot as blue blazes as well, but he'd thought of her dignity and he'd preserved it. Let her walk away with a cash prize that could easily have been his.

Now, here, in the close confines of the storage room, her body was her worst enemy. It craved his touch. Same as his wanted hers. She could feel it. Like they were magnets structurally drawn to one another. "So this is where it all happens, is it?" His smile was mischievous. And inviting.

"If you're talking about catheters, enema packs and kidney dishes, yes." She beamed up at him. From a distance. Getting intimate with Carter Booth would be like pulling open a bag of potato chips. Once you got the taste for him, you would always want more.

The sensation of wanting more was something she hadn't felt in a long time. If she were to believe her last boyfriend's parting words to her—*you barely give, and you definitely don't receive*—she wasn't really a strong candidate for a relationship. At the time, he'd been right. She hadn't been remotely available on the emotional front. Everything she'd had was poured into helping her sister. And physically… Who wanted to make love to someone they knew wasn't really there? She hadn't begrudged the guy for calling it quits. It had meant she'd had more time with April. Three precious months. And, if the rumor mill was anything to go by, her ex was set to head down the aisle this coming Valentine's Day. So, yeah. That ship had sailed. Even so…it wasn't as if she didn't appreciate a bit of eye candy. Looking but not touching was allowed. Right?

Carter pretended to look around. "Where are the personal touches? Fluffy pillows, colored blankets, scrubs with bunny rabbits on them?"

She harrumphed. She didn't know what sort of ERs he'd worked in before, but those sorts of things weren't found in this part of the hospital. Pediatrics? Definitely. Ortho had a blue room for healing vibes. Geriatrics had an orangery and even Imaging had a glassed-in garden room. But here? The part of the hospital where they covered everything from alcohol poisoning to stab wounds and back again? As far as emergency rooms went, theirs definitely wasn't horrible. Not like the ones they showed on TV. But apart from the play area they'd set up in the pediatric waiting area, a handful of potted ficus trees and the quiet zone for people who knew they were waiting for bad news… Nah. Plain scrubs, white pillowcases and ready-wash blankets were where they peaked. "People who come to the ER are in and out, one way or another, before they can admire the soft furnishings. Perhaps you'd be best finding another department if that's your idea of patient care."

He stopped whatever it was he was going to say and looked at her. Really looked at her. "I'd bet every penny I own that you care. Some might say too much."

In that moment, she felt more seen than she had in her entire life. Straight through to her soul.

She did care too much. It was why, after April had lost her life in the very ward she'd dedicated herself to for six years, she simply couldn't do it anymore. Not nursing in general. That was an intrinsic part of who she was. But the oncology ward… Yeah, she wasn't stepping foot in there ever again.

Not all cancer patients were long-termers, but a lot of them were. And, despite her best efforts, she'd got to know them and love them like they were family by the time the inevitable happened. When April had arrived for her first treatment for stage two esophageal cancer, it had just about killed Avery. Not only had life been cruel by giving April cancer, it had taken away that beautiful voice of hers. The one thing April cherished. Being able to sing. If Avery could've done the chemo and the radiation therapy and lost her hair for her, she would have. Donated every pint of blood in her body if it had been a match. Died for her. But life didn't work like that. It was cruel and, sometimes, completely indifferent. Each day that stretched out after April's death seemed to be proof of it...until now. With this man. In this supply cupboard. Who was looking straight into her heart and not running for the hills.

Carter shifted his weight from one hip to the other. "Does it suit you? The drive-through medical care?"

The comment hit its mark. Her conscience. "You like pushing buttons you have no business pushing, don't you?" And then she got angry. "And don't you even dare suggest I give my patients anything other than my best."

She swished out of the room past him and flicked out the light. "We've got patients to see. Chop-chop, Dr. Booth. Time's a wastin'."

CHAPTER THREE

CARTER WOULD'VE HAPPILY walked behind Avery Whittacker for the rest of his life if it would afford him this view—a pert behind that swished beneath the worn cotton of her green scrubs. Shoulders and arms swinging this way and that as if they were about to launch themselves into a dance move. But he couldn't shake the feeling that he'd rattled her cage too hard. Normally, he wouldn't care. Normally, he wasn't in town long enough *to* care. But this time—apart from the fact he might be in Nashville upward of a year—he was getting the feeling he had met Avery for a reason. That the universe had put them together. For him to teach her something or maybe it was the other way around. Maybe both.

Whatever it was, this midnight cowgirl had crawled under his skin and stayed there. The New Year's kiss had a lot to do with that. He hadn't been intimate with a woman in some time and if he'd been the sort to dream of a kiss, it was exactly the type he would've conjured up. Hot, hungry and keen to satisfy.

He shelved the thoughts, knowing they'd only make wearing form-fitting scrubs awkward.

After a brisk walk, they arrived back in the heart

of the internal observation zone. An area, he was informed, where they were to keep patients vertical in easily cleaned recliners rather than beds, because once they were lying horizontal in a bed, it meant more specialized staff would be required, and on New Year's Day they were in short supply.

Fair enough. He'd worked in hospitals more bareboned than this one.

Avery pulled back a curtain to reveal an elderly gentleman who had his hands folded over his heart. He wasn't hooked up to anything, so most likely not a heart attack. His cheeks were more pinked up than your average senior citizen, but his pallor wasn't great. Nor was there a concerned relative sitting by his side. The poor man was either a victim of so-called granny dumping—abandonment by a family who didn't want to look after him—or on his own. Neither of which were good enough in his opinion.

He glanced at the tablet Avery was holding out for him. High temperature. Tight cough. Rapid, shallow breathing. He popped on a smile. "Mr. Blackstone. What brings you to St. Dolly's this fine morning? Something about a cough that won't loosen up?"

Mr. Blackstone looked as if he might be in disagreement with Carter about how nice the morning was, but he could see he'd disarmed the gentleman with his smile and, after giving the man's liver-spotted hand a gentle shake, his touch, as well. It always killed him to let go when he felt the hands hold on a bit longer than necessary. Warming the head of his stethoscope, Carter got down to business. "That's right, if you could just lean forward for me. Let my hand take the weight of your

chest and hang on while I get a good listen." Mr. Blackstone, as he suspected, began to cough as Carter took
his weight in his hand.

He pressed the stethoscope to his back, aware of
Avery's eyes on him as he heard what he'd suspected.
Hints of pneumonia.

He pulled a wheeled stool over so he was at eye level
with the gentleman. No one liked being talked down to.
Literally or figuratively. "Has anyone run you through
the greetings questionnaire?"

Both Avery and Mr. Blackstone gave him a questioning look.

"It's a quick little 'How Are You, Really' quiz I like
to give all of my patients."

Mr. Blackstone frowned at Carter as many of them
did but nodded to go ahead. He took the man's hand
in his and pressed his fingers to his pulse point. Weak,
but steady.

"How are you?"

"Been better. I was hoping you might be able to
change that."

"That's the plan." Good. He was honest and compos
mentis enough to know what was going on. If it was
what he suspected, it wasn't too late to dial back the
symptoms. "Who brought you here today?"

"My niece."

Something loosened in his chest. Okay. So he had
family.

"She coming to pick you up?"

He nodded. "She was finding a parking spot. Said it
was too far for me to walk."

That tight knot in his chest grew looser still. "That's nice to hear. So have you had this cough for a while?"

"No." Mr. Blackstone shook his head. "I had a touch of a cold, but then I thought I'd show the whippersnappers how we used to celebrate New Year's and things got a bit out of hand."

Carter and Avery exchanged a look. "How's that, exactly?"

"Well, we went ice-skating out on the pond behind the house and one thing led to another and when I was showing off my double Axel, I fell in."

"What? Into the pond?"

"Yessir. First time in sixty years, and I'm not a little annoyed with myself."

It was the first glint of humor they'd seen in him and any other concerns Carter might've had were now laid to rest. He was a well-looked-after, lively gentleman who could ice-skate well enough to hoick himself into the air and crash through the ice. Perhaps not an ideal situation, but solvable. He rattled through protocol to stave off pneumonia and, when the niece appeared, desperately worried and with a small child on her hip, he gave them a list of symptoms to look out for which would require a return.

"I don't like hospitals," said Mr. Blackstone. "Never have."

"I am very much in agreement, sir," said Carter. "Best thing you can do is submit to any coddling this young woman here is going to subject you to, otherwise you will end up in a bed here on an oxygen tank."

Mr. Blackstone looked at him in horror. The niece practically glowed with gratitude. And if he weren't mistaken, he'd just earned himself a fractional nod of respect from Avery. Job. Done.

The next patient, a thirty-two-year-old called Mr. Earl Boston, wasn't nearly as obliging. Nor, Carter supposed, would he be if he'd dislocated his shoulder in the process of clambering out of a dumpster after suffering multiple lacerations at the hand—or paw, really—of a raccoon who, it turned out, did not want his help getting out of said dumpster. The cuts were bad. They needed to be flushed. And if his shoulder injury was left untreated, the blood supply to a few critical veins and nerves would be cut off. Mr. Boston also stank to high heaven and had the unsettled disposition of a man who wanted a pain prescription. And not just for the pain. Which made things tricky.

"Have you seen one of these before?" Carter asked Avery.

"I have not." They both tried to keep their expressions neutral. He could tell Avery had also noted what he'd seen in the patient's temperament, because it had taken some assistance from Rocky to get the gentleman from the ambulance bay where the paramedics had clearly had enough.

Mr. Boston was most likely an opioid addict who'd gone dumpster diving only to discover someone—or in this case something—else had got there first. Though dislocated shoulders were common enough, normally they were posterior or anterior dislocations, usually from sporting activities or, in the case of someone like Mr. Blackstone, a fall. But this…this was an inferior dislocation, and it was difficult to keep a straight face, seeing as the guy looked like he was permanently raising his hand to ask a question.

"Stop smirking," Avery growled into his ear.

He had half a mind not to, just to keep her this close, but even a blind man could see she was growing impatient being on babysitting duties with him. She was a nurse practitioner. Could've easily treated the patients they'd seen on her own. But he liked having her near him.

"Sir, if you could please take a seat?" Avery was gesturing to the recliner. "The doctor needs to relocate your shoulder."

"Why don't you do it?" Carter suggested to Avery.

She looked at him in surprise. "Don't you want to?" she asked.

"Not if you haven't done it. This is a teaching hospital, isn't it?"

"Yes."

"Huh," he said when she didn't volunteer anything beyond that. "Guess you're not interested in learning."

"I am so."

"Well, then." He kept his satisfied smile to himself and nodded at her to take up pole position. "Okay, now. Mr. Boston? This might hurt a little, but not as much as it will keeping your arm up like that for the rest of your life."

Earl scowled at him. "Aren't you going to give me anything for the pain?"

"Nope."

The scowl deepened.

Carter took a step forward. "I'll sit on you if you like, to keep you still, but I'm guessing you'll be able to stay nice and still on your own while Nurse Whittacker here does her job."

Earl did a double take. "What? She's not a doctor."

Avery glowered at Carter. It was a look he knew well. One that said, *Wouldn't it be easier if you did this yourself?*

She was right. It would. But then she wouldn't get the practice and he wouldn't be able to tell how high this guy was or wasn't.

He ignored the look and after informing the patient that he was going to be treated by a highly qualified nurse practitioner who knew how to do just about everything short of heart surgery, he began talking Avery through what to feel for and how to perform the reduction. "That's right." He guided her hand along the shoulder, highly aware of the stiffening of her spine. "So, the top of the humeral head is displaced downward rather than toward the back of the body like a posterior one. It's stuck here, under the glenoid rib. Can you feel the difference?"

She nodded, then checked Mr. Boston's other shoulder. They had to cut his shirt off, which created a bit of a hullabaloo that was quickly settled when Avery informed him they'd get him something warmer and cleaner from the lost and found. She returned to his right arm and took ahold of it at the elbow with one hand. Carter stopped her. "You're a leftie, aren't you?"

She nodded, her eyes narrowing briefly as she took on the fact that he'd noticed something a lot of people didn't. He raised his own left hand. "Takes one to know one. If it were me, I'd reposition myself a bit like this."

She flinched just enough to let him know he was too

close for comfort. Completely fair enough. This was work and flirting was something that didn't belong here. Especially if it was digging as deep into her psyche as it was in his. Best to keep things professional.

He struck a pose a good arm's length from her, keeping an eye on Mr. Boston as he did, then guided her through the steps. He watched carefully as she eased the humeral head back up and over into the glenoid fossa. Gave a little fist pump when the telltale clunking sound elicited a yowl from Mr. Boston and an ear-to-ear grin from Avery. She'd done the procedure as fluidly as if she'd done it a thousand times.

"Well, that was a new one for me," she said once they'd flushed out the patient's lacerations and put topical antibiotics and numbing agents on the wounds that required stitches, a treatment which, once again, Carter had overseen rather than performed, enjoying seeing Avery at work. Not for a power trip. It was more… He already knew he could have treated the guy with his eyes closed. Rather it was nice to see another medical professional who clearly took pride in her work and cared about the way she treated the patient, no matter how cantankerous they were or how chaotic things were on the other side of the curtain, which, unsurprisingly for New Year's Day, was the case. Once Mr. Boston had been discharged and they were finishing up the paperwork, she nodded toward the exit. "I saw that you gave him the forms for rehab."

Carter nodded. He had. The poor guy ticked pretty much every box that would make him eligible for a medically monitored detox. No job, no savings, no health insurance and a ranking that no one would fight him for on the poverty scale.

"Think it'll do anything?"

Carter shrugged. "You know what they say about horses."

She smiled. "What? That you can lead them to water…"

"…but that you can't make them drink?" They shared a smile of understanding. The heat of it hit him right in the solar plexus. He wanted more from this woman. More than a mutual love of treating patients to the best of their ability. He didn't deserve it, but he wanted it anyway. "Where'd you learn to ride like that?"

She blinked in a deliberate way that made him think she liked to keep her personal life just that. "My grandparents," she said. "My Pawpaw, really. He used to ride the circuits."

Carter grinned. "Rodeo boy? Was he a bull rider or an all-rounder?"

"All-rounder, but he was a softie, really. Didn't like seeing any of the animals getting hurt, so he only barrel raced toward the end of his career. Did some bareback. Mostly, he took on horses other people couldn't train."

Something flashed through her eyes he couldn't nail down. Something fiercely loyal and edged with pain.

"But he still taught you to hang onto a bull?"

Her jaw tightened, then released. "He taught me a lot of things."

Carter suddenly understood what she was saying. He held his hands to his chest. "I'm guessing he's not with us anymore?"

"No, sir," she said briskly and then, as if a flick had been switched, popped on a smile he'd seen her use earlier with Mr. Boston. The kind that said they were done now. "I think you know your way around well enough now, Dr. Booth. You through needing your hand held?"

He couldn't help himself. "I'll sure miss your caring touch."

He was gratified to see the glint of attraction flare up again, even if only fleetingly. "I'm pretty sure you'll be able to hold your own." She handed him the tablet they'd been using and pointed him toward the board. "On you go. You're a big boy now. No more need for training wheels."

He walked away. Slowly. Normally he would've strode, got on with business, but something told him she'd be staring at his butt right now. She'd been doing it all morning. Was probably itching to give it a squeeze, too, but that was just a guess, or maybe a wish, because he knew his own fingers were struggling to mind their own business when it came to close proximity with Avery Whittacker. They would. He respected boundaries, and a woman's boundaries in particular, but he wouldn't be sad if she let down her guard and invited him back into that supplies room.

He examined the board and felt his jaw tighten as his eyes landed on his next patient. A young man with sickle cell anemia.

Just like his sister. But different, of course. This kid was battling puberty as well as the frequently fatal disease. It had taken Carter's father without too much fight. His sister... She fought it, all right. She fought absolutely everything. Their parents when they'd been alive. The law. Him. Incarceration. Doctors. Lawyers. Anyone who tried to set down some rules. Like, *How 'bout keeping yourself alive, for starters?*

He pulled back the curtain and gave the kid a big old grin. He was African American, which wasn't unusual, the majority of US sickle cell sufferers were. His Caucasian sister and father's diagnoses were comparatively rare.

Poor kid looked wiped out. No surprise given he was in the throes of a pain episode. Those misshapen sickle cells—the ones meant to be carrying oxygen around his body—had got stuck somewhere in one his smaller blood vessels and clogged the blood flow.

"So… Reece Derby… What brings you to my fine ER today?"

"Fainted."

"Just…fainted?" Carter didn't rise to the attitude the kid was throwing at him. His sister had been like this and a thousand times worse, so…better out than in, son.

"Have you taken anything? For the pain?"

Reece shook his head.

His mother sighed. "Reece, I put some ibuprofen in your backpack for exactly this reason! You don't want to have to take the morphine again. Not with your crazy schedule." She sent an appealing look at Carter. "I bet you he wasn't drinking enough water. He never does when he's out playing with the boys."

Teenaged boys weren't really known for paying much attention to their mother's warnings. And sick ones… Well. He knew all about that. Then again, a *crazy schedule* probably wasn't the best thing for a kid prone to overdoing it and, if things went wrong—which they could, and quickly—a candidate for pneumonia, acute chest syndrome, spleen infections and any number of other things.

"Rightio, Reece. I'll just check out your heart rate and a couple of other things if you don't mind."

Reece sat up with a huff and pulled off his shirt. He was tired and cranky, and from the way he kept slumping back, he was ticking off all indicators of anemia. If it was bad, he might need a blood transfusion. If not…a good steak might help kick his iron count back up.

"You having trouble breathing?"

"No, sir."

"Let's see those eyes of yours."

Reece tipped his head back. They weren't jaundiced, but they weren't exactly bright and bursting with life.

The kid didn't look like a tearaway. Not in the way his sister was. Apart from the super trendy sneakers and the latest release phone, he almost looked like a nerd. Christmas presents, no doubt. Or, as they'd been known in his house, contrition. His dad knew buying his sister a new dress or new shoes wouldn't take away the disease he'd passed on, but it was the only way he knew how to say he was sorry.

They ran through a few more tests and, as a precaution, Carter suggested they head on upstairs to his regular doctor in the Hematology Department. They exchanged fist bumps and extracted a promise from his mom to make steak with plenty of salad on the side tonight. When the kid's mother went to fill out a couple of forms, Carter fixed the boy with a stern look. "You know this can kill you, right? If you don't listen to your body?"

"Yes, sir." The poor kid hung his head and shook it. He knew all right. He looked up at Carter. The pain he was feeling inside had worked its way through to his eyes. "I just want to be normal, you know? Be like the other kids."

"I know. And for the most part, you can be. Just... let your mom know you hear her and she'll back off a bit. She just loves you is all and that's no bad thing."

Reece smiled at him and once again they bumped fists. He went and joined his mom, throwing a gangly arm around her shoulders, saying he'd be happy to make dinner if she was tired. The moment hit him in the gut like a well-aimed boot.

Why the hell Cassidy couldn't have been more like that was beyond him. Choosing a life of hanging out with actual friends sounded much more fun than finding a crowd who got her locked up for one to three years, behavior dependent.

She'd never wanted to be *normal* he reminded himself, tapping out the notes on Reece's chart. She wanted to be superhuman. If only there'd been some way to pull all of those deformed cells from her body and put them in his own...

He let the thought wither and die. No matter how much he wished for it, he'd never be able to extract the disease from her body and put it into his. Give himself the curtailed life expectancy. Let her live a normal life. There had been days when he'd cursed his parents for taking the risk of having another child after he had been born free of the inherited disease. But despite her problems, the world would be a less interesting place without his little sister, so...warts and all, he loved her.

Maybe the fact he knew where she'd be for the foreseeable future would change things. Maybe it wouldn't. When he'd gone into med school—a place he'd told her he had to stay in if she wanted her rent paid, clothes to wear, food to eat, that sort of thing now that their parents had passed—she'd settled down for a bit. But the week he'd officially become a doctor, she'd bolted. Stolen some candy or some such, and not for the sugar high. Ended up in juvenile detention. And so the cycle continued. When he was being extra honest with himself, he knew the chances of her walking around free, with an ankle bracelet, or on probation, anytime soon was neither here nor there. Until she stopped seeing her disease as something that put her above the law, it plain old didn't matter.

He caught a glimpse of Avery disappearing behind a curtain with an elderly woman using a walking frame. He liked the way she gave the patient space, but made it clear she was close to hand to help no matter what. He shifted his stance. Who was he kidding? He liked near enough everything he knew about Avery Whittacker. It was a short list, but he knew enough of what mattered. She was a good person. She honored family. She was full of grit. And she cared. About her friends, her patients and, for about thirty very sweet seconds, she'd cared about him.

He'd have to nip whatever was happening between the two of them in the bud. If Cassidy's track record for getting herself transferred to yet another so-called correctional facility—he'd yet to see any correcting—was anything to go by, he'd have to leave again soon. He already had a feeling his heart would be the one that broke if he let himself develop feelings for Avery. He'd made that mistake once before in med school and the fall out hadn't been pretty. That was the way the cookie crumbled when you were a Booth. But how he wished things were different.

CHAPTER FOUR

AVERY DELETED THE "Take your time thinking about it." text from management and switched her phone screen to the realtor's page. She growled when she saw that, for the fifth day running, she'd missed the opening hours. Her shifts had been chaotic and bled well into overtime. No surprise there. They were always short-staffed this time of year with everyone wanting to spend some hard-earned vacation time with their families.

No family to go home to meant she had little to no excuse to ask for time off herself. Not that she begrudged her work. It was more that the change in routine was still new enough—raw enough—to make the loneliness she rarely acknowledged feel fathomless. As families bundled in and out of the ER, she acutely missed being with her own. Hungered for her mom's care packages of leftover Christmas food that she and April used to complain about. *How many turkey sandwiches could a girl eat?* they'd used to complain. What she wouldn't give to have one now.

But, she curtly reminded herself, life was different now and if the experts were to believed, sometimes change could be good.

She still had her weekly video calls from her parents, and to be fair they had invited her out to Arizona to celebrate with them, but…they hadn't exactly begged her to join them. She got it. Being all together again was the most painful reminder that they weren't *all* together again.

She tried not to take it personally. The day they'd adopted her—a scrawny, belligerent mixed race two-year-old with a wild look in her eye—her life had been changed for the better. They'd fed her, clothed her, gave her rules and the room to knee and elbow them into the shape she needed. They'd loved her as if she had been their own. Same as her new grandparents who'd cradled her in their arms, told her bedtime stories and put her on top of her first pony. And, most amazingly, she'd gained a big sister. Her hero from the second they'd laid eyes on one another.

April was the reason behind the adoption. She'd been desperate for a little sister and, despite a few years of trying, her parents hadn't been able to give her one the regular way, so they'd opened up their hearts and brought Avery into their family. So she owed everything to April. The world's best big sister. Voice like an angel. Knew her way around a guitar the way Avery had learned her way around a horse. Dreams big enough for the two of them. Dreams that were meant to have propelled them into the limelight of the Grand Ole Opry. Right up until cancer announced itself in the form of a hoarse voice April couldn't shake, followed by difficulty swallowing, and then a peculiar lump near her collarbone.

When she'd received the diagnosis, Avery had taken to looking after her sister as if it were the sole reason she'd been put on this earth. It had been no surprise when her boyfriend of just over a year had ended their relationship. Told her she wasn't *emotionally available* anymore. To him, she wasn't. To her family, she was all in. She'd moved into her grandparents', helping out with the horses, doing her shifts at St. Dolly's. But mostly she had devoted herself to looking after April.

When April's voice and then her life had been snatched away from her…so had their shared dream of singing professionally one day. Which was why Avery hadn't sung since. Not a solitary note. And why the hospital management wasn't particularly thrilled with her now that it was just a handful of weeks away from the annual benefit that raised money for the oncology ward.

Well, tough. This was Nashville. You couldn't swing a cat without hitting a dozen singers. She got it. There weren't many who'd had sisters die of cancer under their care here at St. Dolly's, but still.

The truth was she was afraid to sing again. Afraid to feel everything that would rise up from that private place only singing tapped into. The place where she held her grief. Her sorrow. Her loss.

It was bad enough that she'd lost her sister and that her adoptive parents hadn't found her reason enough to hang around. But she'd lost her grandparents shortly after April's death, as well. As if life thought she had had too much good luck through the years. Sure. It had given her a bumpy start at the beginning—teenaged birth parents unequipped to raise a child—but from there on out she'd enjoyed the smoothest of sailing for years, only to have it all yanked away over these last eighteen months.

The house she and April had wanted to buy was the one thing that remained. And she'd focused her energies on saving to buy it as if her life depended on it. Praying every night that someone else wouldn't see what she saw in the place. It was a fixer-upper. The kind that was more labor of love than a few rounds with the handyman. And now, at long last, she had the money. For the deposit anyway.

So the fact that Avery still hadn't managed to get down to the realty office to put down the deposit was par for the course. That, or the heavens were trying to send her a subtle hint that she shouldn't buy it. She wasn't so good at reading the signs these days.

"Most health professionals look happy when the patient board is empty."

She didn't turn when Carter slid his forearms onto the same counter she was leaning on, but it was impossible not to respond to his presence. Her body was in total lust with him. Had been for the past week. Handfuls of glitter lit up her insides each time they passed. Butterflies took flight whenever she heard his voice. Her intimate zones had a parade if their hands so much as brushed. Which they may have done. Multiple times.

Even so. Looking him in the eye was another thing altogether. She couldn't shake the feeling that he could read her like a book, and frankly she didn't want to be read. Not today anyway. She was tired and confused and was supposed to be pouring what little energy she had left into making her dead sister's dreams come true. One of them at least.

Carter shifted position to let one of the nurses pass, and as he readjusted that sexy body of his along the countertop, a waft of pine and honeycomb released another fistful of hot sparks in her belly.

An involuntary hum filled her throat, but she caught it just in time, turning it into a throat clearing.

Something about Carter Booth made her want to open up her throat and commune with the songbirds. And it scared her. As if rediscovering that part of herself would be the cruelest of reminders that no matter how hard she'd tried to save her sister's life, she'd failed.

Oh, she knew she alone couldn't cure cancer and that, in the end, no matter how great a nurse she'd been, there was literally nothing she could've done beyond making sure her sister didn't feel any pain.

But it didn't mean she was going to sing again. It would be too savage not to hear her sister's voice wrap around hers like ivy as it always had done. Would it hurt as much as radiation therapy? As much as chemo? As much as dying?

Carter nudged her with his elbow. "You look tired."

"And you look like you could do with a session at the Charm Academy."

Carter snorted.

Avery harrumphed. She wasn't going to admit that he was right. She *was* tired. And hungry. And soon to be homeless as she'd given notice on her tiny apartment rental. She gave Carter a quick glance. He was still looking at her, a smile playing on those stupidly sexy lips of his.

"I don't suppose you can recommend any good places for some Texas barbecue around here?" he asked.

She gave one very slow, very studied blink. "Did you just blaspheme in front of me?"

The corners of his mouth twitched. "What?" He kicked his Texan accent up a notch. "Is mentioning the finest barbecue in the land some form of cussing around these parts?"

"You're damn straight it is! Your piddly little Texas barbecue doesn't hold a candle to our Tennessee slow-cooked pork ribs. Brisket so tender it defies the laws of…um…soft things." She flicked her fingers at him. "Texas Schmexas."

He let out a whoop and clapped his hands together. "That's fighting talk, missy. You do know that barbecue is about as close as you can get to religion where I'm from, don't you?"

"And where is that exactly?" she asked, feeling the vinegar from the sauce she was mentally tasting kicking her energy levels back up to par. "Where you come from."

He eyed her for a minute as if deciding whether or not she was worthy of the information. She jutted out her chin. Damn straight she was.

"I worked at Partridge Hill in Austin."

Wow. They didn't let just anyone walk through those doors and treat patients. It was a good hospital. A renowned one even. "And left why?"

His green eyes darkened, and if she wasn't mistaken, the tiniest of twitches set loose in his jaw. "Family reasons."

She dialed back her aggression. She got that. She also got not wanting to talk about it. The only person allowed to mention her sister was Lia and even then…

Suffice it to say, the two of them were besties because they knew what topics were allowed during their weekly Guac and Talk meets at Gantry's Margarita Den. So even though Carter hadn't explained his family reasons, the way he hadn't moved a muscle but looked as if his entire physique had changed spoke to her louder than the kiss they'd shared, and that thing had announced itself with a bullhorn.

"Guess I'd better learn you up about the finer things in Tennessee, then," she said.

Carter had never been one to put on the plastic bibs most barbecue joints supplied these days but to try to get some sort of reaction from Avery, he tied one on. "What do you think?"

"Cute," she said, her dark eyes dropping back down to the menu.

He grinned. He'd take that as a win. She hadn't smiled or looked all that impressed, but she was sitting across a table from him. Neither of them were talking about it, but that electricity they'd both been ignoring at work was still buzzing loud and clear out here in the real world. Or maybe they'd been drawn together the same way his sister was drawn to trouble. Moths to a flame. The thought sobered him.

He stared at the menu, then feeling shot through with too much choice, set it down again. "What would you recommend, Avery, seeing as you're the expert on regional cuisine?"

She put her menu aside. "I'm guessing that depends upon how hungry you are and how much time you've got."

"Lots and very."

She smiled. "You're a proper wordsmith, aren't you?"

"You want pretty?" He leaned in close enough to smell her—loving the way she somehow wore the scent of sunshine and meadow grass even though it was the dead of winter. "I've never seen a woman ride a bucking bronco—live or mechanical—the way I saw you ride. And to me, that was poetry in motion. Better than grooming a horse. Sending a patient home to heal after a perfect surgery. Or playing lip-lock with a stranger."

She bridled. "Watching me ride was better than kissing me?"

He shrugged. "I suppose they were about equal."

She snorted, then tipped her head to the door. "If that's how you feel, then how about you get your food to go?"

If he'd blinked, he would've missed it, but somehow, he'd caught another glimpse of what he'd convinced himself he'd imagined. A raw vulnerability caught behind walls that instinctively flew up around that tender heart of hers. And something new. Hurt.

He'd pushed too hard. Pushed when he should've pulled. Just like he'd done to a dozen women before her, only those times he hadn't felt the ramifications of his actions in the form of remorse. Well. Once he had and he'd taken it as a lesson well learned. Clearly not that well learned.

Idiot.

"No, ma'am," he said resolutely. "There is no chance I would leave a woman sitting on her own. And definitely not one who's made the type of impression you have."

"And what is that exactly?"

He shook his head, unable, or maybe unwilling, to put into words the fact that she was the first woman to put a chink in his armor since he'd decided relationships weren't for him.

He wasn't a stranger to them. There'd been a girl in high school. Then his dad had died of sickle cell. A couple of long-term flings in college. Then his mother had passed from a stress-induced embolism. Heartbreak if you were to take his sister's word for it. He'd had a long-term relationship in med school. Got too comfortable with things finally going according to plan. Finishing his internship put short shrift to that.

Having a poorly sister hell-bent on getting herself the electric chair instead of dying at the hand of her disease had a way of limiting his options.

Okay. Maybe Cassidy wasn't that bad. A bit of shoplifting here. Some grand theft larceny there. The latest: a DUI after a dine and dash. She never wanted the stuff. She wanted the high. Well, she'd got that all right. And a three-year sentence that she would definitely be serving at least a year of.

And no, he knew he didn't have to traipse along in his sister's wake, but there was no other family around to keep an eye on her, and prison hospitals weren't exactly elite hubs of medical excellence, so he did. Chasing her around the country, making sure he worked in whatever hospital she'd be sent to if things went south. All of which meant over the years on a personal front, his specialty was being an ass. But right now, he was wishing it were something else.

When he failed to answer, Avery shook her head, irritated, and put down the menu. "I don't have time for game playing, Carter."

"And I don't have a single friend in Nashville." Or anywhere for that matter. Getting close only led to saying goodbye and goodbyes hurt. He let out a silent string of cuss words, then decided, for once, to choose honesty as the best policy. He put his hand on his heart. "I could do with a friend right now. One who kisses like you do would be the icing on the cake. Or the Mississippi mud pie they've got here on the dessert menu if that's your preference."

She gave him the side eye, but something told him she was still sitting here because she was interested. "That sounds like a little bit more than your average friendship would offer."

He feigned innocence. "Mud pie?"

After shooting him a look he couldn't read, he saw her lips fighting a losing battle with her frown and eventually twisting through into a smile. "Sounds risky. And high calorie."

He was about to suggest something that could burn off the calories real quick but thought better of it. Avery didn't strike him as the "dine and dash" type in the romance department.

He waved his menu between them. "Why don't we start with the healthy stuff? And then, if we're still hungry, we can see how we go."

He wasn't talking about mud pie anymore and they both knew it.

Avery seemed to consider the doorway for a second and then, when her stomach gave a loud growl, conceded that it was a good idea. They ordered far too much and as such were told it'd be a bit of a wait. When staring at the smattering of people around them grew awkward instead of interesting, Carter asked, "What part of town do you live in? I'm in a serviced apartment right now and it's just about sucked my soul dry."

She arced an eyebrow. "They're that bad?"

He nodded. "I like somewhere with a bit of heart. Character. These are just cookie-cutter apartments that, whilst convenient, aren't exactly welcoming."

"What kind of houses have you lived in before? Did you have a favorite?"

Carter looked away and then drew his thumbs along his forehead as if trying to make room in his brain for the question. If only there were a simple answer. This kind. This house. This town. The end. "I tend not to hang around long enough anywhere to get a mortgage."

She frowned, then shrugged. "Thought so."

He grinned. "Oh, you did, did you? Already got me pegged for a love 'em and leave 'em kind of guy?"

Where the hell had that come from?

She stared at him as if trying to figure out how best to let him know he wasn't her type. "I just got the feeling you moved a lot, but I wouldn't've said it was because you were leaving a trail of broken hearts in your wake."

Despite himself, he laughed. "You're right. It's a bit more complicated than that."

Most people left the conversation there, but not Avery. "Why? Why is it complicated?"

"My sister. She's a bit… Let's just say her health's not the best and she's got a fairly elastic interpretation of the law."

"So you…what? Is she a minor? Are you her minder?"

"No, she's a grown woman, just behaves like a child. As for the minder bit…" He tipped his head back and forth. "Self-appointed. I'm sure she'd rather I did other things with my time."

"Like buy a house?"

It was a pointed question and one he really didn't know the answer to. For the first time in his life, he hoped so. "I don't know. I'm not sure how long I'll be here."

"Why?"

He debated telling her and then thought, *Screw it*. "My sister's in the state pen."

Her eyes widened but she passed no judgment.

"She's got sickle cell anemia. That and a passion for brushing up against the law."

Avery pushed her lips forward. "Sounds like a tricky combination."

"It is if you're her big brother. And her only living relative."

He saw something change in Avery right then. A shift in her body language that altered the protective energy she'd been holding close to her like a shield. "And that's why you left Austin?"

"And Dallas and St. Louis and New Orleans and—"

She laughed and held up her hands. "I'm guessing that truck of yours has a pretty high mileage count."

He nodded. "Wouldn't get more than five bucks for it if I drove it into a car lot."

The light in her eyes dimmed. "I'm guessing she behaves that way because she figures she's going to die anyway, so why not go down in flames?"

"Damn, girl. You know how to get to the point."

She shrugged as if she had some insight in the matter but offered nothing. *Still waters*, as his mother used to say.

"Look." He put his hands flat on the table. "I'm going to lay my cards out. As you know, I'm new in town and you're pretty much the first and only thing I've taken a shine to. If things go the way they usually do, I won't be here long, but while I am, I sure could do with having a friend."

"What makes you think I want to be your friend?"

A solid fifty-fifty combination of nothing and everything about her. The fact she was still sitting here in this pleather booth spoke volumes. As was the fact she'd yet to take off her coat. The way she blushed whenever he brushed his hand against hers. And turned the other direction to grind her teeth once she had. The way she'd welcomed his tongue into her mouth the other night, letting him explore the heat and hunger he knew they were both feeling all the way down to their toes. The part about how she'd insisted on driving her own car here so she could see herself home after.

"Honestly?" he said. "I think that you like me, but that you don't like that you like me. And that's why I'm proposing a fling without strings."

It was a dare. And she knew it.

"So…you want to sleep with someone who isn't sure if they like you?"

"Quite the opposite. I want someone who knows they like me but isn't interested in anything long-term for all the right reasons."

"And what are those exactly?"

There was only one reason, really. Not getting his heart broken. He took her hands in his and rubbed his thumbs across the backs of them. "Look. Life's too short not to enjoy some pleasure. Especially having met someone who I can tell just by looking at her is a kindred spirit." He gave his heart a thump and was gratified to see her blush. He pressed kisses onto the backs of her hands, then released them. "Look. I'm trying my best to be honest. If we get together while I'm here, I know we can have some fun. And it doesn't have to all be adult time. We can… I don't know… What do you like to do?"

"Dance."

"Good. Excellent. We'll go dancing. Then a few months down the line when I inevitably have to up stakes, nobody's heart gets broken. Easy-peasy."

A fire lit in his belly when he saw in her eyes what he felt in his gut. A hunger for something that was more than skin deep. A fear that going there might destroy her.

The energy between them shifted once again. From sparring to interested. Real interested.

She pushed her menu to the side. "I don't know if I want to have a fling with a traveling Casanova."

He belly-laughed, then crossed his heart. "Trust me. Women can see I resist commitment from a mile off, so I try and dial back the 'man whore' aspect of things." His expression turned serious. "I haven't been with anyone in a while. Short-term or otherwise."

She took a sip of her water, then flicked her dark eyes up to meet his. "We'd keep this between ourselves? The sexy-sexy stuff?"

"If you like." He'd sign a contract in blood if she wanted.

"Okay, then. Friends with benefits." She lifted her glass to his for a toast, but because he knew better than most that time was a precious commodity, he leaned across the table and kissed her instead.

CHAPTER FIVE

WHEN CARTER BROKE the kiss, Avery's head snapped back as if she'd just been given whiplash. And in a way, she had.

He was calling a spade a spade and asking her to acknowledge it, too.

Okay, sure. Over the past few days, they'd been wriggling along in this direction. Flirty. Not flirty. Spatting. Making the peace. Carter was being adult enough to put into words what they both knew. There was something happening between the two of them and the only way it could be laid to rest was for one of them to leave town or to go for it.

She thought of the holding pattern she'd been in for the past year. The one she'd landed in once she'd emerged from the initial fug of grief after her sister passed. And even before then, her ex had made it pretty clear she wasn't "ideal girlfriend" material. He'd been right. Even all these months later, filling the void her sister left with a relationship did not seem wise. Her heart and mind were elsewhere.

She'd set her sights on buying this house and having it be the answer to all her dreams, but now that she was within a hair's breadth of it…she wasn't sure that a house without April in it would do what she'd been stupidly hoping for. Bring her back.

She looked at Carter. He looked straight back at her. She could tell he wasn't pressuring her. But his offer was serious. "So…when does it start?" she asked. "Our new arrangement."

"Up to you. I'd happily steam up the truck right now, but I don't want you to think I only want you for your body. Believe it or not, I'd like to get to know the real you, as well."

Despite herself, she blushed. It was one thing to lust after someone, another to have him treat her as a whole person—warts and all. It was more than her ex had done. He never would've said as much but she knew deep down that he'd resented her sister's illness because it took away the time and energy she put into their relationship. He'd wanted a 1950s housewife. Not a woman with a career of her own, a dying sister, grief. Good riddance to him.

She looked at Carter.

Could she do this? Enjoy the physical connection she felt with him, but keep her heart safe and secure?

What if this little experiment pulverized what was left of her inner strength?

What if it didn't?

What if it rejuvenated her? Made her feel alive again? Even though she didn't want her ex back, he'd had a point. She'd been walking around like a zombie and it wasn't until she'd laid eyes on Carter Booth that she'd felt the blood pumping through her veins like it used to.

"I don't even know your middle name," she huffed. As if that were a deal breaker.

"Zane," he said. "That help?" His tone was wry but not unkind. He was giving her the space she needed.

The truth of the matter was she liked the idea. Her grandparents had passed. Her parents were gone, broken by the death of their only natural daughter. She was feeling abandoned and trying to fix it by putting a deposit on an empty house that would never know the sound of her sister's voice.

What exactly was she going to do once she moved in there? Sit in the middle of it and cry every day? Maybe having a "friends with benefits" relationship with Carter would make her happy again. Maybe it would only put her grieving on hold.

To their mutual relief, the food arrived and they began to eat. They were hungry enough for the silence to come naturally, but she had no doubt that both of their brains were whirring like a train heading full speed along the tracks.

Could she trust him with her heart? That was the real question she should be asking herself. Even with a plastic bib on, the man exuded an inner power that didn't seem entirely under his control. But that craving for honesty he was talking about, and desire. Suddenly, she wanted nothing more than to pull her nails down both of their facades and see what was underneath.

She finished a pork rib, wiped her hands on a napkin, then deposited it on the growing pile they had on a plate on the side of the table. "I was going to buy a house tomorrow."

His eyebrows went up, the rest of him stayed still. "Oh?"

"Some of that money from the other night is for the

deposit." She hesitated for a minute, then plowed ahead. "The plan was to buy it with my sister."

"Ducked out, did she?"

"No." She was shocked to feel the tears that she normally kept at bay sting at the back of her throat. "She died almost two years ago."

Carter's whole body reacted to the information and, unlike most people who felt compelled to instantly offer some meaningless platitude, he gave himself the time to truly absorb what she'd said. Pressing one of his big old hands to his heart, he finally spoke. "I've never found an adequate way to express my condolences. Words don't seem good enough to…well…not with my vocabulary anyway."

"Cancer," she said, surprised to hear herself proactively continuing the conversation. Maybe it was the fact he had a sister in trouble, too. Maybe it was just time. She'd kept the topic locked up so tight she hadn't realized how much it needed air. Maybe if they had this *special friendship*, as he called it, one with no-holds-barred, all of the honesty she hadn't realized she craved, she'd find a way to move forward. It would hurt. She might even let loose all the grief and rage she knew was lurking around her insides like a cornered bobcat.

He was strong. Sure of himself. Obviously liked a challenge. She could give him that. And a whole lot more.

It was on the tip of her tongue to tell him her sister's death was the reason she had left the oncology ward. It wasn't because she hadn't loved the job. She had. Very much. She'd had people reach into her life before she'd been old enough to know how bleak it was. This was her version of paying that generosity of spirit forward.

Being there for people during their darkest journeys—it was humbling and hadn't felt like a job so much as a calling. But once she'd been forced to say goodbye to the one person in her life who she'd never imagined saying goodbye to... Well...there were limits to a person's capacity for handling grief.

She'd spent the past eighteen months teetering so close to the precipice of hers... Changing departments and the fact she and Lia had an unspoken agreement *not* to talk about her loss were the only things holding her together. That and earning the money to buy the house.

"Esophageal cancer," she clarified. "It took her voice, her throat and then, finally, all of her."

Carter didn't mince words. "That's a cruel way to go."

"It was." She was pretty sure her face told him everything he needed to know.

He was a doctor so he didn't need the details. And even though St. Dolly's was full to the brim with amazing doctors and nurses, many of whom she considered friends, she felt for the first time since April had died that she was talking to someone who cared. Really cared that she'd loved and lost. Maybe it wasn't even that, because, of course, her friends and family *cared*.

But from the moment they'd laid April to rest, a lifelong fear had resurfaced. The one about being left to fend for herself again. Just as she'd had to when social workers had found her scrabbling around in a dumpster for food when her mother had... Well...her mother had had her own problems. When she'd heard she'd died, the world had carried on as it had before. But when April died... Sea change. So she'd braced herself for the inevitable. And just as she'd feared...the people she held most dear disappeared from her life, one by one, as if she hadn't mattered at all.

So why did Carter Booth, a man who clearly had burdens of his own to shoulder, want to make room for her in his life?

She looked hard into his eyes, trying to catch glimpses of whatever it was he saw when he looked at her. The strength to do the same.

He knew she could ride a bull, boss an emergency room and that her sister had died of cancer.

Not bad for a few days of tactically avoiding one another.

What else?

He knew how she kissed when she wasn't holding back. That she didn't pull punches. And that he unzipped something inside her that made her speak her mind.

"Is that plan still green lit?" he asked after another swig of his beer. "To buy the house?"

"Fifteen minutes ago, I would've said absolutely." She could hardly believe her own ears.

"What changed?"

"You."

His eyebrows dove together. "I wasn't meaning to put a wrench into your plans."

He hadn't. He'd just shone a light on them. "It wasn't you. It was more…" She twirled a couple of French fries around a pool of ketchup. She looked up and met his. "You made me realize I was putting my hopes and dreams into things and you've put yours into people."

He pushed his lips forward, then sucked them back into his mouth. "Person. And let me assure you, doing it my way comes with its own set of problems."

"Sure, but... I don't know why, but you've made me realize that when I buy that house, it isn't going to make my sister come back. It might even make me feel worse."

"Why? Your eyes light up when you talk about it."

"They do?" She felt her cheeks pink up that he'd noticed.

"What do you say you ask for one more tour before you sign on the dotted line? I'll go with you if you want."

She was halfway through saying no when she forced herself to fight the instinct. Shutting people out for the rest of her life wasn't going to bring her sister back, either. He was just another set of eyes on a house he didn't give two hills of beans about. It would be practical to let him come along. "Cool."

"You sure?"

"Yup."

"And..." he swirled a French fry around a puddle of ketchup "...any further thoughts on that other thing?"

She gave him a slow grin. "The 'friends with benefits' thing?"

He nodded.

She felt her temperature spike. Her eyes dropped to his lips.

"You want me, don't you?"

He was grinning as he said it, but she knew if she said no, they'd draw a line under this conversation and never revisit it.

"How far away is your apartment?" he asked.

"You can't swing a cat in mine."

He arced an eyebrow. She blushed. Maybe he thought she was expecting some wild sexual acrobatics. Before she could clarify that she wasn't expecting cartwheels, he said, "Well, then. Looks like you'll be staying with me tonight."

By the time he managed to get the key in the door, Carter was so hot and bothered he was pretty sure he'd go blind if Avery didn't let him pick her up and carry her to the bedroom. Or the sofa. The floor of the tiny living room would do at this point, but not here in the hallway. He had his standards.

Plus, there was always the possibility she might suddenly yawn and say, *Not tonight, honey, I've got to wash my hair.* But if he'd been reading the signals right, he was pretty sure the only showers they'd be taking would be together.

Something had uncorked in them while they'd eaten dessert. Sharing that gooey chocolatey pie had been near enough the sexiest foreplay he'd ever been involved in. Whether it was the sugar rush, the phenylethylamine in the chocolate or good old-fashioned lust, they'd been behaving like a pair of feral teenagers ever since, a lust bubble forming around them as if it protected them from the rest of the world. He hadn't been able to stop touching her. They'd even left his truck at the restaurant because the idea of not being able to put his hands on her shoulders, her cheek, her thighs for the ten-minute drive over to his place seemed a form of torture he didn't have the endurance for. Not tonight anyway.

And judging by the make-out session they'd had in the car before they'd even got in the building… *Mmm…* Suffice it to say, if he'd thought their New Year's kiss had been one in a million, he'd been sorely mistaken.

She had dozens more just like it and some that were even better.

"Hurry," she commanded.

Okay. She wasn't going to be washing her hair, then.

"I am. You got me all flustered, woman."

More than that. She'd got him worried. This wasn't going to be a one-night stand. No chance. Nor was it something he could walk away from all free and easy when the time came. He needed to readjust his emotional settings before things went any further.

Avery grabbed the door handle, gave the key a jiggle and twisted it. It swung open. She arced an eyebrow. "You ready now?"

He grinned. Hell, yes. He'd sort any emotional fallout later. Life was for living, right?

She shoved him into the apartment and began unzipping, unbuttoning and unbuckling everything that held him in clothing. All of a sudden, she stopped and held her hands up. "You cool with this?"

"Honey, I am hot and bothered with this." He took ahold of her hips and pressed them to his so that she knew exactly how uncool he was. Her grin was wicked. She pressed into him as if to confirm she liked what she felt, then got back to work. Why the hell he'd worn a shirt with so many damn buttons on it was beyond him. He could just rip the thing off, but feeling her fingers nip and twist against the fabric and his skin wasn't exactly a hardship. He liked seeing this side of her. In the ER, she was all contained, controlled. Hair back. Scrubs immaculate. Face implacable.

Right now? Not so much.

Her hair had long since lost contact with its clips. Her scarf had hit the floor. Coat had quickly followed suit. Her lipstick had vanished and all that remained was raw, unfettered desire. Her charged energy made him feel a lot less apologetic for all of the plans he had in store for that deliciously curvy body of hers.

"I better ask," he said while she'd freed his chest of fabric and swept her hands across the tips of his nipples. "Are *you* cool with it?" He hovered his fingers above the two ribbons barely holding onto the fabric covering her breasts.

She took ahold of the ribbons and tugged them loose. "Icy."

He could barely breathe.

By the time they had scrabbled around for some protection and were skin on skin, Carter could say in full confidence that Avery Whittacker was the polar opposite of icy. She was hot like lava. Steamy like the tropics. A pool of sunlight on a winter's day. Anything and everything he wanted in a woman. Perfection is what she was.

He'd never known a woman like her. And at precisely this moment, she was ravaging his naked body like he was the last man on earth and her only chance of survival. Something he never imagined being for anyone. Their salvation. He caught the emotions that came along with that and sent them packing. Tonight was about Avery and hearing that delicious groan of hers.

The first time around it was exactly as he'd imagined it might be. Hot. Sweaty. Intense. Enough to blow his ability to think straight clean out of the water.

Nice to see reality catching up to his fantasies for once. He wasn't ashamed to admit it. The nights were long and sometimes lonely. So, sure, he'd closed his eyes and pictured being with Avery pretty much every night since they'd met. They'd had their prelude in the car, so from the moment she'd shucked his jeans off him, turned around and slid him inside of her, the lovemaking, such as it had been, had felt more akin to a sexy wrestling match.

Fast. Furious. A bit angry. A bit not. She might've bitten him. He may have scraped his fingers down her back to find out if she'd moan or scream. She moaned. It had been just about the hottest sex he'd ever had. Right up until the second time. They'd both got their wits about them a bit more and, having used up a fair amount of energy in round one, they took their time. He knew he'd need a lifetime to really know her body. The bits of her belly that made her shiver when stroked. The spot on her inner thigh that, when he licked it, made her grab ahold of his hair and demand he never stop. Her lips. They were point-blank the most kissable lips he'd ever had the pleasure of exploring, let alone tasting. She was honeysuckle and hot sauce. Nutmeg and vanilla. Edible is what she was. Head to toe. But he didn't have a lifetime. He had whatever time his sister's sentence, or her health, would give them.

"Hey." Avery held him out at arm's length and looked at him. "What just happened there?"

"Nothing."

"Yes, it did. You pulled back."

Physically, he hadn't, but emotionally he guessed he had. Just like always, he was already counting down to his departure. So much for carpe diem.

He kissed her instead of offering an explanation. And it did nothing to change the way she felt in his arms—right at home. Already, he felt the storm clouds gathering. He could get a little too used to this. Allow those thoughts he'd allowed himself once before—thoughts about putting down roots, getting a house, the picket fence, even the kids. He didn't know why, but he got the feeling Avery was fighting similar demons for different reasons. So as far as feelings went, arm's length was okay by her. He liked that. Having a tacit understanding of one another. An instinct as to when it was right to push, to demand even, and when it was best to let things lie. He pulled her into his arms and matched his breaths to hers. The lines between where his body ended and her body began blurring as sleep eventually began to seep into both of their pores until, with the scent of her surrounding him like a comforting cloud, he fell into a deep dreamless sleep.

A mug of coffee scraping across the bedside table was the first thing he became aware of. A pair of caramel-colored legs wearing a pair of his boxers was next. He scanned up the length of one of his old country music T-shirts, decided it was much nicer with boobs behind it and, eventually, settled on Avery's morning smile. *Mmm...* He reached out, slid a hand up her thigh and tugged her to him.

"Uh-uh, sunshine. We got work. At least I do." She crossed the room and yanked open the curtains. It was still dark. Winter had a lot to answer for. But at least he didn't have to squint.

She flicked on the overhead light.

He rubbed his hand over his eyes, then forced himself to confront the day. His eyes hit the clock and bolted up to standing. "I'm due at St. Dolly's soon. Why didn't you get me up?"

"I don't know your schedule, do I?" she protested,

then sniggered. "Besides, you looked cute, all snuggled up there. Like a puppy."

She didn't resist when he pulled her close for a kiss. "Is that what you'd like? A puppy?"

Damn. He shouldn't have gone there. He could already see one bouncing around an imaginary lawn he'd just mowed for her. Taking it to puppy class together. Long walks through the countryside.

She tipped her head side to side as if she were seeing the same pictures and giving the notion some serious consideration. "I can't even get it together to buy a house, let alone the puppy to go in it. I think that's one for the *no* pile, bud. Sorry."

Normally, he would've laughed at how thoughts of puppy ownership pulled them in opposite directions, but it didn't feel funny. It felt sad. Sad and lonely that two people who clearly liked one another the way they did couldn't daydream about the future without producing frowns. Pretty much how his childhood had been, he reminded himself. Why daydream when you knew early death was inevitable?

The memory of his mother's face at his father's funeral twisted his gut into a knot. He didn't wish anyone dead, but he had to admit, he'd almost been relieved for her when an embolism took her shortly after his father. She'd hated life without him, and Carter hated that he couldn't take her pain away. Or his sister's, for that matter. All of which fed into the big pool of evidence that he didn't deserve to dream of puppies or anything else with Avery. Well. Sex. He'd definitely be dreaming about the sex. For a long time to come.

Avery took a gulp of her coffee, clearly not bothered

that it was scalding hot, and perched herself on the edge of the dresser.

"Right, my little cowhand. We better set up a few rules and regulations for how we operate at the hospital."

He snorted, then reread her expression. "Oh. You're serious." He took a slug of his coffee, wondering how the hell she didn't flinch drinking something that hot and strong.

She went first. "I don't want anyone to know we have something personal going on."

Fair enough. He wouldn't want to have to leave her to explain everything when he inevitably left, so he was good with that. "Fine."

"If we happen to accidentally meet in a supplies room or an on-call room, we either keep the door fully opened or completely locked."

He suppressed a grin. So they could have hanky-panky at work, just so long as no one knew about it. He would never embarrass her in that way anyhow. Private lives were called private lives for a reason. He put two fingers to his eyebrow and saluted. "Noted."

"And you are never to smile at me like that at work, otherwise my nipples will betray everything."

"What?" Now he was laughing. "Like this?" He tried on a number of smiles.

She wriggled and crossed her hands over her chest, giggling as she screamed, "Stop! It's hard to hide what your nipples are up to when you're wearing scrubs."

"Well, that's something I look forward to seeing." He crossed to her and skidded his thumbs across the soft cotton of her T-shirt just…about… Yup. There they were.

"See?" Avery gave him a warning look. "Nipples are a problem when they are smitten with a hot guy."

"Oh, they're smitten, are they?"

She scrunched her nose and gave a dismissive little sneer. It was cute. Trying to pretend she wouldn't respond if he slipped his hands between her legs and slid his fingers—

She gasped when he carried on sliding his fingers back and forth, back and forth, slow and deliberate as if there weren't a roster full of doctors and nurses waiting for the pair of them. "Carter Zane Booth—"

He stopped her with a hard intense kiss. "Don't you use my full name like I'm in trouble."

"Don't you touch me like that when we're due for work in—" she glanced at the clock "—half an hour."

He didn't stop until she came. When she did, she called out his full name again, but it didn't sound at all like he was in trouble. She pulled him into the shower where they discovered a whole new brand of fast and furious. They dressed, raced to the restaurant to pick up his truck and then made their way to the hospital separately. Her rules would be tough to abide by in the ER. But not impossible. And he was happy with those odds.

CHAPTER SIX

AVERY SIGNED OVER her young patient and, though she hadn't been aware of holding her breath, finally released it as Rocky, who was pushing the child's wheelchair, managed to get her and her parents to laugh as they headed to the oncology ward.

Cancer patients weren't exactly regulars in the ER, but they did come in from time to time and ones like these, little girls who were struggling for breath, riddled with pain… It took its toll unless you shut down part of yourself like she had after April died.

Being too involved was why she'd chosen to switch to emergency medicine. Move 'em in. Move 'em out. Didn't mean she didn't give patients the same standard of care she'd want herself. A top-rate one. It was more…there wasn't time to get attached. Hear their life story. Meet all of their family enough times to know who made peach pie and who couldn't cook for a hill of beans. Who read novels to the patient when they were too tired to do it themselves. Who watched films and constantly whispered spoilers. Who wiped the patient's face clean of sputum and grime whenever they were sick, held their hair, shaved it when it started falling out, all of the things that made saying goodbye to a person so much harder than if you'd only known them for ninety minutes or less. St. Dolly's didn't short shrift their patients, but they'd rather see the backside of a treated patient than the anxious expression of someone walking in. Which was why when the electronic doors opened and Avery's former singing teacher walked in, her heart nearly tore in two.

Bonnie Chisholm was about as close to a second mom as April and Avery had had. Not that they'd needed one. Theirs was great. But Bonnie had seen something in the two of them and nurtured it as if they were her own. When singing lessons were a "twice a week" thing in Avery's life, she felt she'd known everything about Bonnie. One glimpse told her she'd been wrong to stop seeing her. Their friendship hadn't just been about singing. It had been long enough and strong enough to be founded in love. In friendship. Friendship that shouldn't have been dropped like a hot potato.

Bonnie, like Avery, had changed since April's death. Whereas Avery had lost weight, Bonnie had gained it. A lot of it. She was trying to decide whether to rush over to help or hide when a familiar scent filled her nostrils. Pine and beeswax.

Her bottom gave a reflexive wiggle, preparing itself to receive an elicit stroke and her tummy began to form a whorl of delight.

"Hey, there." Carter's voice did what it always did. Tickled some warmth into that sweet triangle between her legs.

Dammit! Not right now.

"What's wrong?" he asked.

She frowned and felt her jaw twitch. How did he manage to appear exactly when she didn't want him to?

Moments like these when she wanted a hug more than anything.

Allowing herself a Carter hug was not going to happen. They were too soothing. Too much like feeling safe and protected. The kind of security that would've been impossible not to want to feel forever.

She'd made the mistake of feeling that with her adoptive family and even some boyfriends, but all of that stood as proof that she wasn't someone people stuck around for.

Carter, at least, had the honesty to say as much up front. Their affair had an end date, something which she had to remind herself of after every time they made love.

Since she was going to be back on her own at some point, sorting herself out when she was hurting was the only option.

But Carter didn't know that the patient walking through the door knew just about everything. He didn't know that when Avery hadn't been able to sing at her own sister's funeral, Bonnie had done it for her. Stood up in front of everyone, put her arm around a voiceless Avery, and put music to all the feelings eating Avery up inside. And that was the last time they'd seen one another.

Nor did he know that Avery needed three seconds to put a clamp on her emotions before she talked to or about Bonnie and he'd caught her two seconds too early.

"What's going on?" He nudged her with his elbow. "You're being weird. Even for you."

Glare. "Nothing."

"Liar."

"So? What business is it of yours?" she snapped,

knowing she shouldn't have, but work was not the place to discuss why her insides were tying up in a knot so tight her blood flow was feeling threatened. Maybe this whole "friends with benefits" plan was stupid. She didn't even tell Lia this kind of stuff. So what was she going to do? Deposit all her broken hopes and dreams in Carter, then watch him walk away so she could be a clean slate? She was pretty sure life didn't work like that.

She looked at Bonnie again. Really looked at her. And her heart sank, finally propelling her into doing something.

She swept her tablet off the counter and grabbed an empty wheelchair for Bonnie, who was clearly struggling. For breath, with her balance, even her focus, and she'd only got a handful of steps inside the waiting room. Heart attack? TIA?

"Bonnie? Hey, there. It's Avery. Avery Whittacker. Why don't you take a seat, here? Let me help you get checked in."

Bonnie all but collapsed into the chair. She was petite in height and had always been plump, but she was definitely on the wrong side of overweight now. As Avery helped ease her feet onto the footrest, she saw that Bonnie's ankles weren't just chunkier than normal, they were swollen. Painfully so.

"Bonnie?"

A man with jet-black hair and an aura of Johnny Cash ran into the ER. He dropped down on one knee in front of her without so much as a glance at Avery. "Bonnie, honey. I told you to wait on the bench outside for me."

"It was cold, Levi. And I told you, you fuss too much."

"You think I'm not gonna fuss over the woman I love? You got another think coming." He turned to Avery. "You a doctor? This here ornery ol' hellcat needs some tending to."

Despite the gravity of the moment, Avery's lips twitched. She'd called Bonnie many things over the years, most of them loving, but never a *hellcat*.

"Bonnie, what's brought you here today?"

"It's my legs."

"So, no chest pain?"

Bonnie shook her head.

Avery pressed her fingers to Bonnie's wrist as she asked, "No discomfort in either of your arms? Back? Neck? Jaw? Stomach?" She got a decisive headshake to each of these. "You seemed a bit short of breath when you came in."

"Avery, darlin'. If you're wondering if I'm having a heart attack, you can stop," snipped Bonnie. "I already said. It's my legs." She tugged up the hem of her long velvet skirt to reveal two very swollen legs with a handful of very prominent varicose veins.

"Let's get you checked in."

Bonnie grabbed her wrist. "I've got lessons tonight, darlin'. Tell me it won't take long."

Avery would've loved to, but sometimes varicose veins indicated a much more serious vascular condition. Which meant Bonnie would need to see her bestie, Dr. Lia Costa, if she was right. She could already imagine drawing a music note on Bonnie's wrist, so that Lia would know straightaway that Bonnie was Avery's patient.

"You know what?" Bonnie started to push up and out

of the chair. "I think I'm feeling better. You folk look real busy, so it might be best if I headed on back home."

Two age-worn hands pressed down on her shoulders. "Oh, no, you don't!"

"Levi West! Since when do you think you get to tell me what to do?"

"Since the moment I laid eyes on you and knew I'd love you forever," Levi humphed. He turned to Avery. "I take it you know Bonnie."

Avery nodded. Explaining why she knew Bonnie wasn't necessary. You only knew Bonnie for one reason: singing.

"Well, then. You'll know she's stubborn as a mule. Would you check her in, please? Her legs have been hurting something fierce lately." He rattled off a few incidents when they'd gone out and Bonnie had been unable to finish getting from here to there. "Not in any comfort anyway. Probably woulda crawled if I hadn't insisted upon us getting a taxi."

Avery started tapping on her tablet, finding the role reversal strange. Bonnie had always looked after her and April. Caught their stray notes and righted them. Soothed their egos when a gig didn't go to plan. Paraded around like a peacock when it did.

"Need a hand with anything here?"

"Well, hello there, young man. Yes. Yes, you can." Levi shook Carter's hand. "If you can help convince the love of my life that it's time she had some *professional help*, I'd be grateful."

"I told you, Levi. My grandmother's poultice was working just fine."

There were sores? Now, that was concerning. Not that the other factors weren't, but...

Despite Avery's annoyance that Carter had come over when she very clearly hadn't wanted him there, they exchanged a knowing look. Sometimes self-care was great. Other times…maybe not so much. And even though she hadn't seen Bonnie since the day they laid April to rest, the thought of losing Bonnie on top of everyone else felt like a razor blade against her heart.

"Why don't we take you on over to number seven?" Carter gave the woman Avery had gone all tetchy about a wink and a country smile and, despite Avery's scowl, took over wheelchair duty. Something had passed through Avery's eyes when she'd finally met his that he hadn't liked seeing. Fear. "Once we get you all settled on a proper exam chair, Avery can check out your stats and we'll see how we go from there."

The scowl twitched into something a bit closer to concession.

He could tell Avery wasn't pleased he'd joined them, but unfortunately he also knew what it was like treating people you knew well. Too well, in his case. From what he'd overheard, Avery wasn't her usual composed professional self. If emotions were going to get in the way of any sort of urgent treatment, it was his job to intervene. It was also his job as Avery's secret boyfriend not to step too soundly on his secret girlfriend's toes. He steered the wheelchair toward the exam area, well aware that Avery was boring two glare holes into his back as he did.

"Right, then." He gave Bonnie a nod once they were in place. "Why don't we get you up here on the exam chair?"

Despite ample protests, Avery and Carter managed to get Bonnie up and out of the chair.

Now that they'd achieved that, something in Avery clicked in and she became the professional nurse practitioner he admired on a daily basis. Whether she was doing it for his benefit or for her own, to calm her nerves, was hard to tell, but there was definitely a brick loose in her foundation this afternoon.

"Okay, Bonnie." Avery held up her tablet while Carter washed his hands and pulled on some exam gloves. "We'll rattle through these, so we can get you in and out of here, all right?"

"Now, that's more like it, darlin'. At least some one is paying attention to what *I* want." Bonnie glared at her significant other. Carter hadn't noticed a ring, but not everyone wore them. He would. If he made that sort of commitment to a woman, he'd want the whole world to know he was taken. His brain stop-started itself and did a little regroup. What the hell? He'd never once thought about himself as the marrying type, and now he was already committing to wearing a ring so the whole world would know.

"Name?"

"What are you wasting your breath asking me that for, Avery Whittacker?"

Avery pursed her lips and said out loud as she typed, "Bonita Sunbeam Chisholm."

Bonnie took umbrage. "Avery! You know how I feel about my full name."

"And you know how I feel about taking care of yourself."

"Bonita Sunbeam?" whooped Levi, covering up Avery's snafu. "I never knew that." He gave Bonnie's arm a squeeze. "Darlin', you just keep getting better and better."

"Deader and deader more like." Bonnie pursed her lips at him, then glared at Avery. "Go on. You said you were going to wrap this up."

To Carter's surprise, Avery became even more brisk. Bonnie was a singing teacher who had been giving a lesson, and when the time had come to show her student out, she'd struggled to get her legs to bring her to the door to wave goodbye as she normally would. Avery didn't comment on the incident, just nodded. Together they whipped through Bonnie's vital signs, which weren't great, but she wasn't having a heart attack, so that was something. When they'd finished, to Carter's surprise, Avery said to him, "You seem to be on top of things, Dr. Booth. Why don't I leave you all to it for the rest of the exam?"

"No!" Bonnie shook her head. "Avery, I know this is uncomfortable but I'm as humiliated as you are hurt, so I'd be grateful if you'd stay."

He watched Avery digest and swallow down the request. What the hell had happened between these two women?

Avery said nothing, but she stayed.

"Pull up your skirt, honey," Levi gently encouraged Bonnie. "Show 'em what you showed me."

Bonnie's bright blue eyes flashed with irritation, but she conceded.

Carter bit back a whistle. This poor woman's legs had been through the wars. She had a fair number of varicose veins, a couple of which were inflamed and one or two of them, at a glance, had caused breaks in the skin.

Bonnie saw where they were looking. "That's not what you think it is."

Levi jumped in. "She says it's her and the cat getting into a scrap, but I'm not convinced."

Because Avery wasn't doing anything, Carter took the lead questioning Bonnie as to whether or not she'd received any treatment for them before.

"No. Like I said, whenever I've had a bump or a break in the skin, I've used my grandmother's poultice as a cure-all. That, along with some rest and elevation, seems to do the trick." She gave them all a supercilious look. "I can read the internet same as everyone else."

Carter refrained from his thoughts on self-diagnosis via the internet. "Elevation's good. As is rest. What's in this poultice of yours?"

"Bread, linseed, baking soda and mustard. You mix in a bit of water, mush it all up and then I heat it in the microwave. Sometimes if it's throbbing, I throw in some honey. Nature's own preservative."

Carter nodded and took a look at the skin breaks. They were clean. No infection. Even so, the scientist in him really wished she'd let him flush them out and put some sterile gauze pads and adhesive bandages on them. But her vitals weren't off the charts, the varicose veins were more stage two or three than stage four when he would definitely be suggesting that it was time for medical intervention. But…keeping patients in against their will wasn't his modus operandi unless their condition demanded it. Which, in Bonnie's case, it didn't. Even so, concern niggled at him. Her blood pressure was high. Her oxygen saturation levels weren't great. Not low enough—or not high enough, in the case of carbon dioxide—to warrant keeping her in for observation unless she insisted, but she seemed more intent on getting out than staying in.

"Tell me, Miss Bonnie—" he sat down on a stool next to her so they were at eye level with one another "—how's your diet?"

"Too full of fat and sugar. I think you know that." She pointed at her generous proportions. "I know, I know. I will start another diet today."

"Try not thinking of it as a diet, more as a—"

"Lifestyle choice," she finished for him. "This ain't my first rodeo, Doc. My lifestyle choice involves baked goods and fried eggs, so…don't worry. I'll regroup. Throw a few carrot sticks into the mix. Is that it?"

"Not just yet."

She huffed in irritation and crossed her arms over her chest.

"Do you cross your legs a lot?"

"Her ankles," Levi answered for her. "She's the daintiest little thing. Always crosses her legs at the ankles like a dancer."

"Do you ever wear compression stockings?"

Bonnie nodded. "Most of the time actually. I got a pair on a flight to New Orleans once for a concert. They were all in the wash today, so I didn't bother. Probably why I ended up in this mess. Look—" she gave Carter's hand a pat "—you seem like a nice young man, but I've got another student coming in a bit, so if you don't mind, I'll just get out of your hair."

Carter wasn't happy with this. He began explaining how varicose veins, particularly ones in the state hers were in could not only lead to further complications but could be indicative of much more serious problems.

Blood clots. Embolisms. Strokes. Any number of things that, if left untreated, could be fatal.

"Indicative, schmindicative. I'm not interested."

"I am," Levi said. "Do you have any pamphlets or things I could have to read up on this?"

"Absolutely."

Avery was out of the cubicle and back with an enormous handful of instructional leaflets quick as a flash. She pointedly explained to Levi about the warning signs to look for when peripheral arterial disease flared up. "It's also known as window shopper's disease."

"Oh, she gets that. Can't stop outside more than one or two stores without needing a sit down."

"Levi West, will you please stop giving away my intimate information."

"It's not intimate if telling these good folk is going to keep you alive longer," Levi protested. "I only just met you, woman. I'm not going to let you go that easily."

Carter smiled. He wished he had half of this guy's guts. He'd found someone he liked and he was going for it. Carter had, too, but was letting fear do half his decision-making. Not exactly the bravest path to follow, but it was the smartest. The most practical anyway.

Okay it was stupid, but Avery didn't seem all that keen on letting him into her life, either, so…birds of a feather and all that.

"Right." Bonnie had clearly had enough. "I think elevating in this fancy chair of yours has done the trick. Time to go."

Carter managed to win a handful of extra minutes. He wanted to put a few stitches into her open wounds and give them some proper dressing. "I would definitely get yourself a couple extra pairs of those compression socks, as they seem to be doing the trick for you, but next time you and your cat have a tussle and the skin starts weeping on your legs, come on in. I'd like to have a second look. Not that I'm saying anything against your grandmother's poultice, you hear?"

"Better not be." Bonnie glowered and then, as Carter carried on wrapping the gauze around her calf, she abruptly turned her attention to Avery. "I know you don't want me to bring it up, but I've just got to ask. When are you getting back up on a stage?"

All of the blood drained from Avery's face. Carter kept on working on Bonnie's legs, but he knew Avery knew he was soaking up every word of this one-sided exchange.

Bonnie continued, "You are every bit as talented as April was, young woman. I know you never thought that, but it's true."

Avery chewed on her lips but said nothing, which seemed to suit Bonnie just fine because she wasn't done yet. "It's a big talent wasted. I understand you needed your time to grieve, and you've had that now."

"Honey!" Levi, who'd clearly heard the background to Avery's story, intervened. "You know as well as I that there's no time limit on these things. Only life."

"Precisely," Bonnie minced. "Which is why she needs to get that cute little tush of hers back in for some lessons, then up on a stage."

Avery put on a smile that didn't come even close to lighting up those dark eyes of hers. "I'm really pleased to see you have someone in your life looking out for you, Bonnie." She switched her gaze to Levi's. "You make sure you bring her back in here if you suspect any trouble."

He said he would and then, without so much as a goodbye, Avery left.

Later—much later, in fact, because the rest of the shift felt like a game of dodge 'em when it came to nailing Avery to the spot for more than two seconds—Carter finally managed to corner her in the small office where they all did paperwork. He sat down in a wheeled chair and whirled hers around so she was facing him. She did not look impressed. He didn't much care. "What was all that back there with Bonnie? About you singing and everything?"

"I could've handled that patient on my own."

"That wasn't what I asked. And for the record, no one said you couldn't."

"Then why'd you go busting in like you did?"

"Because you looked upset."

"Taking care of me is not your job."

He winced. He'd heard that before. Usually during visiting hours down at one county jail or another after he'd drawn up a list of symptoms for the warden to distribute to all the guards. But looking after Avery was different. It wasn't an obligation. It was a choice. And he wanted to do it. The same way Levi wanted to look after Bonnie. Somewhere, down beneath all of the emotional scar tissue he'd built up over the years, Carter knew there was a man who could love a woman the right way. Completely. With all his heart. He just didn't know if he could get there anymore. So, yeah. Avery was right. Even though he didn't want her to be.

He tried to force the depth of emotion churning away inside him out of his voice. Feelings couldn't play a role in this discussion. "I take it she was your singing teacher?"

"You can also take it that it is none of your business." There was a bite to her tone.

"Hey." He tried to give her hand a squeeze, but she yanked it away before he could. "I thought we were going to be friends as well as…erm…enjoying the benefits."

Avery opened her mouth, obviously poised to let him know what a ridiculous idea that had been, then stopped herself. "You want to know what it'd be like being friends with me? Knowing all about me?"

"Yes, I do." He meant it and from the look on her face, she was grateful for it.

"Well, tough. What you see is what you get." And then she walked out of the room.

CHAPTER SEVEN

AVERY AND LIA each heaved huge sighs of relief as two very large margaritas and an enormous mortar bowl full to the brim of freshly pounded guacamole arrived in front of them. Steam was still coming off the basket of salted tortilla chips. And the tang of the vinegary salsa cut through it all.

Bliss.

Guac and Talk night with Lia was sacred and tonight was no different.

Well. Maybe a little different. For some insane reason, she'd actually considered pouring out her soul to Carter earlier today. Maybe it had been seeing Bonnie. Maybe it had been that glint of pain she'd seen in his eyes when she'd refused him access to her past. Maybe she'd just been tired of holding it all in, but...she hadn't given him or herself a chance to find out.

"You look like you've got a secret," Lia said. Not pushing, not pressing, just witnessing.

Avery smirked because admitting the truth probably would've made her cry.

You wanted to talk and cry with Carter. Why not Lia?

She made herself absorb the thought. She guessed with Carter the writing was already on the wall. He'd be leaving eventually so if he was repulsed by her out-pouring of emotion, it didn't matter. The truth was she didn't know if she needed a quiet little sob or a month of ugly cries. The latter was a very strong possibility and at this point in her life she'd lost enough people, so she wasn't about to do anything that might push Lia away. If keeping some things secret and conversation light meant her friendship with Lia could stay as it was that was what she'd do.

They each took long sips of their margaritas and then had a few dunks of guacamole before Lia asked, "Would this secret have anything to do with that sexy cowboy who turned out to be an ER surgeon?"

Avery snorted, grateful Lia's take on things veered away from less comfortable topics. "Maybe?"

Lia laughed. "I'm taking it that *maybe* means *definitely* in this case."

Avery gave up any pretense of being coy. "He's the most delicious man I have ever, *ever* been with." She hadn't been with many, but still. Nashville was full to the seams with eye candy.

"Glad to see you're finally letting yourself have some fun."

Avery squirmed. It was fun. But it was also real in a way she couldn't quite describe. Time to change the subject. "How was your day? Lots of surgeries?"

"Uh-uh." Lia wagged a finger at her. "No, you don't. We're not changing the topic that quickly."

"What's there to know? He's scrumptious. We're having a good time. End of story."

Lia pursed her lips. "Avery Whittacker, you know as well as I do that you are not someone who just hops into bed with the nearest piece of edible man cake."

"Is that what the cool kids are calling it these days?" Avery laughed. "Man cake?"

"Candy. Whatever. The point is, I know you're picky. I also know you haven't so much as looked at a man since…" They both knew since when. She'd been dumped and then her sister had died. "If you're canoodling with this guy after a considerable hiatus in that department, you must see something special in him."

She did. She saw a lot of things. And none of them visible to the naked eye. He had a huge heart. He was kind. Loyal. The human form of emotional scaffolding if ever she wavered—which she had this afternoon—and she had no doubt that he was the same solid rock filled with perspective and lack of judgment for his sister, too. He looked after others before he looked after himself. If that was a flaw, it was one of his only ones. And it wasn't exactly a reason to kick him out of bed.

His inability to put down roots was his secret, and definitely not hers to tell.

Not that she didn't struggle with it. But she got it. Blood being thicker than water and all that.

Besides, she'd agreed to the expiration date for their friendship with benefits, so the way she was looking at it, she might as well keep him in the bed he'd short-sheeted.

Lia was still waiting for an answer, so Avery forced herself to smile and say, "He's great. It's early days. Too soon to make predictions of that nature. Speaking of love lives. How's yours, Lia?"

Her friend lifted up her glass and hooted. "Touché, my friend. Touché."

They both knew it hadn't exactly been on fire. Intimacy was tricky for Lia, and in the same way Lia knew to back off from Avery's sore subjects, Avery knew to do the same for her. "Now. Are you going to tell me how your day was or do I have to drag it out of you?"

Cassidy squinted at Carter as she munched her way through the spicy hot cheese puffs he'd bought from the vending machine. Her favorite. "You look different."

He gave his jaw a scrub and feigned no knowledge of anything being different about him. Externally, she was wrong. Still the same ol' unshaven scrubs-wearing straight-from-the-hospital big brother she'd always known. Internally, she was spot on. He'd crossed a line into rocky emotional terrain and wasn't 100 percent sure he'd made the wisest choice.

Being there for someone meant loving them despite their faults. Like he did with Cassidy.

He wasn't sure he knew Avery well enough to even know her faults. Privacy maybe? Not that that was much of a crime. But the Avery he made love to was a totally different woman to the one he worked with. And the version of her when they'd been treating Bonnie, the singing teacher? Again. Totally different.

He'd run into Bonnie's boyfriend in the waiting room a while later and, unsolicited, Levi had colored in a few of the blank spots in the portrait he was building of her.

This is where it stood now: strong, passionate beautiful woman who was completely on her own after her sister's death; grandparents gone to natural causes; parents who'd lost their minds with grief and up and left as if adopting Avery hadn't meant the same thing to them as it had to her. He knew grief did savage things to people, but he'd been so mad when he'd heard that part of the story, he could've spit nails.

He'd wanted to jump in his truck, drive across the country, find her parents, hitch their mobile home up to his truck and drag them back here to be with their daughter. The one still living with as much pain as they were.

Hearing her story—or part of it anyway—had dragged him through the anguish of losing his own parents afresh. First, his dad to sickle cell and then, as Cassidy liked to put it, their mother of heartbreak. His father's last words to him still rung in his head. *You're the man of the house now, Carter. You make sure you look after your mother and your sister same as I tried to.* His mother had died less than a year after his father, so that had been a massive fail.

The only way he'd been able to make money at that point, as a teenaged boy, was to ride bulls like his daddy had done before him. His dad had done it for the same reason Cassidy stole stuff. To feel alive. Lucky for Carter, he was good at it. It paid for the apartment he and his much younger sister lived in. His med school fees. And everything in between. He'd stuffed away a lot of his winnings for a rainy day, but he'd seen enough guys on the circuit suffer life-changing injuries to step away from it as soon as he could.

Getting on that mechanical bull on New Year's Eve had been his first ride in years and years. Which meant Avery had made one hell of an impact on him and already he knew walking away from her would be harder than walking away from prize riding. So, yeah. He was different. Didn't mean he was going to admit to it.

"Same ol' me," he finally said. "How're they treating you in here?"

She gave him a big smile, her lips coated with artificial cheese powder. "It's just like the Ritz, big brother." The smile dropped away and now, as she turned into the light, he saw the shadow of a black eye. She clocked him noticing. "I'm fine. Don't get all fussed like you normally do. It's all fine."

"How's the clinic?"

She shrugged in that careless way of hers. "Dunno. Haven't been there yet."

"Why not?"

"Been in solitary." She glared at him, daring him to comment.

Carter bit back a remonstration. She'd only been here two weeks and already she'd managed to be in a fight and earn some time in solitary. Fan-freaking-tastic.

"You always said to make an impression." She popped the last corn puff into her mouth and began to lick the orange powder off her fingers.

"Yeah, a *good* one, Cassidy." He was about to say he was going to have a chat with the prison doctor when she looked up at him and he saw something in her eyes that caught him off guard. Regret. She'd never once expressed remorse at her actions, but if he was feeling a sea change in his life, maybe she was, too. He leaned in but the movement made her blink and when she opened her eyes again, it was gone.

She had the same green eyes as his. As their dad's. A man whose advice he could use right about now. He'd always been better with Cassidy than he had.

It was hard to forgive the eighteen-year-old version of himself for being so mad at her when she'd "enjoyed" her first stint in juvy. Their dad had only been dead a few months and their mother had checked out emotionally the day he'd died, so the fact that Cassidy had gone off the rails hadn't been much of a surprise. But he'd had his head too buried in books and his body too wrapped up in testing his own mortality in the bull ring to pay her the right kind of attention.

Bad call.

He should've been better. Which was why pulling the plug on relationship after relationship had been easy. Until now.

He scrubbed his hands through his hair, letting his nails dig into his skull. He wanted to feel Cassidy's pain. See the world the way she did. Understand why the hell breaking the law gave her the high it did. But he knew deep down he never could. He'd been lucky in the gene pool game. She hadn't. Her disease was a time bomb, relentlessly ticking away, and if her number was up when their dad's had been up...she only had about ten years left. So why the hell was spending it locked up the better option to being free?

The guard called time. Groans of disappointment mingled with sighs of relief at the handful of occupied tables around them.

"Same time next week?" he asked.

"If you're lucky." She gave him her cheekiest smile and then, with the prison guard's eyes firmly on them, they shared a quick fierce hug. They both knew it was impossible to predict if this was just a regular ol' visit or the last time they saw one another.

"Love you, sis."

Cassidy stared at him. Hard. He didn't say things like that. Not often enough anyway. She jabbed her finger at him. "Next time, you're going to tell me what's up."

He nodded and rose from the table.

"And Carter?"

"Yeah?" He braced himself for some sort of telling off.

"Love you, too." Then she whirled around and, without a backward glance, disappeared behind the bulletproof reinforced door.

He smiled and shook his head. It was the first time she'd said it back. Maybe something had shifted in that mixed-up heart of hers. And just like that, the promises he'd made to himself to let her get on with her life and deal with her problems on her own evaporated.

CHAPTER EIGHT

THE REALTOR HELD her hands out once they'd circled back to the front door and gave Avery and Carter a winning smile. "Now, if you and your husband would like some time alone in the house, I'm happy to go make some calls. There's heat in my car and my hands are near enough frozen."

Avery was about to interject, explain that Carter was most definitely not her husband, and that she wasn't even sure why she'd invited him along, but he got there first.

"That'd be great." He slung an arm over her shoulders and pulled her in for an awkward side cuddle.

The realtor opened the front door and wagged her finger. "No hanky-panky before we get your signature on a contract, hear?"

Avery squirmed. Carter laughed and said something about how there were no guarantees on that front. Avery gave him a look. She could've guaranteed it.

She hadn't wanted him to come, but he'd met her after her shift at work with a bag of takeout barbecue and a flimsy excuse about having ordered too much. He'd been to see his sister and, though he didn't spell it out, the visit had obviously unsettled him, so, like an idiot, she'd taken him up on his suggestion that he come along.

She looked around. Maybe it was a good idea having someone who wasn't as invested in the place as she was have a look. The place wasn't quite as robust as she'd remembered it. The wraparound porch floorboards weren't just creaky; they had some give in them. The shingled roof looked like it would need replacing in the not too distant future. It would take time and money and most of all love to turn this place into a home. Panic set in that she was short on all three.

Perhaps buying this place was a pipe dream she'd clung to. A means of keeping just a bit of her sister alive. "So?" She heard the false bravura in her voice and did her best not to crumble under the weight of it. "What do you think?"

"Five Acre Farm, huh?" Carter's fingers were hooked on his hips and his gaze appraising the place as if he actually cared.

She could hear the defensiveness in her voice when she answered, "I guess whoever named it didn't have much of an imagination."

"Nothing wrong with calling a spade a spade," Carter said, his eyes catching with hers.

What did *that* mean? He was the one who'd just pretended they were married to the realtor.

Before she could pursue it, he asked, "How far out from the hospital is it?"

"Thirty minutes without traffic." Twenty to her sister's school, she added silently. They'd done the timings a few times before April had had to quit her job and then, eventually, stay at the hospital. But Avery had taken to driving back and forth like therapy. None of which had bought the house, restored it and got her sister living the life they'd dreamed in it, but...

Her shoulders began to wilt. This was an awful idea. And she hated having Carter here to witness it.

Carter cleared his throat. "I think the setting is one in a million, but the house itself..." He turned the kitchen tap on, then off when the water ran brown. "Definitely a fixer-upper. It'll take a lot of work to get this place where you want it."

Her instinct was to bristle, fight back, but he was right. The house had sat empty for five years now. Unlived in. Unloved. Falling apart in bits it probably shouldn't be. Her eyes lit on the stone fireplace in the center of the living room. Each stone carried up from the riverbed by whoever had built the place. And just like that, she fell in love with it again. You didn't get that sort of touch in a new build. That sort of commitment. It was the type of commitment and care she'd want in a relationship, but obviously wasn't destined to get. So... maybe pouring all the love she had to give that no one seemed to want into restoring the house would be the next best thing. Right?

Carter appeared beside her. Ran a finger along the stones in the fireplace. "What kind of life had you pictured living here?"

Avery blinked away her surprise. How did he do that? It was like he'd tapped straight into her brain, her heart, her gut. Telling him didn't feel like giving anything away he didn't already know.

They walked and she talked.

She looked around the house that she had once imagined living in with her sister. They'd each earmarked one of the bedrooms upstairs. The third bedroom was to be for guests. They'd planned to hang old quilts on the walls, fill the beds and sofas with throw cushions galore and the whole house with so much laughter.

"So what's the plan now?" Carter asked. "Since that won't happen apart from the quilts and cushions."

"You don't pull punches, do you?" She was really regretting telling him her origin story.

He held up his hands. "I may be a lot of things, but a realist seems to be the most useful."

"Yeah? Well, maybe some optimism would help you be a bit happier!" she spat back.

"Is that your trick, Avery? Why you're so full of laughter and joy? Why you work in the ER instead of oncology? Optimism?"

His voice hadn't raised, and his tone hadn't changed from the same amiable way he'd asked about whether or not there was a well or a water main for the house. He was doing what a good friend would. Questioning her motives. Didn't mean it didn't hurt.

She glowered, but deep down knew he was right. So, as painful as it was, she pushed the pictures of the life she'd planned on living here with April to the side and imagined herself living here on her own.

Instantly, it felt too big. She glanced at Carter who was tapping on walls and knocking on beams or struts, or whatever the things that held up walls were called, and allowed herself a glimpse of another life. One with a husband and children. A couple of horses. And a puppy, of course.

The images flew into place so quickly she knew they were too perfect to believe so she forced herself to blink them away and, though it was as cold and miserable inside as outside, she suddenly felt claustrophobic in there. She headed to the back door.

All the land that came with the house was out back. A handful of acres surrounded by woodland where she'd once imagined having a couple of her granddad's rescue horses. They'd all literally moved on to greener pastures now. Some in heaven. Some in Kentucky where they'd found another horse rescue center.

"What's this?" Carter pointed at an outbuilding. The bottom half might've been a workshop or a storeroom for horse gear, garden equipment. But the upstairs…

Avery bit the inside of her cheek. She and April had pictured it as a studio. Not necessarily for recording, but a place where they could play music and sing without disturbing the neighbors. They weren't too close to the next house, another few acres and more woodland acted as a buffer, but April was one of those women who thought of absolutely everything. She was considerate right down to her core. *An earth angel* her mother used to sing whenever April brought home another bird with a broken wing or an orphaned kitten or a child she saw getting picked on at school. The fact she'd ended up a kindergarten teacher had been no surprise to anyone.

"Is that your favorite corner of the building?"

Avery gave Carter a hard stare. "It happens to be a perfectly delightful corner."

"Oh, yeah? Even the mouse hole there in the wall?"

She made herself actually look at the corner that, as Carter had clocked, she'd been blindly staring at. Yup. Sure enough, there was a mouse hole. He leaned on the banister that led to the upstairs annex. It gave under his weight.

"You break it, you buy it," they said in tandem. Then

laughed. Some of the weirdness of seeing this house together disappeared as the sound of their laughter melded together like voices in a duet. Just the way she'd pictured it.

Could her friendship with Carter be the thing she needed to feel whole again? To remind her of the woman she'd once been? Or, better yet, the one she'd one day hoped to become?

She looked at him hard. What did Carter Booth bring to her life?

They had really good sex. He made her laugh. He also made her mad. Made her think. Made her want to be a better version of herself and that was no bad thing.

Carter wanted to know her. He couldn't meet the version of her she'd once been. She was finally figuring out that she'd been so lost in her grief she'd made no time to consider the woman she'd become. A shell of a human fixated on buying this tumbledown house.

She had her work, of course. She loved that. But apart from her friendship with Lia, it was as if she'd put every other element of herself in the deep freeze. It'd have to thaw one day. That's how life worked.

She realized it was important to see what it felt like for someone to know both the old Avery and whoever the heck the new Avery was. It felt terrifying, but something deep in her belly told her Carter would be careful with her, whatever happened.

"Bonnie, that patient from yesterday," she said. "The one in the ER I got all cranky about. She was my singing teacher."

Carter nodded. "I figured as much."

"She was also my sister's singing teacher."

Carter nodded, taking a step back as if instinctively

knowing she needed a bit more space in which to let her story unfold. "This building, the house, the stable…it was going to be where all our dreams would come true."

The corners of his mouth shifted into a soft smile. "That sounds nice."

She nodded. "I didn't think it'd be so…so…"

"So much of a wreck?" he filled in for her.

She nodded.

He leaned against a wall after checking it for durability. "I thought you'd been saving for a deposit for the place? Surely you've been in it before?"

She shook her head.

His eyes bugged out a little bit.

"I know." She waved her hands. "I know. I just… We'd been in here years back, April and I. Before we could afford it, so we only snuck onto the property and peeked in the windows and such. It had seemed a little unloved then, but it hadn't mattered. We had our grandparents, our parents, all our friends—April couldn't pass a person without becoming friends with 'em—so the whole place probably could've been leaning halfway to the ground and we wouldn't have cared. We just loved it."

"The way a person loves a scruffy homeless puppy?" His "hound dog" eyes met hers and something flared between them as they met and meshed. Something that went beyond friendship.

A thought bashed into her like a wrecking ball.

Was opening the door to her past also opening up the possibility of loving him?

Heaven knew she'd loved being held in his arms at night. Their bodies seemed to have known one another for years. Instinctively able to elicit pleasure. And safety. Despite his "alpha male" exterior, the man loved a cozy cuddle under the comforter in the morning. The heat of their bodies merging as one. The limbs. Their breath. Their heartbeats.

But puppies—and by puppies, she meant Carter—were difficult. They demanded attention. Wanted things their way. They ate your favorite boots. Tore up the sofa cushions. Wormed their way into your heart in the blink of an eye without anyone having much of a say in the matter. So much of the last few years had been out of her control—she wasn't sure she was up for it. Not holding the reins of her own life.

Was there a middle ground? Did love even work like that?

No. She didn't think it did. Her sister hadn't had a choice in "leaving." Carter Booth did. Sort of. And it was that gray area that made fully opening up her heart to him a no-brainer. She simply couldn't do it.

Carter felt like he was watching someone physically mash themselves through an emotional wringer. This house wasn't just a house to Avery. It was meant to have been her future. He wasn't going to preach to her, but she knew as well as he did that *things* don't make a future, people do. Even so…maybe Avery had to work through her so-called dream plan in order to learn that lesson firsthand. Put in the inevitable blood, sweat and tears this place would require.

Though the price wasn't exorbitant, it was still a lot of money to put down on a dream that would never come true. A dream that had plenty of potential to become a nightmare.

He had enough money saved up that he could buy it

straight-out, but this was Avery's thing. She wanted to put her hard-earned money down. Her graft into buffing up those hardwood floors. Dirty up her clothes painting all those walls into a pretty series of pastels or whatever it was she had planned.

Yeah, he saw that. He also couldn't tear himself out of the picture. Not fully anyway.

"You know," he said, pushing himself off and away from the wall with a booted foot. "I don't know if I've mentioned it, but I do know my way around a hammer and nail." He gave her a wink.

He watched as she rearranged her features into something akin to disinterest, but he'd seen the hope light up her eyes. "Oh, really?"

"Yes, ma'am." He tipped the corner of his Stetson at her. "I partly paid my way through college by using these." He held out his hands. It was what he'd turned to after he'd started seeing X-rays and MRIs of what really happened inside a man who strapped himself to a bucking bull.

She blushed a little as she said, "There's a lot of things a man can do with his hands."

His mind instantly flashed back to the other night when he'd used them to scoop up her bare buttocks and draw her to him, so she had a little elevation to slide onto his erection. The memory began to elicit another one. He glanced around, stupidly looking for a bucket of ice water.

"I used to work on building sites."

She raised her eyebrows.

Okay. Good. She wasn't saying no. He hitched his hands onto his belt buckle and took a risk. "If you're willing, maybe I could give up that soul-sucking serviced apartment, and in exchange for a bed, I could be your handyman. I'm not trying to put myself into your life where I'm not wanted, or into your house more than necessary, but sometimes when you're tackling something this big...it's nice to have a second party to bounce things off. And hammer stuff out."

Her face flashed through a myriad of expressions—fear, panic, disbelief—and then settled on one he suspected neither of them had anticipated.

Gratitude.

And, if he weren't mistaken, she was a little turned on. From the shift of her hips and the way her tongue dipped out of her mouth to lick her lips, he wondered if she was picturing him wearing nothing but a tool belt. It was an aesthetic she liked the look of, if the little noise of approbation she'd just made was anything to go by. *Huh.* He'd never really imagined himself as eye candy before, but Avery looked like she wanted a snack.

He'd taken his shirt off scores of times when he was working before, but wearing nothing but a bit of leather slung around his hips... Too bad that realtor was hanging out front, otherwise, he might just have to break that hanky-panky rule.

"What kind of building sites?" she asked.

Okay. Good. She was fact-finding before committing. This was her baby, not his, so...she got to call the shots on what sort of memories were made here.

"Family homes. Flippers, mostly," he explained. "Investment properties people bought. Fixer-uppers. We'd do them up, sell them for a whole lot more than the original buyer had bought them for."

He'd used some of his prize money to do a few himself. Could move back to Texas anytime he wanted to and take up residence in one with a pool, one with a bit of land attached, or even one right in the heart of Austin next door to his favorite barbecue joint. But he didn't want any of those places right now. Or the hassle of moving the tenants out. He'd bought and worked on them, knowing he'd be moving on. Renting and selling as he went. Doing this—if she let him—felt different. He wanted to be Avery Whittacker's handyman. Help someone else's dreams come true. Dreams of settling down, living in a proper home.

Sure, all of this chasing his sister around the country had an end date. But so did his sister. And he'd far rather keep chasing her than know the reason he'd finally opened the door to his forever home was because Cassidy wasn't around anymore.

Maybe he should take a page out of Avery's book. She knew buying this house wouldn't bring her sister back and maybe every second she spent in it would be torture. But he felt in his bones that she would learn from it. Move on in whatever way she saw best once she'd acknowledged her grief and found a way to move past it—or live with it. He sure as hell didn't know how that worked.

His brain rattled through the hundreds of conversations he and his sister had had over the years. One-way mostly. Him pleading with her to stop her reckless behavior. Begging her to settle down. Bargaining. Raging. It was like going through the five stages of grief every single time he walked through those prison doors. She wouldn't even need to get a job he'd plead. He'd support her. But she should be living her life on the outside. Freely. Happily. Not locked up and counting her days like they were numbered. Which, of course, they were.

"Hey." Avery reached out and gave his arm a squeeze. "What happened there?"

He shook his head. "Just thinking that my sister will never know something like this."

"Like what?"

"Working hard. Saving up. Trying to make a dream come true."

Avery frowned. "Do you think it's stupid? Trying to do something I was supposed to do with my sister even though I know it won't come close to the same?"

He considered his answer carefully. "As long as you know that in advance—that it won't be the same—then I don't think there is any reason why you shouldn't go for it."

A look of helplessness consumed her. "How am I even going to begin? I've had this one dream that I've clung to and—" She lifted her hands up, then let them flop down on her sides. "The place is a wreck. It's not even worth what they're asking."

"Then put in a lower offer." He did a quick calculation, gave her a number that made her blink a few times, then put his offer out again. "I'm willing to help you. If you want to look at this as a fixer-upper instead of the place you're going to live out the remains of your days, it'll make it easier. You can still love the place. Put some of that Avery Whittacker glow into it—"

She laughed. "Avery Whittacker glow?"

"Yeah." He took her hands in his and tugged her a little closer to him. "You radiate something magic. I don't know what it is exactly, but if you poured some of that into this place—" he tipped his head toward the house "—I bet you could get double what you put into it."

"And you'd help me?"

The question was a big one, because it wasn't just a matter of bringing his toolbox over and fixing some squeaky doors. Though they'd only known one another a few weeks, they already had a comfy little routine. She had a key to his apartment. They knew each other's rosters at work. When their paths crossed at "home," such as it was, they ripped one another's clothes off and set the world alight. When they were at work, they worked.

But this place? The one she'd dreamed of for years? He'd be putting an imprint on it. When he left—because that was the one thing they both knew was inevitable—he'd be part of this place. No matter how many layers of paint she put on it. He'd be there.

He looked at her and saw everything he wanted in a woman. Honest. Passionate. Keen to make a difference in the world. Right here in this community. And he wanted a bit of that stick-to-it-ness to rub off on him…

"Yes, I would, Avery. It would be my pleasure."

And probably one of the stupider things he'd agreed to do, but he wanted to help Avery and more than anything he could see buying this place was about closure. Whether she ended up living here until her end of days or until they put the final lick of paint on that gorgeous wraparound porch, it didn't matter. She'd know in her heart she'd done her best by her sister and then could move on in whatever way necessary.

The thought stung.

Yes. He'd be moving on, too. Literally. How and when were the only unanswered questions. He cleared his throat, then nodded toward the street where the real-estate agent sat out in her car. "If you want me to play hardball on the price, I'm willing to do that for you."

Avery threw a wistful look in the direction of the

house, then a hopeful one at him. "Let me see your hardball face."

He showed it to her. She laughed. The next thing he knew, her hands were slipping around his waist, he was holding her in his arms and they were kissing. Soft and light, strong and deep and everything in between. It felt like they were exchanging a silent promise to be careful with one another. After all, this was Avery's dream. Not his. She was welcoming him into her world, knowing one day he'd leave. He was grateful for her trust and would do everything in his power to honor it. Not to hurt her when that day arrived and he drove away. He deepened his kisses, already missing her. Already wishing life were different.

"I thought I said no hanky-panky!"

They pulled apart and threw sheepish looks at the realtor, who beamed at the pair of them. "I take it I need to get out my sold sign?"

CHAPTER NINE

"Whistling while we work, are we?"

Avery looked up from the supplies cart she'd been reloading and grinned at her colleague Valentina, who was doing the same. "It makes the day go quicker."

Valentina raised an approving eyebrow. "I'm guessing that means there is something or some*one* worth going home to these days?"

"Some*thing*," Avery enunciated even though she was pretty sure her and Carter's efforts to keep a cap on their attraction to one another was not quite as successful as it had been a week ago.

"I got Five Acre Farm."

Valentina's face lit up. "Oh, honey. I know you had your eye on that place for a while." Her expression shifted to one of concern. "You sure you're going to be all right in that house on your own?"

Avery nodded. "I'll be fine." And somehow, even though she had no idea what the future had in store, she believed she would be.

Even though they weren't technically buying Five Acre Farm together, they had agreed that Carter would act as her foreman. His offer to pound in nails and patch up leaks had been kind, but the man had a day job here at the hospital. Saving lives trumped caulking window frames. Even though the idea of watching him wander around her house half naked with a tool belt slung around his hips delighted, she knew she'd have to hire a crew. She didn't know a lug wrench from a spanner, so...after pulling off an incredible bargaining session with the realtor, Carter had agreed to help her hire people. All of which had given her the confidence she needed to put her signature on the house deed, knowing her sister's would never be beside it. Though Carter's wasn't there, either, it was in a way. He had her back. And it felt good.

And...she wasn't gonna lie...it felt nice having Carter physically wrapped around her actual back, as well. She'd been on nights for the past week so they hadn't seen much of one another, but they'd managed to tweak their schedules so that they would spend their first night in the house together tomorrow night when the keys would be hers.

Rather than going cheap and cheerful, as she'd planned, she'd splurged on two items. One, a lilac-colored chesterfield chaise lounge she'd seen in a vintage furniture shop and two, the item she was still a bit nervous might not make it up the stairs to her bedroom, a massive sleigh bed made out of Tennessee hickory. It was gorgeous. Big enough for two to sprawl on and with a mattress robust enough to endure a fair amount of bouncing. She knew because Carter had convinced the salesman to let them have a go. Bouncing. Not banging. Although...she was pretty sure there would be some of the latter come nightfall.

"Oh! So we're humming, too." Valentina's smile gave away the fact she wasn't disapproving. "Does that mean we can look forward to hearing you sing at this year's benefit? We missed you the last couple of years."

Avery felt a stillness fill her. One that quickly filled with darkness. The last time she'd sung at the annual Valentine's Day benefit for the cancer department— Love Conquers Cancer—her sister had been alive and the two of them had done what they did best—make beautiful music. Together.

She threw a few more packets of gauze into her cart and stood up. "Guess I'd better get back to it."

She could feel Valentina's eyes on her as she walked away.

"You okay?" Carter was looking at her as if her face were doing something funny.

She thought she'd been masking her feelings, but she guessed she'd made a bad show of it. "Fine."

He made a noise that made it clear he didn't believe her. She was about to tell him to back off when a huge commotion erupted in the ambulance bay.

"Right!" Dr. Chang pushed open one of the double doors with her foot. "I need you and you." She pointed at Avery and Carter. "Someone find Rocky. We're going to need his muscles."

Avery and Carter exchanged a look. A few seconds later, they weren't confused anymore.

It took Dr. Chang and six other doctors to transfer their new patient to the gurney while the paramedic rattled off the transfer information. "Brian Culpepper. Bodybuilder. Was doing warm-up bench presses when he experienced lower back pain. Was on stage preparing for competition when he experienced numbness in his inner thighs."

"I even peed my pants!" Brian yelled. "Right there in front of everyone."

Again, Avery and Carter exchanged a look. Herniated disc. For sure. If he'd lost complete control of his pelvic bowl, things were looking bad. Real bad.

"We don't need this." Dr. Chang ripped off the heat blanket that was covering him.

Despite the gravity of the injury—sometimes it required surgery—she could see Carter struggling to keep a straight face. Brian hadn't peed his pants because he didn't have any on. Underneath the heat blanket, he was wearing nothing but a tiny little sparkly gold swimsuit-type thing. Not even. Two little strings and a bit of fabric to cover up his privates.

"Get me drugs now!" Brian roared. "I want steroids. Painkillers. The lot. I have to get back to the convention center."

"Can someone call ortho!" Dr. Chang barked, ignoring the patient's demand for painkillers. She pointed at Carter. "Get him into an exam room and see how far the numbness has spread. He'll need an MRI."

"MRI's down," Carter said.

"What?" She swore under her breath. It was rare, but machines broke. Even in hospitals. "Then get him a CT scan. Whittacker. You go with him. If he has a compression of the spinal nerve roots, he's going to need to get into surgery. Can someone book a room?"

"Or…he might just need to take it easy for a couple of days and take two aspirin," Carter said pointedly.

Dr. Chang stared at him for a moment before replying. "Back pain a specialty of yours?"

Avery tensed. This was weird. Carter didn't showboat. He stayed calm and collected, but his voice was solid as a rock when he replied, "Just aware that this could be temporary pain, Doc. Nothing a bit of ice, rest and off-the-shelf painkillers wouldn't fix."

Dr. Chang gave him a quick nod. When she was called away to see to another ambulance entering the bay, Carter breathed out.

"What are you doing, man?" the patient asked. "Don't I need painkillers and surgery, like right now?"

"How old are you?" Carter asked,

"Twenty-eight."

"And is this your thing? This weight lifting?"

"It's what I want to do as long as I can do it, and then after that I'll run a gym, training others how to do it. This competition was meant to put my name on the map. Make it easier for me to get sponsorship to find my own space."

Carter nodded. It was easy enough to hear the passion in Brian's voice. The dedication. And the disappointment that today hadn't gone to plan.

"Do you know what surgery will involve?"

Brian looked at Avery for hints. She wasn't sure where this was going so she didn't say anything. Brian crossed his huge biceps over his chest and asserted, "Surgery fixes stuff. I need surgery." He thrust one of his enormous Thor fists into the air. "I demand surgery!"

"Fair enough." Carter's tone switched from his normal congenial self to pure business. "Just so you're aware, a discectomy means a surgeon, like myself, will cut away a portion of the disc that is pressing against your nerve. I might also have to trim away some of the bone from the backside of your vertebrae to relieve pressure on the nerves. That's a laminectomy. Thing is about nerves that have been pressed on like that, they could be damaged by the surgery."

"What?"

Carter nodded. "And not just that. The surgery comes with the risk of lifelong pain, blood clots, infection, leaking spinal fluid. Shall I go on?"

Brian didn't say anything.

"On the plus side," Carter continued, uninvited, "the mortality rate for this type of surgery is real low." He nodded at the orderly pushing the gurney and then at Avery who was steering on the side opposite him. "What do you say? Shall we skip the CT altogether and just go straight to surgery?"

"No!" Brian half sat up, then collapsed back down, the gurney shuddering beneath his considerable heft. "I think I want that scan and then maybe... Do you guys have heat pads or something? Ice packs?"

Carter nodded. "We have both and we'd be happy to help you."

Once they'd got him in for a scan and were waiting for the results, Avery asked, "What was all that about? What if he does need surgery and you just freaked him out about it?"

Carter looked above her head as he spoke, as if picturing something he'd been through before. "You know how I can ride a bull?"

She did.

"Do you know why I did it?"

She did not.

"My father used to ride to feel alive."

She frowned and started connecting some dots. So... his sister's tendency to court danger to feel alive was a precedent set by their father. It didn't entirely explain Carter's motivation.

"I don't get the connection. What does bull riding have to do with Brian's desire for surgery? His symptoms are worrying."

Carter's green eyes flared. "So is paralysis and spending the rest of your already limited life in a wheelchair if you've had unnecessary surgery."

Oh.

The penny dropped.

Carter's father had had surgery courtesy of a "too quick to react" ER doctor.

How awful. No wonder he'd gone into emergency medicine. She felt the doors to her heart nudge open even wider. Not falling in love with this man was hard!

He tipped his head toward the scans, then pointed out a blurry bit. "It's impossible to read the extent of the damage with the swelling. When that goes down, we'll have a much clearer picture. Literally and figuratively."

She got it now. Carter was always going to do the scans. The X-rays, the research. He was always going to book a surgery if he had to. But he was not going to leap to conclusions that could alter this young man's life forever. It didn't answer all her questions, though.

"So…why did you ride if your father suffered permanent damage from it?"

"Research." His eyes didn't meet hers.

No, it wasn't. He'd done it because he'd had to. But they were at work and the topic clearly touched a nerve—no pun intended—so she wasn't going to push, but…she did find his bedside manner with this patient very different from how he treated others. He needed calling on it. That or she needed to find out where it came from.

"And the way you were with Brian? Was that anger at Dr. Chang for being trigger-happy for surgery or anger at yourself for not knowing better than to intervene on your dad's behalf?"

Carter scraped his teeth across his lip and scrubbed his hand through his hair but didn't answer.

"I'm guessing a bit of both."

He held up his hands. "I'm here to fix broken people. Sometimes it works. Sometimes it doesn't. But I think a man who has a choice ought to make an educated one. Not one ruled by emotion or people in white coats being bullied by management to keep the turnover on track or bullying him into something he couldn't possibly understand without a medical degree."

And that, in a nutshell, was Carter Booth. He put himself in the shoes of his patients to figure out where they were coming from and then rammed on his surgeon's shoes and saw it from the flip side. He took into account a person's whole life. Their income, their passions, the miserable future they'd have if it were snatched away. He genuinely cared.

And it wasn't just limited to his patients.

When they were looking at her tumbledown farmhouse, he knew better than to call it a lost cause. He knew as well as she did that knocking it down and starting over would be the smartest option. But he'd seen a need in her. A need to fulfil a promise. So he'd backed her up, but also given her a way out if being there proved too painful. *Do it up, sell it on. Start over.* The solution wasn't exactly rocket science, but since she was in the weeds with all her complex emotions, he'd cleared a path for her. Then another. Let her see the big picture and asked nothing in return.

It made her heart ache for him. A man so used to giving that he never took the time to take care of himself.

She got called away before the conversation could go any further. She gave his hand a squeeze and made a silent promise to find a way to repay the kindnesses he'd shown her. Carter Booth deserved more. Much more than he was allowing himself to receive. Looked like she wasn't the only one who needed the doors to their heart being pushed open. The only question was... what would she do once she got her foot in the door? Move forward? Or retreat?

A few hours later, Carter pulled back the curtain to the bed in the observation bay and kneed a wheeled stool up to Brian's bedside.

Avery had pulled him up on his bedside manner and, though it had taken a few laps around the hospital in the snow to separate right from wrong, he knew he owed this guy an apology. It wasn't Brian's fault Carter's dad had screwed up his back, then seen a bad surgeon. Hell. The surgeon might've been great, but he knew as well as everyone surgeons weren't gods. Even if they liked to think they were. "How're you getting on with that ice pack?"

Brian feigned an expression of being semi-comatose, then grinned. "What do you know? A bit of ice, a bit of heat and not lifting up the equivalent of a polar bear does a man some good."

Carter gave him a satisfied nod. Good. He'd been right to wait. Sometimes it was that simple. Even so, the chances of injuring himself again were high, so he wanted to make sure the two of them were on the same page when this guy walked out of here. "You know masking the pain isn't going to help someone like you."

Brian squinted at him. "How so?"

"You've got enough musculature to get you by with everyday things and, of course, exercise keeps you strong. But the next time you think about picking up a heavy weight or dragging a car behind you or whatever else it is you do to get yourself ripped like that, just remember that none of it will mean a hill of beans if you've not given yourself enough rest time."

"You just said to exercise."

"I sure did. But I didn't mean training. What you're going to need to do is start from the beginning. Retrain the muscles in your back so that they move properly. I can send you some good repetition and resistance exercises to improve your stability—unilateral presses, rows, chops, lifts, side planks. That sort of thing. No twists, squats, deadlifts or overhead weight lifting."

Brian huffed out a sigh.

Through it, Carter continued, "And if you know a good physio, I'd get in touch. You'll need to see one of them before you even think of lifting anything heavier than a pencil."

Brian's features creased. "Oh, come on now, Doc. My next competition is in another week."

"Cancel it."

Brian went to protest.

Carter held up a hand. "A variation of what happened to you happened to my father."

"What happened to him?"

"He pushed it too far and spent the last good years of his life in a wheelchair."

"You serious?"

"Deadly."

"I guess I'll give the competition a miss, then."

Thank goodness. Carter had got through to him. "Do we have ourselves a deal?"

After another aggrieved sigh, they shook on it. Carter had made the impression he'd wanted to, a lasting one. If only dealing with his sister was half as easy. Instead of falling into that rat's nest, he got back to work.

Lucky for him and bad for Nashville, it appeared to be a citywide "slip and fall" day. He'd noticed the roads were icy when he drove in, but he hadn't left the hospital since the sun had risen and set. From the looks of things, the ice had hung around. Wrists, ankles, knees, shoulders, hips. The orthopedic wing was going to be full to bursting if things kept up like this.

His path didn't cross much with Avery's but when it did, she seemed a bit more lost in thought than usual. He didn't think it was anything to take personally, but sometimes you never knew what was going on in someone else's brain. After he'd set and wrapped what must've been his tenth sprained wrist of the day, he found her at the coffee station.

"Hey."

She didn't look at him. "Hey yourself."

"You okay?"

"Fine."

"Don't sound fine."

"What are you?" She finally looked at him. "The 'good mood' police?"

"Nope." He held a carton of chocolate milk he'd been drinking over her cup of coffee. "Want a dollop of something nice in that?"

She shot him a look, then finally cracked a smile. His heart softened at the sight. Funny. He hadn't realized his mood could change with hers.

"Tough day?" He put a good inch or two of chocolate milk into her coffee and she took a long satisfied drink.

"*Mmm.*" She ticked a few cases off on her fingers. "A couple more folk in from the weight-lifting thing. A few whiplash cases from fender benders, three heart attacks and one too many cases of hypothermia than should be allowed in this day and age." She pursed her lips. He'd had a couple, as well. Not good. One homeless guy and an old woman who said she couldn't afford to pay her heating bill anymore. The postman had become concerned when he saw she hadn't collected her mail in a while and hollered up at her bedroom window for about fifteen minutes before calling an ambulance. He was a good man, that postman. If more folk looked out for one another like he had—

"There was a woman in from the prison." Avery looked down, then up at him. "Not your sister. I checked the minute I heard they were bringing someone in."

She didn't say what was wrong with the woman and he didn't ask. "Thanks for checking." He cleared his throat, looked up at the ceiling, then back at Avery. "Would you ever want to meet her?"

The second the question was out, he regretted it. Why on earth would she want to meet his sister—a woman hell-bent on bringing forward her death date—when she was still clearly grieving her own sister, whose life had been cut short far too soon? Not to mention the fact it was letting someone into a part of his life that no one, apart from Cassidy, had ever been in.

"Sorry." He tried to erase the comment. "Don't answer that."

"No, I'd like to." She scrunched up her nose and gave him such a cute smile he was half tempted to give her nose a little boop. "When are you thinking?"

They decided to go that weekend. They paired their diaries, and she began to walk away. Even with a date in his phone, he still wasn't entirely convinced this was a good idea. He called after her, "You sure, now? You don't want me stripped down to my basics, hammering and nailing things?" He struck a pose. "I look extra good in a pair of jeans and nothing else."

She shot an "I'll bet you do" look over her shoulder, then shifted her smile from sexy to gentle. "Family takes precedence over worn-out floorboards."

Avery might as well have reached into his chest, grabbed his heart and popped it into her pocket for the impact the statement had. Of course, he just stood there and said something like, *Good point*, but she was right—and also a little bit not. The way his sister took precedence in his life meant he had no life. If he carried on as he was—putting his life on hold until his poor sweet sister died—he wouldn't be a dad for at least a decade, maybe more. And he wasn't sure that was the right balance of things.

Maybe it was time to break the habits of a lifetime? Put down roots and build a family of his own. He watched Avery swish her way down the hallway— she knew he was watching. He imagined what it might be like, knowing he'd see that sexy sashay every day of his life. Glancing at her hands as they shifted along her thighs and seeing the glint of an engagement ring on her finger. One he'd slipped on when he'd asked her to be his wife. His phone rang. It was the prison. He turned away from Avery so he could give his sister his full focus.

A blunt reminder that this is what family meant in his case. Total sacrifice to keep someone alive who he wasn't even sure wanted to be. As ever, he took the call, accepted the charges and walked away.

CHAPTER TEN

"Whoa!"

"Watch it, pal!"

"Someone call Security!"

"Rocky!"

Avery's instinct was to throw herself between the two men who were throwing punches right in front of her. She had properly sharp elbows when necessary. But in this scenario, she knew she didn't stand a chance. To be honest, she wasn't all that sure the spindly security guards on duty, or even Rocky, did, either. Even though his background was boxing, he was lean and not too tall and these guys were clearly from the heavyweight class at the bodybuilding convention. She was no brain surgeon, but it did seem like the hospital wasn't the best place to end up when you were dedicating your life to fitness.

She'd seen the men coming into the waiting room. One of them had been very agitated, seemingly unaware that blood was streaming out of a bad cut on his forehead. His knuckles were dusted as if he'd done a few rounds and was ready for more, only…bodybuilders weren't boxers. So when the one who wasn't cut told the bleeding guy to wait where he was, and the bleeding guy started hammering into him as if he'd just insulted his mother, she'd been completely taken by surprise and, more concerningly, trapped in a corner.

She saw Rocky appear at the double doors on the opposite site of the waiting room and alongside him was Carter. Carter looked revved up. Ready to take on trouble and show it who was boss. It was two parts sexy to one part scary. There was a wild look in his eye that suggested all his energy was intent on taking down the two men bopping nine shades of testosterone out of one another. Then his eyes met hers and she saw something different altogether. Protection. Care. A silent vow to do whatever he could to make sure she was safe. Now it was two parts sexy and one part scary for a whole other reason. The last thing she wanted was to see him getting hurt.

The nurses and doctors who weren't with patients were busy getting anyone in a wheelchair out of the way. Escorting the elderly to the quiet rooms. Women with children were being hustled into the pediatric waiting room and everyone else was behind the nurse's station or assembling in the minor care triage area. With any luck, someone was calling the orderlies from the psych ward. They were strong and knew how to duck a well-aimed punch. Carter tipped his head and whispered something to Rocky who nodded intently and gave his knuckles a crack. Did they think they could take these two behemoths on? They were insane. Carter was about as strong and sexy as they came, but he wasn't a man mountain, and these two men could throw shade on the Rockies. Carter looked at her then and whatever it was he was lasering at her with those green eyes of his told her she would be okay. He did a quick three count and faster than that had taken, he and Rocky charged the men. A yard or so out, they dove at their ankles. Both men came tumbling down like giants on beanstalks. The floor even shook. One landed in a potted plant and promptly passed out and the other, the bleeding one, crumpled to the floor and began crying, then screaming in a frightening voice, asking why they'd taken all of the ice-cream stands away. He needed ice cream. Now. Chocolate. Vanilla. Strawberry.

The way he was screaming made her never want to eat ice cream again.

All of a sudden it clicked. He had corticosteroid-induced psychosis. She'd heard about it but had never seen it before. It could cause anything from depression to low sex drive to lethargy to psychosis. This guy was out of control, so she was laying her bets on psychosis. Carter had the guy in a bear hug now and was talking to him in a low steady voice. "We gotcha, buddy. We're here for you. We'll get you all the ice cream you need." He glanced up at Avery. "Heart rate is high, body temp feels elevated, and I'm guessing he's dehydrated." His gaze intensified. "Amongst other things." Clever. He wasn't going to hold a man capable of lifting a refrigerator over his head and offer a public diagnosis of psychosis.

Avery knelt down beside him out of the guy's eyeline and mouthed. "I'm going to get you some injectable hydrocortisone."

Carter nodded and tightened his grip, "You're cool, bud. That's right. Long slow breaths."

She hesitated to move away. It was like watching Iron Man trying to hug it out with the Incredible Hulk when the Hulk could erupt again at any moment. "Do you think you can hold him there?"

"I'll do what I can."

She didn't know why but she had all the confidence in the world he could. She asked one of the nurses behind the counter to get the injection ready and to give her a backup bottle, as well. This guy was big. Real big. She could see his vein throbbing in his neck. His blood pressure was likely up near heart-attack levels.

The orderlies from psych arrived. Rather than give him the injection when he wasn't completely secure, Carter and the three orderlies somehow managed to gently encourage him to climb onto a bed that had secure arm straps. They got the injection into him and, on Carter's instruction, prepared some olanzapine, an antipsychotic medication. Someone who'd responded this badly to an overuse of steroids was going to need a few days in the psych ward to come out of it. She watched as his big old super muscly, scantily clad body was wheeled through the double doors and out of sight.

Avery heard a low groan. She gave one of her own. "Plant pot" guy. He was sitting up, pressing his big meat cleaver of a hand to his head.

"Hi." She ducked her head to catch his gaze. "I'm Avery, can I help you?"

He shook his head. "No, I'm good. That was intense, though."

"Are you sure? Maybe we should give you a quick check."

"Nah, honestly. I think I just need some water and maybe... Could I see him?" He tipped his head toward the double doors where his muscled-up companion had disappeared.

When Avery's eyes widened in surprise, he quickly explained, "He's my brother. He keeps taking steroids even though I tell him that's some crazy unnatural shit. And today he literally lost it. Was in the middle of a lifting session, then threw the barbell so hard it cracked the stage floor. If I hadn't tackled him, who knows what would've happened?"

"How'd you even get him here?"

He shot her an embarrassed smile. "Duct tape."

Avery tried to keep her expression neutral.

"I cut it off when we got here because I didn't want you to think I was some sort of psycho."

Fair enough. Arriving as they had had been interesting enough.

She gave him a proper once-over. This guy wasn't exactly tiny, but…he was more…lean rather than inflated. He must be made of protein shakes.

He shook his head and tipped his forehead into his hands, remorse catching in his throat. "I keep telling him he doesn't need to catch up to me."

"What do you mean?"

"He's my kid brother." He looked up at Avery. "He was a reedy little thing all through school. Nerdy. But smart. Helluva lot smarter than me. Sports were always my bag, and not academics, and so I had to punch a few guys out until they knew it wasn't a good idea to shove him in the lockers anymore."

"Sounds like you were protecting him."

He tilted his chin in acknowledgment. "I was, but he hated it. Said he wanted to be able to do the same for me. I said don't be a dumbass. He should be a doctor or lawyer or something that smart folk do. For some stupid reason, he wanted to follow in my footsteps instead of making his own path, and instead of being smarter, he's become stupid. Real stupid."

Avery nodded and tried to give his solid shoulder a squeeze. She failed because of the musculature, but also because there was a ridiculous part of her that was so jealous of him. Having someone to look after. To protect.

Though Carter complained about his sister, she knew his groans of despair came from a place of love. When she'd "won" April as an older sister, she'd followed her around like a lovesick puppy dog as April kept a vigilant eye out for her until she realized she wasn't following anymore. They were walking side by side. Singing as one. Not imagining for one day that either one of them would have to live a life without the other. Losing her had been the most acute way to learn that what they'd shared was one of those precious, precious things that was impossible to replicate without selfless love. It was what Carter had for his sister. What she'd love to do for Carter if things were different.

The thought caught her off guard and pretty much squashed any ability to tell this man that what he was doing was a good thing even if it didn't feel that way. His brother might be a hot mess right now, but he was lucky to have him.

A woman pushed through the double doors and scanned the room. It was Deena Andrews from the admin department. "Quiet in here today."

Avery made a noise that acknowledged the comment, but as her eyes landed on the flyers Deena was about to distribute, her heart lodged too high in her throat to answer.

The Love Conquers Cancer Concert.

With a bright smile, Deena purposefully headed toward one of the notice boards. She tacked up the first flyer and then headed to the next. Avery should've been prepared for this. The calendar worked the same way every year—Christmas, then New Year, then Valentine's Day—but somehow she felt blindsided by the flyer's jolly announcement and, of course, appeal for everyone to give what they could to the Valentine's Day benefit for the oncology ward.

The one she and April used to regularly perform in.

"Looks like fun," said the bodybuilder, then realizing he wasn't going to get an answer from Avery, said something about charity beginning at home and how he'd better knuckle down and find some way to properly help his brother. Get him out of the mess he was in.

If she weren't feeling so out of sorts, she would've tried to think up some advice, but the fistfight topped off by Deena's diligent flyering had loosened something in her. Chipped at the wall she'd built up around her ability to be knocked off her stride. It was all of this talk of siblings. Carter inviting her to meet his sister. This guy, literally and figuratively, torn up over his brother. It made her think of all the variations a sibling relationship could take. Sometimes they kept you safe from bullies. Sometimes they kept you safe from the darker side of yourself. And sometimes they died and took a part of you with them.

All of a sudden, like a dam about to burst inside of her, she began to feel all of the emotions she hadn't been letting herself feel press against her chest wall, demanding more room. More attention. More everything.

She managed to get the forlorn bodybuilding brother

some water from the dispenser and put him in touch
with one of the registered nurses so that he could see
about his brother. Then, knowing she'd used up all of
her stores of bravery, she racewalked into the nearest
supplies cupboard and dropped to the floor, arms
wrapped around her knees, so she could release the
howls of pain she'd kept pent-up for so long.

Too soon, someone came in.

"Hey," she heard. "Hey, now."

She was a mess. Shaking, ugly crying, making weird
noises that might or might not have been words. And
Carter didn't seem to mind at all. He must've grabbed
a blanket off one of the shelves, because she felt one
being wrapped around her, then his arms followed suit,
holding her close, consoling and rocking her, talking
in that reassuring drawl of his. He was so solid. So
kind. If she could've, she would've disappeared inside
of him, but that would be too close to falling in love.
And that was the one thing she'd forbidden herself to
do when she'd agreed to this harebrained "friends with
benefits" thing. They weren't just friends. They were
lovers. And she felt like she was free-falling in the
sea of emotions that came along with the revelation.
If he weren't holding her so close, whispering words
of belief that she could survive whatever it was that
was tearing her up inside, she could've been lost in
it forever. Lost in him. But to her surprise, it was
grounding. Eventually, her breath began to steady,
her tears abated and she was able to open up her eyes
and look into his.

She saw nothing there but kindness. Concern. And
at that moment she realized she was far too late in the
"don't fall in love" department. She already was.

* * *

When Carter pulled his truck into the short drive that led up to Five Acre Farm, he was beginning to have his doubts that his plan was a good one.

The electricity had been on the last time they'd been out here. No porch light today. Could be a blown bulb. He grabbed the pair of grocery store bags from the bench seat of his truck and climbed the porch steps to check it out. Bulb was fine. No electricity.

Damn.

Fuses had probably blown. After filling up the dining room with all the boxes she'd had in storage, they'd asked some workmen he'd heard good things about to come up during the week to start putting the place back together again. Though they hadn't discussed it, they'd both agreed having another team of builders work on the place was best. With a full-time workload, a sister to look after in prison and not much time left...well... he'd rather spend his spare time making love to Avery. He also didn't want her looking at each swoosh of paint and every reinforced wood panel and remember him. If things ended badly between them as they definitely had with his med school ex, he didn't want her to have to hate the house, as well. So, a crew of strangers were doing the work. Ones who left their saw tables and drill packs and piles of tools lying around instead of tidying up each night like he did on a job.

Instead of being mad, he started picking up the mess. He'd promised Avery a beautiful night in her new house and that's what she was going to get. Granted, without electricity, all he had to offer her was a pitch-black, ice-cold house and a mishmash of uncooked ingredients. He checked his watch. She'd insisted upon staying for the rest of her shift, sweet little birdie that she was. His heart ached for her. She hadn't explained why she'd been so upset this afternoon and he hadn't asked, but it was definitely something more than seeing a couple of beefed-up men throw punches at one another. Somehow, he'd known holding her was all she wanted and he was more than happy to do it.

He had an hour and a half before she was due to arrive. A cooked dinner was out. As was the bubble bath he'd planned to draw for her. He did a quick recalculation and adopted a new plan.

When her headlights finally lit up the living room, his heart started jack hammering against his rib cage as if this were the most important night of his life. It wasn't, but his time with Avery felt precious. Worthy of all his attention. All his heart. And though it freaked him out caring so much—more than he'd planned anyway—he enjoyed giving to someone who wasn't used to receiving. Loved seeing a smile light up her face. Feeling her body lean into his the way it had today when she'd been so upset. He'd liked being her rock. As much as it freaked him out, it had also warmed up corners of his heart he'd thought had long since atrophied. Showed him the heart was resilient. Even his. He gave the place one last scan, hoping like hell she liked what he had done.

He heard her light footsteps upon the porch and then, when she opened the door, he felt the quizzical silence before hearing her slightly confused but comedically singsonged, "Honey! I'm home!"

He walked in from the kitchen, struck dumb by how beautiful she was. The firelight cast her in a warm glow that accentuated the curve of her jawline, the glow of her cheekbones, the fullness of her lips. She'd done her hair into two plaits that hung over her shoulders and something about it made her look both young and womanly all at the same time.

She quirked her chin to the side, her lips twitching as if undecided about whether to smile or frown. "It's freezing outside. Why aren't you wearing a shirt?"

He looked down at himself. He'd been boiling hot fifteen minutes ago. Chopping wood as fast as he could tended to do that. He grinned. "Had to make sure my woman came home to a warm house, didn't I?"

Again, her mouth didn't know what to do with itself. "Is that what I am? Your woman?"

If she hadn't been staring at him, he would've sworn at himself for phrasing it that way. A few weeks ago, he wouldn't have ever referred to a woman as his. If one had asked him that question without prompting, he would've answered it with a solid *no*. But the way Avery had asked it—not possessively, not expectantly—just… curious…it all but turned his guts inside out. Instinctively, he felt the word *yes* form in his mouth. He sure as hell didn't want her to be anyone else's woman. But his brain was rattling through his history of abrupt departures and was telling him to say *no*. Any answer he gave was entering a minefield. He took his first step. "For the next twelve hours, you are all mine."

She let the answer sit between them while she scanned the living room, surprisingly warm from only the heat of the fire. He'd laid out a pile of quilts and some throw pillows he'd found in one of the boxes in the dining room, hoping it'd look cozy. Inviting.

She grinned at him, rubbed her hands together and stretched herself out on the quilt. "Well, I guess I'd better start enjoying it then, shouldn't I?" She tapped the watch she always wore pinned to her scrubs top. "Time's a tickin', cowboy."

He heard her unspoken words loud and clear: *We both know each night could be our last.*

For the first time ever, rather than feel slighted, the shared knowledge of his inevitable departure hurt only because he didn't want to leave. Didn't want to have a day when he wasn't looking forward to seeing her. At work. Here at Five Acre. In bed. The unfamiliar ache filled him like energy, and he set himself a task: to do what she was doing. Making the most of it.

An hour later, he was glad he'd torn around to the local store and hacked up that pile of wood and lit the thirty-odd storm candles he'd found in the cupboard alongside a box of jam jars. Because it turned out, roasting hot dogs in the fireplace with a woman who made him feel more alive than he'd ever felt was pretty much one of the best nights he'd ever had. They'd moved on to dessert—a supersized bag of marshmallows—seeing who had enough patience not to stuff the thing in the flames and set it alight. No surprise there, it was Avery. Despite their fiery first meeting, he saw that she was everything he wasn't. Grounded. Focused on doing her best by her community at the hospital. And determined to put down roots no matter how many people left her behind. Her sister obviously hadn't had a choice. That was a cruel strike of bad fortune. And her grandparents. But her parents... He didn't know how they could've just picked up and left like that. Sold the house she'd grown up in. Left her to fend for herself. Maybe it hadn't been like that. Maybe she'd been invited to come along. To join them in putting as much space between them and the pain they'd endured, the losses they'd suffered. And maybe she'd said no. Maybe she'd needed to feel as much pain as she could endure in order to eventually not feel it anymore.

He considered broaching the topic, but the mood between them was so nice he didn't want to mess it up. So he grabbed his guitar, pulled it out of the case and leaned his back up against the raised stone hearth, closed his eyes and began to play.

It wasn't until he was on his third or fourth song that he realized she'd been singing along. Knew every word to every verse. Maybe she hadn't been singing along at first, maybe she had. But her voice wove itself so perfectly amidst his chords and finger work it felt like it had always been there, waiting for just the right moment to make itself heard.

He opened his eyes. Hers were closed but there were tears pouring out of them, glossing up those cheekbones of hers with sorrow. The words she sang were so full of love and truth he felt his own throat choke up with emotion. She had talent. In spades. When the song came to an end, he didn't start another. She opened her eyes and looked at him. "Why'd you stop playing?"

"Why didn't you tell me you could sing like that?"

"Like what?" She looked genuinely confused.

"Like you just walked onto the stage of the Grand Ole Opry and made the whole damn audience reach for their tissues."

She wiped at her face and looked startled, as if she hadn't realized she'd been crying.

Carter tapped his guitar. "You did know you've been singing along with me, right?"

Her brow furrowed and her hand moved to her

throat as if she were checking for some sort of residual sensation. "I guess I was."

She looked as if she didn't know if she were happy or sad about it. She looked at him and their eyes locked together—unspoken words communicating something so powerful he knew Avery Whittacker would always be a part of him no matter what turn fate took.

"I haven't sung a note in almost two years."

"Do you remember what the song was?"

She nodded. "A lullaby."

Goddamn. Singing a lullaby to her dying sister... No wonder she hadn't sung again.

"You must have a magic touch with that guitar of yours," she said, nudging his foot with hers.

He gave a one-shouldered shrug. "I guess it's this cowboy's way of showing he has feelings."

Something that wasn't firelight flared in her eyes.

Before he could register what was happening, she'd moved his guitar out of his lap and replaced it with herself.

CHAPTER ELEVEN

HAVING SEX WITH Carter West was a standout experience at the best of times. Tonight, it was on another level altogether. This, she realized, was what it truly was to make love. He'd seen her frailties and hadn't budged an inch. He'd held her tight, wiped away her tears, made the ramshackle set of walls around them feel like a home and somehow, miraculously, tonight he'd made her sing.

He was half naked already so getting him out of his clothes took half the time. Which was just as well. Because she was *hungry* for him. Judging by the hot kisses he was giving her, kisses that seemed to have no beginning and no hint of an ending, he was feeling the same.

She'd showered at work, but had pulled on some scrubs, and if there was one thing Carter knew how to do, it was how to get her out of her scrubs quick smart. Instead of fast and furious or slow and languorous, tonight was something else completely. Something new. From the moment they became flesh on flesh, their bodies merged like hot molten lava, rocking and moving as if they were one, then two, then one again. Every shift of his body, touch of his lips and caress of his fingertips was mesmeric.

She'd had this big ol' romantic plan to wait. To "christen" the house on the weekend. She'd wanted to make up her new bed—delivery delayed—gussy it up with new cotton bedding—as yet unbought—and for the room to be lit by nothing but starlight. Gray skies were forecast for the next three weeks and the skylight couldn't be installed until April.

But this, here, on the creaking wooden floor in front of a roaring fire filled with logs chopped up by her man—yes, he felt like her man—this was heaven. The house felt like a home, not because of anything the workmen had done or even the nest of quilts and the roaring fire. It felt like home because Carter was in it.

They weren't saying much, but they didn't have to. Singing along with his beautiful guitar playing had uncorked something in her. Opened her up so that there were no secrets anymore. Nothing she wouldn't tell him. Nothing he couldn't tell her. They'd make mistakes and hurt one another, but they'd also care for another. Have each other's backs.

She'd thought she'd been strong these past couple of years. Grief-stricken, sure. But also resilient. Proud. Able to take on new challenges and face them head-on. But what she'd actually been was a shook-up bottle of mixed emotions, no longer able to express herself the way she used to: through music.

The same way April once had, Carter had sensed her mood and played his music soft at first, gentle, then gathering up its pace and emotional punch. April had always made a show of rifling through their songbooks, hemming and hawing over the choices and, as if by magic, picking just the perfect song to lift Avery's spirits or give her that long-awaited cry she might need. She knew when Avery had been upset by a patient dying or happy because they'd gone into remission. She *knew* her. She thought her parents had, too, and though she genuinely didn't resent them for the choice they'd made, she did hope they'd find a way back to one another again. A day when it wouldn't hurt to look at the daughter they still had, a reminder of the one they'd lost.

Being here with Carter, his hands owning her body the way a potter owned clay, she felt cherished. Cared for and appreciated. Desired. It was a potent combination. One that, like it or not, was making its mark. From here on out, everyone would be judged by the "Carter Booth" barometer. And come up short.

The same way her sister had been a rung above everyone else in her life.

But she didn't have her sister anymore and one day she wouldn't have Carter.

Sensing something had changed in her, she felt Carter's hands change their mission. She'd been well on her way to another post-coital orgasm and slightly resented him for stopping what he was doing.

His breath whispered across her lips. "What's going on in that head of yours?"

He was serious. So was she, which was why she didn't want to say anything.

She leaned in to give that juicy lower lip of his a saucy nip, then tried to part them both with her tongue. She encountered resistance. She doubled her efforts. He wasn't playing along. She felt frustrated. Hungry for his touch and, yes, she'd admit it, now that she'd let the earworms in, she also felt scared. Scared of losing this connection she felt. Even considering not feeling his touch at night… It tore at her heart, knowing one

ANNIE O'NEIL   141

day she would have to say goodbye. How was it possible to feel completely whole with someone and know
his presence in her life was only temporary?

"You're looking philosophical," he said after pulling
back, moving one of his hands so that he could trace
curlicues onto her collarbone.

"And you look sexy." She tried to tug his hand back
down to where it had been, between her legs, but he
kept himself solid. Still.

"I don't want you using me just for my body, hear?
I've got two of these." He tapped one of his ears.
"They're good for something, too."

She play-snarled at him, but they both heard the bite
in it. She was falling in love with Carter Booth and until
now hadn't done much to resist it. She thought she had
it in her to keep him compartmentalized, but the fact
he'd somehow made her sing elicited something else in
her. A need to bare herself to him. And she wasn't talking about being naked. She was talking about being an
open book. Being that vulnerable was something she
hadn't done in a long time. Half of her couldn't imagine living without him. The other half felt like being
chest deep in a riptide with the shore getting farther and
farther out of reach. She needed to fight to get back to
more familiar shores if she was going to survive this.

"C'mere, you." Carter tucked an arm around her waist
and easily turned her so that they were spooning, the
both of them facing the fire. He wasn't turning off the
conversation. Quite the opposite. He was pulling a halt
to their intimacies. Not that there wasn't comfort, or intimacy, in lying in each other's arms without so much
as a stitch of clothing between them. There definitely

was, but…if they made love again now, they both knew it would be because they were ignoring the elephant in the room. They had feelings for one another and neither of them knew what to do with them.

He pulled her closer when she began to tremble. "I've got you," he said.

"For how long?"

He wanted to say *forever.* With every pore in his body, he did, but they both knew it would be a lie. He wanted to assure her that they'd get over one another soon enough. That what they were experiencing was that crazy endorphin-fueled rush of lust that made any new couple think they couldn't live without the other, but that would've been a lie, too.

"As long as I'm able."

She whipped around, propped her head on her hand and, eyes blazing, asked, "What exactly am I meant to do with that?"

"We knew this might happen."

"We knew we'd have hot sex," she parried.

Good point. But… "No. We knew there was something more between us than lust."

She harrumphed. He mimicked the sound and, as he'd hoped, a smile flickered across her face. She gave his chest a poke with her finger. Then, with less aggravation, began tracing little designs onto his chest while she thought.

"Why'd you invite me to come see your sister?"

Normally, this was the part where he'd say he wanted her to see what she was up against. Witness, firsthand, the reason why his heart would never be fully open to a relationship. Then the girl would back out, accept that things had come to a natural conclusion and go on to find another relationship.

Cassidy could be vile and though she openly resented Carter's "interference" in her life, she was contrarily embittered toward anyone else who took his time. His affections. So, yeah, if Avery were anyone else, he would've said five minutes with Cassidy was all she'd need to tamp down anything approaching actual feelings for him.

But she wasn't anyone else. She would come to the prison with him, no doubt charm the socks off Cassidy and then he'd be on brand new terrain he wouldn't know what to do with. All of which had to mean something, didn't it? It suggested that they weren't just good at having sex. They were good at being together.

From the moment he'd laid eyes on her, Avery had somehow become a part of him. The same way the knee bone was connected to the thighbone, Avery Whittacker was connected to his heart. And it wouldn't tear when the time to say goodbye finally hurtled toward them—it would break.

She was still waiting for an answer and he owed it to her to be honest. "I guess when I said we'd be friends with benefits, I hadn't realized the *friends* part of it would come to mean so much."

He cleared his throat and stared past her at the fire. It went beyond that and he knew it, but if he declared his real feelings for her, he might as well pull the plug on the whole thing right now. He couldn't tell her he was in love with her. Because then he wouldn't just be walking away from her, he'd be walking away from the man he was when he was with her—the one he'd wanted to become all these years.

"Is there anything we can bring her?" Avery asked.

He shook his head. "Not unless you've got a change jar that you can raid. We can get her treats from the vending machine." He snorted out a laugh. "I've never met a woman who likes cheesy puffs more than my sister."

Avery grinned that open, happy smile of hers. "Cheesy puffs?"

"Yes, ma'am. There isn't a food additive or artificial flavoring that doesn't have my sister's name on it."

Avery pressed her hand to his heart. "It must take its toll on you."

"Her awful eating habits?" He huffed out another humorless laugh. He knew what she meant—watching his sister systematically destroy herself. "If you don't want to come, I understand. After what you've been through—"

"After what I've been through, I should be stronger than I am," she said, her voice hot with feeling.

Enough to pull his eyes back to hers. "What do you mean?"

She kept her hand solidly on his chest, his heartbeats pressing themselves against her palm as if it were a salve. And maybe it was. Maybe love was that simple.

"Do you know why I was crying in that supplies cupboard earlier today?"

He shook his head no, but he had a rough idea.

"After the ruckus with the weight-lifting guys, Deena came in from Admin."

His radar shot up. "Did she say something to upset you?"

"No. She put up some notices." Her lips twitched as

she fought a private battle for composure. "For the Valentine's Day benefit."

"I've seen those. They're putting them up like wallpaper around the hospital. I don't really recognize any of the performers."

Avery looked back at him. "You would've two years ago, and the five years preceding."

"You sang?" He gave her shoulder a squeeze. "I bet everybody loved that."

"They did. They loved both of us."

And then he got it. The singing teacher. The house. The posters. Him pulling out his guitar and unwittingly reminding her of the woman she used to be. The one she could never be again.

"So, I take it they didn't approach you."

"They did and I said no! How could I even have considered saying no when I know firsthand just how much a top-rate cancer center means to people? It's not just money for research. It's support for families, for the hospice. Everything. And I was too wrapped up in myself to help." She reached out and tugged a blanket to her, wrapped it around her shoulders and sat up. He followed suit.

"I think people would understand." He meant the words to comfort, but they only seemed to lance her with more pain.

"But if I were a truly good person, the person April thought I was, I should never ever, no matter what I'm going through, want anyone else to endure a similar amount of pain."

"I don't follow."

"This may sound like humble bragging, but it isn't meant to."

He nodded for her to go on.

"When April and I were on the roster, a lot of people came to the benefits. A *lot*."

"Okay." He wasn't sure where this was heading.

"Including a few bigwigs from the record labels."

"You're going to have to spell this out for me darlin'. I'm about as 'show biz' naive as they come."

She pointed her hands toward herself. "They wanted us."

"For a record?"

He whistled. "If your sister could sing anything like you can, I'm not surprised by that."

Avery's expression turned grim. "She could. And play the guitar. But then she got sick."

Ah. The Lord giveth. Then the Lord taketh away.

"So did they approach you again?"

She nodded. "I said no way. I couldn't do it without my sister."

He didn't mention the fact they were sitting in the house her sister was also meant to be living in.

"I know!" She put her hands up. "You're wondering how I could buy this house without her but say no to a record deal?"

He made a big check in the space between them. "You can tick mind reading off your list anyway."

She smiled, then wilted beneath her blanket. "It's just... I was watching that guy take all his brother's punches and then reminded myself how you have forsaken any kind of permanence in your life to catch your sister every time she falls and all of a sudden it hit me. Even though it's hard, and sometimes physically painful, you're both still doing everything you can for your siblings and I'm not. I let the one thing I know in my heart April would've wanted me to do on her behalf fall to the wayside."

"Become a country star?"

"No. Help people."

"What are you talking about?" He gave one of her plaits a little tug. "You help people. Every day at work."

"I know, but I mean above and beyond. We did that concert every year without thinking because it was that one step further. We also used to volunteer at a soup kitchen once a month. We knew it wouldn't cure homelessness same as we knew singing wouldn't cure cancer, but they definitely helped inch things along." She lowered her voice to something deep and gravelly. "'Some progress is better than none.'" Her smile was soft and faraway. "It was something my Pawpaw used to say when we were training horses and really, life's no different, is it?"

Carter shook his head. No. Life wasn't much different.

Avery was on a roll now, thank goodness, because he was a bit too wrong-footed by the comment to hold the X-ray up to his own life, the decisions he'd made, wondering if what he was doing right now was progress or sheer stupidity. Hobbling himself and his sister? Or helping? There was no easy answer.

"As long as you're going forward..." Avery put her fingers to her eyes, then pointed them out, "...looking forward, it's an improvement. And doing that concert was the first thing I backed away from after she died because it was too acute a reminder of what had been taken from me. It felt personal and I should've realized it wasn't personal. It's just life. It can kick your knees out from under you and what you have to do is get back up again, no matter how much it hurts. I've been sitting on the ground, Carter. Just sitting, waiting for life to happen to me."

"I wouldn't call riding a mechanical bull on New Year's Eve to get the deposit money for the house of your dreams sitting idle."

She tipped her head back and forth. "It wasn't exactly helping society, though, was it?"

Carter had an idea, then backed away from it.

"What?" She poked his knee with her finger through her blanket.

He grinned and gave her cheek a stroke with the back of his hand. "You mind reading again?"

"Trying to, but I think you're going to have to help me."

"I was wondering..." He tipped his head and met her expectant gaze. "What if I were to offer to play alongside you? I won't sing. No one would appreciate that for an offer, but I'd play for you."

She blew out a long slow breath, but her eyes didn't leave his.

"Right up there on stage? In front of hundreds of strangers? You'd do that?"

He nodded. He'd do it naked and upside down if it lit up her eyes like they were now. "Sure would. Any songs you like unless they're heavy metal and then you'd have to find yourself someone who has plugs in their guitar."

She smiled. "I wouldn't want anyone else."

"Is that your version of a yes?"

She nodded, then shook her head no. "It's a can I think about it?"

"Absolutely. Now." He pulled her close to him and dropped a kiss onto her forehead, then just as gently onto her lips. "Maybe we should blow out these candles and get some shut-eye?"

Holding her in his arms that night felt sweeter than any other had. If she went for it, he knew it would be a step in the right direction for her. Only question was could he be brave enough to do the same in his own life?

CHAPTER TWELVE

"THREE BAGS! CARTER, you're spoiling me. What a perfect big brother you are."

Carter rolled his eyes. Cassidy was putting on one heck of a show. Only thing was he couldn't tell if it was a thriller or a chick flick. She seemed to like Avery, but Cassidy seemed to like everyone at first. Before she pulled the knives out. Figuratively, of course. The most lethal weapon she was allowed here at prison was her paper-thin mattress and, surprise, surprise, they didn't let them haul those into the visiting room.

On the flipside, Avery was on top form. Not over the top, not clinging onto him, not overly brightly attentive to his sister. Just a friend along for the ride. A story Cassidy wasn't buying.

"So, what brings you to this neck of the woods?" Cassidy's question was directed solely toward Avery. "Drawn by the catering?" Cassidy held out a half-eaten bag of cheesy puffs.

Carter tipped his head into his hands. Why the hell he'd thought this was a good idea was beyond him.

To his surprise, Avery took a few and had a munch. She frowned at the couple remaining in her hand.

"What's wrong? Not to your liking? I hear the caviar ones are due in on Tuesday, if they're more your style."

She was testing Avery and both women knew it.

"Nah, I'm good. I'm just trying to figure out if I like the crunchy ones with hot sauce more than the puffy ones." She jammed her two remaining puffs between her upper lip and her teeth, then gave them both a good gawk at her orange fangs. They all laughed, and Avery ate her "fangs," pronouncing them delicious. Cassidy's hackles went down, and her body language changed from defensive to genuinely inquisitive. Her eyes pinged between the two of them as if they were divining rods of truth. Before he could think of some way to steer the conversation away from the inevitable, his kid sister pounced. "What's going on with you two anyway?"

Carter said, "We're colleagues," at the same time as Avery said, "We're friends."

Damn. He'd screwed that one up. Rather than bristle, Avery shot him a look that said, *It's cool. I know this is weird.*

"'Outside of work' friends?" Cassidy pushed.

He and Avery shared a look. Cassidy burst into laughter. "Don't even try to lie. I know a pair of 'loved up' people when I see them." She sighed. A wistful look wrapped itself around her so tight Carter felt his own heart constrict.

"You know you're my number one girl, Cass."

Cassidy frowned at him. Avery's expression stayed static.

"You're allowed to have girlfriends, Carter."

As two pairs of eyes lit on him, all the breath in his body felt like it had been hit by liquid nitrogen.

Here it was. The rock and the hard place. Cassidy

knew damn straight why he didn't do relationships. Because the one that mattered most was family.

He felt Avery's thigh brush against his. His instinct was to reach out and grab her hand, but what signal would that send?

The wrong one.

It was like swallowing razor blades, knowing he couldn't give her what she deserved. Hell. What they both deserved. A family of their own.

Knowing there was no right answer, Carter cleared his throat and tried to shift on his stool—the kind that was welded to the table so you couldn't throw it anywhere.

"Do you share a space with someone nice?" Avery asked.

Clever woman. Easing the tension but still staying real. He didn't know what he'd done to deserve her, but at this precise moment Avery felt heaven-sent. Little wonder she'd slid under his skin so easily. He just couldn't wrap his head around why she'd let him slide under hers. An inevitable goodbye didn't seem the best prospect for a romantic partner. It was little consolation, but at least she knew what was coming. With her sister, she hadn't. Maybe losing her sister had made her into the type of person who flipped ahead to the last page of a book before letting herself get past chapter one.

Cassidy shrugged. "She's all right. A bit of a joiner."

"How do you mean?"

"She's always dragging me along to the group activities."

Carter nodded. That was new. And from the way she was avoiding eye contact, he wasn't entirely convinced there was much *dragging* involved. Had something changed during his sister's stint in solitary?

Avery asked something he hadn't caught, and Cassidy was shaking her head. "I don't know which is worse. Solitary confinement or the group activities."

"What ones do they have you doing?" he asked.

She glared at him. "They're voluntary, but I've been going to the—" She hesitated, flicked her eyes at Avery, then told her instead of him. "I've been going to the AA meetings. They're in the chapel." She quickly covered with an explanation. "It's the nicest room in the whole place, so…"

"Cool," Avery said without judgment. "Do they have a choir?"

Cassidy hooted. "No one in their right mind would want to hear me sing." She was about to reach across to Carter, then glanced at the guard and pulled her hands back into her lap. "Has Carter sung to you?"

"Not a note." Avery surreptitiously gave his leg a squeeze. She'd caught that Carter was feeling the sting of not being able to hold his sister's hands in his. In prison, it was a chance to pass contraband. In real life, it was a way to say I love you without saying anything.

This was the first time he'd had someone witness his pain firsthand, then offer him comfort for it. Avery's gesture dislodged something in his chest he couldn't quite put a name to.

Cassidy ran a few croaky notes past them. "Let that be a warning to you. Booths don't sing."

"What do they do?" Avery asked.

Cassidy shrugged, and in the blink of an eye, he watched his sister retreat inside herself to an extent that scared him. Sometimes he thought he knew her better than anyone. Other times he felt like he didn't know her at all. This was one of those times. He ached to know where she went when she disappeared like this.

"How're you feeling these days?" he asked, then from the sharp look on her face, wished he hadn't.

"Peachy," came the terse reply. She stood up and brushed a few crumbs off her blue top. "I think they're about to call time. I'd better get going."

All three of them knew it was a lie. They'd been here maybe ten minutes, max. She got four hours of visiting time a month, which he spread out into eight half-hour visits. Rather than push it, he decided to talk with the warden, see if they'd tack the time onto his next visit. She looked tired. Probably wasn't eating enough if the loose fit of her uniform was anything to go by. She was the polar opposite of Avery—a woman very obviously in the prime of her life, her cheeks still glowing from this morning's run and the shower they might've accidentally on purpose taken together.

He thought bringing Avery here would be... Hell. He didn't know what.

Maybe it was an act of self-sabotage. The only way he could show Avery what a mess his sister was and, by extension, him. Or maybe he wanted to show his sister that life didn't have to be lived the way she was doing it. After all, Avery had experienced some incredibly hard knocks in life, but she seemed determined to get back up again. Cassidy? Not so much.

He didn't know anymore. The only thing that seemed to be coming out of this was the fact that sitting with the two halves of his life made him feel more torn apart than whole. Not the goal at all.

Once they were back in his truck, waiting for the engine to warm up, Avery asked, "You all right?"

The engine choked. He cranked the key again. Too hard. He needed a new truck.

Who was he kidding? He needed a new life. The one he'd been struggling to maintain clearly wasn't working.

He made a noise that might've passed for yes.

"Can't be easy," she said, giving his hand a squeeze as he grabbed ahold of the gear lever and jammed it into Reverse.

He didn't want her pity and she wasn't giving it. Just acknowledging one of those so-called "universal truths." Seeing a sibling locked up made you sad. End of story.

She shifted around so she was facing him. "Want to do something that'll put that Stetson of yours to work?"

Yeah. He did. Anything to take his mind off this disaster of a visit. He put the truck into gear and made a silent promise to pop in on his own tomorrow. See if he could sweet-talk the warden into letting him take a look at their medical facilities.

"What's this plan of yours, then?"

Avery couldn't have wiped the smile off her face if she'd tried. Carter on a horse was like ice cream and chocolate sauce. Biscuits and gravy. Poetry in motion was another way to put it. He and the steed the stable manager had chosen for him—a gorgeous chestnut stallion called Fairweather—were whipping around those barrels as if they'd been doing it for years.

He pulled up to her and grinned. The dullness she'd seen in his eyes after their visit to the prison was now replaced by bright happy sparks of adrenaline and achievement. A bit like he looked after he'd come out of an intense surgery or fresh from delivering someone good news after a potentially life-altering scan. While it was good to have this version of Carter back in the room—or barn in this case—she knew it wasn't a replacement for talking about how things had gone with his sister.

"You think you can beat that time?" he asked.

They both glanced up at the clock.

She fuzzed out a raspberry. "Easy."

He made a noise that acknowledged the fighting talk and then another one that suggested he kinda liked the look of her on a horse as much as she liked the look of him on one. "Well, go on, then."

She tapped her heels into her horse's sides and set off the way she intended to finish, at high speed. When she got back, he had his hat off, pressed over his heart and was blowing out that same low sexy whistle he'd sounded the first night she met him. And just like that night, he took her breath away. Same as he had every day since. It was almost impossible to believe that this man was a stranger a few weeks ago. Now, she felt like she knew him almost as well as she knew herself. She knew his ribs were extra ticklish. And that sliding her hand along the inside musculature of his thigh made him groan. Same as kisses on his throat. She knew when he'd made a diagnosis for a patient and that it wasn't good by the way he pulled up a stool and took their hands in his. She could tell when he'd lost a patient by the tension in his shoulders. And she knew he had feelings for her but that he didn't know what to do with them.

Snap, Carter Booth. Snap.

She'd always wondered what it would feel like to look at a man and think, *My goodness, he's all mine.* She allowed herself 99 percent possession for just this moment, knowing deep down he'd never be wholly hers. Especially now she'd met his sister. Blood did run deep. And in their case, it was "Grand Canyon" deep.

Carter squinted at the timer, then pulled his horse around to the starting line. Her eyes dropped to enjoy the sight of his legs making the most of his blue jeans as he stretched out, using the stirrups as a ballast. Sex god, loving brother and a man who heard the call of medicine as loud and clear as she did. How on earth was she going to let him go? Even thinking about it felt like being wrenched in two. It took her a couple of seconds to realize he was speaking to her.

"You okay?" He looked concerned.

"Fine."

He narrowed his eyes as if he didn't believe her but made a tactical choice not to comment on it. He tightened his grip on the reins. "I'm thinking about going around again."

She forced herself to laugh, hoping it masked the aching feeling that got knocked open inside her whenever she thought about saying goodbye. "Don't tell me you mind being beaten by a girl."

"Oh, I don't," he said, steadying his horse with a big old hand along the chestnut's neck. "Especially when she is all woman." And then he took off.

She reminded herself it was a view she was going to have to familiarize herself with. The backside of him. He'd spelled it out for her before, but now that she'd seen him with Cassidy, it made his promise that he'd be leaving all too real. And who was she to fault him for doing everything he could for his sister?

He was brother and father to her. Doctor. Protector. Everything and everyone a sickly child needed when their parents didn't or couldn't shoulder the load themselves.

She knew that she'd let herself fall too deeply in love with him. Her heart was his for crushing or, more to the point, abandoning when the time came.

He rode back in, his face alight with undiluted joy and flashed her a full wattage smile. If she hadn't begun to let the crystals of fear chill the edges of her heart, it would've melted her into a molten puddle of, *Yes, please, cowboy.*

"Let's go out," he said later when they were racking up their saddles.

"What? For something to eat?"

"No." His eyes were still lit up the way they'd been when he'd managed to tease a few seconds off his time and tie with her. "Let's go dancing."

She looked down at her horsey jeans and thick layering of tops. "Err…"

He pulled her into his arms, nestled into the crook of her neck and whispered, "You look absolutely perfect." He pulled back and warmed her from tip to toe with that perfect grin of his. "Let's go line dancing."

Carter knew it was idiotic. Clinging to a fantasy like this. But holding Avery in his arms, feeling her body respond to his as they both let the music pour through them—it was pure magic. He was as certain as the boots on his feet that he'd never find a woman like this again. It was the first time in his life he wished his sister would actually serve her full sentence. But what, then? Three years down the line, leaving Avery would be next to impossible.

He let a thought creep in that he rarely gave air to. What if he didn't? What if he stayed.

"Penny for 'em?" Avery pulled back and did a little twirl into his arms.

He smiled down at her and pulled her in tight. Intuitive woman. He tipped his head toward the stage where the band was playing. "I was wondering what it would be like to hear you sing up there. See couples swaying like this to the sound of your beautiful voice." It wasn't a total lie. The sound of her voice weaving in and out of his guitar strings ranked up there in the "special moments" department. And his list was short.

She looked up at the stage, then back at him and something deep in his gut told him she was feeling the same kind of sentimental. As if they were practicing their goodbyes so that when the time actually came, it wouldn't hurt as much.

"It's not an open mic night," she said. "If it was…"

His heart crashed against his rib cage. There was a bright light shining in those dark eyes of hers that told him she'd do it if he could make it happen.

Before she could come up with an excuse not to sing, he was walking the two of them off the sawdust-covered dance floor to the bar. He got her a drink then while he was waiting for his and had a quiet word with the barman. He knew this window of opportunity could close real quick. When the band finished their song, the bearded owner went up, had a word and the singer smiled in understanding.

"Ladies and gentlemen, we've got a special treat for

you. We've been told this woman is an angel by day at St. Dolly's Hospital and has a voice to match. Everyone, please give up some cheers for Nashville's own Avery Whittacker."

Carter didn't mind one bit when Avery punched him in the arm for the OTT intro because her cheeks were glowing, her smile was hitting each ear and, most importantly, she was walking up onto that stage. He switched out with the guitar player and once she whispered a song title to him, he let her voice guide him straight to heaven. Because he hadn't been lying when he'd described her voice and by the sound of the audience's appreciative feedback, they didn't think so, either. She'd chosen a love song, which he hadn't really taken in until he realized she was singing it to him, for him, about him. Because it was country music, it naturally involved a healthy serving of heartache, but the overall message was clear. Avery Whittacker loved him. Faults and all. And in that moment, he felt complete.

CHAPTER THIRTEEN

"You LOOK LIKE A happy bunny today." Valentina gave her a hip bump as she entered the nurses' station.

"Do I?" Avery lifted up her tablet and pretended it was a mirror.

Avery was struggling to know if she was floating on clouds or waiting for the ground to fall out from under her. She hadn't exactly told Carter she'd loved him those few nights back when they'd played together at the Cattleman's Bar & Grille, but she knew by the way he'd made love to her that night and every night since that he'd got the message. Between that and the piles of sawdust he'd racked up between shifts, helping her turn her house from an eyesore into something beautiful, she knew that, in his own way, he loved her, too. It hurt, though. Waiting for the inevitable. So, despite all of the happy feels, they were all twisted up with the same sort of pain she'd felt when her sister had received her diagnosis.

"I told you I don't want to be seen by a doctor!"

Avery whipped around toward the sliding entryway. She knew that voice. It was her singing teacher, Bonnie. Her "boy toy," Levi, was pushing her in on a wheeled office chair, and from the looks of things, Levi had tied her to it.

Avery did a quick mental whip through of vitals she should be observing. Bonnie's level of consciousness was certainly fine. Her face was red with rage, indignation, high blood pressure or a heady combination of all three. But the fact she wasn't strictly fighting being in the chair made Avery wonder if there was a part of Bonnie that was grateful her boyfriend had gone to extreme measures to get her here.

Avery ran up to them along with Dr. Chang and Carter.

Dr. Chang set about undoing the ropes and giving Levi what for. "We don't restrain patients to bring them in."

"Oh, yeah?" Levi shot back. "What if the woman you love doesn't have enough energy in her legs to shop for an engagement ring?"

Avery's eyes shot to Bonnie's. Bonnie pursed her lips. They both looked at her ring finger on her left hand. It was empty. "I just didn't want to go through the embarrassment of having none of them fit. I'm starting a diet this afternoon." She whipped a finger in Levi's direction, "Not that I'm agreeing to marry you. Not after this!"

"Hush, woman. You know you love me." Levi clucked, shifting a few of Bonnie's big glossy curls back over her shoulder. "And I love her, too. Even if she is an ornery old mule."

"I am not old!" Bonnie protested. "Honestly. How could anyone marry a man who described them as old?"

Avery took one of Bonnie's hands in her own. Her fingers were plump. Always had been. But today they were cold, pale and a bit swollen. She glanced down. As usual, Bonnie was wearing a long skirt, so it was tricky to see her legs, but Avery would've bet money that they were swollen. Painfully so. Avery could hear a slight wheeze whenever Bonnie drew a breath. Pulmonary hypertension? High blood pressure in the lung's blood vessels could be making her heart work twice as hard, which could lead to long-term damage. Levi had been right to bring her in.

Avery tried to casually check Bonnie's pulse point to see what was going on, but Bonnie was clearly no stranger to surreptitious medical care.

"No, you don't, young lady. You do not have my permission."

Avery held up her hands. "Okay. Fine. We'll do it your way."

"My way is over a stack of pancakes down at the Waffle House, which is where I thought we were going. So unless you're planning on joining me, I guess we'd better say our farewells."

Out of the corner of her eye, Avery could see that Carter had magicked up a proper wheelchair and left it beside her, before turning his attention to Levi who was more than willing to offer up Bonnie's list of symptoms. As Avery tried to extract what information she could from a reluctant Bonnie, she suddenly saw Carter half carry, half guide Levi into the wheelchair Bonnie was refusing to get into.

"It's my arm, not my heart!" Levi protested. But his hand was clutching his chest and it was easy enough to see Levi was either having a massive angina attack or a heart attack.

"Coming through!" Carter took hold of Levi's wheel-

chair and steered him through to the acute care section
of the emergency room. Bonnie was doing her best to
follow but was struggling. Knowing Levi would receive
the best possible care from Carter, Avery took ahold of
her arm and steered Bonnie to a row of chairs outside
the curtained-off area they had swept Levi into.

"I want to be in there!"

"I know you do, Bonnie, but there's no room."

"Tell me every single thing they're doing to him. I
love you, baby! Levi! You hear me! I love you!" Bonnie
shouted through the curtain, then as much as her ample
frame would allow, she turned on Avery. "If I can't be
there, you explain to me what's happening. He's my
man and this is my fault!" Avery knew protesting at a
moment like this was time wasted, so she stared at the
curtain and began to talk. She'd actually seen Carter
deal with this exact situation a fair few times, so she
could picture his calm, exacting movements with ease.
"He'll have Levi's shirt open and will be attaching elec-
trodes to his chest and limbs."

"What for?"

"It's an ECG. An electrocardiogram. He'll be given
thrombolytics."

"Speak plain to me, honey! I don't talk doctor."

"We call them clot busters—they help dissolve any
blood clots that might be blocking blood flow to Levi's
heart. The sooner he receives them, the less likely it is
he'll have heart damage."

"So it's actually a blessing he brought me here?"

"Very much so."

Avery took Bonnie's hands in hers. "He'll probably
be giving some nitroglycerin to help with the chest pain.
It can also improve blood flow to the heart."

"He's got a huge heart. Huge! I love you, baby!"

A weak, "I love you, too, you old mule!" came through the curtain.

Bonnie pursed her lips and glared at Avery. "I'm guessing that's a sign he'll live?"

Nothing was certain in life, but she knew Carter and his team would do their best. "It's a good sign. He'll need some tests to see what's actually going on. They'll take blood samples and probably get him to have some scans. He may need a coronary angioplasty and stenting."

Bonnie gasped. "That sounds serious."

"They are, but they could also save his life."

"They aren't going to put those shocker things on him, are they?"

"Not unless he has a cardiac arrest."

"What's that?"

"When the heart beats irregularly or stops altogether."

Bonnie paled. "No. No, no, no. Levi's got far too much life in him for that to happen." She raised her voice. "And we still got us a wedding to plan, you hear?"

Through the curtain, Avery could hear Carter and his team murmuring soft instructions back and forth, low enough that Levi's response came through loud and clear. "Only if you agree to see that vascular doctor your little friend there told you to see *weeks* ago!"

Bonnie sat back in her chair with a huff. It was easy to see she knew he was right, but the decision still had to be hers.

Avery kept her voice neutral. "Can we take that as a yes?"

Bonnie pushed herself up to standing, took a step toward the curtained area where they were treating Levi, then whirled around. She went a bit unsteady, so Avery leaped up to give her some balance. It looked as though she'd gone into some sort of trance, but realized Bonnie was actually staring at one of the posters for the Valentine's Day benefit.

Her eyes shifted to Avery's. "That's the concert you and your sister used to do."

"Sure is." Avery looked away, practically hearing the wheels in Bonnie's head turning. The curtain around Levi's acute care bed was whipped open by Valentina. Carter was at the head of the bed and a weak but smiling Levi lit up when he saw Bonnie, cheeks instantly streaking with tears. "See what lengths I'll go to get you to marry me?"

Bonnie grabbed his hand and walked along his gurney as best she could, but it was easy to see that their usual pace was too much for her. Levi asked them to stop for a minute. "So I can talk with my beloved."

"Don't you go dying on me," Bonnie scolded.

"I think I could say the same to you, my beautiful young woman."

Bonnie softened at his description. She held Levi's hand in hers, careful not to knock the needle taped into his hand delivering blood-thinning medication. "I mean it. You can't die."

"So do I," said Levi. "Now give me a kiss because the sooner I take these tests, the sooner I can get out of here and bring you to your doctor's appointment so we can go ring shopping."

Bonnie gently pressed a kiss onto his pale cheek and waved goodbye long after he'd disappeared into the imaging department. When she finally dropped her arm, she took both of Avery's hands in hers, a very serious expression on her face. "I will go see that doctor friend of yours. What was her name again?"

"Dr. Iliana Costa. She's great at what she does and if there's a problem, she'll do her level best to help you solve it." Avery pictured drawing a music note onto Bonnie's wrist for Lia, so she'd know Bonnie was one of hers.

Bonnie gave her hands a squeeze and repeated, "I will go…on one condition."

Avery nodded, expecting it to be something about keeping an eye on Levi who would, no doubt, need to spend the night for observation or, depending upon what the scans said, have an operation. "Okay."

"You promise?"

Avery laughed. "So long as it's not committing a crime, I'm in."

Bonnie gave a satisfied nod, then said, "I'd like to see you sing at the concert. For your sister. She'd want you up there, shining like the star you are."

Everything around Avery slowed down. She could hear the *ba-boom* of her heartbeat. The white noise of blood rushing to her brain. The slow-motion slideshow of that awful, awful day when they'd lowered the casket containing her sister's body into the ground, her mother's keening drowning out everything around them. And then, to her surprise, the muscle memory of how she felt when she sang with her sister returned. The warmth she felt in her heart, the smile she could never quite wipe from her face, the love radiating from the center of her truest self. It was a feeling she'd felt recently. Giving voice to her emotions, the only way she knew how. Through music.

To her complete shock, she said yes, then quickly amended. "There's someone I'd like to accompany me."

Bonnie gave a sly grin. "That handsome doctor who just saved my Levi?"

Avery blushed. "How'd you know?"

"I'm fat, not blind!"

Avery didn't contain her grin at being seen. "Shall we pinkie promise on this? That you'll see Lia in exchange for one charity gala?"

Bonnie lifted her pinkie into the space between them. "I thought you'd never ask."

Avery stopped jumping up and down long enough to ask, "Are you sure?"

"With every fiber in my body." Carter started ticking off his fingers. "Hearing you sing. Helping out the hospital. Having a date on Valentine's Day… What's not to love?"

She stared at him for a couple of seconds, started rapid blinking, then said, "Well, then. I guess I'd better go put a set together."

He watched her go and wondered what all that was about, but then realized he'd just walked through a perfect opportunity to tell her that he loved her…and hadn't.

They spent the next week in a happy haze. Working at the hospital and building a beautiful set of songs he knew would get people draining their bank accounts. Avery was a wonder and it felt good to be part of something that was bigger than himself. That would be giving back to the industry that had kept him whole while the rest of his life floundered.

Just a few days shy of the Valentine's benefit, he

could feel the excitement rising like spring sap in Avery. Everything she did had an added zip to it. Bandaging patients came with some cheerful artwork. She hummed while she took vitals. Even signing patients out elicited a playful curtsy or a jaunty cowgirl salute. He liked seeing her this way and was enjoying basking in her glow.

He had just finished booting up a poor guy who'd ruptured his Achilles tendon during an ill-advised game of squash when he heard calls for help from the secure care department. He took off at a run, shooting a quick smile to Avery when she appeared beside him.

The doors to the ambulance bay swung open and the paramedics wheeled in a gurney with a slight figure cocooned in a blanket on it. The patient's hair was dark, making her slightly jaundiced skin seem even more so.

Cassidy.

As he fought to keep his hammering heart under control, Stacy, the paramedic, was rattling off the facts. "Female inmate known to suffer from sickle cell anemia found collapsed in her cell after exercise session at local penitentiary. Hydroxyurea administered on site along with liquid ibuprofen and oxygen. Morphine denied."

Carter ground his teeth together. He'd bet any amount of money they'd denied her morphine because they thought she was faking it. It was a problem in prison hospitals. Inmates faking symptoms. Prison doctors doubting patient's believability. He knew his sister's pride would've had her lying throughout the entire Brief Pain Inventory, the barometer they used for monitoring effective treatment of pain. Only trouble was pain was the main barometer of sickle cell. If you were feeling it, you needed treatment. Immediately. So no wonder she looked like hell.

"Carter." He felt a hand on his arm. Avery. "You need to sit this one out."

"Like hell I do."

Avery flinched at the bite in his tone. He was too upset to fix it. He did what he always did—grabbed ahold of one side of the gurney and said, "Follow my lead. She's my sister. I know what to do." He started rattling off her blood type, her history, the last time she'd had an SCD crisis. He'd made himself a specialist on the topic, stopping short of doing it full time because he knew the ER would always be her first port of call. His sister had never been one to come in on a suspicion that things weren't going well. She always waited until those sickle cells traveled through her tiny blood vessels, got stuck and clogged the blood flow.

"Booth!" Dr. Chang somehow inserted herself between Carter and the gurney. "I don't know what sort of hospitals you've worked in before, but this one recognizes that you have a conflict of interest. Step aside."

Avery mouthed, *We've got this.*

He wanted to feel assured. His brain knew Avery was right. She and the rest of the team were completely capable, if not better qualified to look after his sister than he was right now. He'd been wrong to try to use his rank and his emotions to overpower Avery. He just got so twisted up inside because each time Cassidy was sick like this, it brought him those few steps closer to being the only Booth left standing.

He watched, helplessly, as they wheeled her into the secure unit and began calling for blood transfusions and hooking her up to all the necessary monitors. And then something kicked back into place he'd almost forgotten about. He wasn't the guy who stood by and watched other people look after his sister. He was the guy who had promised to protect as best he could.

He yanked back the curtain and began barking out orders over Dr. Chang's. Cassidy was in a bad state. Worse than he'd seen her in years. She might have splenic sequestration. If she'd been found passed out, those damn cells of hers had had more than enough time to get trapped in the spleen and cause an enlargement. Beneath the oxygen mask they'd rigged up on her, he could see her lips were pale and that her breathing was coming in quick, short bursts. When Dr. Chang palpated her left side, she flinched. Unsurprisingly, the heart monitor was up in the higher altitudes, precisely where it shouldn't be.

Just as he was demanding she be brought in for a scan to see if she needed a splenectomy, he felt two sets of hands clamp onto his arms and the security guys were frog marching him backward out of the treatment room. The door was shut in his face.

He broke free and pounded his fist against the bullet-proof glass window. Couldn't they see Cassidy needed him? *They* needed him. His insight. His point-by-point history of her condition. His photographic memory of her medicines, her frailties, her strengths and the way they could make the most of them. His eyes met Avery's. Seeing the depth of concern in those dark brown eyes of hers should've had a soothing effect. But this time it didn't because for the first time since they'd met, he saw, clear as day, that he'd been an idiot to start something he couldn't finish.

Watching Avery's concern turn to sorrow felt like being slammed in the chest with a pickax.

So he started hollering through the window about

how he hoped they were checking for leg ulcers and strokes and deep vein thrombosis. Pulmonary embolisms. Increased blood coagulation. All things he knew they knew, but shouting was better than sitting around doing nothing.

The charge nurse ran up to him and touched his arm. He whipped around and shouted, "What?"

When he saw fear in her eyes, he knew he'd gone too far. Way too far.

Barely above a whisper, she said there was a little boy who'd suffered a compound fracture after falling off his pony. He gave himself one hell of a shake and forced himself back into the land of common sense. He was here to work. Just like the doctors treating his sister. "Please." He held out a hand to the poor frightened nurse and, with an apology, said, "Lead the way."

When he went to see his sister in the observation bay of the secure unit and found Avery there as well, he forced himself to click into "Carter Booth Departure" mode.

"Hey, Cass." He sat down on a stool on the other side of the bed in sync with Avery standing up.

"Don't be rude," Cassidy weakly chastised. "Say hi to your girlfriend, too."

"Oh, we're—" he began.

Avery waved her hands and said, "It's okay. I was leaving anyway."

He didn't protest.

He felt his sister poke him in the arm. "You're more of an idiot than I thought you were if you're letting her walk away like that."

He couldn't disagree. He was an idiot for a lot of

ANNIE O'NEIL   173

reasons. He pulled her chart up on his tablet, doing
his best to ignore the fact her tiny little hands were attached to the bed by handcuffs and, in as bright a tone
as he could muster, thumbed through the notes and said,
"Now, let's see here…"

When Carter finally came out of his sister's room,
Avery was fuming. How dare he give up on them like
that! Yes, he'd warned her that he'd be leaving one day,
but nothing had prepared her for the way he'd looked
at her when he'd walked in the room and seen her with
Cassidy.

He didn't even look like Carter—that confident,
sexy, cheeky man she'd met on New Year's Eve. The
one who'd bet her a kiss he could ride a bull longer
than she did.

It made her heart physically ache to see him like this.
Slump-shouldered. Bearing the weight of the inevitable.
But it *wasn't* inevitable. Cassidy had already said she
wanted Carter to have girlfriends. She'd just finished
telling Avery that she had begged Carter for years to
quit his hovering. So really, Carter was the only one
denying Carter a girlfriend. And as much as she ached
for him, she hurt for herself, as well.

Carter looked shocked to see Avery, but he set a pace
that meant only one thing: *I'm moving on.* "I thought
you'd be long—"

She cut him off. "I know what you thought."

Carter laughed, but he did not sound amused. "What
are saying, Avery? That you're surprised things turned
out exactly like I told you they would?"

"No," she ground out. "I'm surprised that a man as

strong as you are can't find a way to let himself be loved by his sister and by someone else. By me."

There. It was out there now. The fact that she loved him.

His lips moved as if he were going to say something in return but thought better of it.

"What do you think is going to happen if you let yourself fall in love with me, Carter?" Again, he didn't answer, so she persisted. "Your sister isn't going to die because you find love. You know that, right? If anything, she might be happy for you. Maybe she'd even see it as an example. Something to aspire toward."

He gritted his teeth, a muscle in his jaw twitching as he did. "You don't know what it's like."

She laughed at that one. "Really? I don't know what it's like to have someone I love with all my heart get sick and know that one day, no matter what I do, they're going to die? C'mon, Carter. You're better than that. I know *exactly* what it's like. Only your sister...she's alive! So why don't you celebrate that by giving her a brother who's happy?"

"If you're so smart, how about you explain why building a shrine to your dead sister was such a good idea?"

Avery goldfished for a minute. If he'd physically struck her, it would've hurt less. "You know why I bought that house. And you helped me do it."

He shook his head. "I only gave you the reasons you wanted to justify buying it."

Her breath was coming in short painful huffs now. She knew everything he was saying was coming from a place of fear. Of hurt and a deep well of grief that this might be the time his sister finally lost her battle for survival. She got that. But she'd been through that exact same journey and Carter was the man who'd helped her see things from the other side. The one who'd helped her realize that life wasn't made up of just one single thread. It was composed of all sorts of threads. Beautiful ones. Painful ones. Loving ones. Ones like this that hurt so bad it was almost impossible to bear, but all those threads made a person stronger. And she wanted to be stronger, not weaker. If Carter left now, she knew she'd have lost one of the key threads that had helped put her back together. And that, even though he wouldn't admit it, he had, too.

He kept on walking and yanked a door open to the stairwell. She followed.

A desperation clawed at her, a visceral need to get him to see that the way he was living wasn't working anymore.

Carter didn't stop climbing stairs until they reached the roof level. Mercifully, it was free of any other medical personnel. He looked out into the middle distance, but she could tell he was listening.

"Okay, Carter. Tell me. What if you do leave now, huh? What happens when you follow Cassidy from this hospital to the next one and the next one after that? At some point, it's going to take her, Carter. You know that better than most. And what are you going to do, then? What's your reason for living going to be once that sweet girl in there can't fight anymore?"

It was a blunt way to put it, but she felt she had to say it. She'd made the mistake of putting her own life on hold during April's illness. She'd lost a perfectly nice boyfriend. Some friends. And now her family. She'd hate for Carter to endure the same heartache she had. Or, more accurately, the numbness.

He crossed his arms over his chest. "If you're so wise, why don't you illuminate me? Tell me what *your* reason for living was after April died?"

You.

She couldn't make herself say it. She knew Carter was angry. And scared and hurt and plain old pissed off at life, but it was hard receiving these point-blank blows. Each word hitting like a real bullet.

Carter's eyes snagged with hers and held. She'd never felt pain looking into them before but this time she did. She felt his pain. His anguish. But she didn't hear the one thing she was hoping for. An admission that he loved her, too.

She tried to reason with him, but it felt like she was begging for her own life. "Look. I know you're mad at the world, but have you ever considered that Cassidy might need to make her own mistakes? Scratch her knees. Bruise her elbows. Figure out how to pick herself up?"

"No." He cut her off. "Listen, Avery. I told you this was how I operated. That this is how I deal with things." He looked away for a minute—as if he were having a proper fistfight with his emotions—only continuing once he'd pummeled them into submission. "I know it's not a perfect way to live, and believe me, I wish like hell things were different. But they're not." He pointed to the hospital beneath them. "That woman in there— Cassidy—is my only family. She is sick and I promised her daddy—*my* daddy—that I would do everything I could to look after her. I don't have the big pools of emotional resources you obviously do. I wasn't raised by people who made me feel safe and secure. The only thing I know is loss. So, yeah. You win. Your heart is bigger. Your spirit is kinder. I wish I'd been built the same way, but I wasn't. I'm sorry that it has to be like this, but it does."

She tried to protest, to tell him it wasn't a contest over who had bigger emotional reserves, but he cut her off. "I've got to go. I'm sorry, Avery. I truly am."

It felt almost impossible to watch him walk away, but she knew she had to. Carter said Cassidy was all the family he had. He wasn't allowing himself to believe he could build one of his own with her. She was shivering but going into the warm heat of the hospital just seemed wrong. She wanted her body to feel the way her heart did. Growing so cold it would eventually be numb to the pain.

CHAPTER FOURTEEN

AVERY SENT LIA a text agreeing to meet at their *special spot*, even though she wasn't in the mood to be inspired or have her spirits lifted. She was back in "work is where I shut everything out" mode and was quite happy wallowing in it, thank you very much. But she loved her friend, so…she went.

Whereas most of the doctors and nurses she knew met outside the new babies unit for a bit of an *aw* moment, she and Lia had a different kind of happy. The physio ward. St. Dolly's had received a massive trust from a famous actor who'd fallen off his horse a few years back and had been paralyzed. The hospital had used the money to build a state of the art physio unit that looked more like an Olympic training gym than anything, until you actually started paying attention to who was doing the work and why they were doing it.

Avery went up to the second level of the unit and looked down at the patients. Some were having to learn how to walk from scratch, how to function without a limb, how to live the rest of their adult lives in a wheelchair.

For forty-eight entire hours, she'd been trying to teach herself how to live without Carter Booth.

After his sister had been discharged, he'd "discharged" himself from the roster. Disappeared from her house as if he'd never been there. Disappeared from her life.

It had been awful. Like watching someone flick a switch on their emotions. One minute, you thought they loved you. The next…you felt as if you'd imagined it all.

His departure made her body feel as if everything alive in it had been replaced by an empty void. She'd fallen for Carter. Hook, line and sinker. Let herself believe what she had felt for him was exactly what he had felt for her. True love.

She'd been kidding herself when she'd believed what they'd shared could override a lifetime of packing his bags and walking away. Getting herself to understand that had felt like swallowing shards of glass.

Lia had gently pointed out that Carter compartmentalized his life in order to survive. Just like she did.

Avery got that. He'd not had an easy life, but it still hurt to know he'd shut the door on her without so much as a backward glance. Locked it and thrown away the key for all she knew.

She could find out. She still had his number. But she also had her pride. They'd made a deal and what little self-worth she had right now she was keeping close. And, yes. She knew deep down that pride was a stupid thing to cling to when she was standing here on two perfectly serviceable feet, watching people confronting much greater challenges than a broken heart. She saw the pain on their faces. The sweat on their brows. Heard their cries of agony as their bodies refused to do what they once did with ease. This was why she didn't go to the baby ward. Their lives were shiny and new.

Beautiful blank spaces upon which entire collages of discovery had yet to be drawn.

Hers was a slate that couldn't be wiped clean. She bore the scars of her sister's death and now Carter's departure, as if they were actual physical wounds. But...

She forced herself to rein in the pity party. Even though she didn't have Carter Booth to hold her in his arms at night, she still had her body and her health.

"Hey, you." Lia slid her forearms onto the railing Avery was leaning on. "Are we talking today or just watching?"

"Bit of both." Avery's voice wobbled. When they'd met yesterday, she hadn't been able to talk. Not a word.

But she'd showed Lia the note Carter had left. The one that said he wasn't very good with words, so he was going to borrow a few from a mutual heroine of theirs. Dolly Parton. There was a particular song that spoke to him. One called "I Will Always Love You." He knew he hadn't told her in as many words, but the song covered the gamut of how he felt.

He'd quoted the lyrics that made it clear they weren't meant to be together, but that their time together would always be cherished. She knew her takeaway from his message should be happiness that he had, in his own way, loved her. But how was that going to help her pick up the pieces of her heart and start again? Knowing that she had been loved but hadn't been enough to stay for? Fight for?

They watched in silence for a few minutes until Lia twisted her torso so that she was facing Avery. "Deena wanted me to have a word with you about the concert."

Avery's tongue hit the roof of her mouth in preparation to say, *No way,* when she remembered the promise she'd made was to Bonnie, not to Carter. The vow was to sing for her sister and all the other people who would have to take the same journeys she and April had. Journeys of love and loss. She supposed she never would've been out and about on a New Year's Eve, riding a mechanical bull to earn the money to buy Five Acre Farm if April had lived. They would've been making music somewhere. Watching someone else make it. Or, perhaps, tucked up on a sofa, watching a box set, assuring one another they weren't boring, they were prudent. Saving yet more precious pennies for their house. But the truth was with the jobs they'd had and the money they'd saved…they could have bought Five Acre Farm years ago.

Her mind rattled back through countless memories with her sister. One thing she'd always known, but never acknowledged, became abundantly clear. Avery was the leather to her sister's lace. The country to April's rock 'n' roll. Avery loved horses and the smell of grass after rainfall and country lanes. April loved the heart of Nashville, clothes weighted with rhinestones and the limelight. And boy did she shine when she was in it.

She saw it now as if it were on a billboard for all to see. Her sister had made her feel whole because of their differences rather than their similarities.

As clear as the hand in front of her face, Avery knew April went along with Avery's dreams about Five Acre to make her happy. As such, she owed her sister a concert. One that honored her memory. Celebrated it.

Her heart softened. Though she missed him deeply, wanted him here more than she could ever say, she owed Carter her gratitude for getting her here, to this place, where she believed in herself enough to get up on stage and sing about love again. About heartache. And all the lessons life taught you whether or not you wanted to learn them.

She sent a sheepish smile to Lia. "I think I need to find some musicians."

Lia grinned and pulled her into a tight hug. "You sure?"

Avery gave a nervous giggle. "No. But I've got to start somewhere, right? Remember what April always said?"

In unison, they both said, "Go big or go home!"

Lia pointed at Avery's heart. "Do we need to meet for a Guac and Talk later? Drink some sorrow juice?"

Tears welled in her eyes, but she shook her head no. Even a sip of a margarita would start her ugly crying and admitting that Carter had broken her heart.

She understood why he'd made the choice he had. But it was still a raw wound and the only way she wanted to deal with it right now was to focus on something else. Give her pain some space to do what it needed to in order to heal. It had taken nearly two years of actively mourning her sister to sing again. Less than two months for Carter to gallop into her life, her heart and shake it all up like a snow globe, reminding her that nothing was permanent. No matter how much you tried to hold on to it. The best thing to do was offer gratitude for the good parts and learn from the bad ones. Like losing her sister, she'd need more than two days to get over Carter, but she'd get there, because as painful as it felt right now, she knew there'd come a day when she could look back on their time together with a smile. Bittersweet memories, indeed.

* * *

A tissue box hurtling across the room was Carter's greeting from his sister.

Arms held up in front of his face in case there were more missiles coming his way he asked, "What the hell was that for?"

Though she was still bedridden with fatigue, Cassidy had steam coming out of her ears. "Carter Booth, can you please explain to me exactly how you became a doctor with so few brain cells knocking around that head of yours?"

"What are you talking about?"

"How'd you even find out where I was, let alone get a job here?"

He scrubbed his jaw. Telling her might not be the wisest course of action. Being a doctor in a prison hospital wasn't exactly in the choice pickings department, so that had been easy enough to get. As for finding her... That had been the hard part.

After she'd been discharged from St. Dolly's without his knowledge, he'd called in every favor he'd ever been owed and come up with nothing. In the end, he'd driven down to the barbecue joint where a lot of paramedics hung out and pretty much begged them to tell him where Cassidy was. Somehow, she'd ended up at the Women's Correctional Facility here on the outskirts of Louisville, Kentucky.

"Dumb luck," he finally said.

"Dumb is about right," his sister agreed.

"What are you all het up for anyway? You should be resting."

She glared at him, then at the hospital ward she was in. "You just don't get it, do you?"

"Get what?"

"You should be with that amazing girlfriend you stupidly left behind in Nashville, Carter. Leave. Me. Alone."

He felt the words like knives. "But… I'm your brother."

She saw the hurt she'd caused and softened. "I know that, you bozo. I love you. But isn't it about time you had a life of your own?"

"I do have a life. With you."

"No, Carter." She took his hand and pressed it to her pale cheek before weaving her fingers in with his. "You don't. From the sounds of things, you were just beginning to have a life with Avery and, yet again, you threw it away to chase me around the country." She pursed her lips at him. "You've got to back off. Focus on your own stupid mistakes. I'm great at making my own, and it is high time I started putting together a toolkit to be able to fix them."

Carter could almost hear Avery's voice in his ear. The one that had told him he needed to back off. She wasn't the type to say I told you so, but she would've earned it this time around.

Cassidy was still glaring at him. "Carter. You've got to start seeing what I do."

"What are you even talking about, Cass?"

She huffed out an exasperated sigh as if he really were thick as two short planks. "Knowing you're always around to pick up the pieces of my life has made me reckless. Too reckless."

He was about to say amen to that when he realized

that she really meant it. He got up, yanked the curtains around her bed closed and propped himself up on the end of it. "Talk to me."

And she did. She told him about how the longer sentence had put her in a section of the prison that really opened up her eyes to what she'd done. She was surrounded by women who'd made bad decisions that had years' long ramifications. For the first time in her life, she felt lonely. And no, that didn't mean she wanted him to visit more. It meant she needed to work out how to turn her life around. Spend more time with people like her cellmate back in Nashville.

"Why her?" Carter asked.

"She was the one who convinced me to go to the AA meetings. I went just to get her to shut up at first. But then some of the things they were saying started to sink in. One of them in particular."

"What was it?"

Cassidy's lips did a little twitch, as if she were fighting off some unwanted emotion, but she persisted. "There was a woman in there who'd killed a child when she'd been drunk driving."

Carter frowned.

"That could've been me, Carter," Cassidy said with a gravity he'd not heard from her before. "Behind that wheel. Hitting that child. Taking a life."

He gave a sober nod. It could've been.

"I have no right to take anyone's life and realizing that made me see that another thing I didn't have a right to do was take the life I've been given for granted."

He blinked, trying to absorb what his sister was saying. Was she finally understanding that each minute she had was precious, and as such should be cherished, not frittered away on misguided adrenaline rushes? "If this cellmate of yours was so great, why did you ask for a transfer?"

She frowned at him. "That's now how prison works, big brother. You get taken where you're taken and now that I've decided to start growing up, I'm going to learn from it. I'll go to the AA meetings here. Maybe take a bit more time in their chapel. They've got a real nice one. And maybe see about signing up for some sort of course. They've got me potentially for the next three years, so instead of fighting it like I usually do, maybe it's time to start learning from it. Take advantage of the good things they have." With a twinkle in her eyes she added, "After all, this is a *correctional* institute."

He gave her hand a squeeze. "Wise words from a little sister."

She grinned and, to his surprise, blushed with pleasure. "Want some more wise words?"

"Sure."

"Go back to Nashville and win back Avery."

Now it was his turn to backpedal. "Aw, now what Avery and I had was a temporary thing." In other words, he was pretty sure he'd screwed that opportunity up. Big time.

Cassidy scoffed, "The way you two looked at each other? I'm calling bull!"

Carter feigned being wounded in his chest and then, when he saw she really meant it, he let her words soak in. Hands clasped over his chest; his brain finally connected with his heart. It was Cupid's arrow stuck in there. Not a knife.

Cassidy was right. He was in love with Avery and like a class A idiot, he'd pulled the plug on it without even having an adult conversation with her. He'd basically had a one-way shouting match with her, refusing to genuinely listen to what she was trying to say to him. When remorse had hit for being such a jackass, he'd let the lyrics of a country song do his apologizing for him. And it hadn't even been that. It had been a get-out clause.

Cassidy was right. He *was* being stupid. He loved Avery. Had from the second he'd laid eyes on her. And he owed it to her to tell her how he really felt.

He would always love her. And he wanted to keep on loving her, up close and personal.

More than that, to be the man he knew deep down he could be. One who was reliable. Loving. Wanted a family. Hell. The whole nine yards. He wanted a diamond wedding anniversary with one woman and one woman only. Avery Whittacker.

And Cassidy was right. Avery, too. There were no laws preventing him from driving up to Louisville to see his sister. A city where there were big hospitals with smart doctors who knew all about sickle cell anemia. Doctors who'd taken oaths to care and protect, just as he had. He swore under his breath.

Despite the very real possibility that he'd ruined his chances of Avery loving him in return, he was going to have to try. Even if he made a fool out of himself doing it.

"What?" Cassidy demanded. "What are you shaking your head for?"

"I'm like the worst kind of country song."

"What do you mean?"

"The kind where the singer had the girl of his dreams and let her slip through his fingers because he was stupid."

"I told you that you were stupid." Cassidy looked smug, but also concerned for him.

Carter rose and gave her a little tip of an imaginary Stetson. "It looks like it's about time I started taking advice from my very wise kid sister."

Cassidy clapped her hands. "You going to go all out? Buy the ring? Get the roses?"

Carter had no idea what he was going to do. "I've got a six-hour drive to think about it."

Cassidy gave him a satisfied grin. "Go on, then. Shoo." She flicked her fingers. "Get her back. Clock's a ticking! And bring her next time you come calling. Visiting hour's much more fun with her than you."

"Thanks a lot!" Carter gave her a wounded look, but Cassidy had hit the nail on the head again. It wasn't just visiting hour that was better with Avery. It was everything that was better with Avery.

CHAPTER FIFTEEN

AVERY WAS ABSOLUTELY EXHAUSTED. She'd just pulled a double shift and because it wasn't any fun going home to a house without Carter in it, she'd slept at Lia's and pulled another double. Probably not the winning recipe for sounding her best when she sang at the concert tomorrow night, but a raspy voice worked for Miley, so she hoped it would work for her, too.

When she pulled her car into the drive, she heaved out a heavy sigh. She'd have to get used to walking in here and feeling her own energy fill the place. Not look at all of that space that had been created when Carter packed his bags and headed for heaven knew where.

She forced herself out of the car and, allowing herself just a tiny pity party, stomped up the steps, across the porch and stuffed her key in the lock.

When she pushed the door open, she froze. She hadn't left any table lamps on. Mostly because she didn't own any. She certainly hadn't lit any candles. Or a fire. And she definitely hadn't laid out a thick trail of rose petals that, now that her eyes were focusing, she could see were shaped into an arrow pointing at the stairs... also covered in rose petals.

The table saw was gone. As were the rest of carpentry items the builders had left lying around the living room. In fact, it was all looking really good. Not a bit like the shambles she'd left when she decided she needed some space from Five Acre while she decided whether to keep it or chalk the purchase up to a "good lesson learned" and move on. Before her brain could entirely put the pieces of this very romantic-looking puzzle together… Carter appeared at the top of the stairwell, guitar slung over his shoulder, fingers strumming a tune. And then he began to sing.

He was right. He was an awful singer, but the words he'd written filled her heart with so much joy she would've listened to him forever.

He loved her.

He'd made a bad call. The wrong one. He had never met a woman who'd compelled him to examine how healthy his relationship with his sister was. Whether it did either of them any good. But his sister had set him straight, then turned him around and now here he was, heart on his sleeve, hoping like hell he could make things right. He'd work all day and strum all night if he needed to, but mostly he wanted to spend the rest of his life with her by his side.

"Avery," he sang as he lowered himself to one knee, "you make my voice wavery."

Avery started giggling. Giggling and crying and running up the stairs to him because the space between them was too big and she needed to close it and kiss him and smell him and feel his arms around her again because every pore in her body had ached for him since he'd left. He unclipped the guitar and before he could sing another lyric, they were kissing. Hot, hungry love-filled kisses that only held promises of more to come rather than the bittersweet ache that this was all going to come to an end.

When they surfaced for air, Carter asked, "Can I take it you accept my apology?"

Avery grinned. "You can. I suppose we should talk about exactly what it is you want, though. From us."

"I want all of it," he said. He dug around in his pocket and pulled out a little box. The kind that only held one type of thing.

Her heart flew into her throat as he flicked the box open and revealed a beautiful ring unlike anything she'd ever seen. It had to have been handmade. The band was made of a beautiful warm rose gold, but not in a traditional smooth band with a diamond solitaire. The band looked like tiny flower stems woven together and, as he held it out for her to inspect, she knew there was no other man in the world who would know her well enough to choose this exact ring. There were tiny little gold roses and leaves elegantly binding a trio of basket settings holding three beautiful lavender-colored sapphires in place. It was a country girl's ring. One that she absolutely knew she did not have the power to refuse. Nor did she want to. And he must've seen the answer in her eyes, because before she could put a voice to anything, he readjusted himself so that he was propped back up in the kneeling position. Even though she was sitting on the floor across from him, the gesture felt like he was laying down all the armor he'd worn around his heart for her. This was him in his purest form. Putting his trust in her. His love.

"Avery Whittacker, this may not be exactly the proposal you wanted. I know I'm a frog who comes with a lot of warts, but I promise to do my best by you. My very best. I made myself believe Cassidy was my only family, but of all the people in the world, she's the one who reminded me family were the people you loved. And I love you. I will make mistakes. I will do my best to learn from them. I will never have your beautiful songbird voice, but I promise to accompany you on this life journey to the fullest of my ability. To make you as happy as you make me. Will you let me be your wingman?"

Avery shook her head. "No. Absolutely not." She couldn't bear the stricken look on his face, so quickly finished the sentence. "I want you to be my copilot."

He needn't have bothered with the Tiffany lamps and jam jars filled with candles. His smile was enough to light up the entire house. He whooped and slipped the ring on her finger, and the next thing she knew, Avery was in his arms being whirled around and around with his lips pressed to hers. When they finally came to a stop, Avery saw that they were outside the bedroom. She grimaced. "I'm really sorry, but I haven't been much of a housekeeper lately. I haven't been home for a few days."

"I know," he said, his lips twitching with a mischievous smile.

"You never gave me back the key I gave you, did you?" She grinned because it wasn't like his having access to the house had been a bad thing.

"No, I gave that back. But I might have remembered the spare key beneath the plant by the back door."

She smacked herself on the forehead. "How long have you been here?"

He tapped the side of his nose. "I heard from a little birdie that you were working hard, so I thought I'd put a bit of extra effort into the first time I saw you again rather than appear all straggly and lovelorn and miserable."

She wrapped her arms around his waist and tilted her chin up so she could look into his beautiful green eyes. "You were straggly, lovelorn and miserable without me?"

"Bereft." And then, more seriously, he said, "I was. And I never should have done that. Not listened to you. Walked away angry. If you want me to apologize until the end of time for my behavior, I will."

"No," she said, placing a soft kiss on his lips. "As much as it hurt—it was a good thing."

His eyebrows dove together. "Why?"

She looked away, then realized she owed him as much honesty as he'd shown her. "I think it gave me some perspective on losing my sister."

"In what way?"

"I will always miss her. There is no doubt about that, but I think I went so far inside myself to grieve her loss, I forgot to acknowledge the whole April. The one who would definitely not have wanted me to put my life on ice because she wasn't here anymore."

Carter dropped a kiss on her forehead. "From everything I've heard about her, that sounds about right."

Avery nodded. Then shook her head. "When she got sick, it was like my brain stopped working. All that mattered was caring for her. Making sure every second she had left was precious. I hate that I lost her. And God knows I would've done anything to keep her alive, but that's not how life works. It gives. It takes. And you have to cherish the moments you do have, not regret the ones you never will."

"Sounds like a country song in the making." Carter swept his fingertips along her jawline as she smiled.

"It does, doesn't it?" She grinned. "See! That's what I was saying. Realizing that about April made me understand that loving you was better than not having known that sort of love at all."

He ran his hands down her back and tugged her in close. "I hope this isn't the part where you tell me I can hop on my horse and leave town again."

"Not a chance, Carter Booth. You're all mine!" She kissed him, then pulled back again. "I guess I also needed to realize that love is something that takes all forms. Even frogs with warts," she added with a cheeky wink.

"I'll show you a frog with warts!" He laughed and scooped her up into his arms, then pushed the bedroom door open.

Avery gasped in delight. In place of the air mattress and the mountain of sleeping bags and quilts, was her dream bedroom. Even though it was night, it felt light and airy thanks to the beautiful soft lighting and gorgeous wallpaper covered in tiny little wildflowers. There were upcycled bedside tables and, though she'd only mentioned it in passing, a hope chest at the foot of the bed and a rocking chair by the window. "Did you do all this?"

"Yes, ma'am," he said, gently placing her down on the huge sleigh bed. "Me and the contractors."

"It's amazing!" And it was. Exactly what she'd dreamed of when she thought of spending the night wrapped in her true love's arms.

"Now," Carter sat down beside her, his fingers teasing at the top button of her blouse, "if I'm right, that tiny bird who I've been in touch with down at the hospital says you need to get some shut-eye before your big night tomorrow."

Avery gave him a doe-eyed blink of innocence. "That's true. But I can think of one thing I'd like to do before that."

"Oh?"

"Yes. Practice with my guitar player."

She didn't need to explain exactly what it was she wanted to practice, because Carter knew precisely what she meant. He swiftly began undoing each and every button that stood between them. Making love that night was sweeter than all the times they'd been together before, because this time, with a ring on her finger and a promise in both of their hearts, she felt loved. A "forever and always" kind of love. Exactly the kind the country stars liked to make folk think was unattainable. But she knew it wasn't. You had to find the right guy, work hard at really getting to know one another and then spend the rest of your life making sure he knows you love him. Which was precisely what she planned on doing.

"You ready?" Carter felt more nervous than Avery looked. In fact, she didn't look nervous at all. "There are hundreds of people out there. Don't you feel even a little bit of the jitters?"

"Not with my man by my side."

He grinned and couldn't stop himself from crooking a finger underneath her chin and pulling her in close for a last kiss before they went on stage.

"You're happy with all the songs you picked?"

Avery nodded, enjoying the glints and sparks that occurred each time the stage lights caught glimpses of her engagement ring even from here in the wings. "I picked a half-and-half set."

"What do you mean?"

"Half the songs are ones I know April loved singing."

He nodded his approval. He loved seeing this strength in her. The power that could fuel her love for her sister and the times they shared versus drain and weaken her in the wake of her loss. It was an important lesson to learn. To think he'd almost opted to feel that same pain, that same weakness, made him realize how lucky he was to have a sister who, despite her faults, had enough common sense to call a spade a spade. He'd been stupid, and she hadn't been shy in letting him know.

"What are the other half?"

She grinned and flushed a little. "Love songs."

"Oh, yeah? Now what would make you want to sing love songs all night?"

She ramped up the coquette in her hips and gave him a saucy little swish and turn before saying, "It's Valentine's Day."

"That all?"

"Hmm…" She looked down at her hand, then back up at him, unable to contain her grin anymore. "That. And I just got engaged to the man of my dreams."

"He must be one lucky guy."

"Oh, he is," she assured him. "And I am a very, very happy bride-to-be."

"How happy are you?"

"Want me to show you?"

He lifted his chin. He sure did, but he also had to walk on stage and not embarrass himself in less than a minute, so he said, "How about you show me after we do this little sing song?"

"Here's a teaser." Avery leaned in and gave him a kiss that was sweeter than a perfect peach. It was a nice taste to have on his lips as they were called closer to the stage to prepare for their set. He saw the light catch on Avery's ring and her goofy smile when she noticed it, too.

Buying that ring and putting it on her finger was one of the smartest things he'd ever done. A new start. A chance to provide the type of love and care to a woman—his woman—that he'd never imagined possible. But here he was, living the dream.

The act that was on stage finished up their set and before he knew it, he and Avery were walking side by side onto the stage to rapturous applause. He knew it wasn't for him. It was for Avery. But he basked in the glow because the only person she had eyes for as she began her first song, a love song, was him.

* * * * *

THEIR REUNION
TO REMEMBER

TINA BECKETT

MILLS & BOON

To my husband, who truly makes me feel seen.

PROLOGUE

ILIANA COSTA STARED at the lineup of fathers, her insides beginning to unravel in panic. She tried to remember what Papa had told her to do in a situation like this. But it wasn't working. From this distance, she couldn't spot the small scar at the outside corner of his left eye, and right now all the dark-haired men blurred into one indistinct subset of humans with no defining features. No way to tell them apart other than by their clothes. And she had no idea what Papa was wearing.

She glanced at her classmates, who—with a chicken egg perched on each of their spoons—were laughing and anxious to race toward one of the men on the other side of the room.

Lia was not laughing. All she felt was fear and the remembrance of being made fun of for going to the wrong person. It had happened so many times. With teachers. With friends. With her mom and dad. The worst had been at a mother/daughter tea when she'd gone up and sat with the wrong mom at one of the fancy tables. A little girl had come up to her, chest puffed out and declared that was *her* mother and that Lia couldn't have her. Every head had turned to stare at her. And then came the whispers. Her own mom, who'd arrived late, had come over and rescued her.

It was why her mother now wore a stretchy pink bracelet around her wrist, so that Lia could spot her from a distance. She remembered fingering that bracelet when she was nervous. It was harder with her father, who'd insisted she learn to recognize him using means other than his face. So she used the scar beside his eye. It was his tell…his pink bracelet.

Why didn't other kids have this problem?

Two of the men had beards, so she mentally marked them off the list. One was much taller than the others. Not him, either.

The whistle sounded, and the girls took off, each choosing a direction with a certainty that Lia didn't understand. She ran, too, desperately searching through the rest of the dads, looking for a clue. Then one of the men locked eyes with her, his left hand slowly coming up and forming a thumbs-up sign.

Papa! Oh, Papa, thank you!

Taking a grateful breath, she fixed her gaze on him and changed directions, moving toward him with a sureness she didn't feel. Until she got closer and saw that familiar scar.

Then she knew. *This* man was her father. Her heart swelled with love, the fear slowly trickling away.

When she reached him, she carefully transferred her egg from her spoon to his. And as he moved away from her toward the starting line, her gaze followed his every step, memorizing the clothing he had on. Dark blue shirt. Black pants. Rubber-soled shoes.

Then and only then could she relax with the knowledge that she wouldn't lose him again.

Not until next time, when her sorting process would begin all over again. Just like it did each and every day of her life.

CHAPTER ONE

THE SINGER AT the Valentine's Day benefit concert had something combustible going on with the guitar player seated next to her. It smoldered in the dark glances she sent his way. Sizzled in how he hunched over his guitar, fingers stroking the strings of that hourglass-shaped instrument as if she were on the receiving end of his touch. And the flames they generated spread to the audience as well, who sat forward in their chairs as if they couldn't get enough. As the plaintive notes of a love song cast its spell, Micah Corday perused the space, looking for a vacant seat.

He knew all about spells. Man, did he ever. But hell, he was older and wiser and had no time for those kinds of games anymore. It had been three years and a whole lot of mileage since he'd last been in this town.

The atmosphere here in Nashville was so different from Ghana, where he'd landed after a breakup. These people were not worried about their next meal or where they'd find clean water or medicine. Instead, their attention was fixed on what was happening on that stage. And between the musicians on it.

But despite that, every one of these folks had their own problems. Their own fears. That part was not so different.

His eyes continued wandering, landing on one face after another before a tingle of remembrance forced him to retrace his steps, first mentally and then emotionally.

There. He found her.

Damn. Talk about spells. He'd known there was a possibility she'd still be in the area, that he'd eventually run into her. But he'd hoped it would come later than this. When he'd had time to frame his questions about that time.

Maybe she was just revisiting her alma mater?

Her eyes were closed, and she swayed slightly to the music, but he knew exactly what color would emerge when her lids parted. Tawny tones that seemed to hold the mystery of the ages. He could remember the way that gaze had held his as she studied him in minute detail until he felt nothing was hidden from her.

It had been like that as they sat across from each other on a dinner date. As she'd straddled his hips and carried him to the very edges of sanity. It had been what had attracted him to her. The details she noticed. Details that had nothing to do what other women saw when they looked at his face. It had been…different. She saw what others missed.

At one time, he'd been so sure of everything. Of his feelings. Of hers. Of the certainty they would someday marry. Have kids.

Until graduation day, when those warm eyes had turned chilly with rejection. There'd been no explanation. No hint as to what had gone wrong.

The memory of that moment—of the strained good-byes—made something harden in his chest. He'd had no idea what had happened. But once done, there'd been no undoing it. His pride had taken a huge hit that day. He'd evidently thought things were more serious between them than she had. He'd made certain he never made that mistake again. With anyone. His few encounters while on medical mission had been short and sweet. No unrealistic expectations. Then again, he hadn't felt the pull that he had with Lia.

Was she married now?

It didn't matter. What did matter was whether or not she was practicing medicine here at the hospital or just visiting. If it was the former, he would be working under the same roof as her, if not on the same floor.

So, best to get his facts straight now, before they met by chance in a crowded elevator. Or, worse, over a patient.

With that in mind, he moved toward her.

Lia sensed a presence.

Her eyes opened and she took in the stage, where Avery was still singing, both hands wrapped around her microphone as if needing the support. She knew how hard it had been for her friend to get up on that stage. But wow, it had been so worth it. Lia was proud of her.

The hairs on her nape sent an alert, reminding her why she'd opened her eyes in the first place. Her gaze swung to the right and saw a man staring at her from a couple of rows ahead. He was actually walking in her direction. She blinked, quickly tracking across his face, although she wasn't sure why. That never did any good. A vague sense of panic washed over her when he didn't break eye contact and continued coming toward her.

Maybe he was heading for someone else.

No. He stopped. Right in front of where she sat at the end of her row.

Her thoughts gathered around her in quick snatches, and she finally grabbed hold of the one that held her in good stead most of the time. "Hi. How *are* you?" She infused an enthusiasm into the greeting that fooled most people into thinking she'd recognized them.

His head cocked, a frown appearing between his brows.

Uh-oh. It evidently hadn't fooled him.

"Lia? It's Micah. Micah Corday?"

The second his voice sounded, a sick vibration shuddered through her stomach. *Dio.* Of course it was. How could she *not* have recognized him, of all people? He'd been her lover through most of medical school. And at one time she'd thought, maybe just this once, she would finally be able to…

But of course she couldn't. If anything, this moment in time told her her decision back then had been the right one. The instant flash of hurt in his eyes when he'd had to identify himself had provided proof of that.

She'd almost told him her secret back then. But fear had her putting off that moment time and time again. And then graduation had come, snatching up all her hopes and dreams and crushing them into dust.

She jumped to her feet and grabbed him in a quick hug, realizing immediately the imprudence of that move when his scent wrapped her in bittersweet memories. The stubble on his cheek scraped across her skin in a way that rekindled a forgotten spark in her heart and set it alight. Her breath caught on a half sob when he stiffened under the close contact.

Of course he wouldn't welcome her embrace. Why would he?

Swallowing down the ball of emotion, she took a step back. "I—I thought you were in Ghana."

"I was. I'm back."

Her tongue ran across her parched lower lip, trying to think of a response to that shocking statement. "You're back? As in for good?"

His lips curved in a smile that contained not a hint of humor, and Lia could have cried at how hard he seemed. How unlike the Micah she'd once known and loved.

No wonder she hadn't recognized him.

Her heart branded her a liar. That wasn't the reason, and she knew it. It was the same reason she sometimes needed help recognizing her parents. Her friends. Her coworkers.

Faces didn't register with her. Ever. And although medical science had a fancy-sounding name for it, the reality of it was pretty brutal on relationships. Which was why she'd had so few of them in her lifetime.

Her dad's coaching her about how to blend in—done out of love and having had a brother who was bullied in school for a disability—had backfired in some ways. She'd learned with great success how to hide her own challenges, but in doing so had ended up isolating herself. Like choosing a profession where people were in and out of her life in a matter of hours. No need to go to the trouble of remembering details about them. Relationships hovered on a superficial level.

Except with Avery, who had been the only person in her life who could actually joke about her condition. In fact, her closest friend had a scrap of commentary for every person they met: *Ear stud, right ear. Mr. Fancy Pants. Abs galore.* They were funny quips, but they also provided clues for later recognition.

"Yes. As in for good." Micah's voice brought her back to the matter at hand.

She swallowed, her throat aching. *Dio*, she didn't know if she could handle him being back in Nashville. It had taken forever to get used to life without him. Maybe it was better to know exactly what he meant by being back for good.

"Let's go to the back where we can talk." She glanced up at the stage, where Avery continued to sing. For Lia, Avery's hair was her tell. That glorious mane of curls seemed as untamable as her friend. Avery had pulled her safely from some pretty gnarly situations, like when the hospital's chief of staff had ditched his signature pompadour hairstyle in favor of a simple side part and appeared in front of her in shirtsleeves instead of his regular suit and tie. She'd had no idea who he was at first. As if sensing her struggle, her friend had deftly stepped in and greeted him just before he asked Lia about a patient of hers. She'd been grateful beyond words.

But there was no saving her from her current predicament.

She walked to the back of the venue and found a quiet corner. "When did you get back?"

"Yesterday, actually." His smile revealed his tell— the deep, craggy line that appeared in his left cheek whenever his lips curved. That...and that heady masculine scent that no one—in all her years of interacting with men—had been able to match. He used to chuckle at the way she'd press her nose to his skin and breathe deeply, letting the air flow back out on a sigh.

Dio. So many memories. So many moments lost since...

No. She steeled her resolve. She'd been doing him

a favor by breaking things off. Although there was no way that he could know that. And that had been the idea. All his talk in the year leading up to graduation about doing a stint with Doctors Without Borders had made her nervous. Leave Nashville? Where it had taken forever to learn to separate the people in her own little bubble of acquaintances? Not likely. But she'd gone along with it, hoping he would change his mind. But he hadn't, as evidenced by his work in Ghana.

But he was back? In Nashville, of all places.

He'd only gotten back yesterday, so maybe that meant he was back for good, as in the United States. Maybe this was a stopping place before he continued on to somewhere else, like…say, Omaha.

"So where are you headed from here?"

"Headed?"

"I just meant…"

Dread filled her heart and permeated the ensuing silence.

"You seriously didn't recognize me?"

The dread grew into something that threatened to burst through the confines of her skin as she scrabbled for an excuse. "You didn't have a beard back then. Or that deep tan. Besides, there's a lot going on, and the last time I saw you…"

"Yes." His smile had disappeared. "The last time you saw me was…well, the last time you saw me."

At graduation.

She remembered that day like it was yesterday. The fear. The horror. As she'd stood in front of that crowd of gowned graduates, she'd been transported back in time to the day when she couldn't pick her father out of a crowd.

She'd flat-out panicked. The orange-and-white robed figures all looked the same, although if she hadn't freaked out and had given herself a minute or two she might have been able to deduce which one of them was Micah. *Might* being the operative word.

The thought of going to a country where she recognized no one—with a man she couldn't even pick out of a crowd—sent her into a tailspin. That, and the growing fear that she one day wouldn't be able to recognize her own child, suddenly morphed into a unscalable wall. What about high school graduation? Ballet class? Baseball games? Any event in which a uniform could disguise identities and steal them from her. Yes. She'd broken things off for all those reasons. And she'd never seen Micah again.

Until today.

She owed him an explanation. But where even to begin...

"I'm sorry. For everything."

His enigmatic eyes searched her features. Seeing what? How had he picked her out from hundreds of other people in the crowd? She would never understand it. "Yeah, well what's done is done. But if we're going to be working at the same hospital...*this* hospital..." His brows went up in question.

"Yes, I work here. As a vascular surgeon."

"Well, then. I guess we'd better figure out what we're going to do about the elephant now standing in the room."

She blinked, thinking maybe he'd figured it out, although her prosopagnosia was something very few people knew about. In fact, Avery was the only person at the hospital who actually knew her little secret. She'd become pretty adept at figuring out who was who. Except when she was caught off guard.

Like by the hospital administrator.

And today, by Micah.

She stood a little taller, her chin tipping up a bit. "And what elephant, exactly, is that?" The word *elephant* slipped out with an accent that belied her Italian heritage. Another quirk brought on by nerves.

"That we were once close. Very, very close."

A sense of relief should have washed over her. Instead, her mouth went dry as a few of those moments of closeness flickered across a screen in her head. The most outrageous being the time they'd had a quickie under a stairwell of this very hospital. They'd been fully clothed, and it had taken just a few minutes, but she'd been left with legs that were shaking and molten memories of the urgency of the act for the rest of the day. *Mio Dio*, if they'd been caught…

She swallowed. "Why does anyone have to know?"

The left side of his mouth cocked, carving out his cheek again. "You don't think anyone knew we were sleeping together back then?"

Okay, so probably a lot of the people they'd known had guessed. And Avery definitely knew, because she'd told her. But once she broke things off with Micah, she'd firmly told her friend she didn't want to hear Micah's name come out of her mouth. Her friend had honored her request over the past three years, never mentioning Micah or what had transpired between them. It had made getting over him a little easier. At least that's what she'd told herself back then.

"I vote we say nothing, other than that we already

know each other. And if someone asks, we'll simply say that was in the past and that we've both moved on."

"Moved on. Yes, that's one way of putting it."

Wow, this broody Micah, whose syllables could cut like a scalpel, was going to take some getting used to. But *this* iteration she could handle. If he'd been the mellow, playful guy from her past, she might have had trouble keeping her distance. Might have even repeated mistakes of her past. But this man? Yes. He was a relief. Him she could resist. Could even avoid with ease.

With that thought, she sent him a smile of her own. "Yes. It is one way of putting it. But the terminology doesn't matter. What does is that we're both adults who can work together as professionals." She realized Avery had finished singing and, as a result, her words had come out a lot louder than they might have if the music had still been playing. A couple of people looked in their direction, and she cringed, much like she'd done at that tea party so long ago.

Okay, time to make a quick getaway and find her friend. "There's someone I need to meet, so I'll say goodbye. Enjoy the rest of the benefit."

With that she turned and walked away from him, hoping her steps looked more even than they felt, and vowing she would do everything in her power to make sure they worked together as little as possible.

CHAPTER TWO

AVERY FLAGGED HER down in the hallway first thing Monday morning, making Lia smile. She'd looked for her friend after the Valentine's Day benefit, but both she and her sexy guitar player had vanished. Lia had a feeling she knew why.

"Hey, girlie, sorry I cut out on you at the benefit. But I...uh...had someplace I needed to be."

Her friend's burgeoning relationship with trauma surgeon Carter Booth had been fun to watch unfold, although she knew it had been touch and go for a while.

"You had someplace you needed to be? Or someone you needed to be with?"

"Well...both. And I have some news."

"News? So everything worked out okay?" Lia had a feeling she already knew the answer to that question.

"More than okay. I just never dreamed I would ever..." She grabbed Lia's hand. "Carter asked me to marry him."

She'd had a feeling this was coming. Things had been heating up between the pair for a while now.

"Oh, honey, I am so, so happy for you!"

Avery deserved to find happiness after everything she'd been through. One good part about Lia's inability to separate one face from another was that she had a knack for reading emotions in others without needing to have them spelled out. And Avery's emotion was there in spades. It was in the grip of her friend's hand on hers. In the tremble to her voice as she'd said that last sentence, as if unable to believe her luck.

That ability to read people made Lia hyperaware of how noticeable her own feelings could be and gave her the tools to stow them out of sight.

Although that ability had ended up causing friction between her and Micah, especially over that last year. Whenever she'd submerged her true feelings about signing up with Doctors Without Borders, he'd seemed to sense something was wrong and pushed until she snapped at him that everything was fine. Even when it wasn't. The look he used to give her when she did that stayed with her even now. As if he was so disappointed in her. It had ripped at her heart.

Another good reason to have broken it off. And seeing him again had brought up a lot of emotions she'd thought were long dead.

"I have some news of my own." She looked her friend in the eye. "Remember that name I asked you never to mention?"

Avery's eyes widened. "You mean Slash and Burn?"

Her friend's nickname for Micah made her roll her eyes. Avery had once said that every time that slash appeared in Micah's left cheek, Lia would turn beet red. And she had.

But unlike Avery, who looked like she'd gotten everything she ever dreamed of—her return to singing, finding a man who understood her and loved her for who she was—Lia didn't expect Micah's sudden appearance to cause anything but renewed heartache.

"Yes. Micah." She bit her lip. "He's back in Nashville."

"No! For real?"

"Unfortunately."

"Couldn't this be a good thing? Sometimes things happen for a reason."

Her friend's optimism probably sprang from cloud nine, the place where Avery was currently perched. She was happy, therefore everyone she loved deserved happiness, too. Unfortunately it didn't always work out that way.

"Don't get any ideas. We're not getting back together. That's not what I want." She ignored the little voice inside her that warned her pants were now on fire. "I just wanted you to know, in case you see him around the hospital."

"He's going to be *working* here?" Avery let go of her hand. "How do you feel about that?"

"It's awkward. He came up to me at the benefit and said he had come back to work."

"Did he say why?"

"I was so shocked, I didn't even think to ask. Just got away from him as fast as I could." She swallowed. "Ave, I didn't even recognize him when he came up to me."

"I'm so sorry. But you had no idea he was here— was probably the last person you expected to see at the benefit."

Yes, that was true. But any other person would have known immediately if an ex-lover came and stood in front of them.

"At least we won't cross each other's paths all that

often. I'm in ER for the most part, and he'll be…well, I'm not exactly sure, but probably up in the lab area." She forced a smile. "Anyway, enough about Micah. I'm really am happy for you. You deserve all that and more."

"Thanks. I love Carter to pieces." She seemed to hop down off her cloud. "But that's actually not why I came down to find you. Has a woman named Bonnie Chisholm been in contact with you this morning to make an appointment?"

"The name doesn't sound familiar. Why?"

She sighed. "She's had some problems going on, and I'm worried she's a stroke risk. I asked her a couple of weeks ago to call you, but she evidently didn't, since she called me again last night with a new symptom." There was a pause. "She was my sister's and my singing teacher. She's…special to me."

"Can you give me some details?"

Avery quickly ran down the list of symptoms Bonnie had been having, saying she was now having abdominal pains on top of the leg swelling and shortness of breath she'd had two weeks ago.

"She promised me she'd call you today."

"I haven't heard from her. She does need to see a specialist. If not me, then another vascular surgeon. Maybe she's worried. Any chance you could come in with her?"

"I offered to. I'll go talk to her again. I'll admit, I'm the one who's worried. She's one of the main reasons I got up on that stage at the benefit."

Lia smiled. "And here I thought that was due to my nagging. Or maybe due to that handsome cowboy who was up there with you."

"It was definitely a group effort." She glanced at her

phone, which had just buzzed. "Damn. Sorry, I need to run. One of my patients needs my help."

"Go, I'll catch up with you later. Thursday night for guac and talks? If you can pull yourself away from Carter, that is." Their weekly meet up had become a tradition neither of them wanted to break. It was a time when they could vent, laugh and just generally unload about their week while enjoying the noisy, saloon-like atmosphere of Gantry's Margarita Den.

"Carter knows I need my weekly dose of the best guac east of the Mississippi, so yes, Thursday is great."

Her friend was positively glowing. Maybe someday she would find what Avery seemed to have found. But for now, she would live vicariously through her friend's romance. "See you then."

Avery gave a wave as she hurried back toward the ER.

Her friend knew about Micah and Lia's reasons for breaking things off three years ago, although Avery had pooh-poohed her fears about going on medical mission and about not recognizing her own child. She'd assured her that when the right guy came along, those fears would slide away.

But would they really? Lia had been so sure that Micah was that person. And she'd half wondered if she'd let the one get away. Until Micah had shown up at the gala after his long absence and Lia hadn't recognized him. As much as she tried to blame that on shock or the unexpectedness of his face coming back across her radar, it simply reaffirmed all her reasons for breaking off the relationship.

How fitting that she worked at Saint Dolores, who was the patron saint of sorrows. In Italian, *doloroso* meant sorrowful or painful. Both of those terms aptly described her feelings about ending things with Micah. There was still some *grande dolore* involved when she thought about him.

And now that he was here?

She was going to concentrate on seeing him as a colleague. Someone who meant nothing to her anymore. No pain. No sadness. No longing. If her dad's job as a molecular biologist had taught her one thing, it was that things could be broken down to a scientific set of molecules. Those molecules could then be manipulated to change the way they came together. So if she could change one of the building blocks that had made her want to be with Micah, she could change the entirety of their relationship and make it into something else— something that worked on a professional level but not a deeper emotional level. She just needed to find which of those blocks she needed to change to make that happen.

And if she couldn't? Then the name Saint Dolores was going to be a daily reminder of the hurt she had gone through when Micah had turned and walked away from her, head held high, strong shoulders braced to face life without her.

And from all appearances, he'd done a very good job of doing just that.

She only hoped she'd done just as good a job. Because if not, *dolore* was going to be a hard word to shake. And an even harder emotion to outrun.

"There's someone I need to meet."

Those words had echoed again and again in Micah's subconscious over the weekend. And they were making his first day on the job pretty damned rough.

He thought his pride had taken a hit at their breakup? Well, it was going to take an even bigger hit if Lia had found someone who could give her what he evidently lacked. Every time he thought of her with another man, the crunching blow of a sledgehammer seemed to knock against his ribs.

Hell, the woman had barely even known who he was at the Valentine's benefit, despite their steamy past. So it was ridiculous to even care one way or the other.

Except he was rethinking coming back to the States. Lia's reaction was a stark reminder of his childhood, when he'd felt completely invisible to two busy parents who'd handed him over to a series of nannies. He used to wonder as a kid if they would even recognize him in a crowd.

Ha! Well, he'd seen firsthand that it truly was possible to forget what someone you used to love looked like. It wasn't a fun feeling.

Unless Lia had been faking it, trying to appear nonchalant as she processed the shock of seeing him again.

No. The shock when she realized who he was hadn't been feigned. Neither had the dismay that followed right on its heels, despite her wiping both emotions from her face a second later. Something else she'd been good at when they'd been together, and another thing she had in common with his folks: hiding her true feelings.

A knock sounded on the door to his office just as he reached into a box of books he'd been unpacking onto a shelf. "Come in."

The door opened and a face that he would never forget as long as he lived peered in at him, eyes wary and unsure. She edged inside the door and shut it behind her, leaning against it as if she was ready to rip it open and disappear at the first sign of trouble. Her eyes tracked over his face, seeming to study it before moving on to his body. He remembered how her gaze used to feel like a physical touch and how strangely it had affected him the first time they met.

It was no different this time. But Micah was different. He'd been inoculated against that intense stare. At least he thought he had. "Hello, Lia. Can I help you?" He made his voice as cool and indifferent as he could.

She nodded at the book in his hand. "Well, that seems apropos."

Glancing down, he took in the title. *Preventing Recurrence: It's Up to You.*

"I'm not sure I follow."

"Oh, well, I…um, wanted to talk to you about working together. I know it's going to be weird, but I hope we can somehow figure it out."

He still didn't see how the book… Oh. She wanted to make sure he knew there wouldn't be a recurrence of what had happened between them. No worries there. Because he had no intention of allowing what had happened before to happen again. And she was right. The title was apropos. Because it was up to him—up to them—to make sure that it didn't. "I'm sure we can. Our relationship ended years ago. If you're worried I might be interested in rekindling things, you needn't bother. You made it quite clear that it was a mistake. And I came to realize you were right. We both dodged a bullet."

Her eyes widened before she nodded. "Yes, I think we did. Both of us. I think there's only one person at the hospital who knows we were once an item. And I'd prefer to keep it that way."

"There's not much chance of me broadcasting it over Saint Dolores's loudspeakers."

She seemed to cringe away from that. "I didn't think you would. I just didn't want you to worry about any gossip I might spread."

His smile was hard. "There wouldn't be much to spread. Not anymore."

"No. I guess not."

When that hammer swung against his ribs again, he quickly turned to put the book on the shelf behind his desk. "I agree that we are the key to making this work. So let's just keep our past where it belongs—in the past. There's no reason for anyone to know that we once dated each other."

"And if they ask?"

He turned back to her. "Why would they? I'm new to the hospital, as far as most people know. Would you wonder if I used to date any of Saint Dolores's other employees?"

"Saint Dolly's."

"Sorry?"

"This is Nashville. Surely you remember the nickname we've given the place?"

He'd forgotten about the hospital's second name. "Is that what you call it in front of patients?"

"No, I just…well, Saint Dolly's sounds a little more cheerful than Dolores." She looked down at her clasped hands. "And you might wonder if you heard a bunch of people use the other moniker."

"Okay, Saint Dolly's. Check. Keeping our past a secret. Check." He motioned to the box on his desk. "Anything else?"

"I, um…" Her head came up. "Actually, yes. Why here?"

Was she really asking him that?

"Why did I decide to come here? Why not? It's where I grew up. Where my—" his jaw tightened "—parents live."

"Of course. Sorry. I'm not sure why I asked that."

Did she think he'd come here to restart their romance? Not hardly. If anything, it was the opposite of that. His dad wasn't well, but that wasn't the only reason he was here. He'd come back to the place where his folks lived as a reminder of what it felt like to be invisible. A reminder to be on his guard against getting involved with someone who made him feel like they'd made him feel. Like Lia had when she'd ended their relationship.

And like when she hadn't recognized him at the benefit. Lia was a much more vivid and present image of what he'd gone through in his childhood. And now he wasn't sure he needed a daily reminder of that to keep him on his toes. Actually, he was sure of it.

"Not a problem." He was hoping those words would prove to be prophetic. "If it helps, I had no idea you were working here when I applied for the job."

"It doesn't help. Not really. But it is what it is. Like you said, we'll find a way to make it work." Her brows went up. "And my parents still live here, too. That's why I've stuck around. Besides, I love it here. I can't imagine practicing medicine anywhere else."

"I think you made that pretty obvious." Part of her little speech the night of graduation had revolved around the idea that they both wanted different things out of life. Except he hadn't realized that. Not until that night.

Right now he was wishing he hadn't been quite so quick to leave Africa. He'd done some real good there, but his mom's phone call saying that his dad's health was beginning to fail had prompted him to come home. Although he still hadn't gone to see them. This week, though, he would make it a point to stop in and see if they needed anything.

"And I have no intention of trying to convince you to go anywhere else. Not anymore."

She stepped away from the door, and for a second he thought she was going to move toward him. Instead, she half turned and twisted the doorknob. "Well, now that we've established some ground rules, I'll let you get back to unpacking."

Had they established that? Or had they just agreed that they could be grown-ups and work together? Well, he wasn't going to say anything that might encourage her to hang around his office any longer than necessary.

"Thanks for coming by."

She gave a half-hearted smile and nodded. "Thanks for understanding." With that, she was through the door, quietly closing it behind her. Micah was left with an office that looked exactly like it had before she'd put in an appearance. The space inside his chest was a different story, however. There were traces of her visit painted on almost every internal surface. His gut. His chest wall. His heart.

And like with most infections, sometimes all it took was a minute amount to put someone's life in jeopardy. So he needed to eradicate every stray cell that she'd implanted in him. He thought he'd done that.

The problem was, now that he was back, he wasn't quite sure he had.

CHAPTER THREE

LIA PUSHED THROUGH the doors of the ER on her way to the parking lot where her car was located. She'd had three difficult surgeries in a row and was worn out. Just as she was about to step off the curb, a car pulled up and a woman leaped out. "Are you a doctor?"

She blinked, then realized her lanyard was still hanging around her neck. "I am. What's going on?"

"It's my baby." She threw open the back door, where a chilling sound reached Lia. Coughing. But not the normal cough of bronchitis or a respiratory infection. This was a strangled gasping sound she would never in her life forget. "She just had a cold. It was just a cold." Her words were filled with fear and dread.

An infant who couldn't have been older than two months lay propped in a car seat.

"Let's get her inside. But I want to use the side door." She glanced at the mom. "Were you vaccinated against whooping cough while carrying her?"

The woman's face went deadly pale. "No. My doctor mentioned it, but I wasn't vaccinated with my others, and they were fine."

Vaccination during each pregnancy was a fairly new recommendation. The thought was that when the mother passed her antibodies to her fetus, she would pass them along for pertussis as well and hopefully curb the numbers that were slowly creeping up, even in this day and age.

Dio. If she was right?

Lia unbuckled the child, taking in the red, fevered face just as another bout of coughing racked the infant's tiny body. It was followed by the struggle to draw in breath afterward. With the mom racing beside her, they circumvented the double doors and the crowded waiting room and found one of the isolation rooms. "Sit with her for a minute while I do an exam. What's your name?"

"Molly. And this is Sassy."

The mom climbed onto the exam table, her own cough barking out. Damn. Lia donned a mask, not just for her protection but for her patient's. "Are any of your other children sick?"

"All three of them are, but none of them are coughing as much as Sassy."

All of them. "Who's with them?"

"My mom. My husband went to park the car. I've had a cold and just assumed…"

"It's okay." She quickly called down to Admitting to let them know that a man would be coming in and where to direct him. She also asked them to call Micah and a pediatric pulmonologist. So much for not working with her ex. But as an infectious disease expert, Micah needed to know that there might be a possible outbreak of pertussis in one of the local communities.

She listened to the baby's lungs, ignoring her phone when it started buzzing in her pocket. Whoever it was could wait.

Just as she thought—the baby's airways were clogged.

"I need to get a swab. If it's whooping cough, we'll need to check your other children, and you'll need to alert any kids you've been in contact with."

"Oh, God. My sister came over with her kids three days ago. Her newest is even younger than Sass."

"Were any of them sick?"

"No." The poor woman's voice was miserable.

Within a minute, a man poked his head in. "Are you the dad?"

"Yes, I'm Roger Armour. Is she okay?"

Molly held her hand out, her husband going over to grasp it. Okay, Molly had straight dark hair and her husband had blondish hair that was cropped close. The dad also had a tattoo of some kind of fish on his forearm. She submitted those facts to memory in case she needed to recognize them later. "She might have whooping cough."

His head tilted sideways. "Isn't that extinct?"

"I'm afraid it hasn't been eradicated. Not yet."

It was amazing how many people thought the disease had gone the way of smallpox, when it was still here. Still threatening the lives of young children.

A nurse came in, and Lia handed her the swabs that she'd put in protective cases, which she'd labeled with the baby's name. "Could you run those to the lab and ask them to put a rush on it? Possible pertussis."

"Right away."

She'd just left the room when another man poked his head in. Short blond hair, although the mask obscured his lower face. "Hey, I tried to call."

The voice immediately identified him as Micah. Motioning him in, she said, "Possible case of pertussis."

She glanced at Molly. "I think you may have it as well. We need to start you both on a course of erythromycin."

"Did I give it to Sass?"

She understood the mother's angst, but sending her down the path of self-blame would help no one. "It could have come from anywhere. Let's just concentrate on helping you both feel better." She glanced at Roger. "We'll want to treat you as well, just in case, since you've been exposed."

Micah came over and did his own examination. He nodded. "The signs are there. Labs?"

"Just sent them off."

"Great. We'll need to try to do a contact trace."

Some of Lia's neighbors had gotten whooping cough when she was a teen, and the sound of a coughing baby being strolled down the building's hallways had haunted her for years. One day, the baby left and never returned, and she'd been told by her mom that the infant had died at the hospital later that day. She needed to do something besides just sit here and wait for more patients to be brought in.

"I'd like to make up some flyers to alert folks of a possible outbreak."

"Flyers. Good idea."

There was something in his voice that made her look at him. "You don't think so?"

His glace met hers. "I do. Just wishing we'd had the luxury of those when I was in Ghana."

"Right." She couldn't imagine what he'd seen in his years in Africa. But she was pretty sure whooping cough was right up there. Had she been wrong not to go with him? She shrugged off the thought. There was no going back. Not that she wanted to. She'd made the right decision. Both for her and for him.

The baby coughed again, only this time when she tried to breathe back in, there was only a thin whistle of air. "She's not getting enough oxygen. We need to intubate."

Micah lifted the child from the mother, who sobbed and clutched her husband's hand. He moved the baby over to one of the nearby counters while Lia found an intubation kit designed for infants.

Things were tense for a few minutes while they got the tube into place. Attaching an Ambu bag, he glanced at the mom. "I'm sorry, but we'll need to use that bed to transport her."

"Oh, of course!" Molly scrambled down and sank into her husband's waiting arms. "Can we go with her?"

"Sit tight for just a few minutes while we stabilize her." Placing the infant's still form onto the exam table, they unlocked the wheels and rolled her out. "We'll send someone for you as soon as we can."

Once outside the room, Lia directed him the back way to a set of service elevators, where there was the least amount of foot traffic. "We'll get her up in one of the PICU rooms and institute droplet isolation."

Once in the elevator, the only sound was the squeeze of the Ambu bag as Lia checked the baby's vitals for the third time. "She's hanging in there."

"This is kind of outside your specialty, isn't it?"

Lia couldn't tell from his tone if he was ticked that she had called him in or not. "It is, but I was there when the car pulled up, and all the other ER docs were busy with patients. Sorry for calling you, but—"

"You did the right thing."

She relaxed, glancing at him and reading nothing but concern in his demeanor. He hadn't changed much, outside of his hair and beard, and she again was shocked that she hadn't recognized him right off. But it had happened before, and she was pretty sure it wouldn't be the last time she'd be confused by someone's identity. Especially if it had been a while since she'd seen them. And three years was definitely a while.

Checking the baby's color as the elevator stopped on the third floor, they found Newell Jensen, one of the pediatric specialists, waiting for them. Micah nodded at Lia to fill him in on what had happened so far. She did so with a calmness in her voice that belied the shakiness of her limbs. Whether that was from being in close proximity to Micah or from the immediateness of the emergency, she had no idea. But she had to admit she was glad to hand the baby over to someone whose specialty this actually was. "Her mom and dad are waiting down in ER. They're pretty worried."

"So am I, from the looks of her. Let's get her into a room."

Almost immediately there was a flurry of activity as Sassy was hooked up to a ventilator and her vitals were taken yet again. "We're still waiting on her labs, but from the way she sounded in the ER, I'm pretty sure it's pertussis. Two families have been exposed so far. And I suspect there are more."

"Not good. Let's start her on a course of erythromycin while we wait for confirmation from the lab." Newell glanced at them. "I'll have someone update her parents. Can you notify administration? I'll call the CDC."

"Yes."

The specialist was dismissing them, not because he was being a jerk, but because he had work to do and didn't have time to stand around and talk. Lia could appreciate that.

She and Micah walked back to the elevators, stripping their masks and gloves as they did so and dropping them into a waste receptacle. "Did you see a lot of this when you were in Africa?"

"I was actually there helping with the trachoma outbreaks."

She turned to face him. "Trachoma? As in from chlamydia?"

"One and the same."

She'd had no idea that's what he'd been doing there. Once they broke up, there'd been no need to keep in contact with each other. And for the first time, she wished they had, or that she'd at least kept track of his career. Then maybe that whole embarrassing scene at the Valentine's Day benefit wouldn't have happened.

"Why did you come back to the States?"

His lips twisted to the side in a way that was heart-breakingly familiar.

"Two reasons. My dad and politics."

"Okay, those are two things I never would have put together. Is your dad running for office?"

"No." He sighed. "He hasn't been well for the last year or so. He has cancer, and I wasn't sure how much longer he was going to be around. If I was going to visit, now was the time."

"I'm sorry. I didn't know."

"It's okay. We haven't exactly been close."

She nodded. "I remember you saying that. Did they even come to your graduation?"

One brow went up. "No. But they sent a representative. With a very expensive gift."

Reaching out to touch his hand, she murmured, "I'm so sorry, Micah." She hadn't done a very good job of timing her little breakup speech, had she?

"It's okay. You didn't know."

Fortunately he didn't add that she hadn't bothered to stick around to find out, although he must have thought it at the time. He'd been hurt by everyone he cared about that day. And it made something inside her cramp. If she'd known his mom and dad hadn't come to see him graduate from medical school, would she have broken up with him when she did? She didn't know. And it was too late to go back and change it now that she did. "I'm still sorry. Is there any hope for your dad?"

"I think my dad thinks that cancer is beneath him. That he'll somehow buy his way out from under it, like he's done with most things in his life." He sighed. "And no. According to my mom, he's been given little hope, although he's slated to start an experimental treatment sometime soon."

"Have you talked to him?"

"Not yet. But I'm planning to this weekend."

She could understand his reluctance, but if it had been one of her parents, she would have rushed home as soon as her plane landed. When she and Micah had been together, she'd known that things between him and his parents had been strained, but she'd had no idea it was as bad as it evidently was. He'd never taken her home to meet them, which she hadn't thought was odd at the time, but now that a few years had passed... Had she not noticed out of selfishness? Out of not wanting to know anything about Micah other than how he made her feel?

Dio, she hoped not.

"I'm sure that will be hard." The elevator stopped and she stepped off, waiting for him to exit as well.

"A lot of things in life are hard. But you somehow get through them and move on."

For some reason she didn't think he was still talking about his parents, and a trickle of remembered pain went through her. She knew he'd been hurt when she'd broken things off, but how much more hurt would he have been when he realized why she had such trouble putting names to faces—including his? She'd been able to laugh it off at the time, saying she was terrible with names. But it wasn't the names that stumped her. It was the faces that went with them.

Even his.

She remembered how hurt she'd been when her dad insisted time and time again that she learn a way to get around her prosopagnosia. He'd never let her take the easy way out...except for during that egg and spoon race. But once she hit high school, she finally understood why. He was protecting her from what his younger brother—her uncle—had gone through. Her uncle had been born with a speech impediment that got him ridiculed again and again, and her dad had made sure he was always there to protect his younger brother from bullies. And when he'd had a daughter who couldn't recognize faces, he'd stepped back into the role of protector. It had changed her life for the better and had been a turning point in their relationship. But it had also made her very aware of what could happen if she let people see behind her curtain.

Evidently things were still strained between Micah and his parents, but maybe they would have their own turning point someday. Only if his dad was as ill as he'd indicated, there might not be much time to make things right.

Micah had been right to come back.

They made their way to the administrative office, and she spoke in hushed tones to the hospital administrator's assistant. "We had an infant come in with a suspected case of pertussis. Can we get in to see Arnie?"

Arnold Goff headed up the hospital much like the boxer he'd once been—deftly feinting away from any opponent before coming back with a hard right hook. Other hospital administrators treated him with respect. But the man was also fiercely loyal to his staff.

Arnie's assistant picked up his phone and let him know they were here to see him. "He said to go on in."

They went through the door, and the administrator stood to shake their hands. "You must be Dr. Corday. Nice to finally meet you in person."

"A pleasure."

Arnie hadn't been at the hospital while they had attended medical school there, which was kind of a relief. "So what brings you in?"

"We have a case of suspected whooping cough—an infant—although the labs aren't in yet." Lia paused. "The mom is coughing as well and said her other three kids are sick."

"Hell." He motioned them to the two chairs in front of his desk while he sat back down as well. "What do we know?"

She continued. "Not much. Not yet. Not sure where the family was exposed, but they've been with relatives while displaying symptoms."

He dragged a hand through his hair. "Anyone at the hospital exposed?"

"Minimal. I met the couple just as the mom and baby were getting out of the car. We went in through back doors, and I notified anyone who was going into her room that they needed to don PPE."

"Good thinking. What do you need from me?"

This time Micah spoke up. "Dr. Costa had the idea of putting up flyers around the community alerting the public to the need of reviewing their vaccination records and see if they're up-to-date. The last thing we want in Nashville is a major outbreak of pertussis."

"Agreed. And good thinking. Are you two okay with heading up the push?"

"Us?" Lia's voice came out as a kind of squeak that made Arnie look at her.

"Is there a problem with that?"

"No," she hurried to clarify. "None at all."

The man's gaze moved from one to the other. "I know you both have your own patients, but this is a good opportunity for educating the public, and I can think of no better faces to represent the hospital."

She knew he hadn't meant that comment on faces in the way of grading someone's looks, but it still made her shift in her seat. Because Lia had no idea what made for a more or less attractive set of facial characteristics.

"I'm okay with that as long as Micah has the time."

Too late she realized she'd used his first name rather than his title. But if he noticed, Arnie didn't say anything.

"I don't have anything major scheduled yet. Except this." Micah frowned. "But I'd like to go beyond putting up flyers and see if I can get a handle on where this area stands in the way of vaccinations and contact tracing."

"COVID has given us a little hand up in that area. So hopefully some of those databases can be put to good use."

"That's what I was thinking as well. I can work with the CDC on feeding them whatever info we find out."

Still with the *we*. But then again, she'd have been hurt if Micah had tried to cut her out of the loop, although if he pushed he could have. He was an infectious disease doc, and she was vascular. They weren't quite in the same specialty.

"Can you meet together and come up with a plan and get back to me tomorrow?"

Tomorrow? She'd just been on her way out of work. If she hadn't stopped to assist that cry for help, she'd be home already, soaking in a hot tub. But despite how uncomfortable it might be to pair up with Micah, they'd done fine while treating Sassy. Surely they could handle a couple of hours of planning.

Micah's eyes swung around to meet hers. "Do you have time to discuss it tonight?"

"Sure."

Arnie sighed as if in relief. "Make sure you keep me in the loop."

"Of course." She and Micah said the words in unison.

Lia gave a nervous laugh. That was something they'd always done. And they used to chuckle about it back then. But despite her laugh just now, she didn't find much that was humorous about their current situation.

"I'll leave you to it, then."

She and Micah stood and headed back through the door.

As soon as they were out of earshot, he turned to

her. "Sorry about that. I didn't mean to drag you into anything."

"You didn't. The flyers were my idea, remember?"

"Of course I remember. I wasn't trying to take credit for it."

She smiled. "I didn't think you were. Besides, we both want the same thing—to protect the people of Nashville."

"So where do we do this planning?"

"How about over dinner? I'm starved."

He nodded. "Me, too. Any good guacamole joints around here? I seem to remember you having a penchant for the stuff."

And Micah, who hadn't been a fan, had turned into a believer while they were together. And she knew of a very good spot. But it was the place she and Avery frequented for their guac and talks, and she didn't really relish going there. She didn't want his memories sliding around her every time she and Avery walked into the place. Not like a lot of other things in Nashville after they'd broken things off. She'd even thought about leaving town for that very reason, despite the horror of being pushed out of her comfort zone. And now, just when she thought she'd banished all his ghosts, here he came to add new ones. It had made it easier not to go running to him and take back everything she'd said to push him away. And now that he'd returned?

She needed to stand her ground and remember why she'd ended things.

Was she really destined to be alone? Her whole life? She shook off her thoughts. Avery seemingly finding the love of her life made her feel even more alone.

"Guacamole is still the nectar of the gods, but I'm in the mood for something different. How about wings?"

Although Gantry's Margarita Den also had great wings, there were several other places that sold passable chicken other than her go-to place. And most of them already had...ghosts. Well, she didn't want his ghost inhabiting Gantry's as well. Better for him to roam the kitchen of somewhere that didn't matter to her.

"Sounds good. Is Maurio's still open here in town?"

Maurio's. She hadn't been there since the day before graduation. It was her last wonderful memory of him. Yes. That would be the perfect place, since she purposely didn't go there anymore. And wouldn't go there again after tonight.

"It is. Where are you staying? Or did you already buy something?"

He looked at her. "I haven't bought anything. I'm at a hotel at the moment. They have a shuttle that runs back and forth to the hospital." He shrugged with what looked like an apology. "I haven't gotten a vehicle yet, either."

"It's okay, I can drive and drop you off afterward. Which hotel?"

"Tremont Inn, about three blocks from the hospital. I figured I could walk to work on days I didn't want to take the shuttle."

"I know where that is. It's right on the way back toward my place."

So with that settled, they headed toward the exit before Micah stopped. "Can I check in and see how Sassy is doing first?"

"I'd thought about doing the same thing, so sure."

With that, they both headed toward the nurses' desk and asked the person behind the desk to page Dr. Jensen.

CHAPTER FOUR

MAURIO'S WAS CROWDED. And loud. Louder than he remembered. The sign at the front of the restaurant told them to "chicken dance to a table of their choice." It had seemed cute back when they were dating. And one time, Lia had actually chicken danced to one of the tables, making him laugh.

They'd been young and in the throes of medical school. Laughing had not been high on the agenda, except when he was with her.

Only the Lia of today didn't look like she'd chicken dance anywhere. She seemed more serious now. Sadder.

Because of him?

She'd broken things off, so maybe. The whys had never been all that clear, though. Looking back, she hadn't seemed all that enthused by the prospect of going on a medical mission with him. But Lia had also been a master at covering up her emotions, withdrawing or pretending to agree instead of sitting down and having a hard conversation. It had irked him and brought back unpleasant childhood memories. Like his parents' glossing over the fact that they really didn't have a relationship with their son. All Lia would have had to do was say no, she didn't want to go overseas, and he would have thought long and hard about going.

But she hadn't.

And she hadn't mentioned it in her breakup speech, which had been short and sweet. In his mind, going after her would have done no good. Instead, it had solidified his decision to follow through with his plans of going with Doctors Without Borders.

Ghana had been an eye-opener on what it was like to practice medicine where supplies were hard to come by. He thought he might go back someday, but right now he wasn't making those decisions. He just needed to get through this time with his parents, then he could look toward the future. Whatever it held.

They found a booth at the very back of the restaurant. Immediately memories danced around him—and they weren't doing anything as humorous as a chicken dance. Instead, they were memories of him and Lia crowded together on the same side of the booth, her foot sliding along his leg and her laughing when his face turned red.

Damn. This was a mistake. And he'd only suggested it because it was first restaurant that had popped into his mind.

Lia didn't sit next to him this time, though. She sat on one side of the table, and he sat on the other. Then again, they were no longer a couple, so it made sense. But it also highlighted the distance between them. One of the waitstaff came over with two menus and put them down in front of them, taking their drink orders. He ordered a beer. It was rare that he drank nowadays, especially after the night of their breakup, when he'd gotten so drunk he couldn't see straight. Literally. He'd used alcohol to try to drown his shock and dismay, but the next day it had come roaring back with a vengeance, along with a hangover that wouldn't quit. He was never going that route again.

But one beer wasn't the same as getting drunk.

She leaned on the table with her elbows rather than sitting way back in her seat, something he remembered from the past. And her hair was up in a ponytail, but the end slid over her shoulder and curled near the swell of her breast. And, hell, if he didn't acutely remember how those same breasts had felt in his hands. He did his best not to follow that train of thought, but it was damned hard.

"You said you haven't seen your folks yet. I'm kind of surprised. Wasn't that why you came back?"

The question came out of nowhere, taking him by surprise. It took him a minute or two to think of a response. Mainly because he wasn't sure why he hadn't gone to see them. His mom knew he was planning on coming home, but he hadn't given her a firm date, preferring to do things on his own terms. His dad had cancer, but it wasn't at the critical point yet. But who knew when that could change? Maybe the experimental treatment his mom had told him about during their phone call wouldn't work.

"It is, but it's crazy trying to get things set up with work and housing, etc. Once I get a car, it should be easier."

She didn't say anything, just looked at him. And he realized he'd been home for almost a week. Maybe because he knew once he did that seeing his parents would have to take a regular spot on his agenda. And he wasn't quite sure he was ready for that yet.

"My parents and I still don't have the best relationship." The words were out before he could stop them. He knew they sounded weak, but it was the truth, and somehow he'd always had trouble admitting just how bad thing were in his household. Back then he'd told Lia they didn't see eye to eye, but he had never shared what it was that bothered him so much. Maybe because it had seemed selfish of him to want his parents' attention. As if he'd been the only thing on their plates. They were both wildly successful in their careers. They were in demand by myriad people. He was probably just one more person clamoring for their time. He himself had experienced that in Ghana when there were more sick people than there were medical personnel. It had been dizzying, and sometimes he'd just wanted to withdraw from all of it. Had his mom and dad felt that way?

"Yeah, I remember you saying that. I just thought with your dad being sick that things might have gotten better."

The strange thing was, in a way they had. At least from a distance. His mom had emailed him more while he was in Africa than she'd communicated with him the whole time he'd been in medical school. Maybe because it didn't take as much of an emotional investment to type words onto an electronic device as it did when you stood face-to-face with someone.

Like sitting across from Lia again?

Except there was no emotional investment here at all. Not anymore.

"It's complicated."

A good term for it. And for the mixed bag of feelings generated by being at Maurio's again.

Their drinks came, and they gave their meal order to the waiter. Which, strangely, was like being transported back in time. He got the spicy and she got the honey barbecue sauce. It appeared nothing had changed.

Except for them.

Micah took a swig of his beer, his first drink since being back in Nashville. It was smooth going down, the sensation helping to ground him and sweep away some of his misgivings about being here with her.

"And your folks? How are they? Your sister?"

"They're good. My dad is still working for the same medical lab, and my mom is still teaching music. Only she does it from home now. My sister is in Abilene with her husband and kids. When we all get together, it's a mixture of crazy and fun. I adore my nieces."

Her face showed the truth of that statement. The soft smile seemed to come from a place deep inside her.

"And yet you said you weren't sure about having kids of your own."

Her family was so different from his. And when they'd been dating, it was what he'd aspired to. It had given him hope that he could be the kind of dad her father seemed to be. And that he and Lia could have a relationship based on mutual respect and trust, and that they could love their kids—be hands-on parents. And yet she'd been hesitant in her response to his question about how many kids she wanted. It had taken him by surprise. She'd simply said that if practicing medicine was as busy as medical school, she wasn't sure she could give them the attention they deserved. He hadn't pushed. And she hadn't volunteered anything more on that subject.

"My work is pretty fulfilling."

Said as if having a family would make it less so?

He swallowed. That's probably exactly what his parents had felt.

How had he even thought he and Lia had had the makings of a good relationship? Maybe growing up with apathetic parents had made any kind of emotional attachment seem larger and more meaningful than it actually was. Lia had evidently agreed, since she made it seem like their relationship had been just a phase. Just part of the whole medical school experience.

The aftermath of their breakup had left him reeling. He hadn't had, nor wanted, a relationship since then. He'd trusted Lia with his heart, and she'd handed it back to him without a second thought.

So he'd headed to Ghana rather than face her again. Staying would have been hard. And the last thing he wanted was to find out he was some emotionally needy jerk who couldn't let go.

He was pretty sure he wasn't. Because when he let go, he really let go. Neither he nor Lia had contacted each other again. And although it would have been nice to have true closure, he hadn't gone looking for it. He'd just lost himself in his work.

"I get that kids are hard. I was pretty busy in Ghana, too. Anyway, I'm glad your parents are doing well."

She took a sip of her soda, glancing at him over the rim before setting it down. "Is there anything I can do to help, Micah?"

It took him a second before he realized she was talking about his parents and not about their past relationship.

"No. I plan to go car shopping after we're done here." She set her drink down. "I could take you."

"Why?" He stared at her, trying to figure out where this was coming from. Guilt over the past? Surely not.

She shrugged, but the move seemed stiff, as if she was trying to shift some kind of weight from her shoulders, making him think he hadn't been as far off as he'd thought.

"I'm off. You're off. I have a car..." her brows went up "...you don't. Maybe we can kill two birds with one stone and look for places to put up flyers in between stops."

Ah, so that's why. It had had nothing to do with the past.

She went on. "Pertussis is a subject that makes my blood run cold. When I was a kid, a baby in the next apartment had a terrible cough. I was a teenager at the time, and I still vividly remember the sound of it. And the way my parents tried to keep us away from her. But my sister got sick anyway. Not as badly as the baby, but enough to warrant treatment." She fiddled with her napkin. "Anyway, one day I realized the cough in the hallway was gone. Along with the baby. So when Sassy coughed...that sound... It brought up memories I thought were long gone."

He could relate. Not to the pertussis angle, but to the bringing up memories that he thought were long gone.

Every once in a while, he could almost swear he felt a bare foot sliding against his leg, but it was just a phantom ache, like when a part of your body was missing but that you could swear you felt from time to time.

"The baby died."

He didn't know why he'd said it, maybe because a part of him still wanted to understand where Lia was coming from. Despite how close they'd been in medical school, he now realized they'd actually known very little about each other. He'd withheld parts of his past. And evidently she had, too. He'd had no idea her sister had contracted whooping cough.

"Yes. There were a cluster of other cases in the area, which is why I don't want to ignore this. I don't just want to alert the CDC and let them take over. I want make sure Nashville understands the very real dangers of whooping cough."

"I agree." He felt his features soften. "I'm glad your sister pulled through."

She smiled. "Yeah. Me, too. So you see why I really want to be a part of this."

"I do."

They ate their meal, and Micah found himself relaxing, chuckling when a bit of barbecue sauce landed on her cheek. She swiped at it once and missed, and he reached across with his own napkin and rubbed it away. The gesture felt oddly intimate, forcing him to lean back in his seat to detach from it.

"Thanks," she said. "I always seem to do that."

She always had. And he'd always seemed to be the one to fix it back then.

Only he hadn't been able to fix whatever it was that had happened between them at the end. Nor had he tried. His pride had been so stung that he'd simply removed himself from the situation, preferring to lick his wounds in private. Actually, he'd traveled a long distance to make sure he could do exactly that.

He didn't regret going to Ghana. The experience had been fulfilling in a way that was different than what he was doing now at Saint Dolly's.

And right now, Lia was studying him in that crazy

way she'd always had and making him feel like nothing had changed.

Except it had. So he averted his eyes and stared at the foam on his beer. "What happened between us back then, Lia?"

He wasn't sure why he'd even asked the question, but once it was out, he couldn't retract it.

There was silence for several long seconds, and when he looked back at her, it was to find she was no longer looking at him. And he found he missed the touch of her gaze. He'd forgotten how much it affected him. Until just now.

"I—I just realized I wasn't ready for a relationship. Not one that involved commitment and sacrifice. I know how much you wanted to work with Doctors Without Borders, and I couldn't..." She shook her head. "I couldn't give you what you needed. What you deserved. I love Nashville. And I didn't want to leave my family."

"You could have told me that." He'd been right about her reticence to go. "You never know, I might have chosen to stay."

"I knew that was a possibility. And I didn't want to be the reason you didn't go. I had a lot going on at the time, and it seems I made the right decision." She licked her lips. "You never met anyone over there?"

He gave her a slow smile. "I met *lots* of people over there." He kept his meaning ambiguous, although putting the emphasis where he had may have been a little over-the-top. Especially when she bit her lip as if his words had stung.

Damn. He didn't want to say things just to hurt her. He needed to put an end to this conversation, even though he was the one who'd started it. Downing the last of his beer, he waved away the waiter when he asked if he wanted another.

She glanced at him. "Are you sure? I'm driving."

"I'm sure. I was never a big drinker. It's the first beer I've had in a while."

"I remember that about you."

Man, he did not want to go any farther down that road, where they started sharing remembered stories with each other. "Are you sure you want to take me? I can just as easily rent a car."

Except thinking about it, he wasn't sure that was as easy as he'd made it sound. He didn't have auto insurance because...well, no car. Did they even let you rent one without that? He'd never been in that situation before.

"I'm positive. Like I said, we can scout out places to hang flyers." She glanced at her watch. "Most auto dealerships are probably open for another couple of hours, since it's only four. If you're ready to go, that is."

"More than ready."

When they'd checked on Sassy before leaving the hospital, the infant was still holding her own, and the mom and dad had already been started on a course of antibiotics with a stern warning not to go to the store or anywhere else until the whole family had been on them for twenty-four hours.

Micah tried to pick up the bill, but Lia shot him down by laying cash for her meal on the table. "It's okay. Today is normally the day I go out to dinner with Avery." She smiled. "She owes me since she stood me up at the Valentine's Day gala. She had a good reason, though."

"*She* was the person you needed to meet."

The huge wave of relief he felt shocked him. It shouldn't matter. At all. Unless he wasn't really over her.

He was. He'd spent the last three years doing everything he could to forget her. And while he hadn't completely banished her from his head, he'd at least trapped her in a small corner closet toward the back of his brain.

Seeing her again hadn't released her from that dark room. Had it?

Hell, he hoped not. But at least he understood her reasons for breaking up with him a little more.

"Yep, but she decided to spend time with her romantic interest instead."

"The guy with the guitar?"

"One and the same." She laughed. "Avery swore it would never happen. Swore she was immune. I told her to never say never."

Well, he was pretty sure he could say "never" to his being involved with her again. Once was more than enough.

"I definitely saw something between them when I watched them interact."

Her smile was still there. And this time it was very real. It made something heat inside him.

"Something is an understatement. Carter's the one."

The one. Was there such a thing?

If so, Micah hadn't been it. At least not for Lia.

They made their way out to her car, and his brooding thoughts vanished, a smile taking their place when he spotted her vehicle. It was a little compact model that fit her to a T.

Lia had never been a flashy person, unlike his parents. It was probably one of the things that had attracted him to her. Her dad was a pretty well-known scientist in his own right, and yet she never acted like she'd grown up in an upper-middle-class family—one that had done what a lot of families would have been afraid to do: move here from another country.

Her Italian sometimes still came out when she said certain words or when she got nervous or angry. Her breakup speech had been riddled with little language blips that he was sure came from her background, although he hadn't thought they were cute that time. But looking back, he realized those slip-ups proved that what they'd had hadn't been unimportant to her. Otherwise, she would have sailed through that "I don't think we're meant to be together" speech without a problem. It made the blow that much harder knowing that while she cared about him, it hadn't been enough to make her fight for them. Fight for their future.

Because she hadn't thought they had one.

He crunched himself back into the front seat of her car.

"Micah, seriously, push the seat back. You look ridiculous."

On the ride to the wings joint, it hadn't seemed that important, since he hadn't thought he was going to be in the car for the next couple of hours. But with his knees literally pressed against the console in front of him, every pothole was going to bang them up pretty good.

So this time, he reached down for the lever and pushed the seat back as far as it would go. There. At least if they were in an accident, his legs wouldn't be pushed through his chin.

"Less ridiculous?"

"Much." She took out her phone. "So where to? Any preferences as to car dealerships?"

"Maybe one in this area of town and one over in Metro Center?" He pulled up a map of neighborhoods on his phone. "There's also Music Row, which might be a good location for flyers. I'm trying to think of areas that would get the word out the fastest."

"Okay, how about if we do two car dealerships in the downtown area, since they're closer, and then drive out to the other two spots if it's not too dark. I'm assuming we'll have to make more than one trip. Saint Dolly's is going to call other area hospitals and alert them to what's going on here. Hopefully it's confined to just this one area."

"We can hope." Kind of like his problems with Lia had been confined to one area of his heart. Fortunately he'd contained them in time to keep it from really affecting his life.

When Lia put her turn signal on and headed toward the congested area of downtown, he turned his mind toward helping her navigate and away from everything else.

There had been something heartwarming about seeing Micah scrunched in her passenger seat on the way to the wings joint, but after the strange intimacy that had wrapped around that meal with discussions about their past, she had been loath to carry that intimacy outside the restaurant. So she was glad when he'd pushed his seat back and made the car's interior seem a little less cramped.

Or did it?

The way he'd said he'd met lots of people in Ghana had thrown her for a few seconds. Female people? Or was he just trying to get out of answering what was a rather pointed question? But hadn't his question about their breakup been just as pointed?

She forced her attention to something less personal.

"There are a couple of dealerships off I-40. Do you have a preference of car type?"

He sent her a smile. "Just something a little bigger than a lunchbox."

"A lunchbox?" She laughed, glad things seemed to be heading in a more lighthearted direction. "Are you dissing the big blueberry?"

"Isn't *big* blueberry an oxymoron? There is nothing big in this car."

She looked over at him and raised her brows. "Except maybe its passenger's—"

"Uh-uh-uh. My…er…noggin isn't that big."

She had to hand it to the man. He knew how to make her laugh. And how to leave himself open for the perfect comebacks. "Who said I was talking about your head?"

As soon as the words were out of her mouth, her face sizzled with heat. Okay, so she hadn't been specifically talking about any male parts, although she was pretty sure he was going to take it that way. And maybe her subconscious had thrown that out just to torture her.

Micah didn't reply, although out of the corner of her eye she could see a muscle pulsing in his cheek. In anger? Mirth? Disbelief?

Ha! Well, she had a mixture of all three of those reactions going on herself. But she needed to pull herself together or she was going to do something she regretted. Like wish she was kissing him?

Yes. Exactly like that. Even letting that thought go through her mind had her remembering what it had been like to have the man lock lips with her. And a whole lot more.

Fortunately, they weren't far from the first car dealership.

Five minutes later they were getting out of the car and talking to one of the salespeople. Micah told the man what he was looking for. The salesman glanced at Lia. "Will your wife be driving it a lot?"

"She is not my wife."

He punched those words out in a way that made Lia's eyes widen. It was as if that idea were so far out of the realm of possibility as to be laughable. Only he hadn't laughed. Or even chuckled.

"Sorry. I just assumed…" The man didn't finish that statement. Instead, he dived into a rundown of vehicles that fit Micah's needs.

Lia's mood took a turn for the worse. Maybe she should have let him come on his own.

It didn't take long for Micah to find what he was looking for—an SUV that looked like it would work equally well in town or in the country. "Do you want to take it for a test drive?"

"No, I drove something similar in Ghana, so I'm pretty sure I know what it feels like."

Ah, now that made sense. He would have needed something rugged if he had to travel long distances or over difficult terrain. Her blueberry wouldn't have stood a chance there.

And neither would she, probably. At least not without revealing a lot more about herself than she'd wanted to. Thankfully she'd never had to explain her reasons for not wanting to go, other than what she'd said at Maurio's.

The thought of stepping out of her known world

and landing in a place where she'd have to start from scratch? Learn how to tell a whole new load of people apart? No. It would be like moving the furniture in her house around and then trying to somehow make her way through it in the dark. She might not be physically blind, but face blindness still took away one of the principal means of navigating through the world... through relationships. Not recognizing Micah at the benefit was proof of how hard it was.

Dio, she'd experienced enough angst over that to last a lifetime. Besides, her father's reflections on the difficulties her uncle had faced had struck deep...and stayed there. Would knowing about her prosopagnosia have affected her job prospects? She'd like to think not, but in the real world...

She just wasn't willing to take that chance. And right now, she was glad that she'd kept the truth to herself.

As she wandered through the lot, deep in thought about the decisions she'd made in life, Micah went in to seal the deal. Fifteen minutes later, he reemerged.

"Done already?"

"Yep. It'll be delivered to the hotel tomorrow. Unfortunately that means you're stuck with me for the rest of the day. Sorry."

"It's okay. I figured it'd be easier if we're together."

Together. But only in the most superficial of ways. She'd make sure of that.

"Speaking of which, the owner of the dealership said he's willing to put a flyer up inside the building where anyone who visits will see it."

She hadn't really thought about businesses putting them up, but it made a lot of sense. "That's great. I guess we'll have to figure out what we want on them pretty quickly." Which probably meant there were more meetings in the near future if they wanted to get out ahead of this thing. And Lia wasn't sure how she felt about them huddling over pages of ideas.

They got back into the car and started toward the main area of downtown Nashville. "What about one of the parks?"

"We'll need something a little more durable than plain paper if we put them up outside."

She'd thought of that as well. "Maybe a material like the plastic yard sale signs we see around. I'm sure the hospital would let us have some of them printed up."

A couple of miles ahead, they found a park that had a lot of foot traffic. Was it muscle memory that had brought her this way? She swallowed back that thought. Of course not. They had history in a lot of places in Nashville. She found a place to park the car and looked at the green space, her hand hovering over the key in the ignition, hesitating to turn the car off.

As if reading her thoughts, he murmured, "We used to come here to get away from things. I even remember playing hooky on our classes one day."

She remembered that well. She'd been a wreck after a particularly difficult day, and Micah had talked her into taking a walk to clear her head.

Except it hadn't been the walk that had done that. It had been his kiss. A kiss that had turned into two, and then three. And they'd had their first lovemaking session in a secluded area under the cover of trees and shrubbery. They'd both missed their next class. And she hadn't regretted it. She still didn't. She shivered at the memory.

"Yes, we did." She cleared her throat. "I remember

this place being pretty busy, which is why I think it might be a good place."

"For flyers?" His smooth words made her insides quiver. What else had he thought she meant?

"Yes."

"Do you want to get out and look?"

Did she? Would it cause her to relive memories that should be left in their final resting place? But to balk now would be to confirm that she hadn't gotten over him. Or this place. "I suppose we should."

She turned off the car and tossed the keys into her purse. "Maybe we should take a few pictures of likely spots, so we can remember them later."

"Pictures. Now that's a novel idea."

Was he making a joke about their history in this park? Or was he simply taking her words the way she'd meant them? Actually, she didn't really know how she meant anything right now.

They entered the park, and as soon as they did, she saw everything through the eyes of her past. The greenery that beckoned to hikers and runners alike. The cleared areas that appealed to urbanites who liked the solid feel of concrete beneath their feet. And the small stands of trees that were crafted like mini oases. Those had appealed to Micah and Lia on a day when her stress had been decidedly relieved in his arms.

What were they doing here? This was a huge mistake. She was just about to suggest they turn around and go back to the car when she realized they were...there.

Her shaky legs were thankful for the bench that stood just across the pathway from the dense shade of bushes in front of them. She sank onto it, trying to make it seem as natural as possible. She pointed up at the lamppost.

"This is one of the main footpaths through the park. We could put a flyer up there." To keep her mind on the task at hand, she aimed her phone at the area and took a picture of it.

Micah sat down next to her. "Do you know where we are?"

Pretend you don't. Act like this is the first time you've ever seen it.

Like when she'd seen him at the gala? Only that hadn't been pretense. She really hadn't known who he was. At first.

But now she did. Her eyes shut. *Dio*...now she did.

"Yes." The word came out a little shakier than she would have liked, but that couldn't be helped. She covered with her next words. "We're at Butler Park. I think it will be an ideal place to advertise. We'll have to get permission from the parks department, of course, and then we'll need to design the flyers and figure out how to mount them and protect them from the—"

"Lia." His voice stopped the manic tumble of words that she'd used to keep the pull of this place at bay. It hadn't worked. Because as soon as he said her name, voices from the past came whispering toward her, sliding past her cheek, her ears, familiar scents filling her nostrils.

She half turned toward him, her words suddenly deserting her. All she could do was look at him. Those gray eyes, that short beard that was unsuccessful in hiding a strong chin and square jaw. These were things that she recognized. That helped her differentiate him from a million other people on this planet. That and the way he made her feel.

Both in the past. And right now. Right here.

"Yes?"

"Do you know *where* we are? Do you remember this very spot in this very park?"

He wasn't going to let her sidestep his original question.

This time her "yes" was whispered, and she didn't try to add anything else to it.

Warm fingers slid down her jaw until he reached the point of her chin. He cupped it, tipping her face up to his. "This is where it really began."

Yes, it was. The place where sex among the trees had transformed from a mere release of energy into a relationship that not only released energy but gained it back as they shared with each other.

Suddenly she knew he felt it as much as she did. That the magic this park had woven back then was just as potent today as it had been when they were young medical students.

That's when she knew. Knew that she wasn't getting out of this park without getting what she came for. What she longed for.

And that was his kiss.

A small smile played at the corner of his mouth, denting his cheek and making her lean closer to him. Until at last she felt a completely different kind of magic: one where his lips finally touched hers.

CHAPTER FIVE

HE HADN'T MEANT to kiss Lia. But when she sat down on the bench in front of their spot, and he looked into the bushes and saw in his mind's eye their two bodies twined together in an impossible embrace, he hadn't been able to resist saying her name. And when she turned toward him, lips parted, he'd realized he wasn't going to be able to resist her now any more than he'd resisted her all those years ago.

His mouth covered hers, and he sensed more than felt her melt into his embrace. His arms came up and wrapped around her, pulling her closer, her breasts pressed tight against him.

Hell, it had been far too long since he'd held her or any other woman like this. And that was probably why his tongue edged forward and traced her lips with a question. One that she instantly answered by opening her mouth.

He groaned low in his throat, one hand sliding into the hair at the back of her head and holding her in place as he deepened the kiss. His senses were ignited as memories came at him in snatches, like a set of fireworks that lit the sky for a few seconds before dimming and allowing the next explosion to take its place, each burst more brilliantly colored than the last.

Her fingers gripped his shoulders, clenching and releasing in time with the stroke of his tongue. Just like she'd done hundreds of other times when they'd...

Something between them vibrated. Something that wasn't part of his body.

It happened again, and it took him a few seconds to realize it was someone's phone. Lia's, since his ringer was on.

She jerked back from him, eyes coming up to catch his as she struggled to catch her breath. "What...?"

Damn. He had no idea why he'd just done what he had.

Maybe proving to himself that she'd been as into his touch as he'd been into hers? Had he needed...closure?

As quickly the word popped into his head, he threw it away. Because that kiss had closed nothing. Instead it had ripped wide-open a door from the past, allowing everything he'd stuffed behind it to come tumbling out.

He quickly forced a smile to his lips to cover his musings.

"Saved by a little vibrator."

Wait. That wasn't the right expression. But the burn of red in her face made the mistake worth it. And it helped him realize she'd been just as caught up in the moment as he had.

The buzzing stopped and then started back up almost immediately. Lia fished her phone out of the pocket of her light jacket and glanced at the readout before frowning. "It's Avery."

She pushed a button, then pressed the phone to her ear. "Hi, Ave, what's up?"

Listening for a second, her frown deepened. "About fifteen minutes, why? We had a pertussis case and were looking at spots to—"

She licked her lips. "Um... I'm with Micah."

Evidently she was warning her friend that she couldn't speak freely. Why? Was she planning on sharing all about that unplanned kiss later on? Would she sit there and dissect it with Avery later on?

"Who?" She listened before exclaiming, "Oh, no! Okay, I'm on my way right now. Get her on the list for one of the OR rooms. The sooner the better. 'Bye."

She looked at him. "Sorry, but I have to cut this field trip short. I'm needed back at the hospital. Can I drop you off somewhere?"

"I can just catch the shuttle at the hospital." Field trip? Really? That kiss was more than just a damned field trip. "Anything I can help with?"

"Avery has been treating one of her patients for some vascular issues in her legs. Well, she'd also started complaining about abdominal pains and just showed up in the ER complaining of severe pain in her belly."

"Vascular issues. Could it be an aneurysm?"

"That's what I'm thinking, or aortic dissection, both of which are medical emergencies."

Micah stood and held his hand out to her. "Let's go, then."

They rushed back to the car, and when Lia's hands were shaking so hard she could barely get the key into the ignition, he took the key from her. "Trade places with me."

"Thanks." The look of relief she threw at him screwed with his insides. But he managed to get out of the car and walk around to the driver's seat. He adjusted the seat and started the vehicle.

Then he turned the car around and aimed it in the direction of the hospital.

Lia couldn't believe she'd let him kiss her. Let? *Dio*, if she remembered right, it had been her who'd leaned toward him and not the other way around. But none of that mattered right now. The fear in Avery's voice had been very real. She remembered her friend asking her if Bonnie had contacted her, and she'd said no. Avery said she was going to get her former music teacher to come in and meet her, but evidently that had all changed. It was now an emergency situation. If it was an aortic dissection—where a weakness in the aorta let blood leak between the layers of the vessel—then time was of the essence, because if it ruptured completely, death could occur within minutes. It sounded like it was down low in the abdominal section of the artery rather than up near the heart. She hoped there was a surgeon at the hospital who could scrub in before she got there, because the longer the wait... It was what killed people before they even realized they were truly sick. She could think of actors and dignitaries alike who had been affected.

"Hurry."

"I'm going as fast as I safely can."

It felt like they were crawling, although when she glanced at the speedometer, they were nearing seventy miles per hour. She was a mess, and even though she was worried about Avery's friend, Lia knew that was only part of the reason for her panic.

Her former lover had kissed her again as if nothing had gone wrong between them. And that scared the hell out of her. How could she have let this happen? Micah deserved better than this. And hell if she hadn't tried to give it to him by breaking things off. Once this was over, she was going to have to make sure he knew that nothing had changed. They were not—nor could they ever—getting back together.

He glanced at her. "You okay?"

Really? He was leading with that?

"Sure. Just fine."

"Stop it, Lia." His hands gripped her steering wheel so hard she was surprised he didn't rip it from the console. "Look, I know that kiss was a mistake. Don't read more into it than there was."

What on earth was that supposed to mean? "I'm not!"

"That's not what I'm seeing by the whole 'ready to run and run hard' vibe you've got going on. Look. It was where we had sex for the first time. It's not surprising that we kissed. Exes get caught in that kind of situation all the time."

They did? And just how did he know that?

I met lots of people there. His words from earlier whispered through her skull, pulling pieces of brain matter apart and turning them against each other.

The fact that he'd used the words *had sex* rather than *made love* somehow made what they'd had look cheap and dirty, as if it was just two people with biological urges they'd chosen not to resist.

That hurt worse than the thought of him sleeping with hundreds of other women. But she wasn't about to let him see the truth.

"Sure. Whatever. Just as long as you know it's not going to lead to us having sex again anytime soon."

If she thought she'd shot a well-aimed arrow and hit a spot it might hurt, she was wrong.

"I never thought it was." He shot her a look. "Did you?"

Actually? If he had kept kissing her like that, they might very well have wound up in that same stand of trees doing the same thing they'd done years ago. And dammit, it wouldn't have been *having sex*, either. They would have been making love. At least it would have been for her.

They made it to the hospital in record time, and when he pulled up in front of the emergency room entrance, she leaped out of the car without stopping to say anything to him and headed through the doors. She'd deal with her keys and the whole car thing later on. Once she found out what was going on with Avery's friend. She had an emergency to see to, one that provided an escape that she welcomed more than she could say.

Avery waved to her from behind the double doors that led to the exam rooms.

"Ultrasound?"

"Yes. Looks like it's an aneurysm in her abdomen. Superior mesenteric. She's trying to act like it's nothing, but it's definitely something."

"Thank God." Even as she said the words, she knew how they sounded. An aneurysm could be as big an emergency as a dissection if it burst. But depending on how large the bulge was and how weak the vessel walls were, it could buy them more time. "I thought for sure you were going to say she had an aortic dissection. How big is it?"

"Looks fairly large to me. She's had severe varicose veins in her legs, but like I said, she called me complaining of some kind of twinge in her stomach, and I was afraid something else was going on. I wish she had called you like I asked."

"Me, too. Where is she? I'll want to see the location on the ultrasound and determine the size for myself."

Avery led her toward the back, where the exam rooms were. Before she even got there, she heard singing. Two voices were crooning about falling into some kind of fire pit? No, a fiery ring. She shot a glance at Avery, who just shrugged. "I told you. She's trying to pretend nothing is wrong."

Lia could relate to that. She'd been trying to pretend nothing was wrong for most of her life. Doing her best to hide her condition from friends, family…and from the few men she'd had in her life, including Micah. In the end, her secret had cost her that relationship. So she was going to make sure this patient didn't ruin her life doing the same thing she'd done: keeping secrets.

Avery squeezed her arm. "Brace yourself. Her companion is a Johnny Cash impersonator named Levi. In case they ask if you recognize who he is."

"Seriously? Johnny Cash?"

"Yep. Right down to the scar on his chin."

She stopped outside the door where the a cappella voices originated and then pushed through it into the room. Nothing stopped—the music continued, the room's two occupants seemingly oblivious to everything around them. On the exam table was her patient, and her singing partner was…okay, Johnny Cash, just like Avery had said.

The face meant nothing, but the pompadour was there, as were the dark sideburns, craggy line in his cheek and that scar. And he was dressed all in black.

The song lyrics suddenly made sense.

She waited until they were done with the chorus before moving forward, shifting her attention away from the Johnny lookalike and focusing them on her patient.

Bonnie was in a skirt that was pushed up enough to reveal knee-high compression stockings, one of which was up and the other rolled down to her ankle. She looked again at Avery with a question. Avery shook her head to indicate she hadn't done that.

"Hi, Ms. Chisholm, I'm Iliana Costa. You were supposed to call me?"

The woman's lips compressed, and she sucked down an exasperated sigh. "You're Avery's friend."

"I am. I hear you're having stomach pains?"

"They're not bad right now. Just a twinge here and there. I think they're going away, actually." Even as she said it, her face contorted for several seconds before the pain released her.

"Can you show me where it hurts?" she asked Bonnie, not bothering with the pain scale, since it was pretty obvious she was going to underplay her symptoms and her discomfort.

Bonnie ignored the request, saying instead, "I didn't even want to come to the hospital, but Levi here insisted."

"He was right. And Levi is…?"

"He's a Johnny Cash impersonator."

A laugh bubbled up inside her that she had to disguise with a cough. "I gathered that. But who is he to you?"

"He's my…er, sidekick."

Avery shot her a look that said everything. "So it's okay that he's here, I take it."

"Definitely."

Lia nodded. "Good. So where is this twinge, exactly?"

Bonnie pressed her hand on an area in her abdomen. She looked at her friend again. "Did you save images of the ultrasound?"

"Yep, here they are." She went through the images on the computer in the room. It looked like it was indeed in a section of the mesenteric artery, and the aneurysm had ballooned to about two centimeters. It was a pretty good size. A stent wasn't going to work here. They were going to have to bypass the damaged section, hopefully before it blew out.

She went up to the head of the bed. "Okay, Bonnie, did Avery explain that you have an aneurysm and what that means?"

"She said I probably need surgery. Is that really necessary? It's really not as bad as it was. Can't I just wear a girdle to hold it in, like I do these stocking things?"

Avery stepped forward. "No, because this is deep inside you. If it ruptures, you could very well bleed to death. This is serious, Bonnie. You can't sing it away. You need to listen to Dr. Costa and get it fixed."

The man at her side moved to the head of the bed, his cologne rolling over Lia in waves. "You're the June to my Johnny. Without you, I'm lost. I need you here."

Lia blinked. As odd as this couple might look together, the concern in the man's voice sounded genuine. He cared about her. "Avery is right. We do need to operate. But once we're finished, you should recover well, as long as you're willing to make some lifestyle changes, starting with your blood pressure."

"I'm a singer. It's a high-stress profession."

"High stress can lead to high blood pressure. But I think we can help you with that with medication, so you'll be able to keep singing."

"Ugh. What do you think Avery? Do I really need to start popping pills? I don't want to be a drug addict like some of those rock stars are."

Her friend smiled. "It isn't exactly 'popping pills.' And it's what I've already suggested. More than once."

Bonnie's lips became a sideways slash that revealed her displeasure, but it didn't completely rule out what they were saying. She reached for her companion's hand. "What do you think, Sugar Lips?"

"I think you need to do what they say. You've known Avery a long time. She won't steer you wrong."

His voice was gravelly and low, and Lia couldn't quite tell if it was his real voice or if he was still playing a part. Whichever it was, he was saying all the right things.

Bonnie closed her eyes and nodded. "When does this surgery thing need to happen?"

The next part was touchy. Avery had told her that Bonnie hated hospitals. She didn't want to scare her off when they were this close to getting her to agree to a much-needed procedure. "It should be done right away. You're experiencing symptoms, which means the aneurysm could be very close to bursting."

"Like it could burst inside me right now?"

"Yes. I'm here now, so let's get this done and behind you."

Avery touched her arm, a question on her face.

Lia motioned toward the door. "We'll be right back. We're going to discuss strategy for a moment."

When Levi nodded, the friends exited to the hallway.

Avery pulled her a little way down the hallway.

"What's going on?" Lia said.

"You look exhausted. Are you sure you're up for this? And was that Mr. Slash and Burn that I saw bringing you in?"

"Would you please stop calling him that?"

"No." Avery laughed. "Because I swear right now you're about to do a 'burn, baby, burn.'" Her friend sang those three words, drawing the last syllable out on a crazy combination of musical notes, her hips swishing in time with each change in pitch.

Her antics caused Lia to make a sound that was halfway between a laugh and a screech. "I am not!"

"You should see your face. And I know what it feels like, because I get that way every time Carter gives me a sideways look."

Lia rolled her eyes. "First of all, that is you being caught up in a love mist and wishing happy endings on everyone around you. Micah and I were over a long time ago."

"Sure, sure. We'll circle back to that. Which brings me to the other subject I mentioned. You look exhausted. I can call someone else in."

"No. She needs the surgery, and I'm already here. There's no reason to call another surgeon. As for the circling back, please don't. I took him to look for a car and to scout out places to hang some posters for the hospital."

"And that wasn't a problem at all?" Her friend studied her face. "Being in the same vehicle with him?"

"Not a problem. At all. At least I hope not." Even as she said it, Micah appeared at the end of the hallway, giving her a quick smile.

Her face turned to lava.

"Slash. And. Burn. Right on cue." Avery bumped her with her shoulder.

Micah reached them and said, "I thought you might be back here. I brought the keys to your car. I parked it in the physicians' lot."

Lia gulped, praying Avery wasn't going to say anything else about Micah's cheek, which was still dented from his smile. "Thanks. You won't have a problem getting back to the hotel?"

"Nope. Can we meet up tomorrow to discuss the situation?"

Avery's head twisted sideways to stare at her, brows raised almost to the ceiling. "There's a situation?"

Dio, was there ever. But it wasn't one she wanted to admit to herself, much less to Avery, especially since her friend was right about her reaction to his smile. It had always been that way. Maybe she would confess to her friend at some point about what had happened in the park, but not until she'd had a chance to analyze it for herself. So she quickly broke down the only situation she wanted to talk about: Sassy and the threat of a pertussis outbreak. She ended it with, "But right now I want to focus on Ms. Chisholm's aneurysm. Any other problem can wait until later."

She said that last part with enough emphasis to hopefully convince Avery—and herself—that it was true. Although she wasn't so sure her brain registered her words. It was already taking chunks of what had happened at the park and blowing them all out of proportion.

Micah glanced at her, and the groove in his cheek kicked back up, causing her to sizzle all over again.

He was on to her. Maybe she'd be telling Avery about the park incident sooner rather than later. Because her friend might come up with a worse nickname than Slash and Burn, given enough time.

"Here you go." He reached in his pocket, and the tinkle of her key ring with its little bell sounded. "What's this, by the way?" He fingered the silver jingle bell attached to the key ring.

"That's Samantha's."

His head tilted. "Samantha's?"

"Her cat," Avery said. "Named for her witchy ways."

"Witchy…"

Lia explained, "She's named after a TV show character. She can be a little temperamental. And she's been known to vanish and reappear at a moment's notice."

The indent in Micah's cheek became a full-blown grin, and she couldn't help smiling back like an idiot. "I take it the bell is to let you know where she is. If that's the case, shouldn't it be with her rather than with you?"

"She…um…somehow got it off her collar."

"Well, I guess that means she knows where you are rather than the other way around. Clever kitty."

The low words made her shiver.

"I hadn't thought about that." She'd just put the bell on her key chain so she wouldn't lose it. Although with how smart Sam was, she wouldn't put it past the cat to have turned the tables on her.

She held her hand out for the keys. "I'm planning on putting it back on her safety collar tonight." The words came out a little more waspishly than she meant them to. "And I'd better get back to my patient if I'm going to get this surgery on the road."

"Anything I can help with?"

"No. But thanks for asking."

He looked dubious but didn't argue. "All right. I'll see you later, then. And I'll be in touch with you about tomorrow."

"Sounds good." She'd worry about tomorrow when tomorrow came.

Thankfully, Avery didn't say anything else as they returned to her patient's room. Lia patted the woman on the hand. "I'm going to make sure we're set as far as an operating room goes. I'll be back in a few minutes to give you an update and explain exactly what our plan is."

Bonnie's surgery was off to a rocky start. The second Lia opened her up, the weakened vessel burst, filling the surgical site with a rush of blood. "I need suction!"

"Stats are dropping, Doctor."

She needed to find that vessel. Lia reached in with gloved fingers, feeling around as another nurse continued suctioning the area. There!

"Found it. Clamp."

A clamp magically appeared in her hand, and she somehow managed to get it around the upper portion of the injured artery. When they'd suctioned out the rest of the blood, Lia looked at the screens displaying the patient's vital signs. "Okay, she's stable for now. Let's work fast."

This was not how she'd wanted this to go. If the aneurysm was caused by an infection in the vessel, it could have just released a flood of bacteria into her abdomen. What she'd seen on the scans hadn't looked mycotic, but she would rather have clamped the vessel and bypassed it than have it rupture. She could do an intracavity lavage with antibiotics, but there were mixed reviews on whether it actually helped prevent sepsis or not. What she could do instead was start her on a course of IV antibiotics to ward off infection, just in case. "Is the graft ready?"

Another doctor had been busy retrieving a vein from Bonnie's leg to use to replace the part of the damaged artery. "Yes, although I had a heck of a time finding something decent. Just suturing the site closed."

Lia took the section of vessel and used it to resection the two cleaned-up ends of the vessel. Ten minutes later, it was attached. Looking through her loupes, she checked the suture line, making sure the stitches were close and even. "Let's take the clamp off and see what we've got."

The clamp was removed, and they waited. No leaks. Everything looked well sealed. "Send the removed portion to pathology and have them look for signs of infection. I want to make sure we cover all our bases." She gave a relieved sigh and glanced up at the viewing window, where Avery was watching, and nodded to her. Then she turned back to her team. "Let's get her closed up."

An hour later, Bonnie was in recovery, and they'd allowed Levi to join her. She met Avery in the hallway to give her an update. "I want to keep her for a day or two to give her a chance to recover and so we can monitor for signs of infection." She smiled. "And you might see about getting her a private room, in case she wants to put on another concert."

"I'll work on that."

Hopefully she would have the path results back soon and they'd be in the clear. In the meantime, she gave

Avery a hug. She glanced at her phone and saw it was already after nine in the evening. "I think I'm headed home to crash, unless you need me for something else."

"No. Go. I'm going to head home to Carter in a few minutes, too, before he sends out a search party." Her friend smiled. "And thank you for saving her. She's a special lady."

"I can see that. And it was a group effort. But she is going to need to work on her blood pressure."

"I agree. We'll have another discussion about that. Thanks again."

"You're welcome. We need to set up that guac date." She felt for her keys and found them in her pocket. Hopefully he had made it home. "And please, please don't call Micah by that name again."

"Yes, to the guac. On the other thing… I'm not sure. You'll need to convince me that it's no longer an accurate representation. I could call him Mr. Slash and you Ms. Burn, if you'd prefer."

"No. I don't prefer."

Maybe because it was a little close to the truth. She needed to figure out if anyone else could see what Avery evidently could. And, if so, what she needed to do to change it.

CHAPTER SIX

MICAH SPOTTED LIA and Avery the second they came in.

"Damn." The word slipped out before he could stop it.

The elegantly dressed woman seated across from him tilted her head and frowned. "What is it, honey?"

Honey. It was how she'd always referred to him, but he wasn't sure it meant any more now than it had in the past. In fact, the word itself grated on him whenever he heard it on television or between lovers on the street. Because it brought up a whole host of memories he'd rather forget. In fact, he wouldn't be here at all with her if she hadn't contacted him and asked if they could meet.

He shook himself from his thoughts. "Nothing. I was just thinking of something."

Lia had needed to attend to another emergency surgery two nights ago when they were supposed to meet up about the vaccination campaign. And he actually hadn't seen her since then, since he'd been busy as well. Sassy was still in the hospital. So far no other pertussis cases had come in, but it was still early, and adults tended to fend off the illness better than infants. Sassy had been touch and go, but today, for the first time, it seemed she might be improving.

Something he wasn't sure if Lia knew. He probably should tell her.

While Lia looked straight ahead as if she didn't care who was here, Avery's gaze scanned the faces in the room. Her glance collided with his, and she smiled, then jabbed Lia with her elbow. Great. He'd been hoping he wouldn't actually see anyone he knew here.

The woman leaned close to Lia and whispered something. Lia stopped in her tracks, and her eyes slowly swung in his direction. Okay, well, it looked like he wasn't getting out of here unscathed. He gave her a half smile. Lia's teeth came down on her lower lip, rubbing along it in a move he found fascinating. Why had she done that? Not that he minded.

Actually he thought it was pretty damned...

Inconvenient. That's the word he was looking for.

"Are those friends of yours?" His attention swung back to his companion.

Oh, hell. The last thing he wanted to do was to introduce her to Avery and Lia. Especially since Lia had never met her. Not even when they were dating. Although maybe it had been a sign of things to come.

He struggled to find a way to describe Lia. "They work at the same hospital as I do."

Just then, the pair's trajectory changed, and they headed toward Micah's table, Lia hanging back and looking like this was the last place she wanted to go. Her first reaction to seeing him might have been crazy sexy, but right now she looked pretty miserable. But at least she'd recognized him this time.

Then they were standing in front of them, and he

had a decision to make. So he stood and forced a smile that wasn't real this time. "Hi, ladies. I didn't know you liked this place."

"Best guacamole in the state. It's where we always come," Avery said with a touch of pride in her voice.

He remembered asking Lia for a recommendation of that very dish, and this wasn't the place she'd named. He looked at her. "Is it now?"

Her teeth slammed down on her lip again, and this time a flush leached into her cheeks. "It's only one of the places I eat guacamole."

Avery's head swung around. "*One* of them? I thought you said Gantry's guac was a cut above any other restaurant's? Not that I disagree. It's fab."

So Lia hadn't wanted to bring him here. Why? Did she consider him some kind of infectious disease that would contaminate this place and ruin it for her?

Maybe it was part of the same reason she'd broken up with him. He hadn't bought the whole "We want different things from life" crap she'd thrown at him after graduation. Something had happened. Something that had changed the way she saw him in a nanosecond. But he couldn't force her to tell him if she didn't want to. And he'd been so shocked and hurt that he'd just wheeled away from her and gotten the hell out of there. He'd wound up in a bar very much like this one.

And after all this time, he wasn't going to sit here and second-guess every single thing he'd said or done. Not like he had back then.

"And who is your companion?" Avery gave him a guarded look that he could swear harbored a gleam of disappointment. In what?

He glanced at the woman seated at his table, realizing that through the modern marvels of plastic surgery, she didn't look much older than he did.

Okay, so this was even worse than he'd thought. He did not want Lia thinking he'd kissed her and then immediately gone out and found someone else. Although she probably wouldn't care one way or the other.

"I was just telling her about you both, that we work at the same hospital."

Lia stared down at her feet as if she couldn't bear to look at him. So she'd thought exactly that. That this was his date. That was so far from the truth that it was actually ludicrous.

So with his next words, he allowed a hint of a smile to play across his lips. "Lia and Avery, I'd like you to meet Monica Corday. My mother."

Her head whipped up as shock wheeled through her. This woman was Micah's mom and not his—?

As if summoned, the woman uncoiled herself from her chair and stood. Out came a perfectly manicured hand on which was some pretty impressive jewelry. "I'm so pleased to meet you both."

Her voice was smooth, with a perfect southern drawl that made Lia's remaining accent feel thick and clumsy. She dreaded opening her mouth.

Avery broke in and saved her the trouble, giving back a greeting gripping the other woman's hand. "Pleased, I'm sure." The cool words held just a touch of prickle that no one but Lia would have sensed. It was as if she'd sensed how unsure Lia felt and was moving in to protect her. Just like her dad always had.

A dangerous prickling occurred behind her eyes. She forced it away with a couple of hard blinks.

She appreciated Avery's efforts, but she could fight her own battles. "It's very nice to meet you, Mrs. Corday, I'm Lia Costa."

Although her condition kept her from seeing the resemblance between mother and son, it didn't stop her from noticing that when Monica Corday smiled, there were very few facial lines activated. Botox. A good deal of it, if she had to hazard a guess. Not like her son, whose smile revealed a wonderful network of lines that made her stomach wobble. And that dimple...

Slash and Burn. Hell if Avery hadn't hit the nail on the head.

The insincere curve of lips appeared again. "Would you two care to join us?"

Dio. When they'd first come in and Avery had pointed him out, she'd thought Micah was here on a date. Outrage had gathered in her chest that she'd done her best to banish. It was none of her business whom he did and didn't go out with. But on the heels of that kiss they'd shared? Really?

To find out this was actually his mom had been even more shocking, if that were possible. Micah had said he and his parents didn't see eye to eye. She was starting to see why. This clinic-crafted person was nothing like the man she used to love.

"Thank you, but no. I'm sure you two have a lot to talk about." Too late she remembered that he'd said his father was ill. So her words sounded terrible.

One of Micah's brows crooked up as he smiled.

How could he smile? His dad was sick. "I, um meant, since you've been gone for so long."

Micah was still standing, and his hand slid next to

hers, pinkie finger barely grazing hers for a second as if to reassure her. "I knew what you meant."

Her throat clogged. He was giving her a pass, even though he probably shouldn't have. This man affected her thought processes in so many ways that it wasn't even funny. He'd always done so, but it was disappointing that he still had this effect on her. She should be well and truly over him by now. But she wasn't. Because she hadn't broken up with him because she'd no longer loved him. She'd broken up with him for just the opposite reason. She loved him so much that she didn't want him saddled with someone who would always have trouble recognizing people she'd known for years. It would be even worse if he'd had to drag her overseas with him.

Even if he didn't find her condition embarrassing, she did. And she didn't want him going through what her dad had had to deal with: stepping in to protect his brother from ridicule. And how many times had her parents had to explain and make excuses for her when she tripped over an identity? The thought of Micah doing that made her cringe.

She looked at Micah's mom and tried to pick out things about her that she would remember the next time she saw her. Lack of lines. Long blond hair that was the same color as Micah's. A painted-on mole at the corner of her left eye. Except that might not always be there. Maybe she dotted it on periodically and left it off at other times. Lia's eyes went crazily from feature to feature before finding something else. Her nose was slightly crooked, taking a tiny jog to the left. She wondered if it had been broken at some time in the past. Okay. Blond hair. No lines. Crooked nose.

Avery, who hadn't said anything for a minute or two, spoke up. "Lia's right. We have some business to discuss, anyway, so maybe another time."

"Certainly." Monica's response was as smooth as ever, giving no hint that her husband, who wasn't here at the restaurant with them, was ill. Although that probably was why Micah was here—to discuss things. Although maybe not. Maybe they'd already made their amends. Maybe their family was closer than hers now. In the two days since she last saw him? Hardly likely.

And Micah's eyes held a wariness that she didn't like. She might not recognize him by the parts of his face, but she knew him in a way that no one else would. At least that's what she told herself. Who knew if that was actually true or not. Surely his mom knew him well, since she'd been a part of his life since birth.

So she decided to follow Avery's lead and forced a smile she didn't feel. "It was nice meeting you, Mrs. Corday."

"You as well, dear."

She threw one last look at Micah, who nodded. She had no idea what it meant, so she just turned and went in the other direction, following Avery toward a table on the other side of the room.

Lia dropped into her chair with a sigh, holding up two fingers when their usual waitress glanced in their direction. She would know what she meant. They always got margaritas and guacamole with chips when they came here. She turned back to Avery. "Oh, God. That was one of the most uncomfortable experiences ever."

"You mean with Slash and Burn? He didn't look any more comfortable than his dear old mama did."

Needing something to fiddle with, she grabbed a napkin from the table and worried the edge of it. "I had no idea she was his mother. She looks a little young."

"You never met her while you were dating? And the fountain of youth that particular woman drank from comes at a hefty price tag at the hands of a good surgeon."

She had to agree with her. "I'm sure. And no, I never met her. Not once."

"He was probably afraid you'd run away and never come back. I might."

She kind of had run and never come back. But not because of his mother. Because of her own fears. "He said he and his parents didn't see eye to eye. At least that's why he never introduced us, I thought. But who knows? That was a long time ago. So let's not talk about them. Let's talk about your new life with Carter."

It worked. Avery moved the conversation over to something that was near and dear to her heart. And as she talked about the progression that led to their engagement, Lia smiled. "I saw Micah at the Valentine's benefit, and he thought there was some pretty heavy chemistry going on between the two of you."

"There was. But we're not the only ones who have some wild chemistry going on."

So much for keeping things shifted away from her. "If you're talking about me and Micah, that chemistry is old news. There was some at one time, as you know, but not any longer."

"Are you really sure about that, Lia?"

She crooked one shoulder up. "It's what it needs to be." She paused, torn about whether to say anything or not. But she and the ER nurse rarely kept things from each other. Especially when they were at Gantry's for guac and talks. So she plowed forward. "Except...we kissed. And it was... Let's just say I could be in a lot of trouble."

Avery sat back in her chair. "You kissed! When did this happen?"

She did her best to angle her body so Micah couldn't see her face. Or read her lips. "The day of Bonnie's surgery. We were actually in the middle of it when your call came through." Lia had to admit it felt good to get this off her chest.

"Why on earth did you answer the phone?"

"*Dio*, what was I supposed to do? I figured it was something pretty important or you wouldn't be calling me. And actually, it was a blessing. The last thing I needed to be doing was kissing Micah Corday."

"Why?"

She was stunned. "What do you mean, why? Our relationship is over. Finished. *Terminata*. To dredge it up now would be just plain stupid, since I have no intention of getting involved with him again. It was a mistake last time. It would be a mistake this time."

"You never told me exactly what happened between you last time."

Even though her friend knew about her diagnosis, she doubted Avery would agree with her reasons for ending it with Micah.

"I just realized it was never going to work between us. He wanted to go to Africa, and I wanted to stay here. In Nashville."

She prayed Avery wouldn't keep digging.

Her friend sighed, then slid her hand over hers. "I'm sorry. I remember how hard it was for you to get over him. I can't imagine what it must be like to work with him. But that kiss…"

"It was a shock to realize he's going to be staying at the hospital, for sure. I'm hoping it gets easier as time goes on." She sighed. "As for the kiss, I think seeing him again dragged up a lot of old feelings."

"I bet." Her friend glanced over at the other table. "Don't look now, but Mr. Slash and Burn is looking in our direction."

"Avery, seriously. And I'm sure he's just looking around the room. I do hope he and his mom are getting along better, though. Especially with his dad being ill."

"Is it serious?"

"Serious enough to bring him home from Ghana."

Avery's lips twisted. "So that's why he's here. That stinks."

"Yes, it does." Her heart ached for Micah. He'd rarely talked about his parents. So there must be a huge mess of conflicting emotions involved in returning to Nashville.

The waitress set their drinks in front of them, along with two large bowls of guacamole and chips. "Anything else?"

"Not yet," Avery said, "but we may need some more drinks by the time this is all over with."

Debbie, who had waited on them more often than not, gave them a sympathetic smile. "Just send me a signal when you're ready."

"Thanks." Lia waited for the woman to leave and then blew her breath out in a rush. "Why does life have to be so complicated?"

"Tell me about it." Avery smiled. "But sometimes it works out in unexpected ways. Look at me and Carter. Maybe this is another of those times."

Lia was happy for her friend. Happy that she'd found a person to spend her life with. Happy to see her friend so relaxed and at peace. But things didn't always work out that way. At least not for her and Micah. Even if that kiss had been wildly exciting and crazy good, it was doubtful Micah would ever fully forgive her for dumping him the way she had. And really, nothing had changed. She had the same fears now that she'd had back then. It was why her dating life basically sucked. She didn't see herself settling down and getting married. Having children. Not with the way she was wired.

"It's not, but I'm okay with it." She smiled. "I do hope Bonnie and Levi-slash-Johnny have a happy ending, though."

"They are a wild pair, aren't they? But they really care about each other."

"I'm hoping she'll be released tomorrow or the next day. Did she see you sing at the Valentine's Day benefit?"

Avery nodded. "She did. It was hard getting up there without my sister, but Carter helped me get through it. So did you and Bonnie."

Avery's sister had died of cancer a couple of years ago. It was the main reason her friend had had trouble singing again.

"I think April would be very proud of you, honey."

"I hope so." With that, her friend lifted her glass and said, "Let's toast to new beginnings."

Lia hoped she was talking about her own circumstances and not about her and Micah. Because sometimes there were no new beginnings. Or at least no retreading of old paths. And in this case, she had to believe it was for the best. Even if her heart might disagree.

CHAPTER SEVEN

A KNOCK SOUNDED on the door to Micah's office Monday afternoon. He'd already had a difficult weekend between meeting with his mom and going to see his dad the next day. His dad was a shadow of the strong, commanding man he'd once been. The change had come as a shock and made him realize that though he might not have agreed with the way they'd raised him, he'd been right to come home and try to make peace with the parts of his childhood that had been difficult. That included his parents.

"Come in."

The door opened, and Lia peeked in, a look of uncertainty on her face.

He motioned her inside. "Do you know?"

"Know what?" She slid into the room and perched on one of the chairs in front of his desk, looking like she might like to get up and take flight.

"Sassy, the baby who has pertussis, is being released today."

"That's great," she started, only to stop when he held up his hand.

"It's good that she's better, but there are a couple of reports that other area hospitals have seen some cases over the weekend. One of them is a neighbor of Sassy's family."

Her eyes closed before reopening. "God. I was hoping it was going to be confined to the two families who got together."

"So did I." He picked up a pencil and tapped the eraser end on a map on his desk. "The other cases don't appear to have any ties to the families. But there are always grocery stores or any number of places where a cough can cause an outbreak."

"If this gains speed…"

"I know. Which is why I think we need to prioritize getting some of these posters up. How busy are you today and tomorrow?"

"I have a surgery and a couple of consults to do tomorrow morning, but nothing urgent. I was going to head to the ER after that and pitch in where I could."

"Do you have time to talk about the design? You always did have a flair for putting things like that onto paper."

"Me?" Her voice squeaked in a way that made him smile.

She liked to sketch, and she was good. Micah remembered sitting beside her on the couch while she doodled on a pad. Sometimes the drawings were of things they'd seen that day. Sometimes they were musculature contained within the human body. And sometimes they were things as simple as the fire in the fireplace.

"Yes. You." He hesitated, not sure he should say anything about Thursday night. "It looked like you and Avery had fun at Gantry's."

"We did. Did you and your mom have a productive talk?"

He leaned back in his chair and looked at her. "I don't know about productive. But I think we made a little bit of progress. And I saw my dad."

"How did that go?"

"I'm not quite sure. But we'll see where it leads." He glanced at her. "Let's talk about making a mockup that we can take to Arnie. Can we work on that today?"

"Surely the hospital can hire someone for that part?"

Micah lifted his brows. "I'm sure they can, but all I envision is it taking forever to get all the parties to agree on something. By that time, a few cases could turn into hundreds."

If anyone knew about that, it was him. In Ghana, there hadn't been near the amount of bureaucracy that there was here, and yet it still took forever to get anything accomplished. "If you could sketch a couple cradling a baby with worried expressions on their faces, we can put together a slogan together. The sooner we get this down on paper, the sooner we can hang them around town."

Her features seemed to blanch. "I—I'm not good at drawing faces."

"I've seen some of your drawings, remember? They're really good. We wouldn't need a lot of detail, just kind of neutral features…you could depict worry through their posture, or by how they're huddled together."

She relaxed into her chair. "So just eyes, nose and mouth that could belong to anyone. I wouldn't have to make them distinctly different from each other."

"No." Was it weird that she was hung up on this particular part of the process? Well, maybe drawing faces was harder than it looked. "Just kind of like cartoon characters."

"Cartoon characters." She nodded as if thinking about something. "Actually, that's not a bad idea. If we could make it look like a comic strip, only on a much larger scale, it might attract the attention of adults and children alike."

"I like it." He grabbed a piece of paper and came around to the other side of the desk, sitting in the empty chair and putting the paper between them. "So can we work on it now?"

"You don't have anything else to do?"

"Infectious diseases are what they hired me for, so this needs to top my to-do list."

Her warm scent, probably carried on air currents from the climate control system, drifted over to him, reminding him of that kiss they'd shared. It was heady and made him wonder if having her here in his office with the door closed was such a good idea.

Of course it was. He was an adult. And he would act like it. No mooning over her. No looking for chances to touch her, like he'd done in the past.

Like he'd done at Gantry's?

He reached across her to get to his pencil cup, grabbing two pens and handing her one. Their fingers touched, and a frisson of electricity shot through him. He hadn't tried to touch her that time. It was an accident.

Ignore it. Ask a question. Anything to shift his attention back to the job at hand. "So what are we looking to convey?"

She made a humming sound and touched the top of the pen to her lip, using the pressure to click the mechanism that caused the ball point to emerge.

Micah swallowed, remembering how her teeth had captured that very same lip.

"We want to have a sense of urgency, right? People are getting sick and we want to somehow stop it." Her light brown eyes sought his.

He nodded. "Yes. So how do we do that?"

"Maybe we have a mother with an infant in her arms just as her husband or significant other comes into the room. She's holding the baby close and is looking at the man. We could use a dialogue box to show the baby coughing."

"Would there be actual dialogue between the couple?"

"I don't think so. We have a pretty diverse population here. If we could get the idea across using just the pictures of the cartoon—minimal words—it might be better."

He nodded, trying to think of a way to do that. "So we could have this couple with a sick baby in the first cartoon slide. The next one could be a hospital scene? With multiple couples holding babies, all of whom have the same 'cough' bubble above them."

"That's good. I like it." She turned a sheet of paper so it was horizontal and divided it into three sections. Quickly she sketched a cartoon couple in the first section, just their bodies and heads, and she actually drew them from the behind, so there were no faces at all in them, but you could clearly tell it was two adults with a baby between them. She penned a dialogue bubble above the infant with "Cough-cough" written in bold, jagged strokes. "How about this?"

It was perfect. There was an element of fear in the adults' posture, the merest hint of a nose on each, as their faces were turned slightly inward to look at each other. He'd known she could do it. "That's just how I envisioned it. Can you do the next one? The hospital scene?"

She touched the pen to her lip, tapping it a couple more times. His senses reacted all over again, remembering the slide of his lips across her mouth. How smooth it was. How warm and moist and…

Shaking himself from the memory, he forced himself to focus as her pen started scratching in the next box. Three couples were now seated, same perspective, except for one standing adult who faced them. This character wore a lab coat with what was clearly a stethoscope around his neck. The face was a simple oval, devoid of features or emotion. Three dialogue bubbles hovered over the scene this time, each with the same words in them. It was an ominous scene. Outside the hospital windows, there were dark clouds, and she used hash lines to shade the space to make it look gloomy.

"Yes. That's good, Lia. Very good."

When she looked at him this time, there was a sense of relief on her face. Surely she wasn't worried about him rejecting what she'd put on that page. And the fact that she could do it so quickly was exactly what he'd hoped for. "Are you sure?"

"I am. Absolutely." He nudged her with his shoulder. "This is why I didn't want the hospital to farm it out to a business. It would have taken forever. So the last square…"

"I have an idea. How about this?" She quickly drew the same three chairs, empty this time. There was an empty hypodermic needle in the top left corner. The view outside the hospital showed a couple walking down the sidewalk with a stroller—the top of a tiny head peeking out. The scene was idyllic with trees and fluffy clouds. There was a sense of well-being. Peace even. And no dialogue bubbles.

Across the top of the page she wrote,

Whooping cough
A not-so-silent killer
Save a baby's life
Get vaccinated

"We can put the hospital logo and a number for information. Or even for the CDC."

"Yes." He glanced at his watch. "Fifteen minutes. That's all it took. Hell, Lia, you are amazing."

"No. I'm not, really." She turned toward him. "It's not that great."

It was. And so was she. Her beautiful eyes were looking at him in that way she had of skimming quickly over his face before moving beyond it to dwell on other places, studying them intently. It had always made him feel as if she didn't really see him the way other women did: as in his physical appearance. Being valued for such a shallow thing had made him feel almost as invisible as he'd felt as a kid, only in a different way. Lia had never commented on his face. Except for that line in his cheek, which she'd loved to trail her fingers down.

She'd made him feel seen. Really seen. In a way no one else had.

His hand lying on the desk slid closer to hers before he pulled himself up short. What was he doing? That shared kiss had reminded him of all the things that had been good about their relationship. But when it had imploded…

Yeah. That had been bad. Really bad.

Not a good idea to let himself get drawn back in. He wasn't sure if what she'd said about Ghana was the entire truth or if she had commitment issues or what, but he really didn't want to push replay on whatever had happened at the end. So he did something to drag his attention back where it should be—on the cartoon she'd sketched.

"It is great, and I'm going to prove it to you." He pulled out his cell phone and dialed.

A minute later, Arnie answered.

"Hey, do you have time to look at something? It'll only take a minute."

"Sure. Where are you? Your office?"

"Yep, do you want us to run by with it?"

"Us?"

He glanced at Lia. "Dr. Costa made a mockup for the vaccine campaign we talked about last week."

"Good. That'll save me from having to get a committee together, if it's good. I'll run by your office. I'm on my way out anyway."

"See you in a few minutes, then."

He hung up, only to note that Lia's face was strained. "Are you okay?"

"Are you sure this is good enough to show him?"

"I promise I would have told you if it wasn't."

She looked down. "There aren't any actual faces."

Cocking his head, he looked at the drawing. "You know, I think it's better this way. Those images could represent anyone. Maybe a passerby will mentally superimpose their own image or the likeness of someone they know."

She quickly added a few things to the drawing: a dog on a leash in the last image. A crowd of people outside the window of the first scene, depicting how whooping cough could spread in gatherings.

By the time she was finished, a knock sounded at the door, followed by Arnie coming into the room. He came over to the desk and stood by Lia. "Is this it?"

"Y-yes."

She was nervous. And Lia was rarely nervous. She normally knew her own mind and was confident in her abilities.

Arnie stared down at the picture for a while. Then said, "This is excellent. From one ill child to three, and then along comes the vaccine and empties out the waiting room. I like the touch of showing a happy— and healthy—family walking outside the hospital." He picked it up and went over to the copier and made a duplicate. "I'm going to keep this one, if that's okay. Can you take these to a printer and have them printed, blowing a few into poster-size prints? We'll stamp them with the hospital logo and number and display the large ones here at home and distribute the others to various business. We'll also hang them in places where it's legal to do so."

"I'll need to clean it up a little before we do that," Lia murmured.

"No. I want it left just like this. There's no need to clean anything up. And I know the board will agree with me on this."

Micah smiled at her. "Do you believe me now?"

"I guess so."

Arnie leaned down and took one of the other sheets of paper, scribbling down a name. "This is who the hospital uses for printing materials. Do you think you can get this over there?" He glanced at his watch. "They're open for another hour or so. Order what you need."

"We'll take care of it." Micah glanced at her with raised brows, asking her the question. She answered with a nod.

With that, the hospital administrator opened the door again and thanked them before leaving as quickly as he'd arrived.

"If you can go with me, I actually have my new car, so I can drive this time."

She shrugged. "Well, I guess I don't have a choice, since Arnie made it pretty clear he wants these done immediately. And I do agree with him, it's just..."

"Just what?"

She shook her head. "Nothing. Just wish I had more time to perfect it."

"It'll be okay. You know Arnie better than I do. Would he truly let us print something—something that represents the hospital—if he didn't think it would stand up to scrutiny? I wish I'd had one of your prints in Ghana."

That last statement had slipped out before he could stop it. He'd meant it in a generic way. Right?

Because she'd made it clear back then—and now—that she wasn't interested in him on a personal level.

And that kiss?

He had no idea what that had been about. For her or for him.

Lia glanced over at him. "Thank you." The words

were spoken softly with a hint of meaning that he wasn't sure he understood. Or that he wanted to understand.

"If you're ready?" He grabbed a notebook from the back of his credenza. "Let's slide it in here to keep it from getting bent or damaged."

She handed him the drawing, and he tucked it inside the front cover. Then they moved out of the room and headed out of the hospital.

CHAPTER EIGHT

GORDY'S PRINTING WAS busier than she'd expected. There were four people ahead of them, and it was only thirty minutes until their six o'clock closing time. It must be because some folks were coming right after work.

"Did you find a place to live other than the hotel yet?"

"No. Not yet. But then again, it's been so busy I haven't really had a lot of time."

She thought for a second. "I know you and your parents aren't super close, but—"

"No. That wouldn't work."

He shut her down before she'd even finished saying what she'd been going to say. That maybe it would give him time to be with his dad. Especially since he admitted himself that life was extra busy.

As if realizing how short he'd sounded, he touched her hand. "Sorry. I know it would be a good thing, but my mom and dad... I think it would be hard on both sides. I don't want to put my mom in the middle, feeling like she needs to placate both of us. And my dad— well, let's just say he's not the man I remember, and I don't want to stress him out unnecessarily."

"Is he undergoing treatment?" One of the customers left, and the line moved forward.

"He just started. They're hoping for remission."

He'd said *they*. Surely Micah wanted remission for his dad as well.

Another customer slid out of line, going through the door. Okay, so this was moving quicker than she'd thought it would.

"How probable is that?"

"From what my mom said, there's about a thirty percent chance he'll achieve it."

She couldn't stop herself from looping her arm through his and squeezing it before forcing herself to let go. "I know I've said it before, but I'm really sorry. I can't imagine what that has to be like for your family, and since you're their only child, it makes it hard on you as well."

"Well, as their only child, it's why I came home."

Said in a way that let her know that his return had nothing to do with her. Not that she'd thought it had. She'd just been trying to sympathize with him.

It was their turn, so they moved to the front. Micah opened the notebook and pulled out her sketch. "We need some prints of these. About three poster-size and we need some flyer-size prints as well, but we need them in some kind of heavier paper that's impervious to water."

"We have weatherproof sheets that are about the thickness of cardstock. They're actually plastic, but we can print on them." The clerk was young, with straight dark hair that fell to his shoulders. He looked hip and artsy, a ring on his thumb boasting an ankh symbol.

His nails were painted black. A small name tag on his dark polo shirt read Curtis.

He was definitely different from the cowboy types that Nashville was famous for.

"Weatherproof," Micah said. "Sounds like what we need."

The guy took a look at the sketch. "Who drew this?"

"I did." Her heart was in her throat, wondering if he thought it was ridiculous.

He looked up. "I can't accept it like this."

Oh, God. He did think it was ridiculous. But before she could agree with him, he turned the paper toward her and rummaged through a drawerful of different kinds of pens before finally selecting one. "You really need to sign it. There are people out there who wouldn't think twice about ripping this design off and then claiming it as their own."

"Surely not."

"Hey," said Curtis. "People steal songs and lyrics all the time in this town—you think they wouldn't steal art?"

Art? Was he kidding?

Micah moved close enough to give her hand a squeeze. "Do you believe me now?"

She hadn't. Not really. Until this moment. She looked at her sketch, trying to see what they saw in it. But she just couldn't. She'd always liked to doodle as a kid and had gotten in trouble for doing that in school lots of times.

The young man held out a pen. "Even just your initials with today's date in the bottom right corner will do, but signing your name would be better."

She took the writing instrument and scribbled *L.*

Costa along with the year in small letters at the corner of the last scene. "Like this?"

"Yes, perfect." Curtis blew on the lettering for a second or two before finding a plastic sleeve and sliding the drawing inside it. "And I didn't know that whooping cough was making a comeback."

Micah spoke up. "It's always been here. We're just trying to make sure what's out there doesn't turn into an epidemic."

"Good. My wife is actually eight months pregnant." The guy grabbed a pad of paper. "So three posters and how many flyers?"

"Let's go with a hundred."

A hundred of her sketches were going to be floating around Nashville? It made her a little uncomfortable, but if it saved lives...

Curtis scribbled down their order, his ankh ring catching the light a couple of times. "If you ever need a job, we have a design team that would love to have you on it."

She laughed. Okay, well, that was unexpected. "Thank you, but I think I'm better suited to being a doctor."

"If you ever change your mind, let me know." He added up the costs. "Do you have a requisition from the hospital?"

"No," Micah said. "But if you call in the morning and ask to talk to Arnie Goff, he'll give you a number. He's the hospital administrator over at Saint Dolores."

"Ah, Saint Dolly's. I was born there. My wife and I were actually in the nursery at the same time."

Lia's eyes widened. "Well, that's a coincidence."

"We were both preemies, and the hospital has a kind

of reunion every year for us. We started dating in high school. Went to prom together."

"I've heard of those reunions. That's wonderful." What a romantic way to meet your future spouse. "Are you planning to have your baby at Saint Dolly's?"

"Yes, but we'll hopefully not wind up in the preemie ward."

"Well, I hope everything goes well for all of you."

"Thanks." He touched the plastic sleeve containing her sketch. "I hope everything goes well with this. And I'll check with our doctor to make sure we don't need a booster."

"That's great." Lia fished in her purse and found one of her cards and scribbled her number on the back. "Let me know if there's anything I can do. I'm not in obstetrics, so definitely check with your doctor, but if you have any questions, please don't hesitate to call." She wasn't sure why she'd done that. It was rare that she ever gave out her personal cell phone number, but there was just something about the kid she liked. His love for his wife and future baby were obvious.

"Wow, thanks. I will. Jenny is a little nervous about things. This is our first. We got married last year."

Fortunately there was no one else waiting behind them. "Well, the best of luck to both of you."

"Thanks. To you both as well."

Did he think they were a couple? Surely not.

Micah's quick grin said otherwise, making her face heat like molten lava. He slashed, she burned. *Dio*, Avery really was right. "When do you think the printing can be done once you get Mr. Goff's approval?"

"It should be done in a couple of days. So maybe check back on Wednesday?"

"We'll be here." With that, Micah turned away from the desk and headed toward the door.

He'd said *we* as if it were a given that they'd arrive back here together. Lia wasn't so sure that was a good idea. But she'd address that later. If needed, she'd make sure she had something else scheduled. Because being with him today had really rattled her. Especially when she'd been drawing that sketch, feeling his presence next to her. Feeling his eyes on her as her pen moved over that sheet of paper. It had been unnerving.

And exhilarating. In a way she hadn't felt in a long time. Maybe even since they'd been together.

They walked over to the paid parking garage, Lia pulling her coat around her against the nippy temperatures. Micah showed the attendant their all-day pass as they walked by him. "You know there's free parking not far from here."

"I know, but this was faster, and since I wanted to make it to the shop before it closed, it seemed the best solution. And it's where I used to park when I was in this part of town."

"I remember that from when we were in school."

"Yes, we spent a little bit of time kissing in this garage."

Her face heated yet again. Yes, they had.

They moved into the building and headed toward the back. Even in the paid garage, it had been hard to find a spot, so Lia knew he was right in saying this had been the best option.

They found his car in one of the darker areas, and Micah pressed the mechanism to unlock the vehicle. Going around to the passenger side, she got in, the scents of leather and Micah surrounding her as she sank into the comfortable seat and clicked her belt.

Dio, it was like days gone by.

Micah got into the driver's seat and started the car, waiting for it to warm up for a minute or so before turning the heat on. She turned her vents toward her.

"Cold?"

"It's a little chilly out there." She glanced at him. "You probably should have worn something heavier."

"I actually enjoy the cold after spending some hot days in Ghana."

"What was it like?" She'd been afraid to go, but that didn't mean she wasn't curious.

"The people were wonderful, but it had its challenges, just like every place." He sat back in his seat and turned his torso to look at her. "Seasons of the year were measured more by dry or rainy rather than temperatures, but it was rare for it to drop below the mid-seventies, and hundred-degree days were not unusual."

A shiver went through her, whether from the thirty-degree weather and wind outside today or from being in a warm car with Micah's low voice washing over her. She could listen to the man forever.

"Wow. Nashville gets hot, but we always know there are cooler days coming. Not sure how I would have handled the constant heat."

"Your body actually adjusts after a while. And when there's so much need around you, it's easier to focus on what's important."

Which made her reasons for not going seem purely selfish.

"I can imagine. How hard was it coming back?"

He gave a half shrug. "I needed to. So I did."

The vehicle was warming up, so Lia allowed herself to relax into the seat. "I hope your father's doctors are able to help him."

"It feels kind of weird to say this, but so do I."

"Weird?"

He frowned. "Weird isn't really the right word. Maybe hypocritical would be better. My mom wrote while I was in Ghana, but...well, there are still some problems between us. So I don't feel I have the right to wish one way or the other."

"What was it you disagreed on?"

"Disagreed?"

Maybe that wasn't the right word. "You said you didn't see eye to eye with them, so I just thought..."

"Ah, I see. It wasn't anything specific. We were just never close."

"Maybe now's the time to change some of that?" Lia had felt awful about not being honest with Micah back then. But she'd honestly believed it was the right thing to do at the time. And she couldn't go back and undo anything that had happened. She couldn't undo the hurt. For either of them.

Maybe that's how Micah felt. Like it wasn't possible to undo anything that had happened with his parents. So why bother trying?

Except Lia did want to make things right with him. Not to have a relationship again—she had killed her chances of that. But maybe she could at least let him know that she was sorry. Sorry for hurting him. Sorry for letting things between them go as far as they had before breaking it off.

She took a deep breath. "Hey. I really am sorry for the way things ended between us. I should have stuck around and talked things through a little more instead of taking off like I did. I just realized at that moment that I couldn't be in a relationship. Not with you. Not with anyone else. It had nothing to do with you personally. I really did care about you."

"Really?" His eyes hardened. "It was kind of hard to tell that day."

"I know. I thought it was better to make the break quickly, that it would hurt less. And I knew how much you wanted to work with Doctors Without Borders."

"It didn't. Hurt less." A muscle worked in his jaw, and there was no sign of that sexy crease he sported. "I went out and got drunk that night."

A swift pain went through her heart. She'd known she'd hurt him, but to picture him alone in a bar hunched over drink after drink… She reached for his arm, her fingers curling around it, willing him to feel how sincere her apology was. "I didn't know, Micah. I'm so, so sorry."

He gave a rough laugh. "The funniest thing was to get back here and find out that I'd somehow landed in the same hospital as my ex. Now that was kind of a kick in the teeth from the universe."

"Maybe this is *our* chance to make things right."

"Make things right?"

"Yes. To start off fresh. Not as a couple. But maybe as friends."

He stared at her. "You think it's possible for you and me to ever be friends?"

His words struck a nerve in her. She'd been trying to reach out to him, and to have him bat her words away like they meant nothing… A spike of anger went through her, and she found her fingers tightening on his arm in response. "Are you saying it's not possible?"

His palm cupped her nape, the heat from his skin going through her like an inferno. "Are you saying it is?"

She swallowed, her teeth grabbing at her bottom lip to stop it from trembling. "I—I want to try."

His fingers tunneled into her hair, and a shiver went through her. Maybe he was right. Maybe it wasn't possible, because what she felt right now wasn't remotely close to anything she would define as friendship.

"Yeah?" The gray of his eyes was flecked with much darker colors that shifted with his every mood. How could she ever have not recognized this man when he reappeared in her life? He was like no one else she'd ever met. He wasn't defined by the size of his nose or the conformation of his cheeks, the slope of his forehead or anything that supposedly distinguished one face from another. The difference was there, in his very being.

Suddenly, friendship or no, she wanted him to kiss her. Wanted to feel again the press of his mouth to hers. Maybe that's what all this talk about making things right was really about. Maybe it had nothing to do with righting past wrongs and was solely about what Micah made her feel. Made her want.

So she tipped her chin up with an air of defiance. "Yeah. I do."

One corner of his mouth tilted, and there went that glorious crease. She realized she'd been waiting to see it aimed at her for the last couple of hours. And here it was.

"Well, in that case." He slowly reeled her in, his gaze fastened on her lips.

Dio nei cieli. It was going to happen.

Her body flared to life as that first touch came. And come it did. This was no hesitant, questioning press. No waiting to see how she was going to react. This was war—a mind-blowing battle of one mouth against another. And she was up to the challenge, turning her head so that she could kiss him back, her hands going to his shoulders and dragging herself against him. If she could have climbed in his lap in that moment, she would have, but there was the gearshift and the whole two-separate-seats thing going on.

She opened her mouth as if anticipating exactly what he wanted and wasn't disappointed when his tongue swept in and took her by storm. A shivery need began thrumming through her, her nipples coming to hard peaks that cried out for his touch.

Her palms slid up and curled around his nape, the strands of his hair tickling across the backs of her hands as his head moved in time with what was happening inside her mouth.

A whimper erupted from her throat. She needed more. So much more.

Somehow she dragged her mouth from his and whispered his name.

"Yeah. I know."

She toyed with his hair, fingertips dragging across his skin, and he drew in several deep breaths. "If we don't stop now…"

This was the moment of truth. Did she venture down this path? Or did she retreat and head back to her own corner?

But, *Dio*, she wanted him. So, so badly. And suddenly she knew what she was going to say.

"Come back to my place."

He didn't pull away from her, but he did lean back a little to look into her face. "Are you sure?"

"No. But I know it's what I want right now."

"Hell, Lia." His eyes closed as if thinking it through. And when they opened again, there was a dark intensity in them that gave her her answer. Without a word, he untangled her arms from his neck, put the car in Reverse and pulled out of the parking spot.

He sent her a hard grin that said he was feeling the same thing she was. "In that case, you need to tell me where you live."

CHAPTER NINE

MICAH MADE THE trip to her apartment by darting through the streets and finding the paths with the fewest traffic lights. He hadn't forgotten how to navigate through this city.

Would he remember how to navigate her body with just as much ease?

Somehow she knew he would. Her hands wound together in her lap, gripping each other for support as she waited for him to make his way to the other side of town.

Why hadn't she suggested his hotel? It was closer.

Maybe because she needed to be on her own turf. To be able to keep herself rooted to reality and not go flitting off into some kind of fantasyland.

Wasn't that where she was already? A fantasyland that she'd never dreamed she could visit again.

His hand came off the gearshift and covered hers. "You okay?"

No, she wasn't, but there was no way he could know it was because she was frantic to arrive at their destination. So she wove her fingers of her left hand through his. "Yes. I just never realized how long this drive was before."

His teeth flashed. "I agree."

Then they were less than a mile away. "Turn left at this corner. The complex is about three blocks down on the right. You can park in my space. Three oh one."

Micah swung into the apartment building and followed her directions to the parking garage. It took her eyes a moment to adjust from the sun outside to the lights inside the structure, but her space was just around the corner. He carried her hand to the gear lever and sat it there for a minute, making her shiver as together they shifted the car into first. His thumb trailed across the side of her hand as he looked at her again. "Are you sure, Lia? Very, very sure?"

"Yes." She hoped he was asking about the sex and not just about parking in her space before realizing what a ridiculous thought that was. Of course it was about the sex.

He leaned over and kissed her again, and this time his mouth was softer, exploring her on a level that made her insides knot and her heart pound. She didn't want to leave this car, but she was pretty sure her building had cameras inside the parking area, so she reached over and clicked the door release, the sound cracking through the intimate space.

When he looked at her, she attempted a smile. "Cameras."

"Ah. I thought for a second you might be running away."

Was that a reference to the way she'd left at graduation? But when she glanced at his face, she found it relaxed and sexy. There were no lines of tension that she could see.

"No. I just don't want the security people to get an eyeful." She gave a nervous laugh.

He got out of his door and made it to her side before she'd had a chance to swing her legs out. He reached for her hand and tugged her up and out of the car, one side of her jacket sliding down her arm. He reached for it, pulling it back into place. "Still cold?"

"No, not anymore."

She realized it was true. And although the parking garage was protected, she was pretty sure the warmth was left over from their earlier kisses more than from her coat.

He kept her hand, using his fob to lock the doors of his car. "There's an elevator?"

The way he said it made her swallow. "Cameras," she murmured.

That made him laugh, a sound that rumbled through her belly and drew a smile to her own lips.

"Oh, sorry! You weren't thinking in those terms."

He leaned down close to her ear. "You know I was. Remind me to get a place with no cameras. I'll take my chances."

He didn't elaborate, but she could pretty well imagine what he was willing to take his chances with. And right now, she agreed with him. Sex in an elevator with him would be better than any mile-high club ever invented.

They made it up the elevator without any incidents other than one very hot kiss, his body crowding hers against the wall and leaving her breathless. Then they were on her floor. She led him around the corner of the octagonal building and found her door. She unlocked both the locks and pushed it open. Then she heard a sound. *Oh, no.*

She put her hand against Micah's hip and attempted to push at him. "Wait behind me for a second."

He didn't budge. "Excuse me?"

"I don't want you getting hurt."

She thought she spied a blur of movement out of the corner of her eye. She quickly stepped in front of Micah, reaching for the hallway light.

"What the hell…?" His voice didn't sound any too pleased. But, dammit, she wasn't about to let anything spoil his mood. Or hers.

The light came on, and Lia spied her cat standing just to the side of them. Her tail was fluffed up in alarm. She took a step forward. "It's just me, girl."

"A cat? You're saving me from a cat?"

Samantha spotted him just about the time he asked his question. She stalked toward him, legs stiff, head pushed forward in a way that said she was nervous. It wasn't that Sam was mean. But she was scared of men and had been known to scratch first and ask questions later. The story from the shelter was that she'd been abused by some teenaged boys when she was a kitten. It had made her wary and untrusting.

Lia hadn't been abused, but her prosopagnosia had made her wary as well, so when she'd met the cat—soon after her breakup with Micah—they'd hit it off. Anytime she tried to leave the shelter's cat enclosure, Sam had clung to her leg, looking up at her with huge green eyes, her mouth opening and closing in a silent meow that was more like a plea. She hadn't been able to leave the young feline behind.

"She's not too sure about men."

He laughed, his warm breath washing over Lia's neck and sending Sam scurrying back a couple of paces.

"And you suggested we come back to your place? Were we supposed to wind up in your bedroom or were you more interested in sending me to my doom?"

Rather than changing his mind or suggesting they go elsewhere, though, he stepped out from behind Lia and squatted down on his haunches. He held his hand out and murmured to the cat.

"No, don't—"

"Shh." He kept his arm where it was, and Sam inched forward, her long white fur standing up. "Come here, girl. I promise I'm good."

Yes, he was. And right now, all she wanted to do was grab him, sneak past her temperamental cat and close themselves in a bedroom to remind herself of just how good the man was. Although she remembered just about every minute of the time they'd spent together in the past.

Sam came forward another step as Micah continued to croon to her. His voice was as sweet as any country tune.

The cat came within clawing distance, and Lia tensed. But she didn't scratch. Instead, her neck stretched as far as nature would allow, and she sniffed Micah's fingers, then took another step forward. And another. And then the most remarkable thing happened. Samantha—man hater that she was—put her cheek against Micah's palm and purred.

"*Dio mio*, she never does this. Not with men."

He glanced up. "Had lots of men over here?"

"No, no of course not. That's not what I meant. It's more that the shelter told me she was hurt by guys in the past."

Micah slid his palm over Sam's head and stroked along her back. "Maybe she's checking out her competition."

"Competition?"

"For your affections." He turned to look at the cat. "Looks like she doesn't feel too threatened in that regard."

And she shouldn't be. Micah wasn't here to win back her affections. He was here because things had gotten hot and steamy in his car. And she'd gotten enough of her senses back to be able to back out of anything happening. But she found she didn't want to. She wanted this night with Micah. She wasn't sure why. Maybe for the closure they hadn't gotten or maybe just to spend the night with someone who knew how to please her physically. She wasn't sure. But in the end, it didn't matter. She wasn't changing her mind.

"Micah…"

He glanced up, hand stopping midstroke. "Hmm?"

She licked her lips, ending it with her teeth pushing down on the corner of the lower one. "I'd like a little of what she's getting."

"Would you now?" He climbed to his feet, now ignoring the cat, who was winding herself around his legs and asking for more. "And is that all you want? A little petting?"

She wrapped her arms around his waist and pressed up against him. "No. And she might not be jealous, but maybe I am."

His hands pressed against her upper back, flattening her breasts against his chest before sliding down to just below her hips. His legs were slightly splayed, and when he applied just a bit of pressure, she felt everything. A hardness against her belly. A heat that couldn't be hidden even through layers of clothing.

He leaned down. "I kind of like you being jealous. Even if the other female involved is a cat." The words were said against her cheek, the syllables warming her skin and causing all kinds of yummy sensations to begin flashing in the lower part of her abdomen.

If her being jealous caused that kind of reaction from him, then she kind of liked it, too. "I'm just glad Sam didn't leave you with a present of another kind."

"Me, too. But sometimes old hurts fade and leave you able to trust again."

Something about the way he said that made a little niggle of worry appear in her stomach. Nothing major, just the flutter of butterfly wings. But then again, maybe those butterflies were signaling something entirely different. Maybe it was due to how he was making her feel with his nose sliding along the line of her jaw, the nibble of his teeth as he came up and touched those pearly whites to her lower lip. It was heavenly and soon pushed everything else to the side as she kissed him.

"Let's not talk about Sam anymore."

His hands slid into the hair on either side of her face, thumbs brushing the bones of her cheeks. "Kind of hard when she's down there reminding me of her presence."

His hips nudged her again, sending her thoughts somewhere else entirely.

"I'd like to be down there reminding you of my presence."

His thumbs stopped all movement. Then in a rush, he swept her up in his arms, managing to somehow maneuver past Sam, who thankfully hadn't taken issue with his sudden movement. "Bedroom?"

"There's only one. Straight ahead."

He strode past her living room and into the tiny hallway, moving into the bedroom and using his foot to close the door and exclude Samantha.

"She's not going to like that," Lia said with a laugh.

"Maybe not, but I kind of want you all to myself." He grinned. "And believe me, I need no reminders of your presence."

She reached up to touch that crease in his cheek as he moved over toward the bed.

His brows were up. "Should I play nice? Or naughty?"

"I think I'll need more information." Although she didn't, really. Naughty had always involved some kind of sexy play. And nice…well, that had been all about touch. And caring. And showing her exactly how much he loved her.

Loved her…

No. She didn't want that. Wasn't sure she could bear the way they'd made love during those times. So before he could answer, she blurted out, "I'll choose naughty."

Naughty she could handle. Naughty involved catching her up in a web of sensuality that was normally fast and hot and flamed her until she was sure she'd turn to a pile of ash.

He leaned down and caught her mouth in a hard kiss. "You may be sorry you asked for that."

"Never." She'd never been sorry for anything that they'd done together. She just wasn't sure she could rewind the clock to some of those days.

He kept kissing her until suddenly the bottom fell out. Or rather, she fell, hitting the bed with a soft *oomph* that left her dazed for a second or two before she gathered her senses and scrambled to her knees. "Hey!"

"Change your mind on naughty?"

"No." She could take whatever he dished out.

He leaned down and planted his hands on either side of her hips, his lips within inches of her own. "Good. I need a scarf. Where do you keep them now?"

She swallowed, memories coming back in a flood that almost overwhelmed her. *Dio*, they'd had so much fun back then.

This is not the past, Lia. Just enjoy the present for what it is.

She swung her feet over the edge of the bed and scooted forward, forcing him to stand up straight. "No scarves. Not just yet." With that she hooked her legs around the backs of his knees and crossed her ankles to keep him from moving away. "I think you need a little reminder of my presence."

"Lia..." His voice held an edge of warning that made her laugh.

Her bed was a four-poster monstrosity that she'd regretted getting because of how high the mattresses sat on it. Until right at this moment.

"If it's okay for you to restrain me, then I think turnabout should be fair play, don't you agree?"

She reached for his belt and unbuckled it, sliding it out of the loops with a hiss. "Should your hands be behind your back for this?" She murmured the words aloud, as if talking to herself, while coiling the belt and laying it beside her on the bed. She tightened her legs as if getting his attention. "What do you think, Micah. How still can you be?"

His Adam's apple dipped as he swallowed. "Pretty damned still."

"Good to know." She plucked at the button of his

trousers, sliding her hand along the front of his closed zipper. The air hissed between his teeth as she found the bulge hidden behind it. "Just trying to see if you can keep your word."

Her fingers trailed back up the way she'd come, and his eyes closed, his jaw tight. His hands fisted at his sides as if trying to hold himself together.

This time she didn't pluck. She undid the button and slid the zipper down in a smooth motion that made something at her center clench. She wasn't so sure about the sex play all of a sudden. Wasn't sure she didn't just want him to lay her down and take her.

But, *Dio*, she didn't want this to end. If he could stand the snail's pace, then so could she.

Hooking her fingers into his waistband, she slowly slid it down his hips until his slacks were perched on the muscles of his thighs. He had on black briefs, the hard ridge noticeable against the front of them. And there was a convenient opening right here. She slid her hand into the space and found warm, silky-smooth skin that was so welcome, so familiar that it made her teeth clench for a second. How many times had he used this to bring them both pleasure? How many times had she brought pleasure to him by what she was about to do?

No thinking about the past.

She freed him, glancing up to find his face was a hard, tight mask that made her frown, until she realized he really was trying to not come apart.

Same here, Micah. She wouldn't make him suffer too long, but she just couldn't resist.

"No hands, okay?"

He didn't answer but gave her a quick nod of assent, arms held rigidly at his sides.

They'd done this so many times before, but right now, everything was new with the wonder of rediscovery.

She blew warm air over him, watching as a shudder rolled through his body. Yes. She remembered this.

Giving him little warning, she engulfed him in a smooth motion, the groan coming from above her fueling her need to drive him crazy. He wasn't supposed to use his hands, but she was allowed to use hers, so she slid them around his hips until she reached his ass and hauled him closer.

"Hell, Lia…"

He pulled free, watching her as she sat up. Then before she could do or say anything else, he'd flipped her onto her back, her head on the pillows. Then he stripped the rest of his clothes and donned a condom before climbing onto the bed with her.

He undressed her, pressing his lips to her skin as he revealed each part of her. Suddenly "naughty" was forgotten as his mouth found hers and his kisses grew urgent with need. He parted her legs and held himself at her entrance for several breathtaking seconds, ignoring the squirming of her body.

"Oh, Micah…"

He drove inside her with an intensity that pushed the air from her lungs. He paused, eyes closed, before cupping her head, his lids parting as he stared into her eyes. And what she saw there…

Need. Want. And some sort of longing that made her want to weep. Because she felt all those things, too. But she couldn't. Not now. Not when it was too late to go back.

So before she could get trapped in all those feelings and emotions, she reversed their positions until she was straddling his hips, engulfing him with her body the same way she'd done with her mouth. She moved, letting herself relish how it felt to be stretched and filled again. To take from him and to give back again and again. This time it was Lia who shut her eyes, focusing on the physical joining and praying she could evade anything that involved her heart or her head.

Hands gripped her waist, supporting her rise and fall and guiding the speed to match his need and hers. Leaning forward, she kissed his shoulder, dragging her teeth along his warm skin as if she couldn't get enough of him, and in reality she couldn't. She'd never been able to get her fill of this man.

Her movements grew quicker as she reached a set of rapids that carried her along, trying to remember to breathe as the ride grew wilder.

Micah's eyes were no longer on hers; instead it was as if he was focused on moving toward a goal that he didn't quite want to reach.

His name echoed in her head as she stared at his features, trying to distinguish what it was in his face that made him Micah. But all she could see was the blond hair that fell across his forehead, the hands with those long, talented fingers. His body with its strong arms and shoulders and taut, muscular abdomen. His scent. His voice. The unique gray of his eyes.

Those were the things that made him who he was in her eyes. And she wouldn't trade that for whatever it was that people saw in someone's face that made up good looks. Because what Micah had went far beyond any of that surface adornment of a straight nose or high cheekbones.

She sat up, still moving, and linked her hands with

his, carrying them to the bed beside his head as she continued to move. A wave of sensuality swept over her as she looked at their joined fingers.

Micah chose that moment to open his eyes and look at her. And that was all it took. Her hips bucked wildly as a wave of need rushed through her, propelling her to a point beyond what she could see.

"Lia...oh, hell...yes!" He tugged his hands from hers and gripped her hips, holding her hard against him as he strained up into her. It was a picture she couldn't get out of her mind, of Micah pouring himself into her. Because he had, in a way that went far beyond sex and flowed into the very parts she'd tried so hard not to involve.

Her head.

And, *Dio*, her heart.

CHAPTER TEN

MICAH CAME TO with a sense of disorientation. It was dark, and he wasn't sure where he was.

The hotel? No, this bed was different. Softer. And...

Okay, his body definitely felt spent and heavy, as if he couldn't move. Or maybe it was that he didn't want to move.

Something tickled his face, like someone drawing a feather duster over his cheek.

And then he heard it. A low rumble that immediately identified itself.

A cat.

Then everything came rushing back to him. This was Lia's house. And what they'd done last night...

Was beyond anything he'd ever experienced.

A cold nose pushed against his chin, and he smiled. Hated men, did she?

Not so much. He reached his hand up to pet her, his hand skimming along her back and curling around her tail. He sensed more than saw a dark figure curled up at the head of the bed.

He sat up. "Lia?" A moment of panic came over him. Had he hurt her somehow? They'd made love several times last night.

Moving over to where she sat, he tipped her chin up. "Are you okay?"

She nodded. "Just surprised it happened, is all."

Just surprised it happened. Well, hell, that pretty much mirrored his own thoughts, since he hadn't even known where he was when he sat up. "Me, too. And I'm sorry, but I can't quite bring myself to regret it, though."

"Me, either." She smiled. "And I can't get over the change in Samantha. It's amazing."

"Would you rather she woke me up in a different way?"

"No."

His smile was slow when it came, a sense of lethargic well-being that washed over him in a warm stream. "Would you rather I woke *you* up in a different way?" He glanced at the clock and saw that it was just after five. The sun hadn't come up yet, but it soon would, and it would more than likely chase away the magic of last night.

"I don't think Sam is going to let us go back to sleep. Sorry, but I had to let her in. She was meowing and sticking her feet under the door, and I was afraid she was going to wake you up. So I let her in. And she woke you up anyway."

"It's okay. And who said anything about sleep?" If he pushed in this direction, maybe his mind would stay away from some dangerous thoughts that were rolling around in it like boulders.

"But Sam…"

He climbed out of bed. "I bet we could sneak away and have a nice hot shower. And some alone time. Until one of us has to get dressed and be somewhere."

"Well, I don't have to be anywhere until eight."

"Same here. So that leaves us plenty of time."

"I can't promise Sam won't cause a ruckus outside the door."

He laughed. "I can't promise that you won't cause a ruckus *inside* the door."

"Me?" She punched his arm. "I seem to remember you making a whole lot more noise than I did."

"Did I? I don't remember it that way." He got out of bed and swung her up in his arms like he had at the beginning of the night. It seemed fitting they should end it the same way they'd started it. "So let's see who causes more commotion this time."

With that, he carried her into the bathroom and shut them inside.

Hell, he was exhausted. This was the second night after leaving Lia's apartment that he'd been kept awake by memories of what they'd done. He'd tossed and turned, trying to turn off his damned brain.

It hadn't worked. And Lia hadn't gone out of her way to bump into him at the hospital. Then again, he'd pretty much stuck to his own wing, too, which was one floor above hers. Glancing at the numbers he'd gotten from neighboring hospitals of suspected pertussis cases, he was not pleased. A fourth hospital had reported a case just this morning. A one-year-old girl was in critical condition with the illness.

He couldn't put it off any longer. He needed to call Lia and see when she could hang flyers with him. He picked up the phone. But first he'd call the print shop and see where they were on the flyers.

What was the guy's name who'd waited on them? Curtis, right?

A voice answered, but it was a woman. "Hi. This is Dr. Corday from Saint Dolores. We ordered some posters and flyers two days ago. Do you know if they're in? We ordered them from someone named Curtis, if he's there."

"Your order is in, but Curtis isn't. There was actually a family emergency with his wife, and he's just left to take her to the hospital."

Hadn't he said his wife was pregnant?

"Do you know which hospital?"

The woman's voice came back through. "Why, I think it was yours. It's the closest one to where he lives. And he had a card that one of your doctors had given to him. He called the number on it just as he was going out the door, so I don't know if he ever reached her."

"I'll check. And I'll be by to pick up that order a little later today."

"Okay. Please tell Curtis to call us if he needs anything."

"I will." When he hung up, he called Lia's number, only to have it go straight to voice mail. Damn. Had Curtis even been able to reach her?

Getting up, he headed out of his office. He would head downstairs and see if she was there. He knew he'd have to talk to her sooner or later, so maybe it would be easier if it was when other people were around. Just as he reached the door to the stairwell, his phone buzzed. Looking down at it, he saw that it was Lia. "Hey, I just tried to call you."

"I saw. I'm actually down here with Curtis Matthews from the print shop."

"Good. He did reach you, then."

There was a pause. "You knew he was trying to get a hold of me?"

"I called the shop to see if the order was ready, and the woman there said he was on the way to the hospital with his wife. I also called Douglas Memorial on the other side of town, and they've had a case of pertussis."

"Oh, God."

"What?"

"Curtis's wife. She's here, and she has a bad cough. I was hoping the illness wasn't spreading."

He rattled off a few curse words in his head. "It seems to be the case. She's not vaccinated."

"No. She's not. She and Curtis thought it was no longer a threat, remember? I was just going to ask you to come and look at her."

"I was already on my way down. I'll be there in a minute."

He hung up and took the stairs two at a time before bursting through the door at the bottom.

Lia had recognized Curtis by the ankh ring he wore and by his black nail polish, although she'd already known he was coming by his frantic phone call. For all of Curtis's gothness, his wife was the opposite. She had soft, curly blond hair and had paired white skinny jeans with a loose white top that skimmed her pregnant belly. Her nail polish, unlike her husband's, was pink. They said opposites attracted, and this was one couple that she could definitely see that in. Except they were both really nice and obviously crazy about each other. Curtis sat next to the exam table and was constantly in contact with his wife via touch. Lia remembered a time when she and Micah were the same way when they were outside their med school classes.

Two nights ago, they'd been the same. She'd woken up in a dark room and realized that Micah's arm was around her. She'd flat-out panicked, then realized she could hear Sam meowing outside the bedroom door. It was the perfect excuse to let her in and then crawl back in bed and watch him sleep.

The softness she saw as he lay there—one hand draped over his belly, his muscles loose and relaxed—was a sharp contrast to the commanding man she knew at the hospital and from med school.

She headed back into the exam room when she heard some hard coughing. Curtis looked worried. "Can she bring on contractions? She's feeling something going on in her stomach."

"It's unlikely, but I've got a call in for the obstetrician. It's just going to be a few minutes because she's in the middle of a delivery. I know you said this is your first baby, correct?"

"It is." Jenny was sitting up, blowing in and out. "I should have gotten the vaccine, but I was going to do everything natural. He wanted to come to Saint Dolly's for the delivery, but I wanted to have a home water birth with just Curtis there. We were still in discussions about it." A smile played on her face as she glanced at her husband.

A little alarm bell went off. "Have you been in touch with a midwife or a doula?"

Curtis spoke up. "We always meant to, but we're both so busy with our jobs and work different schedules, so we just haven't yet. And our families don't approve of home births, which is why I wanted to come to the hospital."

That was hard. Lia's parents had always been so supportive of her, outside of her dad really pressing her to get a system together for recognizing people. But once she hit adulthood, her dad had started wearing a bright green crocheted bracelet, a counterpart for his wife's pink one. A wave of overwhelming emotion had swamped her when he'd showed up at her graduation ceremony with it on. She'd cried. Then her mom had cried with her. Her dad had remained stoic, but she was pretty sure she saw moisture in his eyes as he'd hugged her and whispered, "Congratulations, *figlia*. I'm so proud of you."

A knock at the door sounded, and then Micah came into the room. He donned a mask and gloved up. "Hi, Curtis. It's nice to see you again, although not so much under these circumstances."

"I know. Your order is in, by the way."

His eyes crinkled above the mask. "I know. I called the shop and found that you had come to visit us here at the hospital, rather than the other way around."

"Not by choice."

Micah pulled a chair up. "So tell me what's going on?"

He didn't ask Lia, but she wouldn't have expected him to. It was good for him to hear it from Curtis and Jenny.

They gave him a quick rundown with Jenny ending the story by saying Curtis had come home talking about whooping cough going around. "I've had a bad cough for about a week and started to get worried that I could make the baby sick."

This time Micah did look at her. "Did you do a nasal swab?"

"I did it a few minutes ago and sent it down to the lab."

"Good." He turned back to Jenny. "Do you know if you were exposed to anyone with a cough?"

"I make custom cakes at a bakery for parties. There are always people milling around, so I don't know. I've never thought much of someone coughing."

He nodded. "Could you get a list together of people who came in to order cakes?"

She started to answer then stopped when a set of racking coughs went through her. She held her hand to her belly until she was done. Lia handed her a bottle of water, which the patient drank from. "I can get a list, but we don't really write on the order forms if the person called or came in in person."

"I can understand that. Any kind of list will help, because we can check it against people who have come in complaining of a cough."

"I'll call them right now and ask them to text over a list. From how far back?"

Micah frowned as if thinking. "About three weeks. It's not contagious after that period of time. We won't do anything with it until we know for sure that you have it."

"Okay."

He gave her a smile. "Thanks. It'll take a few hours to get the results back. Are you two okay hanging around at the hospital in one of the isolation rooms until then? We can make sure you get something to eat and drink. If the results come back negative for both of you, then you'll be free to go. But we recommend you both get vaccinated, since we're seeing an increase in cases all over the city. The disease isn't as bad for adults, but for babies...let's just say it's bad news."

"Can I be vaccinated this late in the pregnancy?"

"Yes, although we normally recommend it be done sooner. But you'll pass the antibodies to your baby, and it will help protect him or her for the first two months of their life. At which time they can be vaccinated. We had a close call with a baby here at the hospital. She ended up living, but it was touch and go for a while."

Jenny looked at her husband with brows lifted. "I want to get it. For the baby's sake."

"I will, too. I don't think I've had one since I was a kid."

"Great. If you could help spread the word, it would be much appreciated." Micah's glance included both of them.

Curtis nodded. "After you came in, I told my boss what had happened, and he said we can put a flyer up at the print shop."

"And I'll ask the bakery if it's okay. They're kind of stinky about anything that would make people nervous or anxious, but this is important."

"Yes, it is. Thank you both."

Watching Micah interact with the young couple made a sense of admiration swell up in her. She bet he'd done great work in Ghana with his trachoma campaign.

Lia motioned to the door. "If you'll both come with me, I'll show you to a room that's a little more comfortable with this one. And I'll run to the cafeteria and get you both something to eat while you wait on the ob-gyn to get done with her delivery."

"Thank you."

She led them down the hallway to a small private

waiting room that had eight chairs. They normally used the room for family groups that were waiting for news of relatives who were in serious or critical condition. "Don't be alarmed, but I'm going to put a sign on the door stating that this is an isolation room and that it's only to be entered by people who are gowned and masked. Just until we know for sure."

Lia picked up one of the nearby red-framed signs and wrote Curtis and Jenny's names on it along with the date and time. When she was done, she put tape on it and affixed it to the outside of the door. "Now, Micah and I are going to see if we can find something for you to eat. What sounds good?"

Jenny shrugged. "Maybe just some soup and crackers. My stomach is kind of in knots."

"I totally understand. Do you want some juice to go with it?"

"Some apple if they have it."

Micah had grabbed a piece of paper and was scribbling down their order. Or at least that's what she thought he was doing.

"Curtis?"

"I don't know that I can eat."

Lia patted him on the arm. "I know, but it's best to keep your strength up for your wife and baby's sakes."

"Okay, just a sandwich and chips, then. Maybe chicken of some kind. And a cola."

"Great. We won't be long."

She and Micah went out of the room, making sure the door was all the way shut. "Thanks for coming down," she said. "What do you recommend we do?"

"Exactly what you're already doing. Did they come in a side door like Sassy and her family?"

"Yes. Thank goodness Curtis thought to call and didn't just walk into the ER with her. I'm hoping it's not pertussis."

"So am I."

Although whooping cough didn't normally cause complications during pregnancy, there was always the danger of giving birth with an active infection. And the cough could strain abdominal muscles, which were already stretched by late pregnancy, making for a very uncomfortable situation.

They went down to the first floor, where the hospital cafeteria was located, and got some chicken noodle soup and juice for Jenny and a turkey and cheese sandwich for her husband.

"I'm done for the day, so I'm going to sit up there with them and wait on their results. I can only imagine how scary this is for both of them."

"I'll run over and grab the print order and get the posters at least up in the hospital. Then I'll be back to see if we can run down that list of customers from the bakery. Since Curtis isn't coughing, I'm not as worried about the print shop."

Lia took hold of the bags with the food in it. "Sounds good."

Before she could walk away, Micah stopped her with a hand to the arm. "I haven't seen you the last couple of days. I wanted to make sure Samantha wasn't traumatized by her unexpected run-in with a man."

The question made her laugh.

For some reason, she'd expected him to ask her how she was doing, or worse, apologize for what they'd done at her apartment. It was part of the reason why she'd been avoiding him for the last two days. But only part of it. In reality, she'd had no idea what she was going to say if he did either of those things.

"Sam is just fine. No worse for wear."

"And you? No worse for wear?"

Ah, and there was the question du jour. Asking how she was.

"No worse for wear." She forced a smile. "I'm a pretty resilient girl."

"I'm glad. I just wanted to make sure we knew where the other stood."

She blinked. Did he? That wasn't exactly the question he'd asked her. And thank God he hadn't. Because right now she had no idea what her response would have been. Right now, she didn't want to examine where they stood. On a professional level or a personal one. Because if her suspicions were right, she was having an awful time keeping the past and present in their respective corners.

She'd missed him. The last several weeks had proven that beyond a shadow of a doubt. Watching him interact with patients and hold baby Sassy, watching him interact with her cat…and experiencing his touch all over again…well, it made her want to go back and change the way things had ended between them.

But she couldn't. And right now, she wasn't sure if she was going to be able to keep him from realizing that. Or what she would do if Micah somehow guessed the truth.

CHAPTER ELEVEN

JENNY'S TEST TWO days ago had come back negative, and they'd sent the relieved couple home after vaccinating both of them. The hospital had had some names of midwives that worked with the medical center, and they had promised to contact someone on the list.

That was the good news. The bad was that two more area hospitals had called in cases of whooping cough. Nashville was now up to twenty, with most of the cases congregated around Saint Dolly's hospital. Micah and Lia were scheduled to go out once she finished her last procedure of the day and hang flyers in local businesses and in areas where the public gathered. The CDC had also mounted a television campaign aimed at public awareness, and Micah was helping track cases of exposure.

Lia's artwork was also getting some media exposure, after a reporter had spied one of the framed prints hanging on the wall at the hospital. And of course Arnie hadn't been able to resist saying that a member of the hospital staff had done the design on it. Lia had been mortified. But at least they hadn't given the media her full name. But since Curtis had talked her into signing the original, it was probably only a matter of time until someone realized who the artist was.

His phone buzzed, and he glanced down to see a text from her.

I'm done. Ready whenever you are.

He smiled. She always had been short and to the point. Most of the time he'd found it amusing. Except when she'd broken things off with him. That had been a killer. It had taken going to Ghana to get over her. He knew for a fact he couldn't have done it here in Nashville. Seeing her day after day would have been impossible. Running into her after that long of an absence had been enough of a shock.

And sleeping with her?

Well, that had been a much nicer shock than the original. It seemed like they'd kind of gotten their footing again around each other. Maybe sleeping together hadn't been the huge mistake he'd originally thought it was. Maybe it really had given him some closure after all these years and would allow them to do what she'd suggested when she said they could start off fresh… as friends. At the time he'd been incredulous that she could even suggest that. Then of course that had led to them spending the night together, and definitively *not* as friends.

He wasn't yet sure what it all meant. Or how he felt about it. Or her. But maybe they could walk it back and actually become congenial. It seemed like they were on their way to doing just that. And he was looking forward to going out with her this afternoon to hang the flyers,

which was worlds away from how he'd felt when he'd
seen her at that Valentine's Day benefit.

He typed on his keypad to respond to her text.

I'll meet you in the lobby with the goods.

He followed the words with a laughing emoji, smiling when she responded in kind.

See? Friends.

While most of his brain accepted that as a very real
possibility, there was a small portion that was standing back with its arms folded waiting for everything to
implode in his face like it had three years ago. Except
they weren't a couple now. She couldn't break up with
him again. Actually, there wasn't much she could do
other than avoid him. Or quit.

That made him frown. Surely it would never get to
that point? So far they'd been able to remain on decent
terms. So he'd just have to make sure he kept it that way.

He got down to the lobby with an attaché filled with
weatherproof flyers. Hopefully between this and what
the CDC and other hospitals were doing, they'd be able
to prevent the outbreak from spreading even further.
Fortunately, there were still no deaths attributed to the
illness.

She grinned as she walked up to him. "Is this where
I say, 'Hi, honey, I'm home'?"

Honey.

He couldn't stop himself from recoiling at the
word—the empty endearment his mother had used on
him from time to time. Empty because there was no

true affection behind it. She used it on everyone who came across her path. And to hear Lia use it in the same flippant, meaningless way…

It's just a word. It means nothing.

He gritted his teeth and worked past the raw emotions that were swirling through him.

"Micah? What's wrong?"

He needed to just shut up and not say anything. But to do that seemed wrong. Especially since she was apt to use that word again. She used to when they were together, and he'd never complained. But maybe he should have. Should have been more open about how life with his parents had been. Instead, he'd hidden it, thinking that Lia could help him get through it. Looking back, it hadn't been fair to pile that kind of expectation onto her shoulders. Especially since she hadn't even known she was carrying that particular load. The truth was, he'd hidden the truth because he'd been embarrassed, especially after seeing how loving Lia and her parents were with each other. It made his own household seem like a farce. Like some sitcom of dysfunction that never really resolved.

And since his and Lia's connection had weighed so heavily toward the physical, he never bothered to ask himself if he could even have a healthy emotional relationship with her—or anyone. But after that breakup? Hell, he'd asked himself that question repeatedly. Because apparently something had been off that he hadn't been able to see at the time.

And now that they were supposedly "friends"? Maybe it was time to come clean. At least a little bit.

"Nothing. I'm just not overly fond of that word."

"Word? What word?"

Now he was feeling a bit ridiculous for saying anything. "*Honey.* My mom just used it whenever she was trying to talk me into doing something. Or hoping I'd go away."

She blinked. "Oh, Micah. I'm sorry, I didn't know. I'm pretty sure I used to call you that...before. Why didn't you say anything?"

"I don't know. I probably should have."

"All right. I'll try to remember." She paused a few seconds. "She really made you feel like she wanted you to go away?"

He shrugged, stepping closer to her to let someone get past them. "I'm sure all kids feel like that from time to time."

Her brows went up, as if she wasn't sure what to say to that. But she didn't try to pull any more confessions from him, for which he was thankful.

Instead, she finally just said, "I won't use that word again. Thank you for telling me."

There were a few awkward moments while they tried to figure out their footing again. But finally she smiled and pulled her keys out of her purse and held them up. "So...my place or yours?" A little bell tinkled as she shook the keys, making him forget for the moment how his body had jolted to life at her question.

Hadn't he heard that bell at Lia's house the night he'd stayed over?

"I thought you put that back on Samantha's collar."

"I did. But I found it in the bedsheets this morning. I don't know how she keeps getting it off."

Man, the image of Lia sprawled across rumpled sheets was moving through his skull at a snail's pace, refusing to be hurried off his mental screen. The jolt he'd felt a minute ago returned full force. He knew exactly what she looked like when she slept. And so did his body.

To throw his mind off track, he reached over to finger the little bell, forcing himself to look for a spot where there was a fissure or break, but there was nothing. "Has it ever fallen off your key chain the way it does her collar?"

"Nope. I don't know what its deal is."

Avery's earlier words about Samantha's witchy ways came back to him.

"Maybe the problem is with the ring on her collar."

Her teeth worked at her lip for a minute like she did whenever she was thinking. Micah had to glance away when his thoughts veered back to things that had nothing to do with cats or bells.

"I'll have to check it when I get home." She seemed to shake off a thought. "So back to the question. Are we taking my car or yours?"

It was a different question than she'd voiced a moment ago and didn't flood his brain with a rush of endorphins this time. But he'd already known she wasn't talking about homes. Just cars.

"If I remember right, your little blueberry was kind of a tight fit."

Oh, hell. That hadn't come out quite right.

The impish smile she gave him made the sides of her nose crinkle. "Yes. It was kind of a snug ride, wasn't it?"

The words hit their mark, snagging his thoughts and taking them hostage.

She did not mean it that way. But that smile was the same one she'd given him in the past. The exact. Same. Smile.

No matter how many times he tried to banish the memory of just how snug that particular ride had been, a heady, terrifying warmth began to pool in his groin. It had nowhere to go...but up.

Dammit! He needed to pull himself together.

"We'll take my car." He bit the words out with a fierceness that didn't go unnoticed.

Lia's smile faltered. "Are you sure you want me to come with you?"

"Yes, sorry. I didn't mean that to sound the way it did."

"It's okay. My words a few minutes ago didn't come out exactly right, either."

Ah...so had she not realized how her words had come across until now? But she'd had that knowing little grin. When he glanced at her, he could swear he saw a tinge of pink in her cheeks. Maybe she had meant them—as a joke—but his reaction had been so over-the-top that she'd probably had second thoughts about trying to make him laugh.

He sighed. Maybe his hopes of being friends was destined to fail.

Pushing the door, he held it open to let her go ahead of him.

The frigid blast of air hit him in the chest, the cold putting the deep freeze on some very overheated parts. He drew in a deep breath or two, letting the door swing shut behind him.

The weather had taken an unexpected turn, dropping back below freezing, which wasn't too unusual for Nashville, seeing as it was still only the end of February. A severe weather alert had pinged on his phone a while ago, warning folks to look out for slick spots on the roadways due to the rain that had fallen during the morning commute.

Pulling his coat around him as they moved through the parking lot, he unlocked the doors to the car before they got there.

Once they were inside, he realized they should have taken the blueberry. Because they'd had that spectacular kiss in this car. Right before he'd gone up to her apartment.

It was too late now. He was stuck here with her for the next couple of hours. He pulled out onto the road and headed south.

"I spent part of today calling local businesses, and I have the names of some places that are willing to put up our flyers. I mapped them in the order of our route."

"Great. If you want to hand me the map, I can help navigate."

"It's in the front pocket of the attaché."

"Which is where?"

"It's in the back seat. Let me pull over and get it."

Great. Smart work, Micah.

"No problem. I'll just unbuckle for a minute. Try not to send me flying through the windshield with any fast stops, though." She unhooked her belt and then twisted in her seat, hanging over, trying to reach the bag, which was behind his seat. Something soft pressed against his shoulder, and his jaw tightened, trying not to think about what it was. He rounded a curve and sent her bottom swinging into him instead.

"Damn. Sorry."

No choice. He hooked one arm over her derriere to anchor her in place while she reached for the bag.

"Got it."

He lifted his arm to let her slide back into her seat. "Thanks for hanging on to me."

"No problem." But it was. Because his thoughts were right back where they'd started. With her. And him. Doing very naughty things in a very snug place.

She pulled the sheet of paper from the front of the bag and glanced at it. "Oh, wait. The first one is on the next block. Papa's Pizza Parlor."

"Okay. Hold on."

He swung into the correct lane and found the place almost immediately. Parking, they took a flyer in, talking to the owner for a minute before heading back to the vehicle. Maybe they hadn't needed two people to undertake such a simple task, but it was easier and safer to have someone looking for the places he'd called.

They returned to the car, and she glanced at the sheet. "We're headed to the park on Thirty-First next. It's about a mile away."

A drop of sleet hit his windshield. Great. "Hopefully we won't get much of this."

He pulled over to the curb and started to put the vehicle in Park only to have her say, "Let me just jump out and staple it to the information board. You did get permission to hang it, didn't you?"

"I did. But I can do it. I have a staple gun in the main pocket of my bag."

"Just stay here, then you won't have to turn the car off. I'll just be a minute." She hopped out of the car with the flyer and the staple gun and headed to the large plywood structure where people hung notices for different events.

She pushed the stapler, and evidently nothing happened, because she turned it toward her and looked at it before setting the flyer down, stepping on it to keep it from blowing away and giving the gun a shake before opening the cartridge and looking inside. He was just about to get out of his car to help when she picked the flyer back up and tried again. This time she was successful. She'd just turned around to come back to the car when it started sleeting in earnest. Putting her coat over her head, she sprinted toward the car and almost made it when she slipped and went down backward.

"Hell!" In a split second, he was out of the car and jogging toward her. She was already on her feet by the time he reached her. "Are you okay?" He had to shout to be heard as the sleet gave way to torrential rain.

"I'm fine." But when she went to take a step, she grimaced before shifting her weight back onto her other foot. "I think I just twisted my ankle. I'll be okay."

"Put your arm around my waist." The rain was still coming down, and by the time she hobbled to the car, their clothes were plastered to them.

The gutter between the car and the sidewalk had become a river, and there was no way she was going to be able to step across it with her ankle like it was, so, still holding on to her, he reached over and opened the door, then before she could protest, he lifted her, stepping into the rushing water and setting her on the seat. He closed the door, then slogged his way to the other side of the car and got in, turning the heat on high. Then he looked over at her, and they both burst out laughing.

The rain was pounding the top of the car and sluicing down the windshield. He turned his wipers on high. "Well, that didn't quite go as planned, and I don't think anyone is going to let us in looking like this."

She glanced over at him. "*Dio*, your pants are so... I'm sorry you had to get in that water."

"I'll be fine. But I should probably get you home before you freeze and that ankle swells."

Despite the heat pouring from the vents, Lia's jaw was quivering as her teeth chattered. From the cold? Or had she really done something to her ankle?

"Maybe we should get that foot X-rayed."

"No, it'll be fine. I'm just freezing."

And that settled it. He pulled slowly from his spot, trying to watch the traffic as his tires sprayed water in all directions.

"Aim those vents toward you."

She reached forward and did it before widening her eyes. "Oh, no!"

"What?"

Lia held up his stapler. "It may be ruined after hitting the ground and getting rained on."

His stapler. His *stapler*. She was something else. "That's the last thing I'm worried about. We're about three minutes away from your complex."

"Just park in my spot again."

A feeling of déjà vu settled over him, along with a sense of doom. To be in that apartment again... But what was he going to do? Drop her off at the front door to the building and drive away? The least he could do was make sure she was okay. Get her settled in with a hot cup of coffee and check her ankle.

They made it to the parking garage, which, thank heavens, was covered and led directly into the building through a covered corridor. He parked and came around to her side of the door. As she stepped out, she grimaced as she tried to put weight on her ankle again.

"This is so stupid. I can't believe I was that clumsy."

"You weren't clumsy. I almost slipped, too." He smiled. "So, do you want to be carried in—which is my preferred method—or are we going back to the arm around the waist?"

"Definitely arm around the waist. Cameras, remember?"

"I seem to remember it didn't stop us from putting on quite a preshow as we went up the elevator last time."

"Ugh. Don't remind me. Every time I go by the security guard, I picture him watching that scene. Or worse, taping it and playing it for his friends."

"He's probably seen it all before. Keys?"

She handed him her keys and her purse before hesitating and then finally putting her arm around his waist. Was it that hard to touch him? Or was she really just embarrassed about the cameras?

He supported her with his other arm as they slowly made their way to the elevator. She gasped when they had to step up onto a different level once they got inside. Dammit. It would have been less painful to have let him carry her. Not to mention faster. They must look quite the sight. His shoes were literally squelching with each step, and though he didn't look behind him, he was pretty sure he was leaving wet tracks across the pristine surface of the lobby floor. Lia's long ponytail, which had been neat and tidy when they'd left the hospital, was now canted toward the left, and she had a big patch of mud on her left cheek.

A guard came running from somewhere, his hand on his hip—where he kept what looked like a Taser. "Dr. Costa, are you okay?"

"I'm fine. It's okay." Lia frowned as if realizing what

a sight they must be, then shut her eyes for a few seconds. Micah could picture exactly what she was thinking—the preshow was nothing compared to this. "I just sprained my ankle. Dr. Corday was kind enough to help me get home."

"Do you want me to get the wheelchair we keep in the lobby?"

She gave a short laugh. "At this point, I'm afraid of somehow destroying that, too."

"You won't," the guard assured her, his tone worried.

"I'm fine, but thank you for offering."

What had she destroyed? The stapler? That was nothing. Maybe she was worried about his car.

"Hey, my leather seats are pretty tough, if that's what's bothering you. They'll dry as good as new."

"As good as new."

Was she sure she hadn't somehow hit her head? He needed to get her up to her apartment so he could check her over.

They got onto the elevator, and the trip to the third floor seemed to take forever, unlike the last trip, when it had sailed up at the speed of light. Finally the door opened, and he splayed out her keys, searching for the right one, the little bell from Samantha's collar jingling. That's right. Hopefully the cat liked him as well today as she had the last time. The last thing he needed was her adding to the confusion.

He inserted the key into the lock, and the mechanism released, allowing the door to swing in. Helping her inside, he toed off his wet shoes and reached over to turn on the light. He closed the door again, latching it. "Where do you want me to take you?"

"To the bedroom." As if realizing how that sounded,

she said, "I want to get out of these clothes. Why don't you go into the bathroom and do the same?"

As if she could feel his grin, she looked up, and for the first time since her sad little comment to the guard, she smiled. "You know what I mean."

He laughed. "Then maybe you should *say* what you mean. But I get it. The only problem is I don't have a change of clothes here, and I doubt you want me parading around wearing…" He purposely allowed the words to trail away.

"There's a terry robe in there that you can use. If it doesn't fit front ways, you could always pretend it's a hospital gown where the opening goes to the back."

Perfect. "Do you need help changing?"

"I think I'm good. If I need help, I'll yell."

She wouldn't. Of that he was sure. He helped her to her room and left her standing in the middle of the bedroom while he went over to her dresser.

"What are you doing?"

"Getting you some clothes."

"You don't have to—"

"I do," he muttered. "Unless you want to stand here while we argue about it."

"Okay. But don't look."

"At…?"

"The stuff in my drawers."

Did she realize how ludicrous that sounded? "Do you want me to promise to go by feel rather than by sight?" He let one side of his mouth quirk, and her face immediately turned colors.

What was that all about?

He opened one drawer and found socks. The next one had what he was looking for. Hmm…what color? The array before him was dazzling; his fingers ventured in to touch and—

"You're looking."

Yes, he was. But what did she expect a man to do? He grabbed the first pair his fingers had trailed across and started to close the drawer when he heard a screech.

"No, not that pair!"

Hmm? He looked at what he was holding in his hand. Okay, there was barely anything there, except for... strings. What exactly what this used for?

He tried again, taking another pair out, a bit more gingerly this time. Okay, these looked like normal, albeit frilly underwear. He held them up for her approval.

"Yes, they're fine."

He found her a bra and jeans and a comfy-looking shirt with the words *Nashville Chick* splashed across it.

"Avery bought that for me." Said as if he expected an explanation. He didn't. But it had given him a little too much pleasure to pick out things for her to wear. He remembered doing that on some of their "naughty" nights when the sky had been the limit. Those string-a-ling undies would have been perfect for one of those sessions.

Stop it, Micah.

"Are you sure you can tackle putting them on?"

"I am positive."

Something in her face made him dubious, but she pointed her finger toward the bathroom before letting her arm fall back to her side. He doubted she'd call for help even if she landed in a heap on the floor. Giving her a final glance, he made his way to the bathroom, only to find his way blocked by Samantha, who'd—sans warning bell—sneaked up on him. "Hey, girl. I won-dered where you were. Remember me?"

As if answering, she moved in, her purr box starting up immediately as she sniffed the bottom of his sodden trousers and his bare feet. "You don't want me petting you right now. I'm pretty wet."

He tried to go into the bathroom, only to have her follow him inside. Hmm… From what Lia had said, he wasn't sure about reaching down and trying to set her outside, so he let her stay. "Just so you know, scratch-ing at anything you see in here is forbidden, got it?"

As the cat wandered around the small area, he shed his clothes, finding the bathrobe hanging where she said it would be. It was terry cloth all right. But it was pink and had a huge hummingbird on one side of the chest. Well, there was no way he was pulling his soaked clothes back on. So he took the robe from its hook and slid his arms into the sleeves, the shiny ruffled edging coming to the middle of his forearm. Thankfully when he went to wrap it around his waist it was big enough to cover him, although there wasn't much fabric to spare, and the bottom edge hung above his knees.

Hell. This would have been a winner for comedy night if they'd had one when they'd been together.

When he cinched the pink belt and exited the bath-room, Samantha followed him into the bedroom. Ex-cept he was shocked to find Lia standing exactly where he'd left her. In her wet things with the dry ones lying across the bed. Her face was paler than he'd ever seen it.

"Lia? What's wrong?"

She heard Micah's voice through a fog and looked at his face. She realized she'd been standing there, lost in thought about him. About their past. About what they'd done in this room not that long ago.

She was so tired. Tired of everything. Of the scramble for recognition that seemed to go on every time she turned around. Of how other people seemed to sail effortlessly through life, recognizing their friends and family immediately. Not having to pretend until you could finally work out who the person was.

She'd only known who Curtis was because of his ankh ring...the security guard because of his uniform.

Even Micah, who was someone she'd once loved.

Samantha rubbed against his legs as she stared at him. At the hair plastered against his head. At the strong shoulders hidden beneath her robe.

Someone she still loved.

Oh, God. How could she let herself do this all over again? She'd only end up disappointing him when he finally discovered the truth about why she hadn't wanted to go to Ghana, about why she'd really broken things off with him.

"I—I can't. I just can't."

"You can't what? Get dressed?"

She just shook her head, unable to say any of the things that were spinning out of control in her head.

He took hold of her shoulders and studied her face.

Her damned face! The face that she didn't even recognize when she looked in the mirror. She only knew it was her in the reflection because she was standing there in front of it. She could see the features. Knew what a nose, eyes and mouth were, but put them all together on a person, and they all looked the same, with no identifiable differences.

As if he'd seen something that she couldn't begin to

vocalize, he folded her in his arms and held her close. Rubbed her back, skimmed a lock of hair off her face.

"I'm going to undress you, okay?"

She forced herself to nod, even though he probably had no idea what was really going through her head. Hell, she didn't know, either. Only knew that she still loved Micah.

And that she shouldn't.

Gentle fingers were on her skin as he pulled her blouse up and over her head, undid her bra and slid it off her shoulders. She felt another shirt come down over her, covering her chest. He did the same with her shoes, pants and underwear. The old came off and new things replaced them. Things that weren't embedded with cold. A cold that had moved to envelop her soul.

"Do you want some coffee?"

Her head wagged back and forth as if it had a mind of its own.

"You're shivering. Let me get your hair down and get you into bed." He gently removed the elastic from her hair and slid his fingers through it to loosen any tangles.

She sighed and closed her eyes. It felt good. So good.

Arms scooped her up as if she were a precious piece of china and walked with her across the room. This time he didn't drop her onto the surface of the bed. He gently pulled down the covers and placed her on it. When he went to let her go, though, she gripped the lapels of the robe. "Don't leave, Micah. Please."

"I won't." He kissed her forehead. "Slide over and I'll get in with you."

She scooted over, and Micah crawled in beside her. Her ankle throbbed in time with the beating of her heart, but having him next to her was better than any pain reliever known to man. He'd always been a balm to whatever hurt. And right now, everything hurt. Everything…except him.

Wrapping her arms around him to keep him close, the shivering gradually faded away, and she allowed herself to relax fully into him. Closed her eyes and trusted he'd still be there when they reopened.

Then she let all her thoughts and fears float toward the ceiling as she focused on the one constant in her life at this moment in time.

Micah.

CHAPTER TWELVE

LIA OPENED HER eyes with a start. It was still dark, and the apartment was silent. Micah hadn't left. He was lying facing her, one leg thrown over hers, his hand clasping her arm as if afraid she was going to disappear into the night.

She loved him. The realization from earlier this evening sweeping back over her.

Dio. How could she let this happen again?

She hadn't *let* it happen again. It was the same love she'd had for him before. It was why she'd never dated after he'd left.

Her hand trailed down his arm. And Micah. Did he still feel something for her? He wasn't married. Had traveled an awful long distance to get away from her.

Had anything really changed, though? She was the same fearful person she'd been the last time they met. Even if he still cared about her—

He stirred in his sleep and pulled her closer.

Maybe she could put those thoughts on hold for a little while.

She leaned forward and kissed his jaw. The stubble tickled her lips in a way that was more delicious than words. But it was a deliciousness she remembered. A hunger that only he'd been able to satisfy. He murmured something, and then his eyes came open with a speed that made her blink. They zeroed in on her, pupils constricting.

"What are you doing?"

"Kissing you."

He leaned back, a frown pulling his brows together. "I can see that. Are you okay? You were kind of a mess last night."

"Yes, and I'm really sorry about that. I think I was cold and then just got overwhelmed. Nothing that day had gone right, and I—I suddenly realized how much my prosopag…" She stopped. *Dio*, she'd almost blurted out the truth. But maybe he should know. He deserved to know. She'd kept it from people all her life, except for a select few who knew her daily battle. Her parents. Her sister. Avery had guessed the truth and made her spill, but no one else ever had. And no one in her professional realm seemed to notice, thanks to the lanyards they all wore at work and the tells she'd worked out on those she saw on a daily basis. She'd become adept at living a lie.

Her dad would be proud of her.

But she wasn't her uncle, and she was no longer sure her father's solution had been the best one for her.

She would tell Micah and see what happened. Just not this moment. If he rejected her, then she would at least be able to look back on this memory and hold it close.

And if he didn't push her away? If he still cared about her once he knew?

She took a deep breath and picked up her sentence

again, changing it slightly. "I suddenly realized how very alone I feel."

His hands cupped her face, throat working for a second. "Oh, Lia. I am sorry. God's honest truth, I know what that feeling is like." He leaned down to kiss her. "But you're not alone right now."

"No, you're right. I'm not."

One kiss turned to two, and a shuddery laugh erupted when Samantha decided to insert herself between them, purring and rubbing her head on his shoulder.

"Is it safe for me to pick her up and set her outside? I don't want to leave your place tonight missing an eye. I'm going to need all my senses for what I plan to do next."

Anticipation whispered up her spine, and she smiled. "Somehow I think my cat has fallen in love with you."

"Just your cat?" The lightness of his smile took any heaviness from his words.

But what if she wanted heavy?

Her breath hissed in. *Don't ruin this. Let him tell you first.* So she gave a laugh that she hoped was equally light and said, "That's for me to know."

He leaned down by her ear. "And for me to find out."

Climbing out of bed, he scooped the cat up. She curled next to his chest and just ate it all up.

Lia smiled and whispered, "I can't blame you, Sam."

He set her gently outside the door and shut it.

Then he came back to bed and started to slide back under the covers before thumbing the terry cloth collar of the robe he still wore. "I have to tell you, this is the most uncomfortable contraption I have ever worn to bed."

"You never used to wear anything."

One brow went up. "I still don't. But last night, there were extenuating circumstances."

"Those are all gone. So go ahead."

"Are you sure?"

When she nodded, he undid the bow in front, and as the fabric slithered down his body, she couldn't help but run her gaze over him. He was perfect. Gorgeous. And for right now, he was all hers.

And later?

She could worry about that in the morning.

This time when he slid under the covers, she reached for him, finding his mouth with hers. And unlike the last time, there was nothing playful about his kiss. There was an intensity to it that called to something inside her. She answered the challenge and matched his mood kiss for kiss, stroke for stroke, until he finally rolled her underneath him and entered her with a gentleness that made her want to weep. And when it was over, they lay still, Micah behind her, his palm stroking up and down her arm.

He kissed her neck and nibbled her ear before rolling her over to face him. "Hey, I want to tell you something, okay?"

Her heart seized in her chest. Was he going to say what she thought he was? That he loved her?

"Yes, of course."

"I told you I know how it is to feel truly alone. I want you to know I wasn't just saying that."

"Okay." She blinked. This was not what she'd expected, but she sensed something important was going to follow his words.

"I told you my parents and I had some differences, but there was a lot more to it than that." His hand came out and touched her face, stroked down her nose, his thumb trailing across her lips. "You're so beautiful, did you know that? So perfect."

She stiffened slightly before forcing herself to relax. This wasn't about her. It was about him.

"Tell me about your parents."

His fingers retreated, and he reached down to grip one of her hands. "When I was really little, the woman I thought was my mom left and another woman came and took her place. Only that woman hadn't been my mom. Nor was the next. She was one in a long succession of nannies. Each of them was the first person I saw when I got up and the last person I saw when I went to bed. I knew other people lived in the house, but I rarely saw them."

He gave a rough laugh. "Later on I realized these people who slid in and out of rooms were actually my parents. Parents who seemed to avoid me."

"Oh, Micah, how terrible. Did they never interact with you?"

"They tried periodically, but it always seemed half-hearted. I remember one time I was six or seven, a friend came and knocked on the door. My mom answered and actually thought the kid was me standing there. She asked him why he was knocking at his own house."

Lia's heart turned ice-cold even as she forced herself to continue listening. That could have been her, mistaking his friend for her own child.

"I felt totally invisible, totally alone, like they could look at me and not really *see* me. It was as if I were simply living in their house, eating their food, sleeping in a bed they'd bought for some faceless individual. Now I realize that wasn't true, that of course they knew who I was. But back then?" He sighed and squeezed her hand. "It's really hard to have a relationship with people who I felt saw me as a generic human being. Kind of like a Mr. Potato Head doll with interchangeable parts."

The sick feeling in Lia's stomach grew. So she was going to reveal to this man that to her people really were figures with interchangeable features? If she ever had a child, was this how they'd feel? If a neighbor's kid came to the door, she actually might call him or her by her own child's name. Hadn't that happened with acquaintants who'd she'd called the wrong name and then covered it up with a laugh? Only seeing it through a child's eyes, Micah's eyes, it was a terrible, scarring truth that he would never, ever forget. One that still ate at him even as an adult.

She did not want that for her child. But maybe Micah wouldn't want children. Maybe she could tell him her fears and he would wave them away, saying it wasn't a problem. They would just enjoy Lia's nieces.

And if he wanted kids?

"I can't imagine growing up like that. Why didn't you tell me this?"

"I think I was embarrassed. I eventually realized that my family wasn't like other families. And it most definitely wasn't like yours."

She sighed. "My family wasn't perfect, believe me."

"Maybe not. But at least they knew who you were."

Yes, they did. The problem was that without help, she hadn't always known who they were.

"Did you ever talk to them about how they made you feel?"

"No. But I should have. I should have been honest with them at some point."

Well, he wasn't the only person who hadn't been honest with those around him. Maybe it was time. If he realized she didn't want to be like his parents, but that in some ways she might end up acting like them without meaning to... Then what? He would just be like, *Okay, not a problem?*

Maybe she could tackle this from a different angle. "Well, you certainly know what *not* to do as a parent."

He reached out and gripped her hand. "You know, I didn't want children—had convinced myself I'd be the worst parent imaginable, with the role models I had. But now I'm not so sure."

"You're not?" She swallowed, a chill coming over her. "The subject of kids barely came up when we were together."

"I know. I was afraid my decision not to have them might scare you off. But now... Well, in the hospital that day when Sassy came in, I held her, and as I looked down into her face, something twisted inside me. A kind of emotion that I've only felt once before in my life." He carried her palm up to his mouth and kissed it, his lips warm on her cold skin. "I think with the right partner—one who knows how just how important it is to make people feel special—I might reconsider. *If* that partner is willing to take a chance on me, that is."

He was talking about her? She almost laughed aloud. It should be the other way around. She should be asking him if he was willing to take a chance on her. A sense of panic began to rise up inside her. He had no idea who he was talking to.

Her resolution to tell him the truth shattered into a

million pieces as she looked at this man she loved more than life itself. A man she'd loved enough to give up once before. And now?

She didn't know. Maybe she was looking at this scene through eyes that couldn't see the whole picture. But the portion of it that she could see—that of a young child who felt so totally invisible to those who should have loved him—tore at her heart and caused a pain she wasn't sure she could withstand. Wasn't sure she could take the risk of becoming *that* parent: the one who couldn't see what was right in front of her.

Dio ti prego aiutami.

Her silent prayer for help brought no answers. And she couldn't bear to contemplate the subject anymore. So she murmured, "Tell me more about your life as a child."

Maybe Micah would somehow lead her to the answer she so desperately needed.

So as he continued to open up, she let him talk, making sympathetic noises whenever there was a lull in the conversation. But the iciness that had started in her heart slowly encased her in a prison she felt there was no escape from.

Finally Micah was all talked out, and he reached for her again. She held him. Kissed him. Loved him. Hopefully, by morning, she would have her decision and have the strength to carry it out. Once and for all.

Micah woke up in the morning feeling refreshed in a way he hadn't felt in a very long time. He'd poured out his heart to Lia. The very first person he'd ever shared that with. He sucked down a deep breath and smiled.

Hell, he loved the woman. Wanted to be with her. Wanted to have children with her.

When she looked at him, there was no feeling of invisibility.

Speaking of Lia, she wasn't in bed. Maybe she was taking a shower. He rolled out from beneath the covers, finding that ridiculous robe and pulling it on. He ventured out into the hall. The bathroom door was open, and when he went into the kitchen, she was there bent over a basket of laundry, folding it. Her back was to him, but he recognized his slacks. A feeling of warmth went through him.

"Hi, there. You didn't have to do my laundry."

Lia whirled around, holding the pants in front of her almost as if they were some kind of shield. That was ridiculous. Of course she wasn't. He'd just startled her.

"Sorry. I didn't mean to scare you."

"You didn't." She added his trousers to a small stack of clothing. "I think they should all be dry by now."

Her words and movements were quick and flighty, like a bird peck, peck, pecking at the ground and picking up anything it could find. He went to touch her, but she moved away, making it seem like an accident, as if she didn't know what he'd been trying to do. But that initial flinch said otherwise.

What was going on? Last night she hadn't been able to get enough of him, and this morning... Well, if they'd been at his hotel room he could almost guarantee that she'd already be out of there.

He took a step closer. "Are you okay?"

"Fine. I just need to be at work in about a half hour."

"I'm sorry, you should have woken me."

She smiled, but the curve of lips didn't reach her

eyes. "I figured you could let yourself out once you got up."

Ah, so it didn't matter if they were at his place or hers. She was still going to run. Just like she had at graduation, when she said they weren't meant to be together.

Maybe he was reading too much into this. It could be she was telling him the truth. Maybe she really did need to be at work and she was just trying not to be late.

"Okay, how about tonight?"

"Tonight?"

He swallowed. "Do you want to get together?"

Her teeth came down on her lip in that way that drove him crazy, only this time, it didn't. Because something strangely familiar was climbing up his chest and settling there, its spiny surface digging deep.

When she didn't answer him, he nodded, suddenly feeling just as alone as she'd said she felt the previous night. He could stand here and try to get her to open up until he was blue in the face, but something told him she wasn't going to tell him anything. Even after everything he'd told her last night.

"You don't want to, do you? Get together."

A shimmer of moisture appeared in her eyes as she slowly shook her head. "Micah, I am so, so sorry."

He hadn't been overreacting. She was taking the last page from their book and inserting it into their current chapter. And no matter what he might do or say, their story was going to end exactly the same way—with them going their separate ways.

He'd already had this particular dance with this woman, and he was damned if he was going to draw it out any longer than he had to.

"You're right. I would have seen myself out."

He pulled in a deep breath and drummed up the courage to be the one who said the goodbyes this time. "Sorry for unloading on your last night. I think we were both cold and tired and said some things we might not normally have said."

"It's okay."

It wasn't. But maybe someday in the far distant future, it would be. But this time he wasn't going to head to a bar and get flat-faced drunk. He was going to go to the hospital and do his job. He was going to see this pertussis crisis through, and then he was going to sit down and reevaluate his life. He needed to stay here for a while and sort through things with his parents. But after that?

He didn't know. But what he did know was that he wasn't going to let someone make him feel invisible ever again.

And he wasn't going to do this the way she had, simply severing ties. He was going to run this race all the way to the finish line, setting the pace for any future interactions.

His brows went up. "How's your ankle?"

"A little stiff, but it'll be fine."

"Good to hear." He took another step toward goodbye. "I'm planning on going out to hang up the rest of the signs this afternoon, but I can manage that on my own."

This time, she hesitated for a split second before saying, "Okay. Thank you."

And that, it seemed was that. So now he was going to make it very clear. He walked up to her and picked up his pile of clothes. "I know you have to be at work, so

I'll make this short. We'll probably run into one another at work, but I won't make things any more uncomfortable than they have to be. I'll be staying in Nashville for a while longer for my parents."

Her teeth dug into her lower lip again, but this time there was no core meltdown inside him. Just a sad tiredness that wanted this over and done.

"I hope things work out for you in life, Lia, I really do."

Her hands gripped the counter as if needing its support to remain upright before she whispered, "Thank you."

"Okay. I'll get dressed and get out of your hair, then."

With that he took his clothes and, without another look back, headed for her bathroom. Unsurprisingly by the time he was came out again, Lia was long gone. All that was left was Sam, her cat, pacing back and forth in front of the door with a pitifully soft meow. When she saw him, she hurried over, rubbing against his legs. He squatted down in front of her. "I know, girl. But there's nothing more I can do. So it seems this is goodbye."

The last thing he wondered as he locked her door and shut it behind him was how the hell she'd gotten to the hospital without her car.

CHAPTER THIRTEEN

GUAC AND TALKS WAS A pitiful affair. Lia had put Avery off for three weeks before finally agreeing to go. But by the end, her friend hugged her and ordered her to go and deal with the thing that was bothering her. It was as if she'd known exactly what that thing was. Or who.

Micah had made it pretty clear that this time their breakup was permanent. Well, in his defense, she'd kind of beaten him to the punch, opting not to tell him the truth, just like the last time they'd been together.

But it was as if Micah had probed her deepest, darkest fears and stood them up in front of her, saying, "This was how my life was." And when he took her hand and mentioned having kids—implying she was the person he'd choose to have them with—it had been her undoing. The panic from that time long ago, when she couldn't recognize her own dad, had taken her down, paralyzing her.

Dio, the man had poured out his heart and soul to her, and the next morning she'd acted just like the people in his story. She'd barely spoken a word to him other than to say she was sorry. She'd never even told him what the hell she was sorry for.

And it wasn't fair.

Not to Micah, and not to her. But what other answer was there? He'd grown up not feeling seen by anyone in his life. And here was someone who was incapable of seeing him. Not because she didn't want to see him. But because she *couldn't*, dammit. She couldn't!

There was a huge difference between not wanting to and not being able to. But wasn't the end result the same? The odds were that she would one day call him or someone near him by the wrong name. Just like his mom had done to him. How could she live with herself if she did that?

How could she raise a child and have any different outcome than Micah had had?

The questions rolled around and around inside her, and then the loop started all over again.

She plopped into her chair at work and opened a file, staring at it, but not seeing it.

She'd seen her artwork all over town. Micah had indeed hung the flyers by himself. And in the end, his and the CDC's strategy seemed to be working. They were having record numbers of people coming in for their vaccinations, and the new reports of pertussis were beginning to wane.

She had acted terribly when Micah came out of the bedroom.

That had been wrong. So wrong. He'd deserved the truth that day, and she hadn't given it to him. He deserved to know *why* she thought their relationship was doomed.

At graduation, Micah had asked for an explanation, and she hadn't given it to him. This time he hadn't asked. He'd basically told her, "Never mind. I don't need to know. To hell with you."

The thing was, he wasn't the one who'd sent her to hell. She'd sent herself. Time after time. Relationship after relationship, whether it be girlfriends or high school boyfriends. She'd sabotaged every one of them in order to keep her secret. She had very few friends outside of Avery, because no one else could survive the freezing temperatures that came with inhabiting her world.

You owe him an explanation, Lia.

Why?

She already knew why. The man had shared his darkest moments with her, had told her things about himself that she'd never known.

Why now, when he hadn't the last time they were together?

He'd said it was because he was embarrassed.

But maybe it was because he'd finally trusted someone enough to tell them. And that someone had been her. And what had she done? By being unwilling to become just as vulnerable as he'd been, she'd batted his revelation away like it was of no importance.

But it was. It was so very important.

She swallowed. She'd never trusted anyone that much. Ever.

Pushing away the chart, she realized she needed to trust or she would remain that scared woman who'd stood frozen in the middle of her kitchen, too petrified to let down her guard and live life.

Avery was right. She needed to deal with the thing that was bothering her. Or someday, when she least expected, it was going to deal with her.

What if Micah told her to get the hell out of his office without even giving her a hearing? Then she needed to find someone else to tell. And she needed to keep on trying until there was no secret left to tell.

She climbed to her feet, picking up her cell phone and scrolling until she found his number. She should probably call rather than just barging into his office, right?

What would she do if she was in his shoes and had advance notice of his arrival?

She'd make sure she was long gone by the time he got there. Kind of like she'd done when Micah had gone to get dressed that morning.

Okay, then she needed to just go. If he wasn't there, she would camp outside his office until he finally did appear.

So she took the elevator to the third floor and made her way down the hallway until the very end. Then she stood in front of his door for a very long time, her heart quaking in her chest. Then she raised her hand and knocked. Hard enough for anyone within earshot to hear.

"Come in."

Dio, could she do it?

The fact was, she had to. She went into his office and found him up to his elbows in…boxes.

Panic swept through her. "You're leaving?"

"Yep."

"I thought you said you were staying in Nashville to help with your parents."

His brows went up, and there was a coolness to his eyes that made her want to cry out. "I'm not leaving Nashville. Or the hospital. But I am changing locations. The CDC liked our campaign and asked me to come on staff as a representative of Saint Dolly's."

"Oh." The wind went out of her sails.

"Did you need something?"

Her reason for coming here skittered back through her head at his words. Whether he stayed or whether he went was immaterial at this point. But she needed to be as honest with him as he'd been with her.

"I do. I need to talk to you for a minute, if you have the time."

For a second he looked like he might refuse, then he lifted some boxes off one of the chairs and motioned for her to sit. Whew. At least she wasn't going to have to do this standing up, because she wasn't sure her legs would support her.

Micah didn't take another seat, however, he stood over her, a hip leaning on his desk. It was disconcerting, as if he were trying to subtly convey that he didn't want her here and wasn't going to do anything to make her stay more comfortable.

Well, it was working.

"So what is it?"

She'd kind of thought this would go differently. That they'd both be sitting across from each other where she could watch his body language. But where he was didn't change what she was here for.

"You remember when you told me you felt invisible to your mom and dad? That you felt like some faceless entity? A Mr. Potato Head with interchangeable parts, I think you said?"

He shrugged. "I never should have told you any of that."

"*Dio*, Micah, yes, you should have. Because you hit my deepest dilemma on the head. You nailed the reason

I broke things off with you all those years ago, and why I couldn't quite face you the last time we were together."

"I don't understand."

"I know you don't. And I should have told you all this at graduation. But I was… I was too afraid. I've been afraid all my life."

"You?"

"Yes." She looked down at her hands, twining her fingers together. This was it. It was now or never. "People's…faces…they, well, they don't register with me. I see them. I look at you and can see your face as plain as day. But when I look in the mirror, I see the same thing. A face. When I look at Arnie Goff, I see…a face." Her gaze came back up. "But they're indistinguishable from each other. They're Mr. Potato Heads."

He was looking at her like he had no idea what she was talking about.

She tried a new tack. "Ever hear of a condition called prosopagnosia?"

Something in his eyes clicked, and he frowned. "Face blindness? It's extremely rare."

She pointed her thumbs back at herself. "Dr. Micah Corday, meet Extremely Rare."

He tipped the chair next to hers, dumping the contents onto the ground, then turned it so he sat across from her. "You have prosopagnosia? You've had it the whole time we've known each other?"

"I've had it since I was an infant. I had a stroke that affected that part of my brain."

"So when you didn't recognize me at the Valentine's Day benefit…" His eyes closed. "Hell, I thought you didn't remember me."

"Oh, I remembered you. There's a huge difference between recognizing and remembering."

"But how did you finally realize it was me?"

Lia looked at him. "You opened your mouth, and *you* poured out of it. And I normally recognized you." She reached out and touched his face. "Your dimple. The color of your eyes. The way your hair falls over your forehead. There are a thousand things about you that tell me it's you." And she loved every one of those things. Would always love them.

"So why did you break things off?"

This was hard. And real. And scary. She wasn't sure she could make it through the explanation without falling completely apart. "Everyone was in their caps and gowns that day. I looked over the crowd, and all I could see was a sea of orange and white. All the little indicators I used to tell people apart had suddenly been taken away. Including you. I panicked. One of my biggest fears was not being able to recognize my children, and a million moments ran through my head and I realized how many times we wear uniforms and ballet costumes and…caps and gowns."

"If you had told me…"

"It wouldn't have changed anything. That fear was… *is* still there. You described perfectly what any child born to me was going to experience. The sense of invisibility. Mistaking a neighbor's child for my own. You said you felt like a placeholder in your own home. That is the world *my* child will live in. And when you took my hand and said you wanted kids…with the right partner—" Her voice ended on a sob. One she swallowed down before it became a torrent. "I felt like absolutely the wrong person for you to do that with. You deserve so much better. You deserve to be seen. *Really* seen."

"Lia. No. That's not true. God, I had no idea how you would take any of that."

"I know. But it rang so true. It matched what I feared so perfectly."

He grabbed her hands and held them tight. "You say I deserve to be seen. Do you want to know how I felt when we were together back then? I *felt* seen for the first time in my life. Like you could peer inside me and see what no one else could. I felt like more than…" he smiled "…an indistinguishable set of parts. I felt whole and wanted."

"But you're an adult now. If I ever had a child—"

"If you ever *have* a child, he or she will be very, very lucky. Can't you see? That little person will be known in a way that very few people will ever experience. What happened with my parents was willful and hurtful, even if they didn't mean it to be. I felt unwanted. Would yours feel like that?"

"No. Never." She lifted his hand and pressed it to her cheek. "I'm sorry, Micah. I should have told you. Back then. And when you were in my apartment that last time."

"That's why you acted so strange the next morning. You felt like you would doom your child to the life I was describing?"

She nodded.

"I should have seen it. Should have guessed you were struggling with something. If I had…"

"It's not your fault. The only person who has ever guessed the truth was Avery."

He smiled. "I can see how that might be. She's a good friend."

"Yes, she is."

He pulled in a breath and released it. "So where do we go from here?"

Something twitched in her belly. She hadn't been looking for anything more than to just tell him the truth. "What do you mean?"

"Did you break up with me because you didn't love me?"

"No, of course not."

He dragged her onto his lap and planted a hard kiss on her mouth. "Said as if that's a ridiculous thought. Well, it wasn't to me. You put me through hell, Lia."

"I didn't mean to. I was trying to save you. From me."

"What a misguided, unbelievable and totally incredible woman you are. But you didn't save me. You almost destroyed me." He cupped her face and looked into her eyes. "I have a very important question. You said you didn't break up with me for lack of love. Is that still true? That there's no lack of love?"

A veil lifted from her eyes, and she could see him clearly for the first time in her life. "There's no lack. I love you. I always have."

A muscle worked in his jaw. "What can I do to help you?"

"To help me? I don't understand."

"How can I help you believe that what you see when you look at me is enough? That it's always been enough." He smiled. "I have never felt invisible in your eyes."

"I believe you." Hope raged in her chest, breaking free from the fear she'd carried with her from childhood.

"And you believe that your children...*our* children—maybe five or six?—will never feel invisible?"

She laughed. "Five or six? *Dio*, we may have to color code them. My mom always wore a pink crocheted bracelet on her wrist to help me spot her from a distance. She still does, although she probably doesn't need to anymore."

"There's your answer, then. If you're afraid, we'll have a different color bracelet for each child."

"We'll? Are you sure you want to—"

"Have children with you? Yes, and I'm hoping you feel the same way. I love you, Lia."

Love and belief swamped her heart, and she could finally envision a future where she could drop her guard and be herself.

In trusting Micah enough to tell him the truth, she'd given herself permission to be happy. And she was happy. Happier than she'd ever been. And she had a feeling life was only going to get better from here.

His kiss held a promise that didn't need facial recognition software to become reality. Because he'd told her he loved her just as she was. And so would their children. And this time—finally—Lia believed him.

Micah placed a pink crocheted bracelet around their baby's wrist, careful not to wake Lia, who was still sleeping after her difficult delivery.

Lia's mom had fashioned a tiny identification band that looked identical to the one she wore. It wouldn't have any information printed on it like you might expect on one of those kinds of bands, but it would serve as a tell, as she put it, the same way Micah's bright orange wedding band did. She'd sworn she didn't need him to wear anything more than a gold band, that she would always recognize him. But he wanted to. It was a sign that he supported his wife and would do anything he could to make things easier for her. And his band wouldn't be hidden under the sleeve of a coat the way a bracelet might.

He'd almost ruined things by not understanding why she'd withdrawn after their night together, and by not pressing her for answers. Once they figured things out, they'd sworn they would keep no more secrets from each other. Lia had gone to Arnie Goff as well and shared about her prosopagnosia, and he assured her it would have no effect on her job at the hospital.

As for his parents, he'd been surprised and pleased

by their response to the news he was getting married. His mom had actually taken it upon herself to make the bridal bouquet and the one for Avery, who was Lia's matron of honor. Little inroads were being made every time he turned around, it seemed. And his dad's experimental cancer treatment was working better than expected. He hadn't gone into remission yet, but there was a very real possibility it would happen.

The only glitch had come when Lia found herself unexpectedly pregnant a month before they said their vows. It was her deepest fear and the reason she'd broken things off with him. He'd taken her in his arms and reassured her that their baby would not get lost in the shuffle. They would make it work. And with her mom and dad's help, they had.

"Hey, handsome." Lia's tired voice came from the bed behind him, and he turned toward her. "Is she okay?"

"She's more than okay." He perched on the edge of the mattress. "How are you feeling?"

"Better."

Lia had developed preeclampsia in her thirty-eighth week of pregnancy, and because of the stroke she'd had as an infant, they'd decided rather than risk her blood pressure going any higher, they would deliver the baby. Fear had crawled up Micah's spine at the thought of losing Lia so soon after they'd found each other again, and when he'd been kicked out of the surgical suite, he'd found himself sitting in the hospital's chapel. There, with clasped hands resting on the chair in front of him, he'd poured his heart out to whomever in the cosmos might be listening. That's where the surgeon had found him a half hour later. And where he'd learned that both

Lia and Chelsea Day Costa-Corday had made it. He would be forever grateful. And never would he take these two precious gifts for granted.

Micah stroked her damp hair back off her forehead. "You are my world—do you know that?"

She nodded. "Ditto, honey." She frowned and then put a hand on his arm. "I'm sorry. I forgot."

Surprisingly, the word didn't send his world spinning into chaos like it had that other time. Instead, it brought a sense of peace. "It's okay. I think it's growing on me. Especially since everyone in your family calls everyone honey. Well, in Italian."

"It's part of my heritage. I could use the Italian term if you'd rather."

"No. Although there are times when I really do like hearing you speak in your heart language. Like when you're cussing." He grinned and leaned closer. "Or when you're loving me."

"Micah!"

It was a huge turn-on when his wife was so caught up in the moment that she breathed words he didn't understand across his skin. Even thinking about it caused areas that should be quiet to wake up.

It would always be this way. He wanted this woman. Only this woman.

"Sorry. I can't help it."

She slid her finger down the left side of his face. "It's okay." Her eyes shifted to the clear bassinet a short distance away. "Can I hold her?"

"Of course." Micah helped her sit up and propped a pillow across the area where her incision was. Then he turned and reached into the bassinet and gingerly lifted their child, moving with careful steps until he reached her. Laying her in Lia's arms, he moved around to the other side of the bed and slid in beside her.

This was where he belonged. And this was where he would stay.

He saw her reach for their daughter's wrist and touch the bracelet. "Where...?"

"Your mom brought it in while they were doing the C-section."

She gathered her baby close, tears filling her eyes and spilling onto her cheeks. "I just never thought I'd be this lucky."

Micah kissed the top of her head, trying to banish the burning sensation behind his own eyes. "Luck? I don't think so. I think maybe your friend Avery was right."

"What do you mean?"

He leaned his cheek against her temple. "Remember when she was talking about Samantha?"

"Samantha? As in our cat?"

"Hmm... Yes, her little bell jingled on your key chain, and then Avery said you'd named her for her witchy ways."

"Well, 'witchy' was a nice way of putting it."

He laughed. "Well, be that as it may, contrary to her fierce reputation, she didn't exactly attack me that first night I met her."

"Unlike me on that same night." She sent him a look that told him exactly what she meant.

"Don't distract me. But even that kind of proves my point."

"Proves your point?" She tilted her head until it rested against his. "So are you somehow saying that Samantha had something to do with me sleeping with you that first night? With us getting together afterward?"

"Maybe. I'm forever hearing her little bell wandering around our house at night."

"And?"

"I swear I've seen her nose twitch a time or two when she looks at us."

Lia laughed, then her free hand came up and curved around his cheek, turning his face so she could kiss him. "You know, I think I've seen that, too. So you think Sam twitched her witchy little nose and cast a spell on us?"

"Are you denying it's a possibility?"

"No, and now that I think about it, she did kind of force her way into my heart at the shelter not long after I broke up with you. She helped me grieve your loss that first time. And she helped me work up the courage to tell you about my condition."

"That cat deserves a medal for making our problems vanish, if so."

"No. That cat deserved a family. And it looks like she got one. One that isn't going to disappear."

His arm tightened around her. "Good. Because I'm not going anywhere."

"That makes two of us. I love you, Micah."

As he stared down at his little family, his heart filled with love and gratitude. And then he glanced out the window at the skies and beyond and mouthed, "Thank you."

* * * * *

COMING SOON!

We really hope you enjoyed reading this book.
If you're looking for more romance, be sure to
head to the shops when new books are
available on

Thursday 20th
January

To see which titles are coming soon, please visit

millsandboon.co.uk/nextmonth

MILLS & BOON

Coming next month

THE MIDWIFE'S MIRACLE TWINS
Caroline Anderson

The rest of the clinic was busy but routine, with no dramas or crises, and she ended her shift only an hour late.

She went into the locker room to change, found the pregnancy tests strips still in her pocket and put them in her locker, then changed her clothes, dropping the scrubs into the laundry bin. Then she pulled out her bag and a tampon fell out. She bent down and picked it up, then stared at it thoughtfully.

Was her period overdue?

She wasn't sure. Her cycle wasn't an issue, so she never really bothered to make a note, but her periods usually started on a Tuesday, and it was Thursday.

Her heart gave a dull thud and she stared at it for another moment, then put it and the test strips in her bag and shut her locker.

There was no way she could be pregnant—was there? Surely not.

But all the way home her heart was racing, and the first thing she did once she'd closed the front door was run upstairs to the bathroom to do the test.

How could a minute be so long?

She perched on the edge of the bath, staring at the little strip and not quite sure what she wanted to see, one line or two.

One appeared instantly, to show the test was working. Not that anything else was going to happen—

Another line? Really? And a strong, dark line, too, not some vague little shadow.

She got up, her legs like jelly, and walked slowly out of the bathroom, sank down onto the bed and stared blankly at the test strip.

How could she possibly be pregnant? Dan had said it was a tiny tear, and she and Mark had tried for years. How could she be? Unless they'd just been incompatible, but even so...

She slid a hand down over her board-flat tummy. Was there really a baby in there? Dan's baby?

Please, no.

Please, yes!

But...

She'd have to tell him. Not yet, though. It might have been a fluke. She'd do another test in a while.

And then another one, until all the tests were used up.

Four of them couldn't be wrong.

She started to cry, great tearing sobs welling up from deep inside her where the pain she'd hidden for so long had festered like poison, and then the tears died away, leaving only joy.

Continue reading
THE MIDWIFE'S MIRACLE TWINS
Caroline Anderson

Available next month
www.millsandboon.co.uk